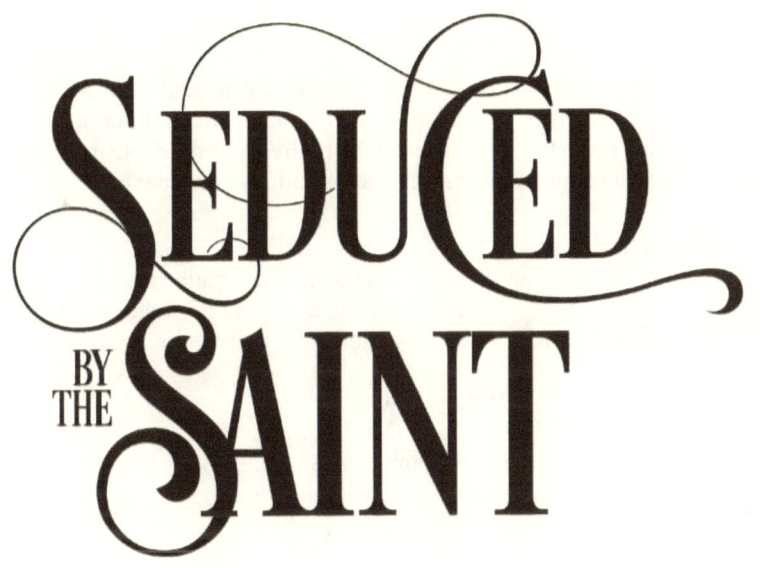

SEDUCED BY THE SAINT

STONE RANCH SERIES

CAYT LAWSON

Written by Cayt Lawson
Edited by Ink It Out Editing Services
Cover Art by © Holly Perret, The Swoonies Book Covers
Interior Design by Ryan Flowers

Also By Cayt Lawson

Ann's Valley (A Stone Ranch Prequel)
Stone Ranch Series
Seduced by the Saint

COMING SOON

Stone Ranch Series
Kissed by a Devil
Wanted by the Ranger
Loved by an Outlaw

Sisters Disreputable Series
Love's Song
Love's Wings

I dedicate this book to my husband and children. Our family has made numerous sacrifices for me to pursue my dream of writing, but through all of our hardships, they have continued to champion and encourage me. If not for their support this journey would be impossible, but if not for their love, this journey would be inconsequential. Thank you, my loves, for always believing in me.

Prologue

High Plains, Texas
July 12, 1851

"I'm dying."

James Morgan wriggled and tossed his head with the pain of his final moments descending upon him.

"Bién. You deserve to die." Antonio Javier García Rivera looked down at James with little pity, certain his brother-in-law wouldn't live another hour longer.

García had ridden out that morning to inform James of cattle hustlers creeping onto their property borders. Although he thought little of his brother-in-law, the man happened to own half of García's ancestral ranch. And while James didn't care about the upkeep of the ranch, other than the little proceeds it brought in annually, García most certainly did.

Apparently, it escaped his brother-in-law that maintaining the ranch was what kept the proceeds coming in.

García was riding the trail toward the settlement near Canyon, certain he would find his brother-in-law coming or going from the settlement's only saloon. About a mile ahead of him, García saw a man fly up out of the banks of the creek where he'd been hidden along the mesquite and sagebrush-covered slope. The rider charged in the direction of another approaching rider. Before García could register what was taking place, a shot

1

rent the air, and without a backward glance, the attacker from the creek bank fled past the man he'd shot, leaving him for dead.

García kicked his horse into a run. As he neared, he recognized the fallen rider to be James. The other rider—presumably a cheated gambler bent on reclaiming his money from James—was already long out of sight.

James now lay in the dirt bleeding from the hole in his chest. And he would most assuredly die. Antonio should feel redemption at such a pass, for the way the scoundrel had ill-treated his sister. His sister, Maria, had died in childbed, after laboring for days delivering James's seventh stillborn child.

James had been in town sharing a bed with a two-bit whore, while his sister had died frightened, lonely, and heartbroken. For that, Antonio would never forgive the bastard now dying in the dirt before him.

"I will finally get to reclaim the other half of my father's ranch that you stole upon your marriage to my sister." Antonio spat down in the dust beside James.

Caustic laughter bubbled from James's lips. "No, you won't."

That revelation caused García's heart to skip a beat. Surely James was delirious.

James took an agonizing breath, and wheezed through his grinning teeth, "The ranch will go to my daughter."

How was that possible? Everyone knew James was sterile. García had never been so happy as the day he learned his brother-in-law had inherited a disease from the whore bed that prevented him from ever having any future children. His wife after Maria had confirmed that before she too had died.

Unless...

Nearly eighteen years ago, García had been playing cards in a saloon in Santa Fe. His brother-in-law had been there, too, sulking. Aware of James's penchant for cheating, García had not permitted him to enter the ensuing card game. A woman charged into the saloon that day and aimed a gun at James's chest. He later learned the woman's name to be Ann Dunneroy. She revealed James had fathered her child, but James cruelly turned the young mother away. Ann Dunneroy, much to Antonio's grief, had left James Morgan alive and whole.

The following spring, García met the same woman yet again at a trappers' rendezvous. Events occurred that led to him becoming a close friend to Ann and her new husband, Grayson Stone. García soon discovered Ann had twin daughters. And they were James's.

In their shared hatred of James, Ann and García agreed to keep the girls secret from him. If James ever asked questions, they were to tell him the baby had died, so he would never learn of the daughters he spurned so callously.

So how had Morgan learned of them?

A clever smile formed on James's lips, "A woman. Ann Dunneroy."

García cautiously responded, "I'm aware of the woman you impregnated before your marriage to my sister. We are friends of a sort."

Shock dawned across James's face. The stricken look brought a small measure of satisfaction to Antonio.

García continued, "The baby died."

The shocked expression faded from his dying brother-in-law's face, replaced by an arrogant smile. "That's a lie."

García tried to mask his surprise to James's confident reply.

"I met the girl."

James continued to speak as if he only had one daughter. García wasn't about to apprise him of the knowledge that he had two.

James continued explaining in short, pain-laced sentences, "At the Cortés Corral. Was buying a horse. A man and woman drove in a fresh herd of young mustangs... I recognized the woman instantly as Ann... Even with her marred face. I didn't feel like getting shot on sight, so I kept back. Learned she was married to a man by the name of Grayson Stone... They had a kid with them... Thought it a boy at first, dressed in buckskins as it was. Looked to be about twelve years old... I did the math. When *Mr. and Mrs. Stone* left the kid with the wagon, I approached him. Had Ann's dark hair. But it was my eyes staring back at me."

Another cocky grin spread across Morgan's face.

"I asked the kid his name. He said, 'Kit Stone.' Wasn't Stone's. Was mine, without a doubt. Only, after it spoke, I realized the kid was a girl. I said to her, 'But it used to be Morgan.' Surprise was evident on her face, but the truth was as well."

García waited while James inhaled a haggard breath before he continued on again.

"Didn't have much use for a daughter. Until..."

Interrupted by a fit of coughing, blood sprayed and misted over James's mouth. The crimson drops remained on his lips as he attempted to continue his sentence.

"Until..." he rasped.

But that was all he could manage before a final gasp left his mouth and his head lolled to the side, body limp and lifeless.

"Damn it, Morgan!"

García wanted to kick his brother-in-law's dead form. He could well imagine the ending to James's final sentence, however. James hadn't any use for a daughter until he realized he could use her to keep the ranch from García. Purely out of spite. The ranch had never meant anything to Morgan, whereas it meant everything to García.

It was Antonio's turn to smile.

James Morgan may have tried to fulfill one last act of treachery upon his death, but he had failed.

James discovered he had a daughter, but he hadn't known of García's relationship with her and the Stone family. He never even learned he had two daughters. Morgan's misfortunes were a direct result of his actions and the life he lived; it was difficult to feel grief on his part. Initially, Morgan's words about the ranch not returning to García unnerved him. But after Kit was revealed to be the new owner, García was feeling quite hopeful.

He ran his fingers over Morgan's eyelids, turning them down to cover the man's eyes. He would take him back to his late sister's ranch (never could think of it as Morgan's ranch) on Hackberry Creek and bury him, though heaven knew the man didn't deserve it. Then he would see about settling matters for Morgan's will and getting to Kit as quickly as possible.

You lost again, Morgan.

Chapter 1

Unorganized Territory
May 25, 1851

Bridles jingled in the night with the quickening pace of the horses. The same eagerness and urgency raced through Benjamin Price, even as he tightened the reins. The familiar aroma of the Mountain Columbine alerted the horses and their riders that they were nearing their destination. The flowers' lavender petals were closed to the night air, but their fragrance remained and floated on the crisp spring breeze, mingling with the earthly scent of pine and filling all their senses with reminders of home. Price looked to Luke and Logan Stone, riding alongside him, and saw their expressions reflected the giddiness of his own. They had all been away from home too long and were eager to return.

Not that it was actually Price's home. It was the home of Grayson and Ann Stone and their children; Luke, Logan, Kit, and Livvy. Price met Luke and Logan during their university days where they all studied at the college back east in Princeton, New Jersey. The three of them quickly became chums and Price, having no home to return to, or one where his return would be welcomed, accepted the Stone brothers' invite to join them on their family's ranch after their final term. His visit turned into an extended stay that never really terminated. He and the Stone brothers went on one adventure after another, always returning to Stone Ranch, where Price was welcomed as if he were another son. The Stone family was dearer to Price than the one that spawned him back in England.

The Stone brothers craved adventure and Price always went along for the ride. Without them he feared he would be without direction or purpose in this life. And their adventures always seemed to end well for the three of them. Such as their most recent one mining for gold in California. The work had been laborious, but the profits lining their pockets now made it well worth it. Unlike the sorry cads that were only just arriving as Price, Luke, and Logan had decided to call it quits and headed out. No, the majority of those men were all headed for grave disappointment.

The stars in the clear night sky began to disappear beyond the dense treetops towering above them, but they knew their way home sure as anything and diminished light was no deterrent. It was a silent, peaceful night, the three of them too determined and focused on their impending arrival and lost in their own nostalgic thoughts of home to make conversation. All that could be heard was the creaking of leather from the saddles, the horses' heavy breaths as they strained against their bits, and an occasional hooting of an owl.

About another hour of riding passed. When they finally exited the thick forest into the clearing, the peaceful silence of the night was shattered into a cacophony of whoops and hollers from Luke and Logan.

The two-story ranch home sat upon a hill, highlighted by the pale moon like a beacon. The three of them let their horses have their head and raced up the path to the stables.

Price raced his mount alongside Luke and Logan, his spirit equally as zealous to be home, but he did not partake in the raucous shouting with them. Benjamin would have felt foolish. Indeed, his reserved nature already balked and had him feeling childish for the large grin he struggled to eviscerate from his face.

The run and excitement of the night was freeing. They had spent a year laboring and living in miserable conditions and been witness to abominable acts of inhumanity, which was what finally drove them from the gold fields.

The words were never said aloud, but Luke had worried for Logan's life on more than one occasion. When lawmen in California put a price of $5-a-head on any Indian, Luke all but forced Logan out of that swill-hole of a mine they'd been living in. Logan, being half-white and half-Indian, often received the scorn of both worlds.

Price had worried for his friend's livelihood as well and was more than happy to hightail it out of there. He'd had enough of the mud and squalor long before their departure but wouldn't abandon his friends. They were the only people in this world who cared for him at all. He didn't treat that lightly, and his loyalty to them was returned tenfold for it.

From the gold fields in California they traveled the Old Spanish Trail to Texas where they resided with Antonio García, a good family friend of the Stones'. They remained on his ranch over winter until after the spring melt, when the mountains were again passable. The living conditions had been decidedly more comfortable than the gold mine they had fled, but their longing for home never wavered.

Having reached the stables, they slid from their saddles with quick succession and the ease of having lived on a horse's back their entire lives, laughter bubbling from each of them with barely contained joy. They were met by Ray, the stable guard, with lantern in hand.

Luke regaled the old ranch hand of their adventure and bragged about the rich state they returned in, as they unsaddled the sweaty horses and rubbed them down. They left Ray chuckling over their exploits as he returned to his barn duties.

"It's going to be heaven tonight, isn't it, boys?" Luke sighed, referring to the fact that they'd be sleeping in their own beds again. He draped his arms over Price and Logan's shoulders who were on either side of him as they walked from the barn.

They barely stepped from the shelter of the barn when another lantern light was thrust into their faces.

"Well as I live and breathe. The three amigos have returned."

Price's ears perked up. It was Kit Stone's voice, but something was different. She no longer sounded like the adolescent girl they'd left some time ago.

Her voice was fuller somehow. She held up the lantern, illuminating herself in the process. Her body had become fuller

7

as well, Price couldn't help but notice. Her natural physique was such that would probably always leave her more lithe and strong than soft and curvy, but she did possess all the womanly curves Price desired. As usual, she was dressed in her brothers' old clothes, and the snug pants left little to the imagination. Ben's throat worked, suddenly dry.

"Baby sister! Is that you?"

Kit ignored the absurd question as Luke pulled her in for a hug.

"You ran all the way out to the barn to greet us?" Luke tugged a lock of her long brown hair that was loose and cascading down around her, stopping just under the small curve of her breast. Lord, why couldn't Price seem to stop noticing her womanly attributes?

"Not hardly," she scoffed, but her gray eyes sparkled with happiness. "I was headed out to check ol' Maggie. She's due to foal anytime now. I hope she didn't fright into labor without me, what with all your hootin' and hollerin'." They all shared a laugh at her jest, before she added, "I'm sure Ma heard you as well and is waiting for you in the house." Kit stepped to Logan and hugged him, too, then passed by them.

Luke turned after her, "Aren't you going to come inside with us? We've been gone nearly two years after all."

"And I missed you all very much, but I need to check Maggie. You best hurry in without me. By now, Ma has probably woken Livvy and is ready to come drag you in by your ears. Besides, Ma will be nothing but a watering can for the next hour anyway and I know you will just be telling a lot of bull-swap."

"Bull-swap?" Her brother's eyes widened with mock reprimand as if Kit were still a child. To which, Kit rolled her eyes.

"That's right. You'll be in there telling fish tales the first thirty minutes at least. By the time I come back in, you'll have settled down and be ready to share the real details." Kit winked at them all and started to turn back to her mission of getting to Maggie's stall, but hesitated her steps to say, "I really did miss you, though." Then she trailed off with her light deeper into the barn.

Price, Luke, and Logan knew that was as sentimental as Kit Stone was about to get. She never did address Price. That stung a bit. Then again, he hadn't initiated a greeting with her either. Perhaps she had grown shy in the time they'd been away.

Or perhaps she'd seen you looking at her breasts like a lurcher, Price ridiculed himself.

They ascended the steps to the wide wraparound porch. Before they could get to the door, Mrs. Stone rushed over the threshold with her arms opened wide, emitting an exuberant squeal.

"Oh, my boys, you're finally home!"

"That's enough, Mama, save some for the rest of us," Livvy squeezed her way into the group.

"Get in here, Benjamin, you're part of the family, too."

Price awkwardly inched closer, happy to be included, but unaccustomed to such outwardly affection. He would never offend Mrs. Stone, however, so he lightly hugged the group before stepping back.

Sensing Price's discomfort, Luke, being Luke, eased the situation with a joke, "Hear that, *Benjamin*, you're now a part of the misfit Stone tribe."

"Oh, what a right wretched way to describe your family, Lucas Rhys Stone."

"Not home for two minutes, and already Mother is forced to use your middle name," Livvy laughed.

"No offense, Mother, but you do seem to collect strays," Logan mitigated.

"Like a dog collects fleas," Luke guffawed.

"Well, is it my fault I have a perpetual need to shower everything with love?" Ann Stone scrunched her nose in a teasing smile and pinched Price's cheek as if he were a boy of eight rather than the six-foot-one towering man he was.

He thought of Luke and Logan as brothers, that was certain. And Ann mothered him just as she did the rest of them. After the stories he had heard, Price concluded, and accepted along with everyone else who knew Ann stone, she was a mother by nature, and a force of nature. No one would stop Ann from loving a child if she deemed that child in need.

"Not a fault at all," Luke placed a tender kiss atop his mother's head. "In fact, it's why we all adore you so much."

A sentimental tear glistened in Ann's eyes.

"Why don't you move the party into the house," Grayson Stone suggested from the doorway.

They all shuffled inside and made their way to the table. Truthfully, Price, Luke, and Logan desperately needed to wash, but Mrs. Stone and Livvy weren't about to allow it, by the looks of them, smiling away as they were, elbows on the table and faces ready for Luke to spin one of his tales.

"You look well," Ann remarked, observing her boys.

"Gee, Ma, I wrote ya and told ya as much."

"I know, but it's not the same as seeing you in person, for myself. You would tell me you were fine, even if you had just fallen off a mountain, and don't think I don't know it."

Grayson Stone walked around behind his wife and took the seat next to her. Folding her hand in his, he gave a little squeeze, their silent communication to one another expressing how happy they were to have their sons home again.

"Well! Tell us all about it!" Livvy cried impatiently from her end of the table, a huge grin dancing across her face. "How was California?"

"You mean, how rich did it make us?" Luke's eyes crinkled at the corners and his smile tugged up at the sides as it usually did when he was about to delve into one of his stories. Luke had a way about him, he could always charm a room. He weaved just enough embellishments into the truth to captivate an audience without technically obscuring the facts.

Livvy giggled, "All of it, I want to know everything!"

"If you did make a handsome return from it, you were lucky, from what I hear," Grayson spoke.

"Luck being the keyword," Luke stated. "If we hadn't been helping García deliver those sheep to Carson, we wouldn't have had the drop on it. Had we arrived as late as most of the poor sods coming in as we were leaving, we would have probably broken our backs for nothing."

Price listened as Luke crafted an animated retelling of their time digging for gold. He painted it up pretty and divulged just enough harrying details to appease his younger sister without revealing just how terrible some of the experiences had really been.

As Luke finished up the story, Livvy asked cheekily, "So where are the jewels you claim to have brought back for us?"

Seduced by the Saint

Luke threw back his head and laughed.

"Oh, Lavinia, do have some decency," Ann reprimanded half-heartedly.

"I think we put them in your bag, Price. Better pull them out, before Livvy attempts to extract them from us the hard way," Luke teased.

"Shouldn't we wait for Kit before we hand them out?" Price asked.

Luke shook his head, "Nah, she wouldn't be interested in anything pretty! She spends most her time in horse shi—"

"Luke Stone, you watch your mouth," Mrs. Stone cut in, scolding him as if he were still a boy.

This in turn caused Logan to grin as if he were a boy. And Price thought things would surely get out of hand from there. Afterall, one didn't spend time with the Stone family and expect anything other than chaos at any given moment; it was all part of their charm—and why Price was so thankful to be included. Price smiled softly; this was what a loving family was supposed to be like.

"A young woman can like both, man's work and pretty lady's things." Ann's words brought Price back to the conversation. Price thought Ann probably referred to herself in that statement, she seemed equally part lady and horse businessman-er-woman. He wasn't so sure Kit had any of the "lady" in her that her mother displayed. But he didn't think it very gentlemanly of her brothers to speak such aloud either.

"So show us, what did you bring?" Kit's twin sister, who seemed all parts lady and the complete opposite of Kit, asked excitedly. In fact, now that Price thought on it, it was as if the twin girls were each one half of Ann. Livvy was the lady half and Kit was, well, Kit was her own brand, but she possessed her mother's strength and grit.

Price reached for his satchel and felt around, but the items weren't there. "Must have left them in my other pack. I'll run back out to the barn and fetch it."

"That's fine, I'll boil up some coffee and put a kettle of tea on while we wait." Mrs. Stone smiled and shuffled to the kitchen, Mr. Stone following close behind her.

Price's boots churned up pea-stone on the path to the barn, just as his mind churned up thoughts of Kit. She was a fascinating creature. Despite her assurance she wouldn't be long at the barn, her family laughed believing Kit wouldn't be returning to join the family, because she was waiting on a mare to foal.

Her brothers had been gone for nearly two years; he knew how deeply she loved, admired and must have missed them while they'd been away. But Kit would never shirk her duty to the horses for her own personal needs.

No one else seemed to take responsibilities so seriously in the Stone family. Perhaps it was Kit's English blood in her? Price smiled at that, liking that they might share something in common after all.

Perhaps he'd mention to Kit that her brothers had brought gifts back with them for the entire family. Her brothers didn't seem to think she'd be impressed, but Price couldn't help feeling that not inviting her seemed like a betrayal. Being ignored was to be excluded, and he was all too familiar with the pain of that sting.

He stepped into the entrance of the barn, intent on finding Kit, but wasn't at all prepared for the sight before him.

The entrance to the barn was enshrouded in darkness and unusually hushed. An odd sound from the back drifted to his ears. He trudged past the tack room where his satchel remained, his boots quiet against the packed dirt of the alleyway. A lone lantern shone midway down the alley and another in a lone stall at the end where the unfamiliar sound was coming from.

Certainly that must be the stall where Kit was assisting with the birth. He'd never seen a mare foal before. He'd seen his father's hound birth a litter of puppies once. A horse, he imagined, would be quite different. Perhaps Kit may even need some help.

He walked softly as he didn't want to spook the mare or interrupt anything, which was why Kit never heard him approach. His grin at expecting to find a miraculous sight slipped from his face in an instant when he took in the tragic scene before him.

Over the top of the stall he saw Kit huddled inside, against the wall, holding a very unnatural looking foal. Then again, perhaps Price, having no experience with newborn foals, was wrong. He wanted to be wrong, but instinct told him he wasn't. Then he heard the noise that had first caught his interest and realized it was coming from Kit.

She was crying.

His heartbeat intensified and raced with the instinct to protect, but his brain stayed him, knowing there was no danger and nothing Price could do.

He looked on. Kit held the foal across her lap, with her head bent against its neck, clutching the wet, spindly-legged form tight to her body. And her body wracked with sobs she was desperately fighting. Price's throat constricted. The foal appeared unnatural, because it was dead.

Kit's red, tear-streaked face raised from the foal and looked on at the mare who was frantically currying the little foal's body with her lips.

"I'm so sorry, Mags," Kit spoke to the mare. "It's not your fault. You're a good mama horse. I'm sorry I couldn't save him for you. He would have been a fine colt."

Kit leaned over the neck of the colt and pressed her forehead against the smooth hard plane of the mare's face. She closed her eyes tightly, silencing the pain she felt. *Poor Kit*, thought Price, *even in her private moments, she won't completely give over to what she's feeling*. A last lonely tear blinked from her lashes and followed the wet path of the others down Kit's cheek.

Price wanted badly to comfort her, but feared Kit would not welcome his company nor be pleased he had witnessed what she would assuredly believe to be weakness on her part. A noise sounded from the other side of the barn, from the back entrance. Price quickly moved back into the shadows and out of sight.

"How's Maggie coming, Kit?"

Ben recognized Kit's father's deep, gravelly voice. Thank goodness, surely her father would comfort her. He waited to hear Kit's voice.

He heard Kit cough twice to clear her throat. When she spoke, her voice was steady, careful not to betray the tears she'd cried moments ago.

"Not good," she said matter-of-factly. All business once more, she continued, "She lost it."

There was a slight pause where Price thought Kit might break down again and reveal her anguish, but instead she recovered and said, "It—he—came out perfectly formed, but already dead. Doesn't even make any sense."

The last sentence conveyed so much. Her father had to hear what she wasn't saying. Ben waited for the confirmation that her father would comfort her.

"Well, maybe next year..." Her father's voice trailed off.

"No. She'll not be a part of the breeding program next year. I told Mother Mags was too old. This was too hard on her."

It was too hard on Kit. *Can't her father hear her?* Price thought angrily. In his mind he urged her father. *Say something. Hold her. Tell her it wasn't her fault.*

Kit was always so quick to take the blame onto herself. Anytime a training horse misbehaved, Kit claimed it was her fault; the animal wasn't ready and that was a reflection of its trainer. How many times had Price heard her say similar things? The animals were her responsibility and she didn't take such charge lightly, but more than that, she just greatly cared for all of God's creatures. Well, at least the four-legged variety, Price amended. Her soft heart was often overlooked by her family. They were oblivious to her sensitivities, believing Kit to be in possession of none. Price ground his teeth together, if her family only paid her the slightest bit of attention instead of showering all of it on her sister, they would know these things.

Then again, Price knew Kit made it easy to ignore her. She didn't like to attract attention. Whereas Livvy gloried in it. Livvy was like a bright shining star. She twinkled everywhere she went, without any effort. Price knew her family probably didn't intentionally give more to Livvy, it just was so. Perhaps it was easier for Price to find Kit in her sister's shadow, because he had always spent most of his childhood in that of his brother's. He recognized its cold familiarity.

Kit's father's voice cracked the night air once more, "Well, let's go bury it, I suppose." Price heard Kit shuffle to her feet.

That was it. No words for his daughter, whose heart had obviously just been broken. Didn't anyone in this family know Kit?

He heard Kit and her father exit the back of the barn with shovels clanking in their hands. Ben took that opportunity to slip back out the front, stopping only to retrieve the gifts from his pack, and back to the house with his presence in the barn never known.

Chapter 2

Unorganized Territory
Stone Ranch
July 12, 1851

"I don't see why I have to go," Kit grumbled. "I'm nineteen years old; a woman grown. Why should I be forced to attend another year at that wretched school?"

Kit's sister Lavinia, or Livvy, as family and friends called her, continued flittering about the kitchen like a dainty, energetic butterfly, serving coffee to their brothers, Luke and Logan, and their brother's friend, Benjamin Price.

Or *Saint Price*. Or some such nonsense. Kit sneered as she was forced to step over the arrogant Brit's shiny boots, crossed at the ankles before her.

"For all you are supposed to be a '*Saint*' your manners certainly do not reflect such."

In the recent, but rare visits her brothers deemed worthy to bestow their family with since their time at university, they'd been accompanied by the smooth-tongued aristocrat before her. And, apparently, the annoying Englishman had decided to attach himself to them for life!

Impudently, Price slanted his green, almond-shaped eyes at her. His eyes weren't the vivid green of fresh spring leaves like her brother, Luke's. They were more the color of the sagebrush that grew to the far north of them by the Platte River along the trail to Independence. The trail that would deliver her back to the Female Academy of Columbia.

Was she never to have adventures of her own? Her brothers used to include her and Livvy on theirs, before they'd left for university several years ago. Prior to that, and all growing up, her brothers had dutifully catered to their sisters' every whim.

Kit scoffed, well, for the most part they had. Other times they were complete rascals.

Their time at university had changed them. Suddenly having their sisters tag along was inappropriate. Kit understood how society worked, but that knowledge didn't prevent her from finding the situation most unfair.

Kit glared back to the Saint for good measure, his dusty blue-green eyes returning the stare with fervor. He'd find out soon enough that no one could beat Kit Stone in a match of stubbornness. She crossed her arms over her white cambric blouse—one of her brother's old shirts, her usual attire—and got ready to stare him out. Then to her shock and dismay, his peach-hued lips quirked up to one side in a smirk and he winked at her. Winked at her! The man was vastly irritating. And far too handsome. He was irritatingly handsome.

It was a new development, Price getting under Kit's skin. It started when he returned from California with her brothers and it was then she noticed him looking at her differently. Before that he never looked at her at all. Didn't speak overly much to her either. She always assumed him a shy sort. Then again, Kit wasn't particularly engaging, herself, as a young teen. Truth be told, she still wasn't. And Kit had never received marked attention from a man.

Unless one counted Russell Martin. Russell was one of the new ranch hands her parents hired on last summer.

Her parents had had to hire help, as her brothers were always gone, making them fairly useless around the ranch they were to inherit.

Russell was one of a handful who stuck around. Kit rather wished he hadn't. She often felt his eyes on her from a distance, and he liked to materialize next to her from seemingly nowhere whenever she thought herself alone at the barn. In those moments, Kit grew gooseflesh and found his presence quite unsettling.

Price was unsettling for an entirely different reason. When he looked at her, his gaze was full of tenderness, as well as something else Kit couldn't quite identify. Sometimes he looked at her in a way that left little fires over her body, wherever his eyes traveled. It invoked strange feelings within her she'd never before felt.

She found it thrilling.

And that was the unsettling part.

Her sister's voice sounded with confidence from the other side of the kitchen. "You're wrong, Kit. Benjamin is simply Benjamin Price. His father is the Earl of St. Vincent. His elder brother may have a courtesy title, however, Benjamin is just a second son and is afforded no title."

Kit heard her brothers chuckle. Luke, the eldest by a mere few months, added to Livvy's insult, "That's correct. Price, here, is certainly no saint!"

"Well, then why do all of you call him 'the Saint'?" Kit tried to disguise her frustration, lest her family realize she was discomfited over being made to look foolish. Not that she could blame anyone but herself. She supposed she deserved to look foolish since she was the one who had resorted to childish name calling.

Logan's sincere voice answered, "Because of the family name he descends from in part, but also, because he made the highest marks at university."

"Yes, and all the instructors fawned over him," Luke interrupted with a grin, then added, "Thankfully, for us! Logan and I would have been sent home early on more than one occasion if not for our association with 'the Saint'."

Kit noticed Price averting his eyes from the conversation, as if uncomfortable discussing his academic talents. Strange, she would have thought him one to preen over such admissions from his friends.

Luke proceeded to laugh at his own jest, and even their far more serious brother, Logan, twitched his lips in a hint of a smile.

Kit noticed Price's lips quirk as if he were forcing himself to smile and join the banter. She supposed the others wouldn't recognize the action as she did. Kit found herself feigning laughter as the butt of a joke often enough to know it well. She watched as Price played into their teasing, attempting a boyish pout at the insult. The look came off decidedly more rakish in Kit's opinion, however, and she felt her belly tighten.

Perhaps she would be ill. She never felt quite steady around the man. Benjamin Price was so damnably perfect—from his tailored gentleman's attire that never seemed to dirty, to his oil-shined boots. His sandy blond hair was short, but not nearly as close to the scalp as her brother, Luke's, blond hair, and yet it never seemed to be out of place or creased from a hat. Of course, he didn't wear a beaver hat like her brothers and she herself did.

His face was perfect as well, with bold brows, a far darker brown than that of his wheat-colored hair, arching over his light hazel eyes. His eyes seemed to fade from a pale green, like the underside of a leaf, one moment, to a gray-blue the next, accented by long, dark lashes. It should be a crime for a man to have such lovely eyes, thought Kit.

As if to offset the prettiness of his eyes, his chiseled features—from his blade-straight nose to his cut cheekbones and flesh-toned lips—practically made women weak at the knees. Well, not Kit; she didn't have time for such weaknesses.

Even as she told herself that, her eyes drew to his lips. The bottom one was slightly fuller than the top. Just like everything else about the man, he seemed a mixture of soft and hard. Dotting around his soft lips and lining his jaw was the dark, new growth of rough hair. It was probably the only feature about him that wasn't impeccably groomed.

His one imperfect feature was one that only made him that much *more perfect*. Kit found everything about the man quite aggravating!

Price's half-pouted, smiling lips spoke then and his eyes lit with more teasing, "I do have a courtesy title actually. There are some occasions where I may be addressed as the *Honorable* Benjamin Price."

His gaze grew intently on Kit and a warm spiral tingled through her body.

"My, my, how humble we are," Kit angled her head condescendingly, ignoring the tingles. "And here I was under the impression you thought yourself a prince."

19

Logan shook his head as if unamused by the others' jesting and brought the conversation back to panning for gold—the topic they had been discussing prior to Kit's interruption.

Price's tongue wetted the bottom of his upper lip as if he planned to continue their banter, but instead returned his attention to her brothers seated opposite him around the table.

Kit made her way to the stove to procure a cup of coffee for herself. Their mother and Livvy were the only ones in the house who drank tea.

From the counter, she heard Logan's steady voice.

"We already mined in California and each made a small fortune. Why should we head to Cherry Creek to work like dogs in mud and slop again?"

Luke scratched the back of his head in thought, a grin growing across his face.

And the Stone household knew that when Luke Stone flashed his pearly whites, and dimples appeared in either cheek, trouble was about to spew forth.

Therefore, his response, "Why, for the adventure!" came as no surprise to the lot of them.

Logan shook his head again. For all Luke was the eldest, Logan was often the more comported.

Price smiled encouragingly to his boisterous friend.

Kit would perhaps have been smiling, too, if her own life wasn't being decided for her and completely out of her control. *She* was not allowed adventures.

Surlier than when she had first come down the stairs seeking her mother, she turned to trek off in search of her once more. Kit was tired of her brothers having all the fun. It was high time Kit was able to decide for herself.

Before she could get to the front door, she felt her sister's slender fingers at her elbow. Everything about her sister was lovely and lady-like, while Kit had toughened sausage fingers from preferring men's chores to her "Lessons of Refinement" as their mother called them.

From all she had been told about her mother's poor attitude toward such lessons prior to having children, Kit gleaned that Ann Stone was a complete hypocrite!

"I don't think you should speak to Mother right now. Perhaps wait until after her tea."

"You are just afraid I will ruin *your* plans to attend the academy again. You don't care for the saddle and you get carriage sick. What could possibly be so attractive about the school that you would be willing to endure traveling all the way back east for it? The very place where, might I remind you, the good *ladies and gentlemen* thereof spurned our brother Logan; treating him so maliciously Luke nearly dragged him home to flee them."

"Yes, well, that was terrible. But not all the people there are of that mindset, or so cruel. Certainly, none of my friends despise Indians."

Kit had forgotten how many friends Livvy had there. They were probably the reason Livvy wanted so badly to return. Not to mention, all Livvy's dance partners. Kit rolled her eyes.

That lifestyle just wasn't for someone like Kit. She was too course. She didn't care about dining cutlery except for which utensils could most swiftly shovel the food to her mouth. She didn't care for dancing either. Although, admittedly, that was due more to the fact that she was terrible at it. She was athletic and direct. Movements that served her well in the Stone stables, where she helped buck out and train the fresh two and three-year-old horses from their mother's proud breeding line. But on the dance floor? Well, on the dance floor she *still* looked like she was breaking out a young colt.

Livvy, however, had taken to the city life like a bird to the air. Kit sighed. She supposed she didn't want to prevent her sister from living as she desired. There should be a way they could both get what they wanted.

"And do call me Lavinia. Livvy is so juvenile."

Kit rolled her eyes. She suspected her sister's recent aversion to her childhood name had to do with the professor Liv—*Lavinia* had grown quite chummy with. Not that Livvy would discuss such harbored affections with Kit.

She and her sister never used to keep secrets from one another. Livvy used to be Kit's partner in mischief and greatest champion. Kit missed those days. She couldn't help but think the lofty school had changed her sister. Now she had her fancy friends and dandy professor. She was too good for the likes of Kit anymore.

21

It didn't escape Kit that there was a shred of jealousy in her heart. Her sister was all that was refined grace and elegance, a true lady. Whereas Kit was course and awkward amongst sophisticated society. Kit was the one who felt the juvenile, especially compared to her sister. But she'd fit pull her own teeth out before she'd begin ordering people to call her by her full name, Catherine, and walk around superior-like wearing stiff dresses.

Let *Lavinia* have her life of sophistication.

And let her brothers go off on their adventures without her.

She didn't need anyone! She had her horses. Horses she understood, and they understood her.

Kit was too late to retort on her sister's snootiness. More than likely, Livvy, knowing Kit would respond with a snippet of her own, had intentionally gravitated back to their brothers to listen to their exciting plans and ignore Kit. Kit shook her head, irritated with all of her family members—including their friends!

Deciding not to heed Livvy's warning, Kit exited onto the wraparound balcony where she knew she'd find her mother sipping her morning tea.

Tea was one of her mother's fondest indulgences and a tradition she adamantly upheld from her life in England before traveling to America in pursuit of Kit and Livvy's father.

As she turned the corner on the deck, she saw her parents against the rail overlooking the stables and horses. Her father stood to her mother's back, with her enveloped in his arms. Kit hesitated. Perhaps, she was interrupting a passionate interlude. Her parents, she thought with equal amounts mortification and disgust, were not shy with their affections to one another. Kit personally felt they could be a tad more private with those affections. They were ever being discovered in less than proper states. She was about to turn around and disappear, when she heard her name in their conversation.

Well, if they were discussing her, perhaps it wouldn't hurt to hang back silently and hear what they had to say...

"I do despair over our children," Kit heard her mother's soft voice.

"Luke and Livvy: charismatic and carefree. A terrifyingly reckless combination. Then there's Kit and Logan."

Kit's ears perked up even more.

"Equally serious and stubborn. Can't tell either of them anything."

Not true, thought Kit. *Logan isn't nearly as stubborn as me.*

"All set to run their own lives even though I could manage them all for the better," her mother's voice continued in exasperated fashion.

Manage them better, indeed. It was all Kit could do to keep from grunting her strong opposition to the idea.

Her father guffawed then, his gruff laughter echoing across the morning air. She couldn't see her mother's face, but Kit rather thought it probably reflected annoyance for having been laughed at.

Her father rubbed her mother's shoulders soothingly, but said, "Lest you forget. You charged clear across an ocean and another continent just to see things done *your* way when you were their age. I'd say our children are smooth as churned butter compared to you."

Not pleased to be reminded of her youthful foolishness, her mother responded, "Well that is why they should heed my wisdom. And *you*, you old goat, had better start waxing some flattering compliments to make up for your insulting tongue."

Her father began to nuzzle the back of her mother's neck. Livvy was right, her mother's morning tea was not a good time to discuss matters. Kit hurried and fled back in the direction she'd come without being heard. She started returning to the kitchen, then thought better of it. She had no wish to be in the company of her siblings, all free, except her, to do as they pleased with their lives.

Not to mention the *Saint* was still in there, with his arrogant smirks and grins he reserved only for her, because he knew how exasperating she found him. Kit didn't have time for troublesome males in her life. Unless, of course, the male in question was a horse. Speaking of which, she had a new colt to see to at the barn, wherein resided the company Kit preferred.

Chapter 3

Shortly after breakfast, Price followed the Stone brothers out to the stables to retrieve their horses. He was eager to get there. He knew Kit would be in the corral out front working another horse. And by god she was a vision when she was with a horse.

It was nearly five years ago when he had first met Kit Stone, formerly Kit Morgan according to what her brothers shared. Grayson Stone adopted the twin girls when he married their mother. Even Logan, unrelated by blood to any of the Stones, chose to be legally adopted and take the Stone name. None of the siblings, except the twins, were related by blood, but they were closer than any he'd ever witnessed.

Upon graduating from university and nowhere to go, Price had accompanied his friends back west to their home in the mountains. He had been shocked to learn a completely different lifestyle. Where Price's family had been cold and distant, a true noble family of Britain, the Stone family was warm and boisterous. His father would have considered them ill-mannered. But Price found them...endearing. In fact, he was glad to have been welcomed into their home to stay. Quite frankly, he hadn't wanted to leave. He'd never had friends like Luke and Logan.

Kit had just been a gangly teenager on his first accompaniment to the Stone home, and hardly worth notice. It wasn't until this past spring that he'd begun to view her in an entirely different light. He and her brothers had left to hunt gold in California and when they returned the awkward teenager had disappeared and in her place was a lovely grown woman. Not that her brothers had noticed at all. Price felt certain Luke and Logan would ever see their sisters as the pestilent children they had been from childhood.

Both Kit and her sister had been little tagalongs to their brothers, even when Price had met them. He'd been surprised to see his friends not put off at all by the girls' continuous, and often chatty, company. Luke and Logan teased and called them parasites, but Price could always tell they didn't truly mean it. In fact, it was plain to see they adored them and took pride in the fact that their sisters were strong, intelligent young women with adventurous souls. It was a remarkably different family unit than Price had experienced growing up. Made him ponder what kind of relationships he and his brothers may have had, if they had been raised in such a warm and relaxed environment.

It was no use, however. He and his brothers had been reared knowing their places in the world, and those places hadn't been as children to be cherished and loved. No, they had been born to serve the crown, the earldom, and their parents' wishes. Back home in England, he would ever only be a spare: a spare to the title, a spare son, a spare brother.

His father had announced one day that he was sending Price to America. Told him he would send word if he was needed to return. That *need* being if his father or brother happened to perish while he was away. Neither of those possibilities were likely, the men in his family derived from a robust and healthy lineage. His brother and father were no exception.

Price's thoughts were interrupted when his eyes caught sight of Kit in the center of the corral. Lately, his heart sped up at the sight of her for reasons of a more amorous nature—not that she returned such feelings—but this time his heart kicked into a thundering beat for an entirely different reason: fear.

He watched as a young stallion reared above Kit, his ears laid flat back and his teeth bared. The whites of his eyes leaving no room for doubt, this horse was out-of-its-mind mad. Without a thought, Price rushed the fence and vaulted himself over the rails. His boots hit the thick churned dirt, but always a natural athlete, his footing was sure, and he raced to Kit, barreling into her and rolling them both out of harm's way.

He heard her breath exhale on a hard thud and knew his surprise action had knocked the air from her lungs. Before he could check her over for injuries, he thought it prudent to get them both out of the pen lest the crazed stallion charged them.

As he shifted his weight from scooping Kit into his arms to readying himself to lift her high over the top rails, her limbs struck out with wild abandon, causing him to release her abruptly.

Kit fell with another loud, "Ooompf!"

At least she had landed on the safe side, he thought, and then despite his now aching jaw from where she had struck him, climbed the rails and jumped down beside her. Before Price could utter a single word, Kit was on her feet facing him down. Red-faced and seething, she quite resembled the horse he'd been attempting to rescue her from.

"Just *what* do you think you're doing?!" she shouted. Dirt mingled with the sweat on her face and streaked over her lips. She spat a swatch of the grime out of her mouth between huffing for another breath.

Confused as to why Kit was angry with him, he looked toward the crazed stallion as if the answer to her question wasn't glaringly obvious. "That rogue horse was aimed to turn you into corral dust!"

Kit's eyes bugged and her mouth twisted cynically, as if Price were the one out of his mind. She opened her mouth, ready to give him an earful, but instead slapped her hands down to her sides in exasperation, sputtering furious incomprehensible mutterings. She spun on her heel and slid effortlessly through the middle fence rails back into the pen with the beast Price had just rescued her from.

As he started after her, he felt a hand at his shoulder restraining him. Luke's chuckling dissipated as he asked, "What was all that?"

Still somewhat dazed from the entire encounter, Price pointed after Kit, "Why, she's mad to be going back in with that horse!"

Luke smiled amusedly, "Oh, she's mad all right, at you most likely."

"How can you just let her work with a savage animal like that? She could be killed, you know that."

Luke and Price stepped toward the rail where Logan perched, facing the corral. Kit stood in the center of it, coaxing the stallion to her. The horse reared and bit out at the air then charged past her, so closely, Price nearly experienced heart failure. How was it her brothers cared so little for her, that they would allow her to risk her life unnecessarily?

Logan's calm, even voice stroked the air, "You don't know much about sisters, do you?"

Price realized now that neither Luke nor Logan seemed worried for Kit's safety in the least, and he must have looked quite the fool rushing into the pen and manhandling her in such a way. Still, he didn't understand why neither of his friends seemed to fear for their sister. And now he felt rather offended toward Logan's comment.

"Being as I don't have any sisters, no, I wouldn't know a whole lot about them," Price grumbled.

Luke laughed outright and slapped him hard in the middle of the back. To anyone watching it would have looked like chummy comradery, however, despite Luke's laugh, Price was the one who felt the blow. And he suspected the force of it was intended as a warning. Perhaps he should apologize for his handling of their sister?

Before he could make a decision as to whether his friends deserved an apology, Luke said, "If you had sisters you would know that they are the only creatures on earth ornerier than that there rank horse." Luke's dimples appeared as his grin widened.

Then, as if to let Price know his actions had been questionably out of character and hinting at an inappropriate affection toward his sister, Luke stated more gravely, "If my sister ever does need rescuin', she has a pa and two brothers who would take care of that."

Price noticed Logan's keen dark eyes slant in his direction, assuring him of that sentiment as well.

"Hey, you don't have to worry on my account. I'd as soon dance with a cobra than court your sister."

"Wasn't courtin' I was worried about." Luke's tone took him aback.

Price's jaw ticked and clamped tight, "I may not be a *saint*, but I am a gentleman. I'd think I wouldn't need to tell you that."

Luke's features relaxed and a smile lit his face once more. "So long as we're clear on the subject." He turned and headed toward the barn alley. Price hesitated before following, wondering if Logan might have anything to add to the strange conversation. But Logan remained on the fence rails, his eyes trained forward once more on the hellion in the center. And the slow loping horse circling her.

Price's eyebrows shot up as he acknowledged the change in the demeanor of the animal. The beast's eyes were still white, but more focused and less wild. His movements were fluid and rhythmic, beating out a slow pace. The animal's ears twitched and listened, trained on Kit. Kit was in control. Price could hardly believe that was the same animal from moments ago.

He saw Logan tip his hat to Kit, and her acknowledge her brother's approval. Observing them, one knew it was a familiar exchange. Kit's eyes took on a sparkling new clarity and Price saw the pride in them. He couldn't help but be in awe of the woman.

"Hey!" Luke's voice hollered from the barn, "You coming, or are you just going to stand there all day gawking at my sister?"

Logan sent Price a glare over his shoulder then, too.

"I wasn't gawking," Price muttered furiously. Bloody hell, how transparent could he be? He needed to get away from Kit Stone. He knew that with a certainty.

Logan climbed down from the rail to join Price, or more accurately, escort Price, to the barn. Luke met them in the entrance way with squinted eyes, seemingly searching Price for answers. His lips parted as if he would say something, but instead he nodded his head, and the three of them saddled their horses.

Chapter 4

Riding alongside Luke and Logan, they checked the ranch perimeters. It was nearly a full day's ride to cover that much ground. Maybe longer at the pace they were setting, Price thought with some annoyance. Luke and Logan were still arguing over whether they should head to Cherry Creek in search of more gold. The idea was rather unappealing to Price, but he didn't have any plans of his own, and he was happy enough to be included. Therefore, he wasn't going to insert his opinion on the matter. He'd go wherever they decided, certain the Stone brothers would meet success in any direction they chose, and Price along with them. As his friends argued, his thoughts wandered back to Kit. Or rather, her family's treatment of her.

Kit's family seemed to think her made of granite, but Price knew differently. Sometimes he wondered if he was the only one who really did know her. Maybe Kit didn't even know herself. Or more accurately, she was too stubborn to admit to herself she wasn't as strong as she let on. She seemed more than content to put on the charade everyone expected of her. He didn't know if that made her brave or foolish. But a part of him was glad for having glimpsed a side of her no one else knew about. Made him feel special, even if it was his secret alone, when he'd rather it be one shared with Kit.

"Sound good to you, Price?" Luke's voice interrupted his thoughts, bringing him from past to present in a murky-minded state.

"Ahhh...sure," Price stumbled. Of course he had no idea to what Luke referred, since he'd been wool gathering the entire ride.

He noticed, as well, that they had circled back to the barn and it was near supper time.

They put their horses up and headed for the house. Angry voices could be heard from inside as they stepped onto the porch.

~

Kit gripped the back of the kitchen chair with linen napkins bunched between her squeezing fingers as her mother continued setting plates around the table.

Her frustration with her mother's decision grew, "I'm telling you, I'm better off here at home."

Her mother responded, "Your father and I are more than capable of managing the ranch in your absence." She cocked an eyebrow, and added drolly, "After all, we managed just fine before you began insinuating yourself into the mix of it."

The grim line of Kit's lips was all that held her back from retorting that her efforts with the ranch had met with more success than her mother's. It was the truth, but Kit would never state such a disrespectful comment aloud.

Livvy, following Kit with the silverware, poked Kit in the side to move her along so they could finish with the table setting. Kit furtively cast an annoyed glare in her sister's direction, but continued on, forcefully laying napkins beside the plates as she went.

"It is true, you are by far the best horse trainer I've met," her mother stated, surprising Kit. "But there is far more to running a ranch than caring for the horses. They will still fetch a pretty penny at the Cortés Corral, even if we ran them into the pens wild as the mustangs they descended from. It is more important that you see more of the world and receive a higher quality education."

Ann held up her hand to silence Kit's next argument that would surely reference her mother's capability to teach her children.

"I have tried to teach you as well as I was able, but between starting this ranch and not having a strong aptitude—or desire—for traditional teaching, I am aware of the deficiency in your education. Trust me, you will thank me one day."

Hardly, thought Kit. Aloud she exclaimed, "For forcing me to attend a school intended to turn young women into presentable brides-to-be?"

A narrowing look of anger replaced the reasoning look in her mother's eyes. "Where I come from ladies are expected to wed by the age of sixteen. I myself was turned out at seventeen. I am providing you with an outsourced education. A college *for women*—something I was never allotted. I am not forcing or even pressuring you to marriage. All I am doing is forcing you to take advantage of an opportunity. I'm disappointed that you would scoff at the value of an education. The American West is opening doors for women. There are female doctors and teachers. Business owners. Are you telling me you are ungrateful for these opportunities?"

"No. But I think you are missing the point, Mother. Women are not fighting for all women to become doctors. They are fighting for women to have choices. To choose to be a doctor or not. Doesn't mean we must all choose to be one."

"Well, no one is saying you have to be a doctor," her mother argued.

"You are deliberately misconstruing my words," Kit said, frustrated.

"The matter is settled. Ben and your brothers are going to escort you to the academy on their way to Cherry Creek."

Ben, Luke and Logan hesitantly chose that moment to enter the battleground taking place in the kitchen.

Luke was brave enough to speak first, "What's going on in here?"

Livvy replied, "Kit is still trying to ruin our only chance for adventure away from this mountain."

Luke attempted to pacify, " I had to go to a fancy school. Don't see why you shouldn't have to." His teasing and sparkling eyes

31

would normally have eased the tenseness in the room, but Kit was too upset to concede and accept his peaceful entreaty.

Kit chewed the inner part of her bottom lip, ignoring her siblings as she thought over what her mother had last said. For the first time, Kit felt less defeated. If her brothers were escorting her, she'd have a lot more freedom on the trail. Perhaps even take her own horse. She knew others who attended the school boarded horses in the town. The male students did anyway. School would be infinitely more palatable with Blue there to ride and blow off steam when she needed.

"So you are saying I can ride Blue to Columbia this year?"

Before her mother could respond, Livvy cried out, "Oh no, Mother, you mustn't let her ride in like a common ranch hand accompanying us!"

Livvy's snobbish ways were really getting on Kit's nerves.

"I AM a ranch hand," Kit inserted adamantly.

Livvy rolled her eyes in response.

Disgusted with her sister's newfound sense of superiority, Kit crossed her arms and glared at Livvy in return. Honestly, Kit couldn't take much more of her sister's attitude.

Ever since they'd attended the academy with the rich elites back east, her sister had grown to be quite the snob. Kit didn't understand why Livvy was so eager to join their ranks, after how the so called "gentlemen" there had treated their brother. Well, technically it wasn't the same part of the country, but all the easterners were the same in Kit's book. At least, the one's whose pockets were lined with inherited money and hands were coated in baby-soft skin untouched by a day's work.

Kit still remembered when Luke and Logan had returned home from school early their first year in a huff, the Saint right along with them. Luke's contempt for the elite personage of Philadelphia was made known to the entirety of the Stone household.

Logan, however, had returned home, his demeanor unchanged. He remained silent, never speaking of his time there. Even now, years later. And Kit couldn't understand why he ever went back to that awful place.

Luke certainly hadn't been happy, Kit recalled that much. Perhaps he was forced to return as Kit was being so now. Logan may have been able to forgive those horrid people, but Luke hadn't and Kit couldn't reserve her animosity either. To Kit, Livvy's actions stank of betrayal. Where was her loyalty?

Grayson shoved away from the wall then, his plate filled with the supper their cook, Rita, had prepared and laid out on the sideboard. Most days the food was brought directly to the table, but when her brothers were home, every meal was laid out like a buffet. There were simply too many bodies at the table and too much shuffling of dishes otherwise. And Rita certainly didn't waiter plates to and from the table.

Her father's low baritone voice grated through their hostile arguing, "There isn't anything wrong with being a ranch hand."

Kit controlled the urge to childishly stick her tongue out in the direction of her sister.

"Of course not," her mother joined in, "but simply put, Kit is not one. You, Kit, are in fact the granddaughter of an English Earl and heiress to a great fortune."

Livvy cut in, "Indeed, she only comports herself like a ranch hand."

"That is enough, Lavinia. You're not helping," her mother replied, her exasperation with the pair apparent.

Surprisingly, it was Logan who spoke next, "Mother's right. It's your chance to see more of the world, Kit. You should take it. Women are seldom granted these opportunities."

All three women in the house rolled their eyes then at the reminder of society's patriarch rules.

"The world that was so good to you," Kit responded grudgingly.

"That was different," Logan replied. A shuttered look crossed his features and Kit regretted her words.

He spoke again in his ever-gentle tone and measured words, "Not all of society was unenjoyable for me. I don't regret having went to the places I've been. All experiences, good and bad, help a person to grow."

Her mother fairly beamed at Logan, pride shining in her eyes as she crossed to where he was seated at the dining table and placed a kiss to the top of his head. There was a time Logan and Luke would have objected to such coddling treatment, but at twenty-seven years of age they accepted it like gentleman.

Mother is the gushy sort when it comes to her children, thought Kit with a shake of her head. For all Kit's childhood was filled with stories of her mother's bravery in the face of her many hardships, she felt Mother had sure grown soft in the years since their family came together.

Livvy spoke up and ruined the moment, "Well, Mother? Are you ordering Kit to attend another year at the academy with me?"

Ann sighed and directed her gaze to Kit, "You are going."

Kit clamped and unclamped her jaw. "I'm finished," she placed her napkin over her plate of barely eaten food and stood rudely, "for I have lost my appetite."

Her mother's voice turned stony to match her gaze, "You may be dismissed to pack your clothes. Your brothers will escort you and Lavinia to the academy on the morrow."

Kits lips remained pursed and face pinched with anger, but she inclined her head with a nod. She was only brave enough to cross words with her mother so much.

As she was making her way from the kitchen, she heard her mother add, "You may take Blue and board him in town while you are there."

The reminder that Kit would at least have her horse was some comfort. As well as knowing it would serve to make Livvy unhappy.

Chapter 5

Price watched as Kit stomped her way around the barn, evidently still fuming over being forced back to the academy. He saw that new hand, Russell, following her with his eyes as well. Price looked around to see if others were present to take notice. Of course if they were, they'd have caught Price as well. Gooseflesh raised the hair on his skin. He didn't like that Russell character. Price didn't have rights to be friendly with Kit Stone either, but this Russell sure as hell didn't have any right to be sniffing around her.

He'd inform Mr. Stone before they headed out today. Let Kit's father deal with the situation as he felt best. Since telling her brothers only garnered their speculation about where his own eyes have been.

They nearly had the wagon loaded down and ready to set off, but first they'd all sit together for breakfast—their last meal all together for months. And it was awfully hard to get mail through the mountain passes come winter. There'd likely be no communication again until spring unless someone happened to be riding through.

The riled foot stomping in the barn ceased. Price peeked his head around the barn door to investigate and saw Kit saying goodbye to each of the front pen mares. Price smiled. *And Kit wants all those around her to believe her heartless.*

From seemingly nowhere, having not heard him approach, Luke appeared next to Price. Luke's eyes squinted with all his harbored suspicions from Price to Kit, but he held his tongue.

Irritated with the continuous accusations thrown *his* way and Luke and Logan's refusal to take the threat of Russell seriously, Price explained, "I saw Russell following her again. Just wanted to make sure he wasn't up to no good."

"Ah. Nothing again, though, I see. In fact, all I see is you following her."

Angry heat fused through Price's body at the accusation, but his English blood cooled it before it made its way to his mouth. Instead he said, "I'm telling you, you need to be keeping an eye on him."

Price saw the moment Luke's shoulders unstiffened. "Yeah...I agree," he relented, much to Price's surprise, "something's a little off with him."

Just then, they both heard the thudding sound of something heavy hitting the packed dirt floor within the barn.

When they turned their heads, they saw Russell lying on the floor at Kit's feet, grimacing in pain.

It was clear Kit had sent him there. Russell's face, unmarked by blood, evidenced Kit had used her favorite tripping method–a trick she'd learned from her brothers and had perfected over the years.

Price had never been on the receiving end of it himself, but he had seen her employ the tactic on Luke once or twice. It was a simple hook-behind-the-leg motion, but it was effective.

As Russell had surely just learned.

Kit looked down, "I told you, you were bound to get hurt sneakin' up on me like that."

They watched as she offered her hand to assist Russell to his feet.

Luke sauntered forward, in his usual slow, cocksure gait and greeted the ranch hand, "Howdy, Russell. What brings you up to the barn this morning?"

The smirking of Price's lip was barely discernible, in fact, many would never have noticed, the movement was so small. He had been on the receiving end of this deceptive calm of Luke's— more lately than ever—and he couldn't help feeling pleased

Russell had been caught out. The figurative firing gun was finally aimed where it belonged.

Russell addressed Luke, "Thought I'd head out a little later today. Stay close to the house for now, in case you all needed an extra pair of hands loading up the wagons."

"My father give you that order?"

A hard glint crossed Russell's features, like a snake tightening its coil ever so slightly.

Luke didn't wait for a response, just tipped his hat, "Well, run along now. And get to the duties you were hired to see to. I think four grown men can handle packing up two little ladies, without any extra *help*."

Russell nodded with dark eyes below slanted brows, a mean grimace on his face. He didn't counter Luke, but all present knew the man was not happy with his humility check. Once Russell was out of hearing distance, Kit said, "I don't know if that intimidating peacock display was necessary. I handled him just fine."

Price spoke almost before he knew he was doing so, "But you shouldn't have to."

Kit looked to him as if just realizing he was there. Her lips gaped slightly, taking in his presence and the words he'd spoken.

"Russell just wanted to say goodbye," she said, shrugging off the young man's bold and inappropriate actions.

"I know what Russell was doing," Luke spoke.

A little harshly, if one asked Kit. Her brother's mood seemed a bit absurd considering.

"Okay," Kit spoke, "then you know there was no harm in it. Well, other than the harm inflicted on *him* when I threw him to the ground." She chuckled, hoping to lighten the severe expression on her brother's face. "Besides, it's all the touching he does that makes me uncomfortable, not the thought of him shirking chores to say goodbye."

Price and Luke both stiffened at Kit's innocent revelation. Her smile was unwavering as she finished oiling the leather strap on her saddle, completely oblivious to the fury coursing through both men beside her.

Looking to Luke, this time it was Price wearing the superior all-knowing look. Price had been right all along about Russell panting after Kit.

"Just what kind of touching?" Luke growled.

The fierceness of Luke's tone took her aback. Kit stammered at first, "N-Not any romantic type touching if that's what has you looking like a rabid coyote fixin' to tear the hind end off a lamb." Her eyebrows scrunched and Price knew she was fueling up for another speech about her fending for herself and not needing her brothers breathing down her neck.

Of course, ironically, it's the opposite of the speech she delivered to them when they first arrived after any of their long adventures. That's when she released her guilt speech about her brothers not being home nearly enough. Price quite enjoyed the intricate relationships and bonds between the siblings, often entertained by their madcap antics.

To Price's surprise she held her tongue.

"Just stay away from that kid. He's no good for you."

Then Luke had to go spouting another bullying big brother dictation. All the Stones were similar in that respect, from Price's observation. Each fought to have the last word.

"I'll talk and touch whoever I damn well please. And you can just stay out of it." Kit poked her brother in his puffed-with-over-importance chest. Price rather thought Luke's sisters may be the only people on the planet he'd allow to get away with that.

"The hell you will. You won't be touching anyone and vice versa. That's one good thing about you and Livvy heading back to that girls' school."

Kit snorted a laugh.

"And what's that supposed to mean?" demanded Luke.

"There may not be any male students, but there's plenty of male instructors. Not to mention, there's a men's college right at the other end of town. They always get invited to the holiday and going away balls. Plus, they are always about the town. And there's far too many of us girls to be adequately chaperoned ALL of the time."

With a final tug of her saddle bag strap into place, Kit smiled gleefully and headed out the back side of the barn, leaving Luke furious and Price more surprised than ever at Kit's knowledge of the male proximity to the female academy.

Price and Luke exchanged flabbergasted glances with each other before a flustered Luke turned on his heel out of the barn.

"I'm going to go see to that Russell getting his final dues and a ride outta here on the morrow. You mind loading up those stacked barrels by yourself?"

Price gave a quick assertive nod, leaving Luke to the business Price had been trying to get him to do for weeks.

He had loaded up the last barrel from the barn and realized Kit hadn't yet come back to saddle her horse. Curious, he stalked to the exit near the back of the barn. His blood came to an instant boil when he heard Russell's voice.

"Sorry about that. Hadn't meant for your brother to interrupt. Just wanted to say a proper goodbye was all."

Price, still hidden in the shadows of the barn, inched slowly along the wall until he could see Russell. He couldn't see Kit, but he heard her.

"Well, that's kind of you, Russell. Thank you." She regarded Russell with impatient directness, speaking the polite words, but not actually lending any of the warmth that typically accustomed such. Price knew that tone. Kit was set on a task and she didn't have time to talk to anyone when she had duties to attend to.

Price saw Russell's body shift as if reaching his arm out and it took all manner of self-control not to lunge from the shadows.

"Well, by proper goodbye, I kind of had something in mind."

Price, somehow, found the strength within to restrain himself. It wouldn't do any good to go rushing out like a mad bull and infuriate Kit further. He waited, sure Kit would set Russell in his place as she would have himself or her brothers.

There seemed to be a suspicious hesitation. Price risked angling his head to better see Kit's position. Instead, he saw the back of Russell's head as his face was bent over Kit's with his lips locked on hers. And then he only saw red.

~

Her brothers could be complete asses sometimes. They were gone, sometimes years at a time, on some fool errand or another, leaving Kit and Livvy completely to their own devices and then think they can show up and act the gentleman chaperone. Ha! As if they needed chaperoning. Like she'd been trying to tell her mother, she and Livvy were full-grown women who could make decisions and take care of themselves.

Once she was sure Luke and Price were no longer in the barn, she returned to saddle Blue—her one boon in this pending nightmare of a trip. At least she could test Blue's endurance. She'd never had him off the ranch before, it would be good experience for him. He might just turn out to be the best horse this ranch ever produced. Too bad he had been gelded as a colt.

Kit was caught up listing all her horse's excellent attributes in her head when she ran into someone before reaching the back entrance of the barn.

"Sorry 'bout that, Kit."

She looked up to see Russell's blue eyes smiling down at her. Well, his whole face was smiling, but his eyes definitely had an odd happy gleam to them. It was those strange tendencies that made her feel uncomfortable around the man for some reason. She didn't fear the bumbling fool by any means, she knew she could take him down in a gun fight, and probably a physical fight, too. She'd wrestled her brothers before in fights and come out on top, and they were far more stout of build than Russell.

Russell had somewhat of a lean physique. Well, no, lean wasn't right. Price was lean; lean and trim, but muscular and strong looking. Russell was, well, wispy. Like a good wind might blow him away. And the brown lanks of hair that fell around his face under his hat looked unclean. Kit much preferred the close cut of Price's hair.

Kit shook her head, how did she come to comparing Russell to Price in her mind again? Thoroughly irritated, she tried to focus on what Russell was going on about. She just wanted to get to her horse, so whatever she needed to say to appease him and get him out of her way, she would. She tried to smile and nod her head as if listening, while saying as little as possible. She knew speaking would be taken as an invitation to continue talking. If she held her tongue, she was sure he'd talk himself out. *Any second now*, she thought.

Wrong.

One moment he was uttering some nonsense about a proper goodbye and the next his wet mouth was covering hers.

Her first reaction was to shove him, but she held back, for a thought occurred to her. She wasn't any great beauty, and she didn't have plans to ever leave Stone Valley, so this may be her only opportunity to see what the big deal was about kissing.

Russell's eyes were closed as his mouth pressed against hers. She finally realized he was trying to pry her lips open with his tongue. The idea was repugnant to Kit. When his teeth gnashed into her teeth, she'd decided that was enough experimentation. She knew enough now to determine kissing was disgusting and thoroughly uncomfortable.

Just as she was about to push him away, Russell went flying through the air, as if her thoughts alone had been strong enough to force him from her.

What in God's name—?

Then she saw him emerge from the shadows like an avenging storm. Ah, the Saint. Of course he would appear from nowhere the one time she decided to dabble in the female arts.

She started to speak, but the look on his face made her rethink that wisdom. She'd never even seen her brothers look that furious. Russell, however, seemed to be lacking the brain cells required to know that he should be in fear for his life at that moment.

Russell stood, brushing the dirt from his clothes. He repositioned his hat and had the audacity to smile, "Why hey, Saint. What brings you out here?"

Price didn't utter a word. His stance and silence were more threatening than any words. Kit rather thought it foolish of Russell to do anything other than run at this point. She really ought to say something in Russell's defense, after all, she had let the man kiss her.

Russell's smile faltered. "I was just, ah, telling Kit goodbye." He sent a smug look toward Kit that only made her want to wallop him.

"Thought you did that already," Price stated. All present knew it wasn't a question. "Fortunately, that was your last one."

Russell's blue eyes squinted, "I wouldn't be so sure about that."

"Oh, I'm bloody damned sure."

Taking Price's meaning, and without another glance to Kit, Russell scrambled off hastily.

Kit thought it a good time to interject something, but then Price turned his stony gaze to her.

"What about all that nonsense back at the barn, when you told Luke you could take care of yourself?" he demanded

41

Kit crossed her arms and quirked her brow. She wasn't as easily cowed as Russell, plus she knew to show fear to her enemies was to lose the battle before it ever begun. She widened her stance and settled in for the argument.

"What makes you think I can't?"

Price pulled a face and cocked his head in the direction Russell had fled as if that was answer enough.

"I had the situation completely under control. There was no need for you to come growling like a protective mother bear."

Price was taken aback by the comment. *A mother bear*? Oh, now that was emasculating in the extreme. He'd felt rather more like the warrior coming to the princess's rescue. Perhaps he should remind her of the "situation" she seemed confident she was "in control of."

"Were you aware then that Russell had his lips and hands on you as if you were a two-bit whore he'd paid for?"

The words were harsh, but he thought she needed a good dose of reality. That reality being she had been in danger and hadn't even known it.

Anger flickered in her eyes. "So any woman who receives a kiss from a suitor is a...is a...is behaving immorally?" She could swear with the best of them, fully trained in the art of a sailor's tongue—compliments of her brothers—but she couldn't bring herself to say the word *whore*. Which made her feel childish and irritated her further.

"Are you saying you welcomed his advances?" Price looked more unsettled than she'd ever seen his English airs allow.

"Are you saying I shouldn't be flattered that a young, handsome ranch hand finds me desirable?"

Price suddenly felt as if he'd been transported from land. How had he ended up in this strange territory with Kit? Since when was Kit Stone "flattered" to be found "desirable?" And since when did she decide she wanted to be desirable?

Hell, if that was what she wanted to know, he could set her straight on the matter.

Kit smiled smugly.

Price knew she thought she had flustered him in a way that would have worked on her brothers. Her brothers would have been embarrassed to be discussing their sister's desirability with her and would have disguised that embarrassment with a bravado show of brotherly protector.

But that saucy minx of a smile of hers affected Price a whole lot differently.

He decided to play her game and call her bluffs instead.

"You didn't much care for it, did you?"

Her confident smile wavered, "Didn't care for what?"

Price smiled, feeling he firmly held the upper hand, "Russell's kiss."

He watched as her smile slipped completely and the familiar irritated scowl crossed her features again.

"What makes you think that?"

"Because Russell is barely more than a kid. Doubt he knows how to *properly* kiss a woman." He watched Kit's eyes lower to his lips.

"And I suppose you consider yourself man enough for the job?"

Price lowered his gaze to her lips and saw the moment she softened under his perusal of her. That was all the invitation he needed.

He filled the space between them in a quick stride, tipped her head back gently to meet his and pressed his lips to hers.

Her arms circled around his neck encouragingly, and his controlled movements were quickly lost as he gave in to his hunger for her.

His soft exploration of her lips turned ravenous. He coaxed her tongue to join his in nature's dance of desire.

The satisfaction he felt when she melted against him drove his need to fulfill all she was seeking.

She moaned her pleasure against his lips and, unfortunately, reality came crashing back to him.

Dear God, what was he doing? He was supposed to be lecturing her about allowing Russell to take liberties. Instead, here he was dallying with her; Kit Stone, sister of his two best friends. Quickly, he forced her from him and stepped back, effectively breaking the kiss that never should have happened.

~

Confused at the sudden separation, and still dazed with the passion he'd stirred within her, she looked to Price for answers and read horror on his face. Shame and embarrassment coursed through her. She must be terrible at kissing. It had felt marvelous to her. Shocking, but marvelous, all the same. Obviously, Price hadn't felt as she had.

Anger came to her rescue, vanishing her feelings of embarrassment. With pride smarting she snipped, "I don't know what you think you're doing but I'm not interested."

~

This had not been in Price's plans. He had given some thought to a proper courtship, one day far later in the future. And maybe a little thought to stolen kisses during such a courtship. Okay, a lot of thought on that score. But he never intended to act on it so soon, perhaps not ever.

This was not ideal, especially with a two-month long trip ahead of them with forced close quarters. Effecting a cool manner and appearing unstirred by the kiss seemed the best course to deflect any suspicions and unpleasantness. Considering her irate stance, invoking a sense of calm could prove easier said than done.

He would deliberate on the fact later that she had melted into his kiss like she had in every dream he'd ever conjured of their kisses since he'd been taken under her spell.

"Don't flatter yourself," he said, "it was a temporary lapse of control. Nothing more."

She flinched visibly, and Price contemplated telling her the truth. No, she didn't feel the same. It would destroy his place here, the only place he could call home, with the only people who cared about him.

"Well, you were the one who initiated the kiss. I was just a hapless victim."

"You kissed me back."

Her face reddened, with embarrassment or anger, he wasn't sure.

"If I did, it was reactionary and certainly no indication of a response to you."

Definitely anger.

"Reactionary? Have you been making it a practice to kiss men behind the barn?"

"I'll have you know that there *are* men who find me attractive and desirable. And they aren't afraid to show me."

Now it was Price's turn to see red. "If you're referring to Russell, you can be sure he will have touched you for the last time. I'll see to that. You stay away from him."

"You don't get to tell me what to do. I have plenty of bosses already. But your order shall be obeyed, for now at least, since we are leaving within the hour!"

"Good."

"If you will excuse me. I still need to carry out the last orders I was given," Kit snarled. "And for the record, you may want to work on *your* self-control."

Chapter 6

Female Academy of Columbia
March 21, 1852
8 Months Later

Kit stared out the window in her chambers, recalling Price's lips on hers. And the awkwardness between them in the weeks that followed on the trail to the academy. It had been a long two months of travel—what with a sickly Lavinia, two bickering brothers...and the Saint.

Luckily, she and Price spent most of the trip avoiding one another. That endeavor helped some to make the time pass more quickly. Being preoccupied with every detail of Price and how to covertly keep her distance from him, kept her from dwelling on the boredom of trail life and from acknowledging her sister's complaints.

Time passed quicker still the closer they got to Independence, as the roads became more passable and easier to maneuver. So many new settlers were on the move. The trail was hardly recognizable from the year before. It was now packed earth, none of the prairie grasses even attempted to return growing under the steady crunch of wagon wheels.

Kit agreed with her brothers—too many people were making their way west. Soon the entire land would be broken into states and people would be covering their mountain home in no time, filling it with the industry and noise of the east. Kit curled her lip in disgust at the thought.

She wondered what Price thought about that. And was he planning to stay on at Stone Ranch indefinitely? Lavinia had actually sparked this question the other day, stating that their brothers would all be starting their own families soon, and where would that leave Price?

Kit didn't think her brothers would be setting their caps to marry all that soon, but the thought it would happen one day was unsettling. As well as the words Livvy had spoken next, "And surely Ben will return to England for a proper wife, then."

Kit touched her lips again. A proper wife. Yes, one as cold and English as he was. And why should Kit care?

Just then the door to their room flew open and her sister fled in a flurry of skirts.

"I'm so fed up with that ogre, Gabriel Hart. He thinks he can do anything or say anything he likes."

Kit rolled her eyes. This was not a new topic of discussion. For some reason Gabriel Hart made it a hobby to irk her sister. She often found herself agreeing with Gabriel, however. Her sister was a snob, it was great fun to get a rise out of her.

"Why were you standing so solemnly by the window? My goodness, Kit, cannot you even scrounge up an iota of cheer for the holiday?"

This, too, was not an uncovered topic. In fact, it was one of great contention between the two of them. So much so, they had switched rooms so as to share as little space with one another as possible. Kit was glad for it, mostly. She'd switched to be paired with Kate Kerryton, a girl who kept to herself mainly, reading books in all her spare time. Lavinia was still across the hall, though, so it wasn't as if she was free of her entirely. And, lately, her sister's activities had become more than a bit suspicious...

Kit wasn't about to bring that topic up, however, and she surely wasn't going to disclose that she was thinking about Benjamin Price!

"It's not fair," stated Kit instead. "After tonight, everyone else will get to go home to celebrate Easter with their families and we'll be stuck here."

"You know it would be futile for Pa to come all this way through the mountain passage this time of year. Why, there wouldn't be enough time for such travel anyway. It's a short holiday break; only the ones whose families live nearby are leaving. The rest of us shall make do. The end of the school year is but a short two months away. I dare say you shall survive it."

Kit knew all of this. She wasn't a complete ignoramus. She could STILL express her dislike about it all.

"I wish Great Uncle Rupie hadn't whisked our cousins out of the country. We could have stayed with them over the holiday break. Besides, I miss them all terribly."

Livvy's annoyed expression softened, "As do I. However, you know Grandfather's health is ailing and he needed Uncle to return home to England."

"I still say cousin Suzannah could have stayed on with us. England wasn't *her* home after all."

"Your petulance has taken another selfish turn. Stop whining over every little thing and try to enjoy the remaining time we have here."

Had Livvy been looking Kit's direction, she would have been seen the daggers Kit's eyes shot toward her. As it was, she was spared their cut.

Kit decided to shake it off and ignore her sister in hopes she would leave all the sooner. She was wholly unprepared for her sister's next idiotic sentence: "Maybe you will meet someone."

Kit heard the excitement through the cautious reserve in her sister's voice. The question left Kit looking like a bluegill after a worm on a hook.

"Meet someone! Like a man?"

Livvy smiled, pleased with the comedic reaction she'd elicited from Kit. Then she grew serious again.

"Yes, of course. Don't you want to marry someday? Don't you believe in love?"

Kit answered with a roll of her eyes and effectively kept her private, inner thoughts to herself. If she loosened her tongue and spilled the truth, that she *did* believe in love, but didn't believe anyone could actually love *her*, her sister would have been on the next brain train trip to the altar. And Kit would have been her hostage passenger.

"Don't tell me you're still mooning over Price."

Kit had thought her sister was through shocking her, but apparently not. Just what did her sister know about her and Price, anyway?

"I don't know what you're talking about. I haven't the slightest interest in 'the Saint'."

Livvy studied her sister with lips pursed and narrowed eyes for a moment, then shrugged, saying, "I suppose that must be true. I didn't think him your type. He's not the rugged sort you would go for. He's far too sophisticated for your tastes. Not to mention, as far as looks go, he's not the most appealing male specimen in general."

Kit felt offended on so many levels she could barely sputter forth a sentence. She couldn't be certain whether Lavinia was insulting her or Price, so she decided to be insulted enough for the both of them.

"Firstly, I would hardly consider Price 'unappealing'—just because he's not built like a reed shaft as is your precious professor. Secondly, you have no idea as to what I find attractive in a man."

To that Lavinia raised an eyebrow, "Oh, so you're telling me you don't intend to marry a ranch hand? Someone to help you buck out the next crop of young horses?"

Kit clamped her mouth shut. She couldn't argue against that, for if she thought about marriage at all, in which she hadn't in the least, the man her sister described did seem the adequate partner she should aspire to acquire.

Price certainly didn't fit that description. Kit could never picture him working brassy young colts alongside her. He didn't know a thing about raising horses or training them. He would never be a suitable partner for her.

And yet...his kisses felt branded to her lips...

Livvy was bent over the little beauty table, the topic of Price forgotten, applying rouge to her lips. *Rouge?* That seemed a bold move, even for her sister. Why, she was dressing like a harlot! What had gotten into her sister lately, anyway? Kit looked on with mild curiosity and disgust, trying to decipher her sister's mood.

49

"What do you think of this dress? Well, not of the dress, I know you care not for fashion. But rather, how do I look in it?"

Livvy didn't give Kit a chance to reply.

"Aunt Cora and our cousins sent it from England. All the other ladies here tonight will be quite envious," Livvy's eyes glowed as she continued her perusal of herself in the looking glass, "Last year, they tried to snub me, because they had the latest fashions from the East coast. But not this year. Places like Boston and Philadelphia haven't even seen the newest trends from Paris or England. Notice the neckline is slightly lower."

Kit had noticed. In fact, everyone was sure to notice her sister's scandalous décolletage. Her breasts were practically spilling over the green silk.

"And," Livvy asked as she spread her arms wide and turned slowly for Kit's viewing, "did you notice my new waist?"

Kit had not noticed her sister's new waist, whatever that could mean.

"Honestly, Kit, look," Livvy blew an exasperated breath. "My waist is entirely slimmer. It's called a bone corset. It required quite a bit of effort lacing. The poor morning maid worked up a sweat tying it, but it sucked me in nearly an entire hand length!"

Kit looked again. This time she did see, where normally her sister's womanly frame filled out a bit more, it was cinched in dramatically, enhancing an hourglass figure. Her sister, apparently, did not require a response from her, however, as she returned to focusing on her face in the looking glass once more.

Kit was still trying to wrap her head around all of her sister's changes when Livvy said excitedly, "This night is going to be glorious. Don't you agree, Kit?"

"If you call wearing all the extra weight in material of a ball gown and trying not to make a complete fool of myself the entire night 'glorious'."

Livvy appeared to be tugging hairs one direction, only to place them back exactly how they were before. She was acting like a crazy person.

"Yes, well, if only you would show as much enthusiasm for the dance floor as you do working a horse, I think you'd quite enjoy it."

"Livvy, is all of this," she gestured with her hand in circles about her face, implying the mad artistry taking place, "for that professor you've been moon-eyed over?"

Livvy smiled coquettishly, "Maybe." Then she looked over the mirror with no trace of playfulness, "And, it's Lavinia. How many times need I remind you not to call me by my childish pet name?"

"Why did you barge into my room?"

I'd like to borrow the brooch Mother packed you."

"Mother packed me a brooch?"

"Oh, honestly Kit, did you even look through your chests after our belongings were unpacked?"

"Why would I, when our clothes are laid out for us every day, as if we were incapable of dressing ourselves?"

Kit went to a small set of drawers where she perceived any packed jewelry would be and easily discovered and retrieved the brooch.

The plain ivory brooch on ribbon. Not nearly eye-catching enough for her sister's usual taste...

Kit's brows drew together, "You came into my room, only to borrow this?"

Livvy gave a quick glance to the floor before returning her gaze to Kit, "Of course." Kit watched her sister's focus turn rather intently to clicking back her cuticles. "Oh, and will you be attending the ball this evening?"

Kit had been undecided, although with her sister's out of ordinary behavior of late, she rather thought she should attend just to keep an eye on her. There was something Kit couldn't quite determine about the professor that she didn't like. Livvy seemed to believe Kit was simply jealous because she spent more time with the professor than with her, but that was absurd. Kit had switched rooms to be away from her. She wasn't jealous.

And she wasn't jealous that Livvy had a beau, either. It's just, shouldn't a professor, especially of a young ladies' academy, be more circumspect about his students' reputations? Instead he seemed to be putting her sister at risk. It certainly didn't seem an honorable or gentlemanly action to take, even if he was courting Livvy; which seemed wholly inappropriate if one asked Kit. And probably, if one asked their mother, too...

"Actually, I am going," Kit said, prepared to gauge her sister's reaction.

"Oh. Oh, well, that's wonderful, dear. I'm happy you have finally decided to partake in ladies' festivities. Perhaps you will even convince your hermit friend to join as well. To keep you company." Livvy's tight smile told Kit all she needed to know. She was up to something and wanted Kit to be otherwise engaged. That could only mean a duplicitous activity. Well, Kit would see about that.

Kit smiled, "I'm not sure she is going. In fact, she is currently to the library fetching a good book to keep her entertained for the evening. But at least I shall have your company."

"Er—yes, that is, when I'm not dancing, I will try to see how you're faring." She held her manufactured smile in place as she backed out of the room.

"Oh," Livvy held the brooch out toward Kit, "you know, I think I will wear something else. Afterall, you should wear this as I know it's the only adornment you have here with you."

She dropped the brooch into Kit's extended hand and fled the room.

Damn her sister to hell. Now Kit would be stuck babysitting all night and be required to dress in layered taffeta while she did it.

Chapter 7

Kit really abhorred these fake gatherings. She rubbed the bare expanse of her arms between the puffed dress sleeves at her shoulders to where the silk gloves began above her elbows. Not so much because she was cold, but more to distract herself from her own humiliation. She should have been cold, but whether she was cold or not, she didn't know, because she was too anxious to feel anything inflicted from the physical environment around her.

She *hoped* she appeared cold. Cold would be normal, being it was mid-March already. Her eyes searched once more over the chatty young ladies occupying the edges of the dance floor and the pairs twirling about to the beat of the orchestra. Where had Livvy gone off to? The skeezy professor had yet to make an appearance tonight, so at least he wasn't behind her sister's odd absence.

Just then, she felt a presence to her right.

"You seen your sister around?"

Ah, Gabriel. "She was here a few moments ago, but then she dodged out of the room and I haven't seen her reenter."

She noticed a pink stain rising over Gabriel's Hispanic colored features. She slanted her eyes to the side to study him more closely, then hooked an eyebrow in mock accusation, "Why? Have you seen her?"

I'm afraid she may have fled the dance floor due to...due to a conversation we were having." Gabriel looked away guiltily.

"A conversation? Or another argument? I can tell you which one I think more likely," Kit supplied sarcastically.

"Well, your sister is a stubborn one."

Hmm, interesting.

Gabriel seemed riled beyond mild irritation with her sister, which was rare. In response to his comment, she said, "That's not new information to either you or me. What exactly caused this row?"

She watched as his features tightened and a hardness crossed his eyes.

"Just don't let her wander off alone with Sidney. I—" Gabriel brought his voice down to a whisper, "I've heard sinister things about the man, and I don't believe he is to be trusted."

Just to play devil's advocate, Kit said, "The professor? At a female academy? Not to be trusted? Are you implying, sir, that this institution is ill fit for delicate, proper young ladies?"

It was Gabriel's turn to give Kit the side eye.

Kit quirked her lips, the most smiling she had done since arriving to the blasted academy, and relented in her false support of the professor. Then added seriously, "I happen to agree with you. Which is why I am searching so heartily for her. Perhaps we—"

"Well, as I live and breathe! My sister, all spun up in silk and shimmering like a freshly hooked rainbow trout."

Luke's voice? Kit inhaled her shocked breath and turned her head over her shoulder in search of him. There striding toward her were her brothers Luke and Logan. And the Saint. Nervously, she swallowed what felt like a dry ball of air. His hazel green eyes were piercing through her. Did everyone see him looking at her like that? It could hardly be appropriate.

She was about to ignore his look and rush her brothers eagerly with a hug, when her brother's words dawned on her. *A fish?* Had her brother just referred to her, in front of a ballroom full of Saint Louis's finest, as a *slimy fish?*

Kit's twisted face must have revealed her revulsion to such a comparison, because Logan dipped in for a hug and rushed to correct Luke's so-called compliment, "Our sister would look lovely even if she were draped in a burlap sack. As it so happens, the silk gown is even more flattering." Logan's soft-spoken words caused her to blush. He had never said any such thing like that to her before. She didn't know whether to be embarrassed or to embrace the compliment like a warm cloak. Then her eyes met Price's and her blush deepened. Definitely embarrassment. Oh, where was Livvy, who always knew exactly what to say, and could always come up with witty conversation that smoothed the most awkward of situations?

"That's what I said." Luke appeared affronted. Kit couldn't help but notice the slightest roll of Price's eyes toward the rafters and a small smile tugged at her lips.

"Where is our other beauty of a sister?" Luke searched the room.

"She must have escaped back to her rooms, for I haven't seen her in quite some time."

Gabriel had shuffled away when her brothers arrived to allot them some space, but she felt his return to her side, now.

"I don't mean to break up your family reunion, but I think it imperative that you go check on your sister. See if she is in her rooms. I saw Sidney briefly enter near the library wing before disappearing into the crowd. I can't be certain which direction because I was waylaid by Miss Porter."

Instantly the cheery mood turned dark. Her brothers' smiles transformed to glowers. And they were directed toward Gabriel.

"Exactly what are you implying, Mister...?"

"Hart. Gabriel Hart. And I'm not trying to be insensitive. I fear for Miss Stone's safety."

This raised surprised brows from her brothers and dread settled in Kit's stomach like a bad omen.

"Livvy has been...being courted, I believe, by Albert Sidney," she explained hesitantly. " He is a professor here. I believe the courtship started last year."

Her brothers turned angry faces toward her, "And you didn't think it imperative to divulge that bit of information to us? Or Ma and Pa for that matter?"

Kit crossed her arms defensively, "No, I did not. There was no harm in it. And why should she be denied love if she finds it?"

Gabriel cut in, "Well, I don't think he loves her. And I don't think he's been courting her either. Charming her more like."

Gabriel raised his eyes over Kit's head to communicate some kind of manly code to her brothers.

Kit shivered, "Well I will go check our rooms. More than likely she came down with a megrim and needed a break. I'm sure Livvy would never plan anything untoward..." Only, that was a lie. Kit wasn't sure what Livvy would risk at this point. But she wasn't about to allow her brothers to cause more of a scene. Everyone was already staring on at the uninvited guests.

"I'll check the library," Gabriel supplied.

"I'll go with you." Luke followed Gabriel through the crowd.

Kit descended toward the exit to the courtyard. The sleeping quarters were not attached to the main hall. Her slipper-clad feet, as she was yet unaccustomed to the thin soles, felt every crack in the paving stones that marked the path to the Senior Hall dormitory rooms. The night air chilled her as it had not done before. How often had she crossed this walk? Alone, even? But suddenly there was something sinister about it. Like monsters hiding in the bared branches of the trees and the thin smoky clouds drifting over the face of the moon, leaving little light at all to travel by. She was happy Logan and Price were with her.

To break the eerie silence, Kit placated, "I'm certain Livvy is fine. In fact, I'll bet Luke found her in the library. Come to think of it, I doubt she would have traveled all the way back to the dormitory for a headache. If she even had one. Perhaps she has been in the ladies' retiring room." She knew her excuses were weak, but she felt if she didn't keep speaking the silence would engulf them all. It was completely unlike her. Usually she was the silent type, preferring silence to useless conversation and prattling on like an idiot, as she was currently.

Through the satin of her gloved hand, she felt a warm, comforting touch. She turned her head slightly and slowed her step, surprised at Price's gentle squeeze of her fingers. She looked to see if her brother had noticed, but Logan's fast pace distanced him a step ahead of them. Price's hand then moved to the small of her back, guiding her forward and back into step with Logan.

She risked a glance back at Price. With a single look he conveyed his understanding of her aberrant chatter. He read her fears. And in that same look, offered comfort. An odd feeling washed over her. The secreted small graze of his hand to hers had touched her more profoundly than she could consider at present. She would perhaps examine those feelings more closely later. Livvy was her priority now.

Reaching the entrance, Kit dashed up the two steps to the door. The patioed area where they stood was sheltered by the balcony above and the grand white pillars that held it.

"It wouldn't be appropriate for me to allow gentlemen into the ladies' dormitory. You'll have to wait out here."

Before Logan could protest, Kit held up her hand, "If I encounter trouble, I will scream my lily-white head off."

Kit didn't leave room for debate. She stepped inside and closed the door behind her. Luckily, she and Livvy's room were on the ground floor, but they were to the very end of the hall.

Kit wondered if her roommate, Kate, had stayed up reading. It seemed not as not a single light burned in the entire place. Surely someone should be patrolling the building. If nothing else, Mrs. Barnaby could usually be counted on to be lurking about, ready to break up any innocent shenanigans the girls got up to.

Kit never partook in any of it, that would require too much chummy conversation with women she had little in common with, but she hadn't begrudged the others their childish antics. The early bedtimes made for boredom and if the institute leaders thought to treat grown women like children, then why not have a little fun breaking some of the rules?

"Mrs. Barnaby?" Kit's voice crackled a bit in her tentative call for the head mistress. There was no response and no sign of the old biddy anywhere. A few more steps brought her to their doors, Kit's room to the right and Livvy's the left.

To Kit's surprise she did hear muffled sounds coming from Livvy's room. Her heart pounded as her hand found the knob to the door. She pushed her shoulder into it as she turned and entered the room.

To her utter horror, she found her sister crumpled to the floor, her back against the wall, her once pinned to perfection hair disheveled and falling around her face. Her bare legs were exposed, with her dress layers bunched awkwardly at her waist. Kit could hardly take in the sight before her. Her sister's chest shook with silent tears streaming down her pale face. Her eyes were the most soul-haunting sight of all. Livvy hadn't even acknowledged Kit entering the room. Her eyes stared listlessly ahead as the tears flowed steadily down their constant path.

Then Kit saw him. Professor Sidney. Her defensive hackles raised in an instant and she reactively reached for her gun, but her hands slid to an empty spot at her hips, down the smooth useless gown.

A low growl sounded in her throat and she knew she must resemble a snarling wolf. But the vile snake before her tucked his shirt back into his breeches and straightened the lapels of his formal jacket, without the slightest rush, fear, or urgency. He barely acknowledged Kit other than with the smug look he tossed her way as he walked coolly from the room.

Kit should scream, but she couldn't find her voice. This was not what Kit had thought to find. She had feared finding her sister in the company of the odious man, perhaps sneaking some stolen kiss, but never this. She never expected to find her sister harmed.

"God! Livvy!" Kit rushed to her sister, kneeling beside her on the floor. "Livvy, Livvy, look at me. Shhh..." Only nonsensical muttering came from her lips. Her sister remained shaking, lost in her own tears, even with Kit's arms wrapped around her.

Kit felt dizzy, as if the world were spinning so fast, she couldn't make sense of it. She needed to get to Price and Logan. They were still waiting at the back entrance.

She brushed her sister's hair from her face and pulled her dress down over her legs.

"Livvy, I'm going to get Logan. He'll know what to do."

Of course, Livvy had no idea their brothers had shown up to surprise them this night, but her face revealed little awareness to Kit's reveal. The haunted look in her sister's eyes scared her more than anything. She had an uncontrollable need to hold her sister. It was as if she could feel her sister's pain coursing through her own body. Sometimes, their twin bond was closer than ever and though it had been months since Kit had felt the connection so strongly, this moment was reeling in full force.

Kit offered soothing tones once more, her hands petting her sister's hair, face, arms, as if her touch might somehow pull her sister from her grief-stricken trance.

"I'll be right back," Kit cooed reassuringly. She didn't want to leave her. Just then she heard the click of the side door at the end of the hall and knew it was Professor Sidney sneaking out the emergency exit door. The world stopped spinning in that moment and offered Kit red clarity. She was going to kill that son of a bitch.

She stood, renewed strength coursing through her with her determined sights set on one goal.

She didn't make it far down the hall when four figures emerged from the shadows: Logan, Price, Luke and Gabriel.

Logan read something on her face and the slightest flare of his nostril alerted Kit to his edgy state.

"You didn't scream."

"It was too late. We were too late."

Luke shoved past her.

"Where is she? What do you mean?"

Kit trotted forward in effort to outpace her brother to lead him to Livvy's room. Luke pushed past her into the room as she was opening the door. It did not take him long to assess the situation.

He stopped the others from coming into the room, but his veneer was hard, stormy, colder than she had ever seen her brother. She recognized the slate for revenge, nay justice, glittering in his eyes and knew he'd arrived at the same conclusion as she had moments ago. The man who did this to their sister needed to pay...with his life.

"He went out the side exit, here," Kit pointed toward the door just beyond her and Livvy's room. It was normally locked from the inside this time of night, Mrs. Barnaby having the key. Professor Scum must have had a key as well.

Luke spun the chambers in his revolver to ensure they were full and snapped them back into place. He looked dangerous.

He barely looked to Kit as he spoke, "You stay here with her." His voice sounded tight, as if he were choking and Kit saw his throat work.

The deadly glint in his eyes frightened her. It occurred to her suddenly that hunting Sidney down and taking his life in cold blood would only worsen the state of their family. Kit agreed the monster should die, but if her brother pulled the trigger, he would surely hang. She touched Logan's arm in a plea for help to stop this madness. To make sense of everything.

"No, Luke. You mustn't go after him. You'll hang."

"Whether I hang or not is of no consequence. That man is going to die tonight. Of that there is no doubt." And with that he strode out the door in angry, purposeful steps.

Gabriel called out to him, "She's right, Stone, Sidney is an exalted member of the community in Columbia. He's like a god here, the city worships his feet. His family is the leading benefactor of this school, and the entire town."

Luke's steps never slowed.

Suddenly the world was spinning into chaos again. Logan darted off after Luke, but Kit wasn't certain if it was to join him in murderous pursuit or to stop him. She knew what she needed to do. She needed to stop this. She fled across the hall to her own room in search of what she knew would get the job done.

~

Price could hardly believe what was happening. He was torn between remaining behind with Kit—who seemed as lost and helpless as he'd ever seen her—or following after Luke. He knew Logan would need help calming Luke down enough to see reason. As much as he knew they all wanted to see the man responsible for whatever unspoken crime he had undoubtedly committed to Livvy, Price and Logan knew murdering the town leader and getting hanged wasn't the right answer.

Mindlessly, he pushed his fingers through his hair. This was a nightmare. Although none of the implied details had been confirmed, Price was certain he knew what had taken place. Only one hideous crime could have affected Luke so. How could this have happened? Out of the corner of his eye a flash of blue silk rushed across the hall through the other door. What was Kit up to?

The man Kit had introduced as Gabriel stared as if boring a hole through Livvy's door. Pain and fear radiated from the man. Price couldn't understand what this chap was doing here. Livvy shouldn't be his concern. *Ahh.* The realization dawned on him. Price should not have had trouble recognizing that look. It was the same feelings he harbored for Kit: that of unrequited love. Poor bloke.

Price wished to speak with the man, as he was certain he'd drawn the same conclusions as had the rest of them. However, if he hadn't, Price did not want to apprise him or anyone of the details. He was not precisely certain himself yet at any rate. But the less people who knew of Livvy's compromised state, the better her reputation would fare. He hoped Luke would come to his senses and realize this himself. Drawing attention by killing a man would only ensure the world discovered what had happened to Livvy.

He could see the man before him suffering for the young lady he loved, and wanted to give him something, but just when he thought to placate him with soothing words, his attention got turned to a lone cloaked figure exiting the opposite direction of the hall. *Kit!* Dear God, she was going after them. And there was no telling what cock-eyed plan she had in mind.

"Excuse me." He started to rush off after Kit, but thought to turn back with, "Do not disturb Miss Stone. A-and do not let anyone else disturb her. Please." He growled his frustration as he saw Kit turn out of sight. "I'll return shortly. Just guard her door." Price took off after Kit without any reassurances from the-essentially-unknown man, but he hoped he was right to entrust him with safeguarding Livvy.

He dashed around the corner to see Kit sneaking around the hedges undetected. The buildings circled a manicured expanse of lawn, that could have been a field had it not been tilled for landscape. The buildings were all connected with paved stone pathways. Shadowed alleys formed between some of the buildings that were near to one another.

Price hurried after her through the dark night air. Amidst the fog and trees, he could discern, though barely, some figures standing along the shorn grass in the courtyard. His heightened awareness and pounding heart told him it was the Stone brothers and something terrible was about to happen.

Where was Kit?

That's when he saw light glint off metal and directed his gaze to find Kit's cloaked figure hidden deeper in the shadows, gun raised. She didn't seem to notice Price. Quickly, and as quietly as possible, he rushed to her and pushed the gun downward.

At that same moment, a shot fired.

A man screamed out in agony.

"No!" Kit yelled from beside him. Dazedly, his eyes met hers and recognition dawned on her face.

"Price! Do you know what you just did?!"

"I stopped you from committing murder and getting yourself hanged!"

She shook her head, fear filling her eyes, "No, they wouldn't hang a lady. But Luke..." She covered her mouth with her hand, the shock and pain too great. "Now, Luke will hang!"

Luke and Logan turned to flee. Surprise and shock lit their faces when they saw Kit and Ben behind them.

"Get out of here, Kit!" Luke yelled furiously. "Price, get her out of here!"

Price felt helpless and confused. There was no way Kit would go willingly with him. Especially not now that she thought he aided in sending her brother to an early hanging. Luckily, Luke's disoriented, angry state scared her into submission.

"Luke, no..." She shook her head, unable to form the words.

"Get out of here!" he yelled.

~

Logan looked to his sister with sad, knowing eyes. His sister had shot the professor. Luke or Logan would have to cover for her now. Logan had been doing all he could to get Luke to see reason. The professor's arrogant mewling hadn't helped at all. Even so, while Luke still had his gun raised, Logan had seen sense begin to return to him. He'd thought Luke was ready to put his gun away.

Then the shot rang out.

Luke hadn't fired, though. As soon as they turned around and saw their sister Kit standing there with a gun and Price looking frightened and dazed, they realized what had happened. Kit had fired the shot.

Someone would hang for sure now. It didn't matter that the professor deserved to die for what he'd done. He was a respected member in the community and an entire political team would stand behind him and mete out injustice declaring his innocence.

Oh, Kit. What have you done...

When Price tugged Kit away and she fled with him back into the school, Logan ran with Luke to the professor to see if he was yet alive.

He was dead.

No one saw the other hidden form in the shadows beyond—the only one with a gun barrel still smoking—retreat back into the darkness.

Cayt Lawson

Chapter 8

The ending to that evening had been amassed in a fog of all their senses it seemed. Kit had rushed to change out of the confines her layered confection and into the familiar woven trousers she had missed greatly every day spent at the academy where she wasn't allowed to wear them. She then helped a listless Livvy change into warm, comfortable riding attire. Normally Livvy wouldn't have been happy about riding, let alone at the speed of which had been required to flee town, but her sister had remained mute during their escape.

Gabriel Hart had assisted Price and Luke with readying the horses that had been stabled across town, even saddling his own for them to take along for Livvy. Livvy wasn't in any state to ride, however, and was tossed up into the saddle in front of Logan. They took Gabriel's horse to help alleviate the other horses when they tired, so they could continue at a heady speed. Even so, it was winter, and the mountain passes would surely be shut up with snow.

The journey was long and arduous. Livvy slept the majority of the trip. They had been forced to stop several times due to weather conditions and while the roadways were surprisingly passable due to the military convoys using the trail for their purposes, it was still weeks later when they finally arrived at the ranch. Each of them exhausted to the very marrow of their bones.

It was the dead of night, but they made no effort to be silent and soon the barn and house were alive with activity. The air seemed charged with dread and everyone sensed this was not a happy reunion. Old Ray helped them care for the horses without speaking a word, his experienced hands deft and quick to take over the untacking of the horses and softly ordering duties to the waking ranch hands, allowing for Kit and her brothers to escort Livvy and their belongings to the house.

Her mother and father stepped out onto the porch in the night air and Kit breathed a sigh of relief at the sight of them. Her mother gathered the wrap on her arms more closely to her, her eyes wide with alarm to see her children unexpectedly before her. Kit longed to run up and throw herself into her father's arms. She'd felt lost and scared ever since the tragic night of the ball.

While Livvy had finally come around to mimicking the motions of the living and nodding in response to everyday meaningless questions, such as, 'would you like another cloak? Or another biscuit?' she never actually spoke, and Kit could sense the invisible thorny shell calcifying over her sister.

Then again, no one had spoken more than two words to one another beyond civil necessity the entire journey home. Kit longed for the nightmare to end, for it seemed a perpetual loop.

Instead of running to her father and the embrace she knew would allot her necessary comfort, she assisted Livvy up the steps. Her mother's wide, perceptive eyes darted eagerly over her daughter searching for immediate answers. She then looked up and met Logan's eyes.

Luke wouldn't look at her.

"What has happened?" she demanded.

Kit felt Livvy tense beneath her arm at their mother's questioning. "Let's get Livvy to her bed, first. It's been a long, hard ride. We're all exhausted."

Her mother nodded curtly, holding back what must have been a terrible urge to know her daughter's obvious pain and comfort her. Their mother, to her credit, did not speak further, only quietly took up Livvy's other side and aided her into the house.

Kit was surprised to see Uncle Tonio sitting solemnly at their table. The mood of the night hung in the atmosphere like a thick cloud and their family friend, whom Kit and Livvy had grown up calling "Uncle" even though he was of no relation, pulled his lips into a sad slight of a smile and bowed his head in a respectful hello. It was obvious there was no cheer or welcome in this return home. Kit wondered if their lives would remain lost in this dark cloud forever.

No, surely her parents would set everything to rights. They always fixed everything, there wasn't anything they couldn't do.

Kit helped her mother lay Livvy onto her bed. If possible, her sister looked even more pale and exhausted. Kit looked to her mother and saw the worry evident on her face, which worried Kit all the more. There wasn't much their mother didn't take with a grain of salt. No matter the injuries sustained as children, their mother told them the best medicine was to toughen it out. As much as their mother was known for her compassion, she was also an ardent believer in tough love. For their mother to be unable to disguise her fear—although it was apparent to Kit that she was trying—truly brought home how severely injured Livvy must be.

She helped her mother wash and dress Livvy in a clean night rail. Then her mother shooed her from the room.

"Go. You too need to wash up and find a fresh change of clothes."

Kit hesitated briefly at her mother's demand, wondering if her mother needed her further, despite her claims to the contrary, but decided to heed them in the end. She could always return. Wiping the trail grime from her body was more desirous than she would have liked to admit.

As she neared the door, her mother called her name.

Kit turned slightly to acknowledge her.

"Are-are *you* well?"

Kit nodded and managed to croak out, "Yes."

Her mother exhaled what must have been pent up breath and nodded a few yes shakes of her head. Knowing that was her mother's dismissal, Kit took her leave. As she was stepping into the hall, Rita burst through.

"Miss Stone!" She grabbed Kit by the shoulders and looked her over frantically, then surmising Kit was unharmed, only fatigued, pulled her in for a quick embrace. Something completely out of the ordinary for the surly cook. She then stepped past Kit into Livvy's room.

"Oh, Miss Lavinia..." Kit heard Rita's voice trail off, and barely heard that of her mother's join Rita's as Kit made her way farther down the hall to her own room. Kit had dreamed of her return from the academy since discovering she was being sent. But this was certainly not the circumstances she had wished the reunion to be under.

She cleaned herself as best she could with a rag and wash basin Rita had so kindly brought to her room. A flannel night rail and the wish to curl up in her own bed and sleep for days would have to go unanswered, for she heard the commotion downstairs and knew her desire for sleep would have to wait. She wasn't about to miss out on whatever plans were being made. So instead, she dressed in a clean pair of trousers, pulled a cambric shirt over her head, and called it good.

She was just traipsing down the last steps into the kitchen when she heard her mother's voice, unusually raised, "What do you mean he's gone? How could you have let him flee into the night? He's not in his right frame of mind. He needs sleep, and food, and, and—" Her mother failed to conceal the break in her voice and the anguish of tears trying to escape, "his mother. How could he have left here, after everything, and not spoken a single word to me?"

Her father pulled her mother to his chest. Kit's constricted. She was confused with no reference to her mother's words, but she knew the night had taken another dastardly turn. Logan looked guiltily away. Where was Luke? And where was Price and García? By all accounts, they were considered family as well and should have been present. Nothing was resembling any normalcy.

"He wouldn't listen to reason. Once he cools, he will realize that and come back." Logan's words went ignored.

"And you are certain it was Kit?"

"Yes."

"Certain what was Kit?"

Logan glanced furtively to the floor, ashamed. *Ashamed of her?* Kit wondered. What on earth was going on? What had she done, exactly? She looked around at everyone's faces, searching for answers.

Logan met Kit's questioning gaze, "We know it was you who shot Sidney." Regret and sadness shadowed his eyes, and he couldn't hold her gaze long without averting as if it pained him.

What nonsense was this?

"Are you saying Luke *didn't* shoot him?"

Logan looked up to her then, puzzled by her question, "He didn't shoot him. You shot him. I was with Luke, he never fired off his gun and you were the only other one there with a gun. We saw the smoke from your barrel, Kit."

Kit's eyes grew big. "You're telling me Luke did not...he didn't..."

All eyes turned to Kit expectantly.

"I didn't shoot Sidney. I-I was going to, had planned to. I knew the town would be less willing to hang a young woman than a rough cowboy from the mountains, which is how I knew they'd see Luke. It wouldn't have mattered that he was defending our sister's honor, because no one would have believed us."

She was prattling on, her nerves taking over her lips as if out of her control. She hoped the words she was stringing together were making sense. But she could see they weren't because Logan appeared confused as ever.

"But your gun went off. We heard it go off, and we saw the smoke."

"No. I-I mean yes, I fired, but Price, he pushed my gun aside and I fired wide. The shot didn't go anywhere near the professor."

Just then, Price appeared through the main entrance from the balcony, "It's true. I did divert her shot. I didn't want her to be hanged for murder." Price's voice rang accusingly.

"But what about the second time you fired? There were two shots."

Now it was Price who appeared confused. Kit looked from him back to Logan, "We thought that was Luke's shot."

Logan's raven-wing brows slashed over his deep brown eyes staring across the room intently, "Except Luke never shot."

∽

Two days later, the house was still in upheaval. Though Price, Logan and her father had searched for Luke, they hadn't found him. If only they would have spoken about what happened on the trail. Then Logan and Luke wouldn't have quarreled, and Luke wouldn't have run off.

Everyone was solemn again this morning, quietly sipping coffee around the breakfast table. Again, no one communicating with one another. Price kept sliding glances in Kit's direction, which she ignored. She was in no mood to decipher his looks.

Livvy had spoken with their mother, apparently, but every time Kit tried to comfort her, she was cold and silent. Kit wasn't sure how to perceive that, only knowing that it hurt deeply.

Just then, her mother entered the room. She squared her shoulders and placed her hands strongly at her hips—a determined signaling, and one Kit knew meant an impart of instructions was forthcoming. For once, Kit looked forward to her mother's dictatorship ways. It was familiar and would hopefully provide Kit with something tangible to do. She needed to take action and have the repetitive thoughts of that night eviscerated from her mind by occupying herself with a task. She was ready.

Everyone at the table looked to Ann, the leader of the family, and waited for her directives as if in attendance to an important meeting. Which Kit supposed it was.

"We all need time to heal. It is difficult to put this behind us with Luke's absence and move forward. I wish he had trusted us to figure out a solution, no matter what he believed had transpired at the time, but we must take action now.

"I know you are all wondering how Lavinia is faring... I won't lie, she is still most pained. It is her heart that took the worst of the battering. We will not know for some time yet if..." her mother's tongue darted her lips nervously, a habit she'd had as long as Kit could remember, "if Lavinia is with child."

A baby! Of all the things Kit had thought about, whether or not her sister had been impregnated by that odious scoundrel had never crossed her mind. *Her*, a woman whose specialty was rearing foals, how could such a concern have never crossed her mind? *Oh, Livvy.* Sorrow for her sister filled her. And her eagerness for a directive diminished under its weight.

She felt Price's hand find hers beneath the table. She nearly jumped from the unexpected touch. When she cast a look his direction, his eyes remained focused on her mother still delivering her speech. Kit realized no one else in the room had any idea that her hand was in Price's. Months ago, she would have been abhorred by the very thought, but now, whether she was weak from the turmoil her family was drowning in, or her own despair, she found it comforting.

"Kit," her mother's voice stating her name shocked her back to attention. She dropped Price's hand from hers as if it were a hot coal and a furious blush heated her cheeks.

"Kit, García has some news for you. The rest of us are going to get on with chores but you should remain behind to discuss matters with García.

She looked to her uncle who was studying her. What matters could he possibly have to discuss with her?

∿

A ranch? She could barely process all of the information García explained to her. Her biological father—whom she hadn't thought about in years—left her his ranch? Her mother had allowed her father to believe the children he had sired perished. But somehow, he had discovered that not to be true. Since he never knew there had been twins, he left his ranch to his child, singular. The one he had apparently met at a horse sale in Canyon, when Kit had been just a girl. The memory was too foggy to recall his face, as she hadn't known at the time she had spoken with her father. She had spoken with so many people, he could have been any of the men around the corral that day.

So that was why her uncle had been here upon their return from what Kit had begun to call "that night." He'd been here to deliver what he had thought would be good news, but it wasn't. It was all too much to take in. Kit wasn't certain she would have regarded it as good news even had she learned of her new inheritance under happy circumstances.

Her mother entered the house then. It was nearing luncheon. Logan and Price followed in behind her.

"Did you tell her about her inheritance?" her mother directed toward García.

Peeved her mother refused to address Kit as a grown woman when discussing her own life, Kit inserted, "He told me. Some big ranch in Texas."

Ann nodded faintly, "Good. You will leave with García on the morrow."

"What?!" Kit exploded, "I can't just leave!"

"You can, and you will."

"I see. You just ship me off whenever and to wherever you're so inclined."

"I really don't have the time or strength to deal with your selfishness right now."

Kit clenched her jaw. Fury and pain mingled within her body, sewing her lips tight.

~

Price stood watching the scene from the doorway. He could read Kit's face so easily, why could no one else? They saw her set features as mulish, stubborn anger. How did they not see the fear in her large glossy eyes, the heartache for her family in the flare of her nostril as she struggled to breathe against her inner storm?

Her mother called her selfish. Could she not see Kit's love and loyalty to her family took precedence over everything else in her life? Couldn't her mother see Kit *couldn't* leave her family behind, knowing they were all broken?

Price wanted to cross to her. To hold her. Let her know she wasn't alone and bear what pain he could for her. She glanced his way briefly, he hoped to convey his support to her silently with his eyes, but hers only stung with embarrassment.

Without a word, Kit skid the creaky wood of her chair across the hard floor and left for her room. Price couldn't follow, as that would be inappropriate, though he desperately wanted to. Instead, he excused himself lamely, to check the situation at the barn. He too needed an escape. He'd never witnessed such brutal deconstruction of his family. He had a feeling of dread they'd never recover.

He decided to check on Blue, Kit's pride and joy. He wasn't around when the colt had been born, but she'd written her brothers about him. The colt's dam was sister to another mare who foaled a filly on Stone Ranch the very same day. Like Kit and Livvy, the colt and filly shared a birthday. She wrote she was so thrilled over the duo that she named the pair after Washington's two prized war horses: Blueskin and Nelson. It took her some effort to convince Livvy, who had never been all that fond of horses, to keep the red dun filly for herself, while Kit kept the grullo colt. They were able to keep the pair together. Price remembered Luke reading the letter to them four years ago while they had still been at university and smiling over her exuberance. Letters from Kit, unlike Livvy, were a rarity, but when they arrived, they almost certainly contained news of progress with whatever new crop of horses she was turning out.

Price patted the silver-hued horse. Blue was a stout, handsome gelding now and Kit was more attached to him than most humans, he figured. Except for her sister, perhaps. He sighed, what a terrible predicament they found themselves in. Especially terrible for Livvy.

He continued to work his brush over Blue, until enough time had passed he thought it safe to return to the house without risk of running into any of the grieving family members. As he was about to exit the stall, bad luck would have it, he heard the voices of Ann and Grayson Stone nearby. From the tone of their hushed angry voices, he gathered it was intended to be a private conversation, but at this point Price wasn't sure his interruption would only cause embarrassment, so instead of exiting he hunkered down in the stall and waited. Hopefully they moved on quickly.

"You think Kit is okay riding with Price all the way to Texas?" Hearing Grayson speak his name piqued his interest.

"Of course. Logan will be there as chaperone along with García," Ann stated. "Plus, Price is the perfect English gentleman. It's ingrained in his bones. They call him 'the Saint' for Pete's sake."

Grayson responded dryly, "I don't think that's the inference behind the name, dear."

"Pish posh, you're worrying about the wrong kid. Kit is a competent woman. She can handle this move. Have a little faith in her, Grayson."

"It's not that I question her resolve or capabilities. I just worry..."

"I know, dear. Kit has always been your little shadow around the barn and you're not ready to give her up." Through the slits between the stall boards, Price saw Ann reach for her husband's hand and give him a comforting squeeze.

"I just didn't think she'd leave."

"Surely you knew she would someday?"

"I don't know, she expressed building a house on the property..."

"Grayson, she's young. But once her brothers are having kids and starting families here, she's going to want a family of her own, too." Ann paused thoughtfully, "I know you want to go with her. To keep her safe," Ann smiled, "but this is her adventure. You have to let her have it."

"Christ, Ann, not everything is an adventure. This isn't a jaunt to one of the forts for supplies or a night out camping. She'll be riding through what's left of Comancheria. She could be killed before she even gets to her ranch. And if she does get there? What awaits her there? I loath to think what kind of men a man like James Morgan would have associated with."

"I'm going to forgive you for that outburst, because I know it comes from fear for our daughter and heartache. But Kit is going to be fine. She is as good a shot as you—"

"Better than that, I'd say she's as good as you."

Ann smiled, noting his changed tone for the apology it was.

"Well, I was trying to be humble for once." Her lips quirked up on a saucy grin. Price heard them embrace and figured the discussion was at an end, so he scurried along while his escape was sure to be unnoticed.

Kit ensured both her parents had reentered the house before she fled. She needed to escape. Needed to be in the barn where she could think.

The sweet scent of hay greeted her, and she inhaled deeply, welcoming its pleasant aroma. A ride would clear her mind all the more. She grabbed her saddle from the rack and carried it to Blue's stall. Always a curious horse, Blue broke from his contentment of munching hay and placed his muzzle over the stall door to see what Kit was doing. He playfully nudged her arm.

"You're ready to stretch your legs and I'm ready to outride this anger. We always make a good team." Kit planted a soft kiss on the white star marking between his eyes; the same place she'd been delivering kisses to him since he was a gangly-legged colt.

"Can't believe they are making me accept an inheritance from a man I never knew. And what little I do know of the man who sired me isn't very commendable," Kit muttered as she stroked the smooth plain of Blue's face. Blue twitched his ears, listening intently as Kit complained her woes to him.

It was a common enough scene over the years. Kit didn't hear Ray gradually walking his old bones up beside her, although she should have expected as much. He and Blue had ever been her best listening ears over the years. Once she realized Ray was beside her, she waited for him to speak, knowing he would have something to say.

"You know, Miss Stone, I knew your daddy. Your sire, that is. I'm not talking 'bout Mr. Stone."

Kit looked to him, shocked.

"Yep," he continued, "Rita was Maria's nursemaid and went with her to the new ranch when she married your-er-Mr. Morgan. He wasn't a good man, that's for sure. And I'm right sorry to have to say it."

"Well, you're not the first to say so, so that comes as little surprise to me. I didn't know you and Rita worked for him, though. Who is Maria?" Kit admitted, she'd given little thought to how Ray and his wife Rita, both hired to help the ranch, had come to be here. They'd simply always been here in her memory.

Ray released a hearty sigh, "Maria *was* García's sister. She married Mr. Morgan, long ago. It's my understanding you was just a babe at the time, brand new into the world."

Kit tried to wrap her head around the strange ties overlapping in her family, ties she'd never known about, as Ray continued on.

"When Maria died in childbirth, Senior García, he brought us—me and Rita—to Stone Ranch. Knew your mama would find a place for us, he did. The Stones was in need of a cook at the time. My Rita, she'd never had cookin' duties afore, but she was mighty glad for the change." Ray paused to chuckle. "I used to be a foreman, but too old for that. Happy to piddle here in the barn these days."

Kit looked at him as if seeing the gentle old man for the first time, taking in his tightly coiled silvery hair in contrast to his dark wrinkled skin around his kind eyes. Shame burned through her for never having truly understood her friend, never having known about his life before Stone Ranch, and for never having bothered to ask. She guessed now that he and Rita perhaps hadn't enjoyed a very liberated life while in service to Mr. Morgan. But she wouldn't have imagined García would treat humans disrespectfully.

"Why did you work for Mr. Morgan?" she asked now, curiously.

"Rita had a fondness for Maria, and she feared for the girl, knowing what kind of man Morgan was an' all. And I wanted to remain near to my Rita."

Kit smiled wanly, better understanding the two people who had been like family to her her entire life.

"And I want to be near my family," Kit stated, hoping for a champion in her corner who understood.

"Yea-t, yea-t, I know this," Ray's gentle, but toughened hand settled comfortingly on her shoulder. "But this family ain't going to be the same forever. Your brothers and sisters, they've all got their own changin' to do, too."

Perplexity wrinkled Kit's nose as she thought on his words.

Ray spoke again, "I guess what I'm trying to say is, life, it ain't like those fancy trains bein' built all over the country; it don't follow the track you lay, no matter how good you build it. It blows its own way like a leaf in the wind, and there ain't no predictin' it.

"Was a time I thought I'd always live in Mexico on Antonio's daddy's ranch, then that part of Mexico turned to Texas. And Don Antonio's pa died. I met a lovely señorita and made her my wife in those years. And we ended up moving to Morgan's ranch with Don Antonio's sister. And then ended up here. But all in all, I've had a good life full of moments that have made it grand."

"So, what you're saying is, I should seize all the opportunities that come my way, and don't be choosy."

Ray tapped her on the head with the dry end of the hay-grass he'd been chewing on, "Naw, that ain't what I'm sayin'. I'm sayin' don't put so much importance on the 'where' and the 'when' in life. Put more on the 'who.'"

"On the who? I fear you're not making a lick of sense, Ray. Perhaps you've been inflicted with the old timer's."

Ray looked to her like he was about to bonk her on the head again with the hay-grass.

"I'm sayin' it ain't got ta make sense now, because when ya find that special someone, none of the other stuff will matter. Perhaps this new ranch is where yer supposed to be right now, to meet that person. And when ya do, you'll finally learn what it is to live."

"Why, Ray, I never took you for such a romantic."

"Well, I reckon I am that. Yes, I reckon I am." The old man laughed as he hobbled away in his familiar aged gait.

Kit saddled up Blue. She had a lot of thinking to do.

Chapter 9

Later that night, an unexpected pounding at the door woke everyone from sleep. Kit and her parents scrambled down the stairs together in a rush. Logan and Price entered from the hall off the kitchen that led to their rooms.

They could hear ol' Ray's shouts. Her father opened the door quickly to let the man in.

Ray looked wide-eyed to her father, "Riders approaching!"

"Luke?" her mother asked desperately.

Ray shook his head, "Don't think so." Ray wrung his worn hat between his hands before adding, "Jenkins an' Petey are escortin' 'em, but they fired a shot, so I knows whoever it is w' 'em ain't welcome."

Ann's eyes met Grayson's, "I'll be right back."

Her father nodded knowingly, in that manner most annoying to Kit, when they seemed to speak in code to one another and no one else knew what they were saying.

Kit had managed to slip her trousers on under her gown, but rushed down in her stocking feet and now realized her night rail was bunched up in her pants in ridiculous fashion.

She searched the room discreetly in hopes of confirming no one had witnessed her display, but caught Price looking her direction.

Oh, of course he would notice. Damn him and all his looking. Angry and embarrassed, she huffed back up the stairs after her mother to don different attire.

~

If not for the intensity of the moment, having been awakened in the night to strangers approaching—something all but unheard of in their isolated ranch that allowed for no one to enter—Price would have cracked a smile at Kit's irritation with him for seeing her in her half-garbed night rail.

She had been embarrassed, but what she didn't know was Price hadn't noticed her silly attire until she stomped off in obvious humiliation. He'd been gawking at what had been left exposed from it.

Of course, he didn't think she would have been any less mad if she'd known those details.

Price, along with Logan and Grayson, ensured their rifles and pistols were loaded and strapped to their waist belts, then headed out the door. Grayson waved for Price and Logan to remain behind on the porch, but they could hear the conversation taking place below.

"Hello, gentlemen. What brings you this-a-way?" Grayson's voice carried.

"We're Pinkertons, from St. Louis, Missouri. We're investigating a murder that took place, about two months back. Tracks led us to Stone Ranch. Not easy people to find."

"Getting easier by the day, it would seem," came Grayson's acerbic reply.

"I take it you know of the murder to which I refer?" Pertinent arrogance sounded in the voice of the lead Pinkerton.

"Jog my memory," Grayson replied.

The Pinkerton looked annoyed.

"If you don't mind, we could surely use a bit of coffee. We could discuss events then, while we rest our horses."

"I'd love to invite you fellas in, but truth is, this is my wife's ranch, and she's not near as friendly as I am."

"Your wife's ranch?" The man turned to his partner looking ready to share a laugh over that bit of information.

"That's right. Do you find something amusing about that, gentlemen?" Ann Stone was a sight to behold. She marched into the early, biting spring wind with her rifle barrel leading the way, pointed directly toward the two strange men.

"Now, wait a minute, little missy, you'd better take care who you're pointing that gun at. We here are lawmen. Sent from the great state of Missouri."

"Well, you can head right on back to the great state of Missouri. Out here, you aren't lawmen. See, out here," Ann perused the isolated fortress of their ranch home in a slow shift of her eyes, "you're just trespassers."

The irritated Pinkerton tried once more to appeal to Grayson, "Listen, we have witnesses to the scene. Nobody wants any trouble with your boy, Mr. Stone. They all agreed, it was the Injun boy who done it."

"That 'Indian boy' is our son, and he didn't murder anybody. In fact, you have come a long way out here for nothing, because not one of my children has ever killed a man." Ann paused, before drawling, "I, on the other hand, well, my record isn't so clean. Then again, when one lives in these destitute parts of the world, one does what one must to survive." Ann tilted her head slightly, knowing the angle would allow the moon to highlight the disfigured side of her face. She learned early on how to use her scars to her advantage.

Sure enough, she watched the first man's partner recoil and tighten his grip on his reins. She wanted them to know, she wasn't jesting about embracing the uglier side of life. The pompous man doing all the talking was taken aback at first, but was apparently dimwitted enough to continue climbing down from his horse.

Ann fired her gun toward the sky. The loud shot caused the man's horse to shy during his dismount and he ungracefully scrambled back up into his saddle.

Grayson had his gun pulled beside her, as she recocked the lever and readied to fire again.

The lead Pinkerton gave her a venomous look before declaring, "We're leavin' now, but you haven't seen the last of us."

The men turned their horses around and spurred them back in the direction they'd come. Four more ranch hands had dressed and been ready with guns from the barn, they along with the original two escorts followed the Pinkertons to ensure they didn't miss their exit.

Price was the only one remaining on the porch when Ann and Grayson Stone made their way up the steps.

He watched Ann's face blanch white, her eyes searching panickily, as she asked, "Where's Logan?"

"It's okay, he's safe in the house," Pen assured her. "Once he heard they were after him, he ducked back inside. We figured it wouldn't do to be seen by those men who were looking only too eager to haul him away."

Ann visibly slumped with relief. And probably not a little weariness from that show of bravery. Price smiled, he knew exactly where Kit got her fire from, not that there had ever been any doubt.

A long discussion ensued following the visit from the Pinkertons. Everyone had been too jittery to go back to sleep, so they instead went over their departure plans and set to work.

Price could scarcely believe how this once bonded family unit, one of the tightest-knit he'd ever witnessed, was snagging and unthreading like the loose ends of a scarf.

Their love for one another remained strong, however. Price hoped that would be enough to hold all the broken pieces of them together. If only Luke hadn't run off. Price couldn't help but think Luke and Logan were better as a team; together they could solve any problem.

Price had, of course, felt the tensions between the brothers growing for some time, Logan chaffing more and more under Luke's protective cocoon. They couldn't have chosen a worse time for their rift to come to a head. It seemed the final blow to shattering the fragile bruised pieces of their family into pieces. Price worried the pieces would be too small to recover and rebuild.

Restless energy ate him, wondering if he would be of more help to the Stone family by going after Luke himself. But, no. As much as he wished to help, Kit was currently his main concern.

Livvy was being cared for, and rightly so, and Luke and Logan were a main worry as well. Especially after last night's confirmation that both brothers were being hunted down for the murder of that scoundrel, Albert Sidney. Well, not the Stone brothers, precisely. Mostly the "Indian one." That very particularity was the driving force in Luke's argument with Logan. He had wanted Logan to flee with him, because he knew, he *knew* the "lawmen" would be out for Indian blood. And Luke had been exactly right. Bloody hell, everything was a goddamned mess. And amidst all of it, he saw Kit left to care for herself again.

Ever the strong one, Price knew she'd not complain. In fact, he was quite sure she would reject the need for comfort and bury herself in training her horses.

Only, she was to be denied her own methods of self-preservation. With her parents' focus on her siblings, Kit was being shipped off yet again. With no thought to her desires. Similarly to when Price had been shipped off to America.

Indeed, that had turned out to be the best thing his parents had ever done for him. Price was glad the decision to go after Luke or remain with Kit had been made for him and he'd been included in the order to escort Kit to her new ranch. He planned to make sure she had someone to look out for *her* for a change. Whether she knew or wanted his protection, she had it.

The day's goodbyes brought gloomy frowns and silences. Ann was too preoccupied, with Livvy still unwell and Luke on the run not knowing he was innocent and needed at home, to be her usual encouraging self. She did still manage to wrap Logan in a hug before he could climb into his saddle.

"This is for the best," she said. "The further south you go, the harder it will be for them to find you. They'll give up eventually. The man may have had good stature in the town of Columbus, but in the whole of things he was a nobody. It will all blow over soon."

Logan, oddly quiet even for him, only accepted his mother's attendance on him and nodded his hat. His actions raised Price's suspicions. From a distance, he discreetly scrutinized his friend. Logan seemed to be secreting something in his mind. Though what it could be and why he wouldn't divulge important information, Price didn't know. Ann was usually quite perceptive when it came to her children, but the weight of recent events had clearly taken its toll on the brave woman. She squeezed Logan one last time and parted with, "You look after your sister. That's your job now."

This time, Logan gently returned his mother's embrace, before climbing into the saddle.

No hugs for Kit, Price noticed.

Of course, that wasn't entirely a fair judgment, perhaps they had said their goodbyes earlier behind closed doors. Grayson stood next to Kit, who was mounted on her horse. Price watched her father pat her buckskin-clad thigh affectionately and Kit place her hand on his shoulder, returning the gesture.

Did she always have to be so bloody stoic? Price wondered. She and her parents behaved as though Texas was a short jog away, when in reality, none of them knew when next, if ever, they would all be together again.

If Kit decided to remain at her new ranch...

The heaviness of the moment sat fully on Price's chest. And apparently, he was the only one acknowledging exactly how vastly their lives were being altered. Either that, or everyone else were made of far sterner stuff than he. And he was bloody English. Raised an aristocrat where feelings were expected to never be exhibited.

Then again, he'd never been made of stone, like the rest of his ilk; which was why he'd never been happy until coming to be a part of *this* family. They'd shown him what unconditional love was from a parent to a child and it was with them he'd witnessed the warmth of bonds between siblings.

Of course, love had never directly been his to feel, but it was enough just to know it existed. Price hoped someday he'd have a family like this of his own.

Right now, he just hoped *this* family found its way back to that place. And Kit was his main concern.

Chapter 10

After eight weeks on the trail Kit still couldn't believe the turn of events that had taken place forcing her to leave her family behind. Worry for her sister ate away at her. Would Livvy ever recover from the traumatic experience? Could she? What her sister must have endured was unimaginable. Kit couldn't help but feel glad the bastard who'd hurt her was dead.

If only her brothers weren't being wrongfully accused of the murder. Luke was off who knows where believing he had a bounty on his head, and Logan, who truly did have a bounty on his head, was coming with her to lay low in Texas. Thoughts circulated in her mind, landing on another question she'd often asked herself over the past weeks: if she'd inherited a ranch when her family wasn't in distress, would she have been happy? Kit honestly didn't know.

She had been chaffing lately for her own freedom. But mainly she had just wanted to be left alone to continue her work with the young horses. Kit wasn't a good student. She wasn't a good dancer. She was abysmal at flirting. And apparently, if Price's reaction was any indication, she wasn't good at kissing either. All in all, Kit wasn't much good at anything. Except training horses.

She loved the rewarding satisfaction of taking a completely wild horse or raising a young foal up and seeing it transform before her eyes. She seemed to have a special connection with every horse she worked with. They were all unique in their personalities and all came to her with their own set of fears and talents. She built their confidences and eased their fears. She gained their trust, helped bring out their most favorable qualities and expound on them until they were the best athletes they could be.

Kit kept thinking back on her and Livvy's conversation when Livvy had deftly pointed out Kit's precarious position at Stone Ranch. When her brothers took wives and built homesteads on the property, where would that leave Kit? Livvy was adamant she herself would be married and probably living a life back east.

Kit had begun to imagine her own little cabin built amongst the family homesteads at Stone Ranch. After all, if her brothers could have their own houses built, why couldn't she? She could be the eccentric spinster aunt to her brothers' children. She smiled, liking that image. She never continued the dream to the parts where she might get lonely. And she tried not to think about her sister being so far away. It had hardly mattered, anyway, because at the time, plans seemed to be far off into the future.

Then seemingly overnight the future had become the present, and Kit was the one hying off and building a life somewhere away from her family...

At least Logan was with her. Of all her siblings, he understood her best. They were both comfortable speaking only when they had something to say. There was so much to be read from nature and the surroundings at any given time, and they both knew that language well. A whole lot of words never seemed necessary when they could communicate through observation alone.

Admittedly, Kit reminded herself with a roll of her eyes, a whole lot of trouble for Luke could have been avoided had they all communicated verbally.

Kit took in the changed scenery around her, so different from her verdant mountain home. The land here resembled tall mountains of stacked dirt, dotted with shrubbery, and made her feel a stranger. Which she was. She was riding in the wagon next to García. He was driving, thankfully. She hadn't really needed the break, but her horse had. Blue was unaccustomed to the dry heat this far south.

It occurred to Kit that while she'd been distracted with her thoughts, they had traveled farther than expected and were no longer headed in the right direction.

Curiously, she turned to García, "Aren't we headed to Santa Fe? If I remember correctly, it was southwest of the Cimarron Cutoff point."

García had been uncharacteristically silent this trip as well. She supposed no one was terribly happy with the predicament they were in. He sighed, before answering, "No."

"But I thought my-my—" Kit cleared her throat, uncomfortable using the word father in regard to the man that sired her, "Morgan's ranch," she settled on, "was near Santa Fe?"

García turned his gaze toward the sunlit hills west of them and studied them with a nostalgic gleam in his eyes.

"My grandfather's land, granted to him by Spain, used to be just east of Santa Fe. 48,000 acres from the mountains into what is now Texas."

Kit felt Price and Logan's presence nearer to the wagon as if happy to hear the sound of voices break the mundane silence of the trail.

Price spoke, "Your family must have descended from Spanish royalty, then?"

"Not royalty. My grandfather was of noble ranking, but not so high up he wasn't easily sacrificed to aid in the settling of Mexico.

"You're like Saint, then," Kit said, referring to Price with a smirk.

~

Price had to keep from rolling his eyes. Talk of García's prestigious ancestry was yet another reminder to Kit of his own not-so-humble beginnings—to which most women found greatly appealing, he thought caustically. But not Kit. No. Somehow, he'd fallen for the only woman on two continents ill-impressed with titles and nobility.

García acknowledged them with a nod and continued, "When Mexico took over, the land was broken up and redistributed." He harrumphed, "Seems to get smaller every time it changes hands.

"My father inherited and divided what was left between my eldest brother, myself, and our sister. My brother inherited the ancestral homestead."

He paused and guilt crossed his features, "While I was away, enjoying the pursuits of a foolish young man, my brother was killed trying to defend that land. He lost his life as well as the land closest to Santa Fe." He swallowed the painful memory, "My father rebuilt on the land between Vegas and a little settlement called Blue Water."

García looked to Kit, then, "My sister married James Morgan before I returned home, and they moved onto the land farther east. They built a home on Hackberry Creek."

~

The ranch Kit was inheriting was farther into Texas than she'd thought.

García continued, "The border between Mexico and Texas kept changing. A few years back when Texas got annexed into the United States, I had to choose again, which land to lose and which to keep. The bigger portion was in Texas in the staked plains, so I gave up the land in New Mexico territory."

What must it have been like to constantly be rehomed? Kit wondered. It occurred to her, the Native Americans weren't the only ones in this land being treated unfairly. She tried to imagine wars and governments splitting up Stone Valley and parceling it off to strangers. She shuddered at the thought. She was struggling to leave her ranch home, even knowing it was still in one piece and safe with her family.

García's voice interrupted her thoughts.

"As it turns out, your—Morgan—wasn't all that wise with money. I ended up selling more land in order to pay off his gambling debts. Now I've got a small house built south of the settlement of Blue Water."

Logan spoke up, "Though I wouldn't call it small."

The lines by García's eyes crinkled as he smiled, "Well, compared to what my ancestral home once was, it seems small to me."

There was a beat of silence and then, "I'll be parting ways once we get to Onieda."

Kit's head whipped around to face Logan. Surely, she hadn't just heard him correctly.

"What do you mean, you'll be 'parting ways'?" she demanded. She looked around to the others and realized none of them shared her shocked expression.

"I've been speaking with García," Logan said.

Kit cast a furtive, accusatory glance to García, who had the grace to look guilty.

Logan continued, "He is friends with the Texas Rangers in these parts and thinks I can join them."

Kit sent a look to Price silently asking for his appeal in this, then asked Logan, "But why would you wish to join the Texas Rangers?"

"To clear my name."

Kit pondered this, still bewildered.

Logan expounded, "Albert Sidney was killed and none of us are responsible. Which means someone else was there that night and wanted him dead."

"Well, that could be a lot of people," Kit replied, disgruntled."

"I have someone in mind."

That took Kit aback.

"Gabriel Hart was there that night as well."

"Gabriel Hart! No. I can't see him murdering someone—"

García interrupted, "He has in the past."

Kit shook her head, "Those were just horrid rumors."

"No. It is true he murdered his own brother," García added.

How would García know of such information? "How do you know Gabriel?" Kit asked.

"His father owns the ranch south of mine."

Kit was surprised to learn Gabriel Hart lived so close to where she would soon be making her home. It pleased her, she considered him a friend of sorts. At the very least, they had both despaired over her sister's snootiness while at the academy.

"No, no. Not the Gabriel Hart I know," Kit spoke up, "There's no way he would kill someone, let alone his own brother—not without just cause. And surely he wouldn't pin the murder on someone else?"

Her remarks didn't make sense even to her own ears, but her mind was whirling with all of her conversations over the past two years with Gabriel. There could never be just cause in murdering one's own brother...could there?

Price spoke then, "And he was sweet on Livvy. All the more motive."

Kit shook her head, "No, he wasn't. They argued all the time. Livvy couldn't stand him."

Price's eyes caught hers and the intensity of them reminded her of the kiss they'd shared behind the barn before leaving for the academy. There certainly seemed to be a lot of heat between them and they didn't much care for one another. Could Livvy and Gabriel have been of the same ilk?

"I plan to find out who is responsible, whether that man proves to be Hart or someone else."

Kit didn't have long to absorb Logan's surprise, for they entered the town of Onieda moments later. The town appeared disorganized and messy. The boardwalks in front of the shops were broken apart and some of the lumber lay in disarray in the street. Kit watched as people stepped over and walked around the boards, ignoring the mess.

"It floods here often," García explained, "I still don't know why they ever built so near to Amarillo Lake."

Some riders approached and tipped their hats to García in greeting, but they addressed him by another name. One unfamiliar to Kit.

"Howdy, Rivera. I see you made it back in one piece, and your company, too." A man with an unruly beard and tired but kind eyes spoke.

"McCulloch." García greeted in turn.

"And, Lone Wolf," the ranger addressed Logan with a pleased grin, "it's good to see you again. You didn't stick around California long."

Logan smiled, "No, sir. And it appears you didn't either."

"What can I say? Texas has a way of pulling a man back to her."

"I hear you're about to be appointed Marshall in these parts," García revered.

The ranger tipped his head in humble affirmation, "Looks that way."

"Have the Comanche attacks been worse?" García asked.

Seduced by the Saint

"No," he answered with a bored sigh. "No, they are mostly subdued these days. It's the surprise of the attacks that creates the biggest problems 'round here. I'd advise heading straight through to Canyon, to be safe." His eyes darted in Kit's direction.

"We plan to. This here is Kit Stone, daughter of the late James Morgan and heir to his ranch, as you might have heard." García smiled and introduced Kit to his friends.

Kit's cheeks flamed with embarrassment at being announced as James Morgan's daughter and heir, as she was well aware of her blood-father's bad reputation. García's smile and his friends' glittering eyes implied they knew more about her than she did them. The disadvantage made her uncomfortable. And just why was García being addressed by a different name? Kit didn't care for all the mystery. And her scowl left little misinterpretation of that point.

García continued the introductions to Price who said, "It's good to see you again, Major. And this time not under fire."

"Ah, yes, same to you, Saint."

Then to the entire group the ranger said, "Though I cannot promise how long the streets shall remain peaceful today. Best not waste time moving through."

"I'd like to speak with you privately," Kit heard her brother speak up. "That is, if you have a moment?"

Kit watched another silent communication pass between the men.

"Well, I have some postal errands and I'm sure you have some business as well. How about we meet up at the saloon in a half an hour, shall we?"

"Thank you, sir," Logan responded firmly.

A nervous feeling was coming over Kit and she greatly wished to be free from the wagon and returned onto the back of her horse where she would be more likely to shake the unfamiliar wave of vulnerability she was feeling. As they parted from the group and traveled down the main street, Kit could hold back her curiosity no more.

"Why were those men calling you Rivera? And why did you tell them I was James Morgan's daughter?"

García sighed wearily as he directed the cart toward the general store.

"Those men were Texas Rangers."

"Yes, so I gathered by the shiny stars pinned to their chests," Kit sniped.

García ignored her testiness and continued, "They are also friends of mine and well aware of your situation as well as mine."

"I gathered that much as well," she crossed her arms petulantly. "Does everyone know about my 'situation'?"

With zero hesitation, García responded, "From here to Buffalo Springs and all the way to Fort Belknap, I reckon."

Kit didn't pretend to know where those places were, but it sounded a great distance. She wasn't used to her personal life being spread so publicly. Growing up in her valley on Stone Ranch, her personal life wasn't even completely known to her own family. She certainly didn't like that everyone here seemed to have access to her business. Not one bit. Kit decided to change the subject away from herself.

"And how did you know the ranger?" Kit directed to her brother.

Logan answered, "I served under him toward the end of the Mexican war. He was first lieutenant under Colonel Hays' First Regiment and later named chief of scouts under General Taylor—that's where I served with him. He was used as a tracker, and a damned good one he is. He was promoted to major after the battles of Monterey and Buena Vista. Luke, Saint, and I ran into him from time to time in the gold fields after the war, too. Major McCulloch was sheriff of Sacramento, then."

Kit understood the special connection her brother must have had with the ranger, for Logan was an excellent tracker himself. He was also exceptionally well at going about untracked.

It was odd for Logan to share about his time in the war. In fact, none of them ever discussed it overmuch, not even Luke. War seemed very unreal to Kit, as she had never truly been touched by it, but just hearing her brother name the battles he fought in sent shivers down her spine along with the realization of just how real it had been. She thanked the stars her brothers had been spared. She knew she mostly had their schooling at the university to thank for that, since it kept their adventure-seeking souls out of danger longer. They hadn't lived in Texas, so Kit felt that hadn't been their war, but seeing as how García—or Rivera, or whatever his name was these days—was like family, she supposed that was small of her to think so. Thankfully those days were past. She now had other sorts of battles to contend with and focus her worries on.

Once they reached the hitching post in front of the store, Kit jumped from her seat in the wagon, eager to stretch her legs and get back to her horse.

She turned to Logan, who had dismounted from his horse, "What if the Rangers won't help you?" She hoped she didn't sound too selfishly hopeful that her brother might be forced to continue on with her instead.

García spoke with certainty from where he tied the horses, "They will." His tone brooked no room for argument or doubt.

So that's that, thought Kit. Her brother would be abandoning her.

García spoke again, "Kit, I could use your help inside. I'd like to get supplies and head out of Onieda as quickly as possible."

Kit understood the order for what it was. She was wary to leave Logan, for fear he, like Luke, would take off without so much as a goodbye before she made it out of the store. She eyed her brother with as threatening of a glance as she could muster. Logan nodded his understanding. That was as good as a promise in Kit and Logan's book, so she followed García into the store, knowing her brother would be there waiting for her when she returned.

~

Price knew Kit must've felt as if her entire world kept unraveling. He felt guilty for having known this information in advance and been a part of the party that kept it from her. After Kit followed García into the store, Logan turned his attention to Price.

"Remember your promise."

"Of course. I'll look after her as if she were my own sister, you know that," Price assured his friend.

Logan studied him for a moment and Price feared his friend could see through to his soul and was reading therein his attraction to Kit Stone. "I'll do my best," Price assured him again, hoping that would break the close scrutiny.

This time Logan nodded and shook Price's hand.

Kit came out of the store then, eyeing them both warily and trying to guess at another surprise coming her way. Kit always thought herself so closed, when Price could read her like an open book.

"Price will be going on with you and Rivera."

A flash of surprise crossed Kit's features, but she was quick to conceal it.

Logan continued, "I need to get on to the saloon and meet with Ranger McCulloch. I'd like to get an early start on the hunt tomorrow, so I need all the plans settled tonight."

Neither she nor Logan were good at goodbyes, both awkward. Price laughed silently to himself thinking they'd both have made excellent English peers the way they believed emotional expression to be a great weakness.

Instead of hugging in the public street, the stoic siblings shook hands. Then Kit swung up into the saddle on her horse and stared silently ahead, awaiting the direction of the wagon to follow.

Logan led his horse farther down the street to the bawdier side of town where the saloon was located. Neither of the siblings looked back toward the other, but Price knew they were both feeling a painful goodbye. Logan was feeling the guilt of abandoning his sister, and Kit was harboring fear and disappointment in those around her.

Price vowed not to add to the growing list of disappointments in her life.

Chapter 11

They had already passed through the little town of Canyon and would reach Hackberry Creek and Morgan Ranch before sunset. Nerves were twisting around in Kit's guts like a spring nest of garter snakes. She'd felt trepidation all along the journey, but ever since her brother had abandoned her, the sickly feeling had worsened. She knew his reasons were just for leaving her, but she selfishly wished he had at least waited long enough to help settle her in before taking off.

To keep her mind from her own fears, Kit decided to pepper García, or should she say, *Rivera* with questions.

"All right, now that we're out of town, explain to me why everyone in Texas calls you Rivera instead of García."

"My full name is Antonio Javier García Rivera."

"Gee, crimany, that's a mouthful."

Rivera chuckled, "Yes, it's common with Spanish names. García was my father's surname and Rivera, my mother's family name." His smile faded then and his face saddened, "I made foolish, foolish mistakes in my youth. Here in Texas I was Sebastian Rivera, but north of here, where I went hunting for trouble, I began going by García in order to protect mi familia."

Kit, eyes wide with astonishment, pried further, "What could you have done that required you to use an alias of sorts? Did you break the law?"

"Not any man-made laws, no. Still, I am not proud of the things I did."

Kit was more curious than ever but knew she shouldn't ask further. They rode in silence for a while, each contemplating their own inner thoughts.

As they grew closer to the ranch, García broke the silence, "There are some things you should know before we arrive."

His ominous tone caused Kit's brows to quirk as she braced herself for more complications. As if her life needed aught else in the way of problems.

"The ranch is not in peak condition..."

Kit waited for him to expound on that remark. She noticed Price's expression had changed from merely conversational interest to alarm as well.

"To put it mildly—"

"Put it accurately," Price spoke the words Kit was thinking but was afraid to say for fear of the answer.

"Well, it is not financially sound at the moment. You'll have your work cut out for you."

Kit rolled her eyes skyward, of course asking for less problems would almost certainly result in a steaming, piling heap of them.

García, who was driving the wagon, turned to his left to address Price atop his horse, "I hadn't known at the beginning of the journey that Logan would not be staying on to help her. I know you graciously accepted the duty from Logan and promised to look out for her..."

Price shifted uncomfortably in his saddle. His friend had thought he had relayed upon him a heavy burden to look after his sister and placed great trust in him, not knowing he had his own selfish reasons for undertaking the "duty."

"As will I," García continued. "When I can, that is. My own ranch is not faring well either. Morgan had many debts that demanded be paid off after he died. It has put both our ranches in a poor position. And I'm needed at home."

Kit spoke up, obviously disliking being discussed as if she weren't there, "I'm not completely addle-brained. I know the runnings of a working ranch. In case you've forgotten, I was raised and taught those duties. I can assure you I won't need any assistance from Price." She scoffed, "What does he know about ranching, anyway?"

Price sent a scathing glance her way.

"Si, Kit, you are familiar with the operations of ranching. No one is questioning your capabilities in that regard. Although, you may find a cattle ranch to be quite a bit different than the workings of a horse breeding farm." García spoke those words kindly and respectfully.

Kit knew only an idiot would reject assistance when it was offered. Assistance from someone more experienced than herself she would welcome. Kit would gladly take guidance from García, he knew this land and the ranch. But, Price? Certainly not. He'd been raised a pampered English dandy. And even after all the years spent traipsing around the country with her brothers, he still wore his dandified English clothes and looked as out of place as a piano in a field.

One had to be tough to survive life on the frontier. Gentlemanly mannerisms and soft hands would get a body killed.

García spoke again, "It would behoove you, Kit, to pretend Saint is your new ranch foreman, hired by your brother who will be returning soon."

Multiple problems with this falsehood arose in Kit's mind. For one, her brother *wasn't* expected back soon, and until this very second, Kit hadn't given a thought to this being the first time in her life she would ever be unaccompanied by someone considered a guardian or respectable companion. For all her gruff speech about not needing protection, she suddenly felt very vulnerable. Despite such feelings, she was certain this was the wrong action to take.

"And when the other hands realize Price doesn't know the first thing about ranching? Then what?" Kit asked cockily.

"It does not matter that Saint knows less than you about running the ranch."

Kit passed a pleased glance to Price at García's confirmation she was more capable than he. The look earned her a bored expression that she'd come to know was Price's equivalent of an eyeroll, and she delighted in it.

García continued, "The men will not take orders from a woman."

Kit couldn't recall a time she was more offended and was about to unleash her fury when García said, "These are not gentlemen. They are the rough associates of your dilapidated, gambling sire. They are all you have, however, so I suggest you don't alienate them or agitate them. There's not a lot I like about this situation. But you are your mother's daughter, and therefore I have every faith in you. You'll have them all whipped into shape and taking your orders before the year is out. Gain their respect first, if that's even possible. At least until we can find replacements. And until then, Saint will mete out your orders. Things will go far more smoothly for you if you stick with this plan."

Kit didn't like it, but she could see the sense in it—for the time being. Plus, she'd get to boss the Saint around. That should prove interesting... She quirked her lip up and directed a sly grin in Price's direction to let him know she would enjoy her reign over him. But instead of earning a look of displeasure from him as she'd intended, his eyes took on a smoky glaze, the intensity of which seemed to start a fire low in her belly. Kit quickly averted her eyes in an effort to ignore him—and the blaze he'd set forth within her. How could the man stir her so with only a simple look?

❧

García informed them when they crossed onto her land. *Her land*, that was a heady feeling, she sighed. Kit made a study of the surroundings as they rode, wondering if she could be happy in such a place. From the north entry her land was divided by a great gorge and she couldn't prevent roving a skeptical eye over the rocky earth and believed she'd inherited a ranch that couldn't sustain itself. It didn't appear to be at all practical for grazing and it was difficult to ride on horseback. The terrain began to even out, however, as they rode and the flat, patchy land met with taller, greener buffalo grass and rolling hills. Eventually they came across some rough fences made from stumps and tree limbs. It was obvious they had been arranged in way of fence rails.

"It's mainly a border to warn others of trespassing. Your men should patrol the grounds in order to keep the livestock in," García explained after watching Kit eye the rough property.

Kit nodded her head and hoped she didn't appear unimpressed. Her stomach was in knots. She couldn't help comparing Morgan's ranch to that of Stone Ranch and the security Stone Ranch offered surrounded by steep mountain walls on all sides. Fences hadn't been necessary. And trespassers were almost unheard of.

As they neared the outbuildings they'd viewed from a distance, Kit noticed the twisted branches and stumps fade into true notched fences. And even a tall, wide arch over the entrance to the ranch welcomed them.

Kit studied the new surroundings. Yucca plants bordered all the buildings and hackberry shrubs grew along the fence line. García had explained how the hackberry shrubs would soon produce sweet fruits as they headed into summer. The ground before them between every building was dirt. A whole lot of dirt.

García whistled as he crossed the entry arch and some men came forth to assist him with the cart. One of the men stepped forward and lashed out his hand to halt the progress of the men seeing to the cart. He was missing more than one tooth in the front of his mouth and he appeared not to have bathed in a month. Kit began to believe García hadn't exaggerated when he described her men as a tough lot.

"We don't work for you," the angry, gap-toothed ogre growled.

"I'm the one paying your wages at the moment, so yes, José, you do work for me," García replied, unintimidated.

"Your wages are not fit for gin rot!"

"As if Morgan paid you better," García drolled. "Besides, you should stay away from that rot anyway."

Before the man could argue further, García began speaking Spanish and Kit no longer understood the conversation. The belligerent man speaking to him finally nodded, however, and two men took the cart and horses to a barn to unhitch. García untethered his horse from the cart before they took it away and climbed up into his saddle.

Kit watched him curiously, finding it strange he wasn't unsaddling. García didn't wait for the two men with the cart to return before he began addressing the group of ranch hands spilling forth and congregating in front of the long building they'd been resting in.

Once they stood before them, García began what sounded to Kit like a speech. However, since García continued in his native Spanish tongue, she caught very little of what he was telling the men, other than her name.

The fifteen or so men scattered in a half circle before her, Price, and García didn't look like ranch hands. Kit rather thought they looked like bandidos, especially with their sneers and leering eyes directed her way. Many of them missing teeth and all of them appearing as if they hadn't bathed in a fortnight. Kit worked to keep her lip from curling at the brood before her.

García turned toward her, "They all speak Spanish, only some speak English. Do you know any Spanish?"

Kit shook her head, deflated that she was already an inferior leader. How was she to direct these men if she couldn't even communicate with them?

"No worries," García flashed a smile, "your ranch foreman knows enough Spanish to carry out your orders."

Kit whipped her head around to look at Price, "You know Spanish?"

Price didn't bother looking at her as he answered, "Some. Picked it up while in California panning for gold with your brothers. And then after that, we stayed on with García until spring and he was kind enough to teach us a bit more."

Kit gave a small look of betrayal. García, a man who had been like an uncle to her all her life, had never bothered to teach her his native language, but he had taught Price. Well didn't that beat all, Kit pouted.

"Saint here is quite modest. The truth is, he picked it up rather easily. I'm sure he'd be glad to help you learn as well."

With a tip of his hat, García pointed to the buildings, naming each of them. The long building housed the hands. There was a barn for the horses, a barn for harvests, a small slaughter shed, a chicken run, pig pen, a well, a privy, and the building behind them at the end of a long winding path he pointed to was her new home.

The house was too far from sight for Kit to get a very good impression of it.

"I'm sorry to drop you off and run, but the men informed me a tornado touched down while I was away and tore through some of the buildings on my ranch across the way. I need to get back right quick and see to matters there. As soon as all is handled, I'll be back. You just get settled in. The housemaid, Sofia, will take care of you up at the house. Tomorrow, one of the hands can show you around the property."

García added, in an unmistakably serious tone, "Do not go anywhere on this property without Price. I don't trust many of these men, if any."

With that, García and Price shared a knowing nod.

Kit had been abandoned by her brother, and now her uncle as well—with all these rough characters, after weeks on the trail, and never even introduced to the house staff. She felt fear creeping in like a frost over fresh sprigs of grass. But the heat of her anger melted it away before it could make its kill. *So, everyone would just abandon her, huh?* Well, she didn't need anyone.

She couldn't afford to appear weak by allowing her fears to show or anger take over. Instead she concentrated on exhaling a slow steady breath to regain her control. That's when she felt Price ride up beside her, so close the calf of his leg rested against hers and the leather of their stirrups scraped. She recalled the times he'd comforted her with the merest touch and just as it had those instances, his presence now calmed her, reminding her she wasn't completely alone after all.

"Oh, and Kit?" García looked to her beseechingly and Kit knew he was about to divulge something serious in nature. Thinking he planned to tell her of more misdeeds her sire had been responsible for, she began imagining various atrocities Morgan had probably committed, to prepare herself. But what he said was much worse...

"There's more information I didn't tell you before. That I didn't tell your mother, either." He looked away guiltily. "I had wanted to give you some time with the ranch first but seeing as how I must now return to my own, I think you should know."

The anticipation was killing her, but she remained quiet so García would continue. She slowed her breathing near to nothing, afraid the tiniest motion or sound of breath would distract him and delay parting what could only be terrible disastrous news.

"There are specific stipulations regarding your owning of the ranch. Your fath—Morgan, that is—made them in part to ensure his blood would always have a legacy, and because he was in a tight spot with some of the neighboring ranchers and this was a way out... He, well, in order to keep the ranch, you must marry. And you must marry within six months' time or the ranch reverts to Kingston. Kingston loaned your father quite a bit of money. One could say he practically owned Morgan himself and awaited gleefully for the day he could collect his debt. That debt being this ranch.

"One good thing Morgan did for you was not force you to marry Kingston. It's a small blessing, but something of which to be thankful for, nonetheless. There are some good young men in these parts. I'm sure they've heard the news by now. Since we passed through Onieda and Canyon on our way and those are the only towns within hundreds of miles, I'm sure word will carry quickly that the ranch heiress has arrived. Men will be showing up at your doorstep soon, I imagine.

"I am sorry to be the deliverer of such news. And I wish you had time to truly love this ranch before making a decision. Know that you do not *have* to marry. But if you choose not to marry, you will be unable to obtain the ranch."

García looked out into the distance, studying the land. Love for the remaining pieces of his ancestral property shone in his eyes. He continued his perusal and avoided looking in the direction of Kit and Price, for he did not desire witnesses to his emotional grief as he spoke. "I was happy when your father announced he left the ranch to his lone child. He thought he was cutting me. Even at the end of his life he was a rotten bastar—sorry, forgive me. He was not a fair man. But instead of causing me a lifetime of unhappiness in seeing my father's lands shrink yet again, he did the opposite. I was overjoyed to learn someone I love and see as kin would be inheriting this land.

"I will understand if you are unable to bring yourself to care about this pile of dirt as much as I, myself, do. But I beg of you to make your decision fairly and honestly. That is all that I ask."

And with those weighing words, García spurred his horse and took off, leaving a dust cloud chasing after him under the ranch arches.

Marriage? Her? Her mind raced. Who would ever be willing to marry *her*? Well, being heiress to a ranch would probably help, but this ranch didn't really seem to be all that alluring... Kit looked around again at the dilapidated buildings and graying boards giving way to rot. She winced, knowing she didn't add a lot to the pot. If García had stuck around she may have asked him what the will stipulations were if no men offered marriage? She couldn't very well force anyone to marry her.

And, oh heavens, what if all the men in these parts looked like those hairy, rough characters she'd met at the barn? How was Kit going to be able to turn up any marriage prospects she didn't shudder at?

No. She set her shoulders. She was being preposterous. No man may want her, and her ranch may not be financially or physically sound, but land was land. Someone would want her for the land. Hopefully lots of someones, thus providing her many options.

Realizing Price was next to her witnessing her silent storm, and in order to cover up her embarrassing show of vulnerability, she shrugged and said, "Six months? Shouldn't take that long, I imagine."

~

Price looked to her in shock. He had been waiting for Kit's outrage. Her nonchalant reaction was completely unexpected.

Kit's eyes traveled her new pile of ruins. "I suppose it wouldn't hurt to have a husband."

"'Wouldn't hurt to have a husband'..." Price repeated, stupefied. "So, just-just any husband?"

"Of course not. He'd need to be—"

"I'll marry you," the words blurted from his mouth.

Kit looked to him as if HE were the one that had just grown two heads. Then, worse, she laughed. Sputtering, she said, "You? Ha! I don't think so."

Well, that was certainly a blow to his pride.

"Price, are you serious? You don't know the first thing about running a ranch. I need a partner who can sit the saddle all day and wrestle calves during branding season. I mean, you were raised practically like royalty."

Anger piqued within him. How could she stand there and treat him like a dandy from the east coast? Had he not spent the previous year in the muddied pits and dried up, rock-bedded rivers mining for gold with her brothers? For that matter, had there been a day where the majority of his time hadn't been seated in a saddle, since meeting her family? He'd dare to say he lived a far humbler lifestyle than Kit had ever imagined, cocooned in her lily-white sleeping gowns, and quilted bedsheets warmed by bricks from fires she'd never had to go without.

She ignorantly tossed accusations his way, when she didn't have a solid patch of ground to stand on! He was too incensed at the moment to attempt a response. And quite honestly, he was too hurt. All this time, living in the harsh west with her brothers, and she still saw him as little more than a soft, titled nobleman from England. *Bloody hell!* He kicked the toe of his boot into the dirt and stomped off toward the horse barn to see to the care of his horse. Kit followed.

"Careful", he heard her call after him, "you'll scuff those shiny boots of yours."

Oh, is that so? he grumbled to himself, trying to keep in mind that Kit didn't realize how badly her teasing cut.

They curried down their horses. None of the ranch hands came to the barn to speak with or assist them. Price was having a hard time digesting everything they had learned in the short time. He had just blurted out an offer of marriage that had been shot down in cold blood. He was glad there was no company in the barn.

Kit seemed to be in deep contemplation herself. He supposed that made sense. Although he was sure she wasn't giving any thought to his proposal. She'd thought it a joke.

Oh, the cruel irony he had been saddled with. The woman he loved thought him less than a man—certainly not man enough for her. She also happened to be the sister of his best friends to whom he swore he would protect. And he was quite certain they hadn't intended for him to marry their sister.

Although at this point, would not it be considered protecting her? She didn't know these other men, the potential marriage candidates. It could be looked on as Price making the ultimate sacrifice to protect Kit. He wondered if Luke and Logan would buy that.

Of course, he would have to convince Kit to marry him first, before he could justify it to her brothers.

Oh, what a bloody mess.

～

Kit was meticulous with her care of her horse, so the process of brushing had taken quite a while. She also voiced her fear that someone may attempt to steal the gorgeous animal, so she had been loath to leave the barn. When she finally decided to head to the house, he followed, though he couldn't bring himself to utter a single word to her. He considered whether he should pass his proposal off as the joke she obviously believed it to be, or to press his suit harder.

His thoughts over his internal struggle came to a halt as they neared the house, for even the dim evening light couldn't disguise the ruinous state it was in. Kit's steps slowed as she stared at the weathered boards in surprise.

The step up to the small planked porch leading to the entrance was broken.

He watched her sharp intake of breath as she swung the door open and it fell off its hinge in the process. The floor was dirt and there were few furnishings inside. The house looked abandoned.

Kit called out for the maid García said would meet her at the house. No one responded. Kit seemed to be daring herself to step farther into the crumbling abode.

She called out again. No answer. He followed her across what he supposed was the den area to the kitchen. Soiled and rusting iron pans sat about as if they had prepared a meal and were never properly washed and put away. The old fat building up in the skillet had a repugnant smell that made Kit cover her nose with her arm and shake her head in horrified disgust. Flies buzzed around the instruments.

"Well, at least some dishes were spared," Price suggested helpfully.

Kit disagreed with how helpful his comment was and glared balefully at him as she turned from the room. One other room existed off the side of the den. All in all, Price knew this to be fair accommodations. With some elbow grease the place would be a home to be proud of.

Kit obviously didn't see the potential in it.

Price smiled, taking great joy in watching Kit's distasteful reaction to her new home. It was definitely not what she was accustomed to. Price, however, had slept in far worse conditions. Standing at what was obviously the one bedroom in the house, staring at the lonely cot on the floor, he watched her throat work to swallow.

She turned to him, as usual her eyes unreservedly displayed all her thoughts. She tried to mask her uneasiness in the next instance when she tipped her nose stubbornly into the air, appearing every bit the "dandy" she'd accused him of being.

"Well." She sniffed, "Well, this certainly is a work in progress."

He cockily tipped his hat, "My lady, I'll bid you good night and leave you to your castle."

He and his arrogant smirk faded away with that last dig, leaving her alone, and feeling foolish, indeed.

Chapter 12

Kit spent the night tossing and turning in the empty, squalid quarters of her new home—on a cot no less—and awoke to the realization she had overslept. Thankfully, when she had changed from her trail ragged clothes and prepared for bed the previous evening, she had decided against donning a night gown. Instead she dressed into a fresh set of working clothes to greet the morning ready. And was she ever glad for it now.

She couldn't deny she was accustomed to more comfortable living arrangements; however, she had slept many a night on the ground while traveling to and from the academy and even on her journey here. *You simply need to adjust your expectations,* she told herself.

She would not fail.

If *the Saint* thought to see her squirm over a hard cot on a dirt floor, she would ensure him doomed for disappointment.

True, she'd not been able to hide her initial shock upon first learning the state of the house. An unfortunate reaction on her part, as it had brought Price no end of amusement. She mustn't give him more reason to judge her as incompetent. Nor the group of vaqueros outside awaiting her failure. She would prove to all of them just what Kit Stone was made of.

Which meant she'd better get her tail out there and face the day.

No sooner had she jogged down the steps from the house, was she met by the arrogant Saint, himself. Her mood soured instantly upon seeing the knowing smirk on his face. Her irritableness only served to remind her she'd missed taking her morning coffee. *That's what came of sleeping in,* she chided herself bitterly. The Saint would do well to keep his distance, if he knew what was good for him.

But, of course, he did not.

"Sleep well?"

Kit rolled her eyes and kept walking. She could see the men already lined up in front of the bunkhouse. The sun was already cracked over the horizon in a fiery line. No doubt the men were accustomed to being issued orders before the sun was fully risen. Kit mentally kicked herself and promised to wake earlier on the morrow.

"Good morning, gentlemen."

The men remained in the cool shadow of the bunkhouse, staring back blankly. *Right, many of them don't speak English.*

"Which of you speak English?"

A sandy-haired man not much older than Kit's brothers raised his hand.

"Excellent. What's your name?"

"Frank Perkins." His curious blue eyes watched her closely.

"Nice to meet you, Mr. Perkins. And do you speak Spanish?"

His reply of 'yes' sounded more like 'yacht' as he crossed his arms. Kit could sense his mulish demeanor wouldn't bode well for her.

"Excellent. This here is your new foreman. He goes by 'the Saint.' He speaks Spanish as well, so between the two of you, I expect my orders to be carried out."

He spoke Spanish to the crowd of men and their faces turned churlishly toward her. Kit knew she needed to stand tough if she was going to win this hard group over.

Out of the side of her mouth, she asked Price, "What did he say to them?"

Price rubbed his bristled jaw and answered, "You don't want to know."

Kit addressed Frank again, "Have them line up and when I point to them, say their name. Just their first names or whatever they wish me to call them."

It seemed juvenile, and indeed the men expressed as much on their faces, but Kit needed to begin somewhere and knowing what to call everyone seemed as a good a place to start as any.

Instead of fanning out into a line, however, the men dispersed.

"Where are they going?!" Kit shouted in disbelief.

Frank, called over his shoulder as he was walking away with the other men, "They say they don't have time for childish games. There's work to be done."

Kit wasted precious little time. She reached for the pistol at her side and fired a shot into the air. As expected, the men stopped in their tracks and turned back toward her. Price slanted his eyes at her with a questioning hook of his brow.

"Whatever your plans for the day, cancel them. I want repairs on all the outbuildings started immediately. Beginning with this bunkhouse."

Their glares turned to looks of surprise with the order.

One of the older Spanish-speaking men spoke to her and Frank translated, "He asks, what lumber would you have them use for these repairs?"

"I saw some already cut and piled out behind the barn where the carts and wagons are being stored. Why not use that?"

The older Mexican sneered and spit at the ground, his dark eyes challenging.

Frank studied her, his eyes dancing with laughter or ridicule, she couldn't tell, as he said, "Rivera ordered that lumber to renovate *your* house."

"Well, as good intentioned as my uncle is, he doesn't give the orders around here. I do. Let's get started, shall we?"

Kit left no room for further discussion as she walked out in front of them and led the way to the outer barns where the horses and carts were.

~

Price watched with astonishment, and more than a little pride, when the men followed after Kit. He never expected anything less of course, but he was rather surprised to see her turn this viper pit around as quickly as a charmer with a pungi.

When they reached the lumber, Kit pointed to the gap-toothed ogre, "You. Big, tall man. Price, how do I say bear in Spanish?"

"Oso."

"Oso," Kit repeated, pointing at the looming man before her. He stared back, mouth parted in confusion, displaying just how few teeth he had and pointed a finger to his chest.

"Yes, you. Go hitch up the cart."

Price quickly translated. Before the big man could respond or not, Kit moved on and pointed to another man. She seemed to notice that for all his clothes were grimy and stains soiled the shirt below the pits, his boots were either new or kept well-conditioned.

"You with the fancy boots. Go help the bear."

The man glared at Kit defiantly before Price could finish the translation.

Perkins attempted to intercede in that moment. Seemingly hesitant to speak and disrupt the hostile stare off, he pointed to Fancy Boots, and stuttered, "H-his name is—"

Kit cut him off coldly, "Ohhh," she stretched the word, her sarcasm apparent, "the time for the name game has passed. I will now be assigning them," she finished on a tight grin.

She heard the men mumble amongst themselves, disgruntlement apparent throughout the group. Then Frank laughed.

"What?" Kit asked curtly.

"They would like to know what they should call you." Frank eyed her rebelliously.

"They can call me *Boss*."

Kit spun on her boot heel and headed to the horse barn, back straight as an army general, leaving Price and the other men staring after her in reverent awe.

The entire week proved to be a struggle between her and the men. She earned the respect of some of the ranch hands when she insisted on fixing the men's quarters first. They gradually introduced themselves over the course of the days, but many of the nicknames Kit initiated had already stuck and were being used by many of them. Not all the men were so easily accepting of their new boss, though. And the men weren't the only obstacle.

One problem after another arose. Kit's buildings were all deteriorating and in need of repairs. The garden was in an atrocious state if their meals were any indication. They had dined on nothing more than beef and mealy potatoes since she'd arrived, and Kit had a feeling this had been the men's diet for quite some time. It was no wonder they were all a bunch of sour grapes. She was fast becoming as ornery as they were. She hoped assigning the boy—Samuel—to the task of gardening would improve their food state. It seemed he knew more than the others about such matters.

Kit suspected the boy's grandfather was the true font of information behind the gardening, but he was the crankiest of them all and certainly didn't like Kit. Kit had started calling him Badger and his was one of the names that stuck, so clearly her opinion of the grump was shared by them all. While the old cuss was curt and gruff with Kit, and even the other men, she often saw a gentler side of the man expressed to his grandson.

That wasn't the man's only redeeming quality. He obviously had the respect of the other men and seemed to be their ringleader. As much as he butted heads with Kit, the fact that the other men looked to him carried a lot of weight with her opinion of him. So, despite the man's apparent joy in insulting her every chance he got and his condescending speech that ground her teeth to powder, she kept in mind the respect he garnered from her men. It seemed a mystery to her, for the man seemed in a constant state of orneriness.

Price had the impression that ol' Badger had a soft spot for Kit, though Kit didn't believe that for a second. What the old man enjoyed was having someone to bully and ridicule. It didn't escape Kit, however, that while ol' Badger always had a critique at the ready for her, he was also the one teaching her the most. There was guidance in his curt words and so she bore the insults and learned.

Whatever it took.

Because Kit didn't intend on tucking tail and giving up her very own ranch.

The man creating the bigger raucous was the one she had deemed "Fancy Boots." She later learned his name to be José and that he could speak English fairly well—in fact, she'd learned quite a few of the men could speak English. Apparently, José had taken his nickname worse than the others and resented Kit mightily for it. He seemed particularly intent on causing trouble for her; he was either blatantly disobeying orders or taking his sweet time with tasks in a challenging fashion. He also let his ill opinion of letting the ranch fall into the hands of a "mere girl" be heard far and wide.

For the most part, Kit tried to ignore it. But today, her temper boiled right along with the scorching sun above.

"José, I warned you, if you don't get those boots dirty by doing some work, I'm going to revert back to calling you by your nickname. Now, why don't you fetch another pouch of nails."

"I don't take orders from no gringo las chica."

Kit let the end of the rough-cut board she was holding fall to the dirt and forced her aching back into standing position once more. She looked directly into José's dark eyes glinting like gun powder.

"Listen, if you don't want to take orders from a woman, that's fine. Gather your belongings and head out. I'm sure an able-bodied man, such as yourself, will have no trouble finding employment elsewhere."

A leering smile carved its way across José's face, "Do not make threats lightly, señorita."

"I don't make threats, José. And I don't pay ranch hands who don't carry their fair share. So, either get to work or ride out. Now."

José straightened from his resting position against the corral post but continued to glare at Kit. She waited for him to storm off and fetch his horse, but to her surprise he snarled and headed to the supply barn to fetch the nails. She wiped her brow and glanced around at the other men who had paused in their work to watch the spectacle. As her eyes met theirs, they quickly resumed their tasks of replacing the damaged boards on the barn.

~

Price worked alongside Kit and the ranch hands all week rebuilding and repairing the outbuildings. The only remaining project after their current reconstruction of the horse barn was to sturdy up the corral and the stock holding pens.

Earlier in the week, the weather had been mild to cool, especially in the evening, but today the sun was punishing. Price knew Kit had a lot to prove and her pride would never allow her to display something she would consider a "weakness."

Such as heat stroke, he shook his head at the woman's stubbornness.

Price began to wonder if anyone present was sensible enough to cease work in the middle of the day rather than frying like lard in a pan. Apparently, today's goal was to sweat to their imminent deaths.

He knew one thing for certain, Kit wouldn't be the one to give in. He'd never met anyone who worked as hard as she— including her brothers! And these ranchers weren't about to speak out so long as a woman continued laboring beside them without so much as a peep.

Deep down he believed Kit knew her humanly limits, but he wasn't sure if her stubbornness might dominate her good sense and end them all. He wasn't so prideful as the rest of the lot. If Kit didn't put an end to this misery soon, he *would*.

With every discreet glance her direction, he noticed the areas where her skin was exposed turning pink. Her beat up, wide-brimmed hat protected her face well enough, but her arms were sure to blister soon if she didn't roll her sleeves down.

She straightened then, took off her hat with one hand and wiped the sweat from her brow with the other. The movement caused her sweat-dampened shirt, tucked in at the waist of her pants, to stretch tautly over her breasts. Price's mouth went dry at the sight and suddenly standing was very uncomfortable. Irritated with his body's reaction to the woman, he quickly surveyed the other men to ensure they weren't staring inappropriately at the same spectacle he was. Apparently, the rest of the men were too tired to notice. *Thank God.*

He struggled to avert his own eyes, not wanting to be caught gawking. His efforts mattered little, however, because as usual, Kit barely noticed his presence—luckily for him in this instance.

The stubborn woman repositioned her hat back atop her head and reached for the next board to hand up the ladder to Perkins. He could tell by her crimped movements her back ached, yet she persevered.

Price continued his task of prying off a low, damaged board, distracted though he was, and the heat of the day wasn't entirely to blame. He imagined placing his hands on the small of Kit's back and massaging her aches away. Of smoothing his hands down over her hips, while the soft curve of her arse pressed against him.

Damn. Those thoughts would not do. Price adjusted himself. Out of the corner of his eye, he watched Kit cast another concerned glance Samuel's way.

Of course, Kit would never firstly be concerned for her own health and safety. As always, her duty was to those in her care; the employees and animals she was responsible for. That was precisely why Price made Kit *his* responsibility.

Her eyes were still on Samuel. The boy sat on a tin bucket pulling precious cut nails from the old slabs of rotted boards they'd pulled. The task required diligence to preserve as many of the nails as possible for reuse. Price knew she was taking in the boy's slowed movements and wilted position. Samuel was a hard worker, but he was still just fourteen years old.

"Samuel," Kit called, "I have another important duty for you."

The boy pushed the board from his lap and stood attentively, clearly happy for the opportunity to escape his current role.

"Si, boss."

Kit smiled appreciatively. He was one of the few workers she had who were willing to take orders and was eager to please. Price knew Kit admired the boy's spirit, as did he.

"We all need our canteens refilled. How about you run ahead, pull up the water from the well and get a start on it. I assume you can locate everyone's canteen?"

"Si."

"Make sure the water is chilled, first, then bring them 'round."

Price grinned, Kit had effectively ordered the boy to drink first and issued a work break for all in a way that allowed no one to feel inferior.

"The water is deep in the well underground, of course it's cold," Price grinned slyly. "You may as well have asked him to ensure it was wet."

Price noticed some of the other men cracking smiles. None had been fooled by Kit's orders. And all were greatly pleased.

Kit sniffed, assuming an air of indifference, "Well, that was so the boy didn't dawdle."

"Ah, yes, clearly," Price smirked before turning back to prying another board.

She was winning them over with her natural leadership qualities, even if she didn't yet realize it.

Their benevolent queen, he thought.

And, oh, how he would love to worship her so.

Chapter 13

Kit silently congratulated herself for surviving the first week on her new ranch as she helped mend the corral. She looked around and saw the fruit of their labors and smiled; she was proud of all they had accomplished in just seven days. There was something about putting one's own blood and sweat into a place that made it feel more like home. *If only the blasted weather was tamer*, she thought, then she might feel more fondly about her new home.

The scorching Texas air caused trickles of sweat to dampen her shirt, while the awful dry dust adhered to it, making mud. She swore the air in Texas had more dust than vapor in it. Every time she moved, she kicked more up onto herself and coughed. Her white shirts were all ruined and stained brown because of it.

And, to think, García had told her this was the rainy season. *Hah!* Spring was never this hot in the valley. In fact, often there was still snow coating the ground this time of year. It was a difficult adjustment and she wondered if she would ever find the climate bearable.

Fair to suffocating she had long since untied the soiled bandana from her neck and shoved it into the waistband of her pants. It left her neck exposed to the sun, but in the high of the afternoon, she could tolerate no more breathing restrictions, and decided it needed to go. As filthy as it was, she should have tossed it to the ground, but she hadn't wanted to forget it and leave it behind. Eventually, she would have to wash all her dust and sweat-laden clothes.

Which was another contention she had with her new ranch. Back home, she hadn't performed her own laundry duties, Rita had done it for the family.

She had a feeling Price knew her predicament, because he kept commenting on her stench, the cursed devil. She'd have to wait until he wasn't around before attempting a wash day on her own. After all the accusations she had thrown at him about being too dandified to hack it on a ranch, she sure wasn't going to allow him the pleasure of seeing her, once again, in such an embarrassing state. Him laughing at her shock when she'd learned of her housing conditions was quite enough.

The problem was, the man was always around. Like the addle-brained barn cat back home that was always underfoot, oblivious to the peril he put himself in.

Price made his way to her side. She rolled her eyes, *think of the devil and he will appear. What does he want now?* she wondered. She was fast becoming aggravated with his constant hovering. Then she noticed what he'd already spied—an unknown rider was approaching, entering under the ranch archway.

Price didn't say a word, but Kit could feel an edgy anger permeating from him.

"Do you mind?" she barked. "No need to hover directly over me. It's hard enough to breathe in this blasted part of the country as it is."

Price's hazel eyes thinned to slits at her orneriness, but she noticed he did take a step back. The rider swung down off his mount in a swift motion. To Kit's surprise one of her men rushed over to him as if he were royalty and took his horse for him. They hadn't done that for *her* the day she arrived, she thought, disgruntled.

Just who could the man be? José led him to where she was. Great. She was in no state of dress to be welcoming visitors on her ranch yet.

Pulling the bandana quickly from her waist band, Kit made short work of attempting to clean her hands. The man was before her in an instant, however, so she quickly thrust the rag into Price's hands, hard enough to deliver a punch to his gut at the same time.

He expelled a grunt behind her at the unexpected aggressive contact.

Hmph, that might teach him to stand so damnably close, she thought with a satisfied grin.

"Hello," the stranger before her extended his hand to her in greeting. Kit absently shook it. This man looked as if sculpted from stone. The sun shone off his pearly white teeth when he smiled, teeth perfectly arranged in a neat row. Most women, she was sure, would find his smile attractive. And indeed, there was certainly nothing *unattractive* about the man, but Kit had always thought teeth that big and straight belonged on a horse.

Even so, she smiled in return, hoping the gritty sand she felt in her mouth didn't show on her teeth. She suddenly had the urge to spit but knew that would be unseemly. So she swallowed the grime, instead.

"You must be Catherine Morgan."

"Catherine Stone, actually. My stepfather adopted me when I was a child. And, please, call me Kit. Everyone does."

The man's crafted smile turned up more in the corners, as if charmed,

"Well then, Kit it is. It's nice to meet you."

"And who are you?" Price inserted with the manners of a horse's behind.

Kit had to stop her eyes from bugging out. Price was normally cool and collected. She couldn't count the number of times she had tried to irritate him into showing emotion and failed.

In fact, the only thing that had seemed to heat his cool English blood was when they kissed. He'd been furious that day. Kit blushed for recalling the memory at such an inappropriate moment. Then she blushed again for having blushed in the stranger's presence in the first place. And it was Price's fault. She resisted the urge to stomp on the toes of his boot. If she could have gotten away with it without anyone being the wiser, she would have done so.

The man barely spared Price a glance. That would have gotten Kit's dander up had it been she, but Price here probably didn't even recognize the slight.

The man took off his hat, exposing a full head of brown hair, so dark it was nearly black, matching the thin mustache styled above his lip. Normally that sort of grooming would make a man look too genteel for Kit's tastes, but on him it was rather dashing.

He smiled again, "I am Whitney Kingston, Cornelius Kingston's son. You may be familiar with the name?" he queried.

"I'm afraid I'm not familiar. Please do enlighten me." Kit gave her best imitation of how she imagined Livvy would address the handsome man.

"The Kingston Ranch is to the east of you. My father has actually invested quite a bit of money into Morgan's ranch. It is my understanding that señor Rivera fetched and delivered you."

It took Kit a second to recall the people from García's home region knew him as Rivera.

"He did go over the terms of your inheritance, I hope?"

A derisive snort escaped her lips before she could prevent the unladylike action. One could hardly call García's announcement of her inheritance stipulations just before abandoning her to her fate as 'going over the terms.'

"He mentioned them, yes, but did not divulge many details, I'm afraid." She wanted to ask if he was here to offer marriage, but that seemed a bit forward.

She did want to curb this meeting, though. Daylight was wasting, and she was hoping to check the herd over after fixing the corral. Many of the first-time heifers were due to calve soon. Having always been in close contact with her mares during foaling season, Kit wanted to be nearby during the calving process as well. Even though Badger had laughed in her face at such an idea and informed her Mother Nature would handle everything. Perhaps cattle weren't as finicky as horses, but Kit wanted to be nearby just in case.

"Rivera had an urgent situation to deal with upon our arrival. He had to leave in a hurried state, but is expected to return soon," Price voiced in his smooth, proper English.

Whitney Kingston eyed Price as if he were a servant speaking to royalty. How ironic, Kit thought, since Price came from a line of nobility—unlike, she was certain, this pompous Kingston fellow.

"And who are you again?" Kingston eyed Price shrewdly.

Deciding it would be fun to further nettle Price, Kit interjected, "This is my ranch foreman, Mr. Price."

Price narrowed his eyes at the introduction that alluded to such an impersonal relationship. Not about to allow Price to expound otherwise, Kit hooked her arm in Kingston's. She had to suppress a pleased smile from forming at the utter shock and dismay shown on Price's normally inscrutable face as she steered Kingston in the opposite direction.

"That guard dog you were with, he's just your ranch foreman?"

"Well, truth be told, he is a close friend of the family and is temporarily assisting me while my brother is away on business."

"He doesn't seem at all pleased to have you walking with me." Kit missed the calculating curiosity in Kingston's tone. "He looks a man of jealousy."

"Saint? Heavens no. He's near as much a brother to me."

You wouldn't have passionately kissed your brother, she admonished herself. She smiled to Kingston in hopes of disguising her guilt over the white lie.

~

Price couldn't believe what he was witnessing. Kit was ever the stoic, quiet sort. Direct and poignant, preferring efficiency in minimal words. She abhorred unnecessary chatter. Kit was normally so tight-lipped that even civility and politeness was a rarity.

To see her attempting to charm and flatter a stranger was quite unnerving. Especially when the receiving party was likely to have a weighing interest in Kit's charms. She knew the man was after her ranch and she was seemingly throwing herself at him.

And if the man's winning smirk was any indication, Kingston was quite enjoying Kit's marked attention upon him. Price growled. How could Kit possibly be trying to woo this man? Those words didn't even belong stringed in the same sentence. Kit didn't woo. Kit worked. She didn't have romantic interests in men, and they shouldn't have interest in her.

Except, he knew that to be false, for he wasn't the first man interested in what she had to offer... But damn it, he was likely the first interested in *her*, rather than her grand inheritances. Of course, he was wrong about the other notion as well.

Kit *was* interested in the romantic arts. She had expressed as much to him before leaving to that blasted academy. Unfortunately, she just wasn't interested in *him*.

An unusual sound pricked his ears. Price looked up to see Kit's head tilted back with soft, tinkling laughter. He wasn't sure what the over-oiled gent could have said that was so amusing, but Kit tittered in return. *Tittered!* Price hadn't thought Kit capable of behaving so coyly.

He didn't like it.

If he was going to convince Kit he was best suited for her as her husband, he was running out of time. Price knew this was only the first of many swains who would be knocking on her door.

~

Kit couldn't stand the promenaded prig at her side. Whitney Kingston could talk of nothing but himself, it would seem. But she knew Price was watching on, expecting her to botch things as usual, so she feigned interest. For some reason, it irked her that Price didn't find her desirable and for reasons unknown to even herself, she wanted to prove him wrong. She would find someone willing to marry her, and she *would* keep this ranch. She didn't need any false, sympathy proposals from *the Saint*.

Kit attempted meaningful conversation with Kingston, "You've lived in Texas your entire life?"

"Yes, even before it was Texas."

"Did you fight in the war against Mexico?"

"I did."

Kit wasn't sure why she was surprised, other than the fact she just couldn't picture this man risking his life for something larger than himself. Her first impressions of people were usually correct. She excelled at silent observation as she was normally overlooked in most social situations where she and Lavinia were presented together.

The fact that Kingston fought in the war did raise her respect for him. Perhaps she needed to look beyond the promenade and pomp.

"My brothers fought in the war as well. Although just the very end of it. They attended school back east for the better part of it."

Dust kicked up where Kit nudged loose a small shrub with the toe of her boot, "So, ah, did you know my-my, ahem," she cleared her throat, "James Morgan?"

"Not well, I'm afraid. He mostly did dealings with my father. And I, like your brothers, was sent off to school as well when I came of age."

"What do you know about this ranch? It's my understanding that it doesn't quite border yours, so I find it strange your father would be very interested in it. And as you must know, it's finances are not in good condition at the moment." Of course, Kit knew the reason behind Kingston's interest, for García had already revealed to her the Morgan Ranch was greatly indebted to Kingston, but she wanted to know what the son knew. Or rather, how honest he was.

Kingston smiled, flashing a lot of teeth her way, "No need to worry your pretty little head over something as gauche as finances."

Her *pretty little head?* She brushed the insult aside for the time being.

Eyeing him keenly, she said, "Strange thing to say for a businessman."

"Precisely; the running of a ranch is a *man's* business. You will do well to heed your father's will and marry quickly."

Before Kit could recover from the surprise of receiving such an unsurpassed degree of condescension, the man turned back toward the barns where is horse awaited him.

"Well, I think I should be on my way. But I will be back to visit before long, my dear. In the meantime, there's no reason to worry about finances. I'm sure your future will be secured in no time. After all, the decision is up to you, is it not?"

Did the man just presume she would marry him? Disgust curled her lip before remembering Price surveilling her in the distance.

She tried to recover by forcing pleasant words from her mouth, "That was a lovely stroll, Kingston. I can hardly await your next visit."

"Perhaps you can ready some refreshments the next time I come calling. I'll send round a note in advance, so you can better prepare for my visit."

Oh, God, please just leave, she thought. Her smile was involuntarily transforming into a grimace. She thought it better to wave, silently, than to open her mouth for fear of what might slip out.

After he rode off, Kit walked straight past Price back to the corral and assisted the men fixing another rail. Cowardly of her to avoid eye contact, yes, but necessary.

She hoped more marriage candidates appeared besides Kingston, or she feared this ranch would not be hers for very long, indeed.

Chapter 14

Another sunny day she awoke to. Another day of work ahead of her. She stretched her achy muscles. Sleeping on a cot was more bothersome than the actual work. She was accustomed to ranch work.

She grumbled, she wasn't, however, accustomed to housework. Her clothes were more soiled than ever they had been, and the stench was a tad debilitating. She stepped out onto the broken porch, hoping the fresh air would mask some of her odor.

"Dear God, Kit. You want me to show you how to wash your clothes?"

Price.

She rolled her eyes.

"Did it ever occur to you, I'm letting them accrue some stink, so you won't hover about me all the time?"

Price grinned at her cantankerousness, while handing her a cup of fresh brewed coffee.

Her weakness.

"I suppose your hovering does come with some perks every once in a while."

"I rather thought so," he replied, amused.

Just then Samuel trotted up to them, "Grandpapa wants to know if we are to work fences again today or if we can get back to cattle wor—oh!" Samuel finally arrived within a foot of Kit and caught a whiff of her clothes.

The unfortunate boy instinctively thrust his arm up to block his nose. Once he realized he had just insulted his boss he tried to lower his arm, but Kit watched the struggle on the poor child's face.

"Is, is that smell you?"

Price shook with suppressed laughter beside her.

Placing his hand strategically to block his nostrils, but not his mouth, Samuel offered, "I could wash your laundry for you if you would like, when I wash mine and Grandpapa's clothes."

Kit's expression must have been fierce because the boy retreated a few steps. Though that could have been self-preservation from her stench.

Now Price was out and out guffawing.

"Oh, do shut up," Kit barked at him, then to Samuel directed, "Thank you, but no, I am capable of washing my own clothes, I'm sure."

She threw a scathing glance to Price who was now using the door frame of the house to hold himself upright against the bellyaching laughter.

"Tell your grandpapa, that I would love to see to the cattle today and tell the hands to saddle up. Thank you."

Price was wiping tears from his eyes as he trotted down the steps to join her all the while dramatically displaying his safe distance-keeping.

Kit could only roll her eyes in response.

Kit discovered she quite loved hunting for new spring calves. The ranch had required a lot of groundwork, leaving little time for riding and it felt marvelous to sit a saddle again. Blue had felt the restraints of late, too. When she fetched him from his stall and led him to the corral instead of the pasture—as had become customary—she'd felt energy ripple through him as he nickered with pleasure. They both needed this day.

Kit wasn't even cursing the hot sun today. In fact, she was rather enjoying it. Tearing off after strays and keeping the herd

123

together as they crossed over the rough terrain was sweat-inducing physical work for her and the horse but sweating in the dirt pounding nails into boards didn't allot for the same feeling of accomplishment. Work from the saddle was freedom! And every chase gave way to a breeze strong enough to dry the sweat from her face and she was refreshed once more. It was as if her soul was cleansed with each run.

"That is one fine horse you have," Badger's Spanish-accented voice sounded at her side, surprising Kit. Though it wasn't his appearance next to her she found startling, but the compliment.

"Thank you," she replied almost cautiously. When she didn't see signs of sarcasm or foul comments forthcoming from the older ranch hand, she continued, "He was bred and raised at Stone Ranch," she smiled proudly and patted the slope of Blue's shoulder.

"Si," Badger continued, his dark eyes softening, lending him a cordial manner usually reserved only for his grandson, "Most all señor Rivera's horses came from Stone Ranch; known for their quality horse flesh. Morgan wouldn't allow horses with the Stone Ranch brand on the property. Many of us old cow pokes had to live in envy of señor Rivera's men." Badger's silver-ticked moustache hitched up on one side and Kit realized the man had smiled. Something she never thought to witness from the ol' cur. At least not directed toward her.

"But now that you are here," he nodded respectfully, "running things, I don't foresee that being a problem." His smile grew wider as he swept his arm gesturing toward his horse's rear flank, where an SR brand shone proudly.

Kit looked closer at the gelding but didn't recognize him from the breeding program. "He must be born from Comanche's line, my mother's favorite stallion, before I was old enough to work the young ones."

"Si, he is an old man like me." Badger winked.

Kit smiled, enjoying the unexpected camaraderie.

"It is my understanding that you train all of the young horses that come from SR, these days."

"Most, not all." Her mother still enjoyed finishing out some of their new stock herself. Kit wondered, had her mother given more responsibilities over to Kit for Kit's sake, or her own? She was beginning to think it had been for Kit, rather than her mother slowing down and preferring a relaxed lifestyle.

Which was just another reason keeping this ranch was so important. It wasn't everyday someone received opportunities like this, especially not women. As a woman, and belonging to a family who loved her, she knew she would always be taken care of. Her brothers were *expected* to build on to their empire or start fresh with their own. *Kit* was expected to marry or live out her days at Stone Ranch as a spinster. A lifestyle she always thought she would be contented with.

Until *the Saint*.

He'd just had to come along and show her exactly what she would be giving up. *The abominable man.*

The terms of the ranch were shocking and appalling at first, she admitted, but slowly Kit realized how it had worked in her favor. On her own, she wouldn't have attracted a man, but now she had something to covet. So long as she used her good judgment, she was sure she could secure an agreeable partnership. Someone who shared her vision for the ranch, and also someone who didn't find her completely undesirable.

Badger's voice floated back to her, "This is where the men typically break when gathering."

Kit recognized the questioning tone in his words. She nodded her affirmation and Badger nudged his gelding into a jog to spread her orders to the rest of the men.

It was little surprise why they were partial to this spot for breaking. It was a lovely shady area along Hackberry Creek that offered drink as well as respite from the high afternoon sun.

Instead of discussing the ranch, she learned a bit more about her men. The relaxed manner as they sat around enjoying the welcome breeze brought forth easy conversation. It was the first since her arrival, and it felt more like progress than any of the rebuilt buildings. The only ranch hand still tight-lipped and resentful of her presence was José, but he was no longer blatantly disrespectful, so she counted that as progress, too.

Reenergized, they packed up and climbed back into their saddles, ready to drive the cattle the finishing stretch to the front pasture.

Feeling more hopeful than ever about her ranch, Kit stepped into her stirrup and started to swing her leg over the saddle, when suddenly, she was hauled off into the air!

She recognized the strong arms wrapped around her in an instant.

"Price! Price, you oaf, put me down!"

"Gladly," he responded and then tossed her forward, right into the cold creek depths below.

She emerged sputtering and, quite literally, spitting mad. All the cowhands around who had witnessed the man-handled display were chortling amongst one another.

Why, she'd never been so humiliated!

And there *he* was.

With the nerve to appear completely relaxed, wearing a big smile, while resting against the trunk of a twisty oak.

"Sorry, but you refused the nice clothes-washing lesson, and the men couldn't take much more of your rankness."

She couldn't believe he'd done such a thing. The small respect she'd worked for from her men all out dissolved in a snap, she fumed. Her hands struggled for grip on the spindly grass as she tugged to pull herself up the steep bank.

She ignored Price's hand and scrambled up on her own, completely coating her drenched clothes in dirt, which in turn, created a cake of mud down her person.

She stood and fervently brushed the mud from her form while thinking of how to handle this situation in a way that might salvage some of her pride. But, when she looked up to address the laughing mass, she realized to her horror, they had left, taking the baying cattle with them.

Her head swiveled to where Price had been. He was still there. *Of course,* she growled. She was never rid of that fool. Since no one else was around, she decided to tell him exactly what she thought of his little display.

"Well, thank you. Do you have any idea of the damage you just caused?"

Price continued smiling, "Calm down, they all thought it great fun."

"Oh indeed! And now they will never take me seriously!"

"Here," was all he said before tossing her a wrapped bundle.

"What's this?" she demanded testily.

"Clean garments. You're welcome."

"Welcome? Welcome—ha! This is soooo...so...*un*welcome."

Price arched his brow at her weak argument.

"It was unnecessary. I told you I would wash my clothes. Now, you've made me look the fool before all those men, when I was only just getting them warmed to the idea of me, *a woman*, being in charge."

"Trust me, you looked—or rather, smelled—more foolish going days without a wash. It was a clear indicator you weren't familiar with the simplest of daily tasks."

"Well!" Angry and pride still wounded, she was unwilling to give up on the insult, "It was more than unwelcome and unnecessary—it was inappropriate!"

"Just get dressed."

She looked appalled at the very suggestion, "I can't change into these. The men will know!"

Price laughed, "That's the point."

"No, I mean, they'll know I-I...disrobed in your presence." Her cheeks colored to crimson.

"I'm not even going to be near you. I'll stand on the other side of this tree and promise not to peek."

"It doesn't matter whether you do or not, because there is no one to say otherwise..."

"Exactly, there's no one to say otherwise. Now do get dressed."

She gritted her teeth in fury once again at being ordered about. However, she decided not to allow her stubborn pride to stand in the way of fresh laundered clothes. She would never admit such to Price, but the clothes he'd given her smelled heavenly.

"Fine!" she barked. "But you had better not come out from behind that tree, or there'll be consequences."

Price chuckled, "Don't tempt me. I may just like the consequences."

At the implication of his words, the rest of Kit's body felt as though it had tinted the crimson her cheeks had been painted with moments ago.

And despite the cold muddied material clinging to her body, she suddenly felt warm.

Price must have sensed her aroused state, for although he did move to the other side of the tree, out of view, his voice when he spoke next was low and smoky, "Just change your clothes, Kit."

She shivered, recalling their last kiss and it occurred to her that perhaps she should take advantage of the opportunity to be had in this private moment, to learn more about the art of seduction. Especially if she was to entice a husband before the next six months were up. Price insisted before that he hadn't enjoyed their kiss. But she certainly had. And she wondered if the husky turn of his voice was indication he might be willing to try again...

A plan formed in her mind. A test of sorts. And if she could pull it off—if she could get Price, who couldn't stand her, to want to kiss her—then perhaps there was hope for her. Perhaps she wasn't as unappealing as she believed herself to be. And perhaps she could save her ranch.

Garnering up the false confidence had her stomach in knots and her legs feeling hollow.

Deciding she didn't want to be in a state of undress when she approached him, she changed quickly. The waist of the pants he'd given her were too large even with the blouse tucked in. And the fasteners, she realized, were in back. If she wanted them to fit her waist, she'd have to take them off to resize and then try to squeeze the tightened waist back on over her hips.

Or...

"Price?" she called, weakly at first. Did she really want to go through with this? Could she? It was a stupid plan. Idiotic.

"What is it, Kit?"

He had heard her then. Suddenly her palms were damp with sweat.

"You finished?" she heard him ask from his position by the tree.

"Y-yes." What was wrong with her voice? If she was this nervous about seducing *Price*, how would she ever be able to seduce a potential suitor into marrying her? Before her mind was altogether made up, she heard herself say, "I mean, almost. Could you help me?"

There was a pause.

Her breath held, suspended as she searched for something else to say. Too late. When she spun around to tell him never to mind, he was already before her.

He was an indolent aristocrat. An English dandy. He should be built lean and wiry, or soft from living a life of privilege.

Only he wasn't those things. He was tall, far taller than Kit's petite height, though she hadn't truly noticed before now. And though he was leaner than her brothers, his muscled chest and arms hardly depicted a man who lived an idle lifestyle.

He may not be the ideal partner when it came to running a ranch, but Price certainly wasn't averse to the labor required to do so.

Her heart thundered in her chest as she took in his towering frame. The golden hairs sprinkled over his bronzed forearms below his rolled shirt sleeves matched the exposed part of his chest where he left his lawn shirt undone to accommodate the Texas heat as he worked.

Her eyes traveled upward over his strong jaw sprigged with the rough growth of stubble on a face used to being clean shaven. The butterflies in her stomach fluttered all the more. She tipped her head back, daring to meet his hazel eyes.

It was difficult to think with him so near she could smell the faintest hint of his cologne mingled with her favorite scents of leather and horse. His hazel eyes were mesmerizing as they seemed to change color even as she was looking into them

"It-it's the fasteners," she managed to find her voice. "They're in the back." She turned, presenting her backside to him for assistance.

There was another pause and she thought she would need to clarify that she required his help, but then she felt his hands at her waist, and it was as if her entire body sprang to life like the licking flames of a fire.

Suddenly her body was sensitive to his every touch. Where his thumbs rested along the top of her buttocks as his knuckles brushed against her lower back where the straps were. She felt his fingers working the buckle and then slide along the material at her waistline, drawing them more snugly to her body.

All the blood in her body seemed to be drumming a beat through her, but she thought she heard his breath, warming her neck, become more labored just as she felt his hands rest briefly

Caytt Lawson

at her hips. She closed her eyes, welcoming the touch and was left chilled when he withdrew.

Not wanting the rush of feelings building within her to disappear, she turned to face him and placed her hand on his chest, silently telling him to stay.

Was he feeling what she was? This overwhelming surge of pleasure? The need to touch more and be touched; was this desire? And could she invoke these feelings in him as well?

She stepped forward, bringing their bodies closer together. He did not step away but remained still. The proximity of him and the fear he would reject her caused her lungs to take shallow, rapid breaths. She forced her eyes to meet his gaze.

His smoky green eyes searched hers, then he bent his head and lowered his mouth. Gently, his lips brushed hers, teasing them open. She felt the tip of his tongue trace her lower lip. She met hers to his. She followed his lead, learning the intricate dance he guided.

His hands started at her hips and glided over her cambric blouse as if the material wasn't there. A jolt of electricity shot through her as his thumb grazed the underside of her breast through the thin material, made thinner with the absence of her camisole. Heat pooled between her legs as he caressed back and forth, his tongue mimicking the actions in her mouth. The combined sensations set her afire. It was pleasure unlike any she'd ever known.

She stood on her tiptoes and leaned into his chest, hungry to take what he was giving. If this was what marriage would bring, she would try a lot harder to secure a partner before the six months deadline!

Kit smiled against his lips at the thought. "This isn't so bad," she said, "I think I could get the hang of this, with some more practice."

~

Price wasn't sure how it had happened. He knew he shouldn't have settled his hands at her hips. He should have tightened the fasteners as she'd asked and then released her. But Christ how she had fit in his hands. Her back turned to him, with her round arse below his fingertips, he'd wanted desperately in that moment to rub his hands down those hips and cup her in his hands.

He'd wanted to press his face against her lovely neck and inhale the sweet scent of her freshly wetted hair, already drying in the honeysuckle-scented breeze. Then she turned to face him, and her tongue darted out to wet her lips and he lost all control and restraint not to touch her.

When she stepped close to him and pressed her palm to his chest, it was all he could do not to ravish her like a green lad with his first willing milk maid.

He wanted to show her what a kiss should feel like. How it should build and anticipate the coupling it resembled.

She pressed even closer into him and still, it wasn't enough. He wished all the fabric between them to hades.

Then she spoke. Her words featherlight against his lips. His mind slow to waken to the words she was saying.

Practice? He kissed her more, willing her back to their web of ecstasy. Where there was no talking. Just glorious, glorious touching.

But she spoke again.

"If this is part of the deal, marriage to one of those ranchers wouldn't be so bad."

~

Price's body stiffened against her, his hands dropping from her sides as if burned, abruptly ending the kiss. He backed away from her in one angry step, leaving them both panting for breath.

Confused, her heavy-lidded gaze had trouble meeting his. He appeared nearly as disoriented as she. Surely, this time he had enjoyed the experience as she had? But then, why had he stopped it?

"I'm just your practicing tool? To help you land a husband?"

Kit couldn't understand his anger. He seemed to enjoy kissing her, despite what

he claimed last time, so she didn't see much hardship in it for him.

"I didn't figure you would mind all that much," she spoke guardedly, not wanting him to know his rejection of her hurt. "I thought men liked that sort of thing. I know I'm not the most appealing package, nor am I very experienced, but I didn't think you were all that abhorred by the idea of kissing me.

"If I'm going to entice one of these ranchers to marry me, I think I should learn...how to get a man to want me.

"And who better a teacher than you? I know I can trust you not to take things too far."

His teeth looked gritted enough to break. And if she didn't know him better, she would be a little afraid. He did little but stare back at her, seething through his teeth.

"Well, if you're this disgusted, then I'll find a different teacher. Perhaps Frank. I think he has all of his teeth at least. Or maybe the next time Kingston pays a visit, I'll just give it a go. He's the likeliest candidate anyway." For some reason, she couldn't find the words to make this situation less mortifying and her addled brain was fit to let her mouth continue on despite it.

"Like hell."

"Excuse me?"

"Like hell, you'll 'find a different teacher'," he growled.

Was that jealousy in his voice? She couldn't be sure, but the prospect was less damaging to her own ego. Adopting a nonchalant attitude in order to preserve her pride, she pushed past him toward her horse, and as she did, tossed back breezily over her shoulder, "Careful, Saint, or I'll start to think your marriage proposal wasn't a joke."

Chapter 15

The ride back to the ranch was uncomfortable to say the least. Price's silent fury permeated the air. Kit's confusion had her mind in a whir, until she decided to be angry with Price for being angry.

The men already had the cows penned up in the front pasture by time they joined them. Kit thought the men would be yet snickering about her surprise plunge into the creek. Instead, none of them offered conversation, judging accurately the foul mood their boss and foreman were in.

Kit tried to adjust her attitude to spare it from her men. After all, it was Price she was angry with.

Before Kit turned toward the stable, she asked the group before her, with great effort to mask her humiliation, "Does anyone know how to go about hiring a cook and a maid?"

It was as good as admitting she didn't know how to properly see to house tasks. Then again, so had the dunking been privy to such revelation. Kit's role had always been overseeing the horses and the barn. She'd never had to assist much with household chores. She hadn't wanted to. Livvy had been happy to play the part of wife-in-training, whereas Kit found every opportunity to be at the barn. There was no necessity for her to learn practical hygiene practices, because—and this she admitted to herself with disgust—as Price had pointed out, she had been privileged to the point of ignorance.

She was certain the men would view her query as conceding defeat, but they surprised her by responding otherwise.

Price eyed her, but wisely held his tongue.

Badger's keen brown eyes caught hers and offered encouragement. As if he could sense how difficult it was for her to voice her vulnerabilities. And she gained strength from his assurance.

Then he surprised her yet again when he declared, "I can cook."

"Bloody hell, Bernardo," Price sputtered the dismay they all felt. "Are you telling me that all this time, you could have been preparing edible meals for us? Why the hell didn't you?"

"It wasn't in my job description at the time." The cantankerous man gave a wily smirk, "Besides, we haven't had any decent grub to cook other than the beef."

"Would you know what sort of groceries we'd need to stock in order to have some good meals around here?"

"Si. I have instructed Samuel what produce and herbs to plant. They've already taken root in the garden."

This impressed Kit and she laughed happily, "Thank goodness for you, you ol' devil. We'll get together later and work out a list. Someone can ride on to Onieda soon to get supplies."

"With what money?" José spoke.

"I'll take care of it." That pronouncement seemed to stifle the men. They hadn't been prepared to learn Kit had her own means to pay them. Of course, she didn't quite at the moment. But she knew how to get it. In the meantime, she could make an account with most mercantiles under her last name Stone. She was certain no one would offend her mother and father. They were known far and wide to have money and were always good on their word. Certainly most stores would be willing to lend her credit based upon that alone. Aside from that idea, she hoped to soon learn from García exactly where her ranch stood financially, and how to make it profitable.

"Okay, we have the position of cook taken care of, now where do we stand on acquiring a housemaid?" she asked, returning her attention back to her initial problem.

The men snickered and Kit realized the oafs were *giggling* like schoolgirls over the prospect that one of them might be commandeered for the role. As if one of them could be stuffed into a dress and made to keep house. Not a one of them looked as though they knew their way around cleaning practices, any more than Kit herself did.

Thank goodness, before things got too out of control, Frank began winding through the crowd to the front. "My sister would work as a housemaid."

The men quieted down, and Frank continued, "She is working in the town of Canyon at the moment. But for a fair wage, she could be persuaded to work here and tend after the household duties."

Canyon? Kit wracked her brain trying to remember the small town they had passed through on their way to the ranch.

"Where could your sister possibly work in Canyon? If memory serves correctly, the town only had one inn and a saloon."

Frank gave her a hard stare and the other men looked quite uncomfortable. That's when Kit realized exactly what profession Miss Perkins was employed in.

Price stepped to Kit's side then, "It would not be appropriate to hire someone of your sister's—"

Kit cut him off before he could finish his sentence, "How old is your sister?"

Frank's eyes never left hers, "Seventeen".

Kit closed her eyes and inhaled to ensure her lungs continued breathing despite her heart breaking for the girl. "Go fetch her. Today, now, if you're ready and able."

They all stared back at Kit in stunned silence.

Frank stuttered his surprise, "Are...are you certain?"

Kit nodded sternly. "Take the cart and fetch supplies as well."

She turned to Bernardo, "Badger, are you able to write up a supply list for Frank and help him set off quickly?"

Bernardo's nostrils flared with a deep inhale, as if unhappy with Kit's decision to hire Miss Perkins, but he didn't voice his objections. He instead responded only, "Si."

Frank nodded as well, affirming his consent to her plans and both men set off toward the barn to prepare the cart and list.

"Everyone else, take a break." She barely issued the order before Price pounced on her. Grabbing her arm, he tugged her to the side.

In a harsh whisper, he cursed, "Are you out of your mind? You can't bring a soiled dove, a-a *whore*," he spat the word in hopes

135

of shocking her into her senses, "onto the ranch. What about protecting your reputation? What will all your *prospective grooms* think?" He bit out the last with cutting sarcasm.

Kit hadn't thought about what her decision might mean to the men who might court her. She may very well have risked her ranch. But damn it, after seeing her own sister abused in such a violent manner, there was no way Kit would leave another woman in such circumstances. She couldn't imagine any woman working in a line of profession that required her to sell her body for any other reason than pure survival.

Price's angry words continued to assault her ears, cataloguing all the many reasons why she had just made a colossal mistake.

Finished with listening to him spit vitriol in her ear, she held her hand up to cease his lengthy speech. "Listen up, *Saint,* I don't take orders from you. You take orders from me. If the girl wants to work here, then by all the blue in the sky, she will."

~

Price's anger faded and his eyes softened, the realization of what truly spurred Kit's decision dawning on him. How could he have not seen before that she was thinking of her sister? And how she hadn't been able to spare Livvy...

Even so, she didn't know what he knew about the darker side of the world. She'd only glimpsed a piece of it, always sheltered and cared for, her innocent mind couldn't possibly fathom its depths without having witnessed it.

"Listen," he spoke tenderly, "I know you think you are saving this girl from a life of depravity, but odds are she has already been shaped by it. How do you think the men here will treat her? They know what she is."

"They had damned well better treat her with respect." Kit's silvery eyes flashed like the cool flames of a fire.

"You are correct, they should. But will they?"

Kit paused, her dark brows knit with concern, pondering his question.

It wasn't that he was heartless, but this country was hard. People did what they had to in order to survive...but they often didn't come about unscathed by the sacrifices they made. This particular hardship was one experienced by many women young and old; it wasn't fair or right, but Kit couldn't go around saving all the downtrodden in the world. Price felt for the girl, he truly did. But his main concern was Kit and protecting her. If she was known to be associating with prostitutes, she would be regarded as much the same. Issued the same mistreatment.

And the girl wouldn't fare any better herself, trying to build a new life near the same town she worked in as a prostitute. It would only cause problems for the both of them.

Another matter clawing at the back of his mind was the question of why Frank hadn't better protected his sister? There were plenty of possible reasons, Price supposed. Perhaps the girl had been persuaded it was a grander lifestyle than it truly was and couldn't be made to see reason soon enough. Price didn't have time to enumerate all the possible reasons Frank may have for, what Price believed, his dereliction of duty to his sister. He had to worry for Kit's safety instead.

"You won't be doing her any favors bringing her here."

"We shall see," was all Kit replied before a ruckus at the barn ensued, capturing both their attention.

"García!" Kit squealed and took off at a quick pace.

"Thank God," Price muttered under his breath. García had returned, perhaps he could talk some sense into the stubborn woman.

❧

Kit was obviously attempting to subdue her giddy excitement over García's appearance and failing. Price smiled, glad she couldn't mask all of her emotions despite her efforts to appear an ice queen.

He took in García's lack of supplies, single horse, and no cart. It appeared he didn't plan for a lengthy stay. The man climbed from his horse in one swift motion and affectionately pulled Kit in for a brief hug, before turning toward the crowd of men. Osa's polite attempt to care for García's horse was denied. As Price drew nearer, he realized García's face was screwed up in angry disgust.

"You lot should have told me there was no housemaid the day we arrived," García directed angrily to the group of rancheros.

137

The cowhands shuffled their feet guiltily. Bernardo "Badger" Delores, however, replied, unashamedly, "You didn't ask."

García glared his sentiment in return over the absurd reason given. "I especially expected more from you, Delores."

Kit thought it a good time to interrupt, "All is well on that front. In fact, we just sent out a man to hire and fetch a maid."

"Indeed," García spoke, ill-impressed, "I ran into Frank Perkins just a moment ago and he informed me of exactly who you have planned to hire."

Kit didn't allow García's intimidating scowl to affect her. In fact, Price was rather astonished at how maturely she composed herself. Instead of stepping back into the role of a dependent young woman, she rose up as the boss and ranch owner she had been proving herself to be. "We shall continue this discussion in private. Shall we first see to your mount? Osa is patiently awaiting to attend to him and the gelding looks as though he could use a cooling down.

García nodded graciously. Price thought the man may have been a little surprised by Kit's growth, himself.

"Si," he conceded.

Kit nodded to the men, allowing for them to disperse.

Out of habit in way of treating guests, Kit led García toward the house; not that she knew at all what to offer in way of amenities. It wasn't as if she had clean dishes or even a meal prepping.

As they neared the house, she heard García swear under his breath.

"It's worse than I remembered." García scratched the back of his neck uncomfortably. "I would never have allowed you to stay on here had I known the conditions were unlivable."

"Hardly unlivable, I should think." Kit tried to rain down positivity, less her "uncle" try to toss her over his shoulder and forcibly remove her from the property. "And once we have a maid, the housing condition will improve in short order. It simply needs cleaning. Of which I have not, yet, had time to see to."

"It also needs quite a bit of repairs..." García said, taking in the broken steps, rotted entryway, and poorly patched roof.

Kit quickly barred him from continuing inside the house. "On second thought, I'm parched, let us head to the well for a cool drink."

When Kit began walking the path back toward the barns, García said, "Why not use the well by the house?"

"Well by the house?" Kit asked sheepishly.

"It's outside of the kitchen, around the back side of the house, where the bathing tank is installed."

Kit tugged at her already loosened shirt collar, "Ah, yes, the bathing tank. Of course."

García looked from Kit's face, flushed with embarrassment, to Price.

"We weren't aware of the second well on the property," Price finally answered. He then added cheekily, "Kit has been making use of Hackberry Creek instead."

This earned him a hard glare from Kit, "Indeed."

García seemed to think it best to change the subject. "Have you toured the property yet?"

"No," Kit sighed, "there hasn't been time. We've been repairing the bunkhouse and barns."

"Well, who better than I to show you? How's say, we saddle up?"

Kit smiled her agreement.

~

They rode in silence for a time. With the exception of García occasionally pointing out property borders and the land's history. Then, quite out of the blue, he inquired, "So, have the neighboring ranchers been stampeding the property and offering up marriage proposals?"

Kit was decidedly uncomfortable with the question.

Discomfited by the question, or rather the answer to it, Kit's skin began to feel as though it was being wrapped in a scratchy wool blanket. Why she felt ashamed of the response, she didn't know. It wasn't as if the lack of suiters could be attributed to her. Unless Whitney Kingston had decided her unworthy and told the others...

She gulped nervously, before replying, "No, no they haven't."

Price, who had been trailing silently alongside them, spoke then, "A Whitney Kingston dropped in. He seemed awfully sure of himself in regard to becoming the next one to own this ranch."

Kit noted the irritation in his voice.

"Ah, Kingston, yes." The lack of enthusiasm behind García's words appeared to gratify Price. García continued, "Kingston is the man responsible for this mess you're in. Your ranch is indebted greatly to him, thanks to Morgan." García all but growled the last part. "Trust me, he wasn't happy to learn the stipulates of the will didn't include the ranch being signed over to him. There is a lot of pressure for you to marry and pay him off. For that, I am sorry."

"It's not your fault," Kit gave a wan smile.

"I would not have thought Kingston's son your type, but if he interests you, I suppose that would be an easy transaction."

It was incredibly frustrating that everyone kept professing to know the type of man she should want to marry.

"Well, he didn't propose, and I'm not too keen on him," Kit responded testily.

"All *but* proposed," Price grumbled.

They rode in silence again for a time, allowing for the uncomfortable topic to fade.

"García, have you ever been in love?" Kit's question interrupted the silence and both men seemed completely caught off guard by it.

Kit looked down, suddenly shy for asking such a personal question. And to avoid Price who was eyeing her strangely.

"I married very young to a woman I loved very much."

"You're married?" Kit exclaimed.

"*Was.* A long time ago."

He paused, seeming to breathe in his nostalgia.

"Isabel," he finally said. He spoke her name as if she had been a dream. Then anger crossed his features, "She was taken from me. Stolen away by bandidos while I was involved in a meeting político in town.

"It took me months to hunt them down, and by time I got to them...I was too late. My wife and our unborn child had been killed.

"They scattered when I found them, and I wasn't about to let any continue drawing breath on this earth after what they'd done. I discovered the leader, Calhoun, and many members of his gang had bounties on their heads from previous thefts and murders. This allowed me to hunt him down legally.

"After that, I fully immersed myself in the bounty hunter life. I became obsessed with tracking down and killing every last one of Calhoun's compadres. I wasn't successful. For years I pursued them, as well as other outlaws because it turned out, one could make a good living doing that kind of work."

"But you aren't in that line of business anymore," Kit spoke after García had paused for some time. "I mean it would have been pretty hard to run a ranch all these years if you were never around to run it."

"No. I finally came to my senses and returned home."

"And did you ever remarry?"

García sighed, "For a long time, I didn't think it fair to keep a woman tied to this wild land. My mother died from snakebite. My wife was abducted by bandidos. And my sister died during childbirth."

Kit bristled a bit at the insinuation, "You think women too weak to live in Texas? There are women all over the frontier."

García gave her an aggrieved look for interrupting. "You didn't let me finish," he reprimanded. "I used to think that. But then I met the strongest, craziest, bravest woman I know: your mother."

Kit's eyes widened with her smile, not seeing Price's shrewd gaze fixed keenly on García.

"So my mother proved to you women were capable of surviving out here..." It was more statement than question. Pride glittered in Kit's eyes.

"So once you realized how foolish your thinking had been," Kit tossed a teasing smirk García's direction, unable to allow the insult he'd paid to all womenkind go without a little nettling, "then did you fall in love again?" Excitement and curiosity shone brightly on Kit's face.

"Si," García answered solemnly. "Yes, I did."

Detecting his sadness, Kit's excitement dimmed, "Did you marry?"

"No," he stated, " I did not marry her. I could not. For she was in love and already married to another."

"Oh." Kit seemed to contemplate that.

Price had a sinking feeling he knew exactly the woman responsible for García's unrequited love. He kept his eyes intently on García, but the man wouldn't meet his gaze. Price cast a cautionary glance Kit's way to determine if she realized García was speaking of her mother, but Kit seemed oblivious of Price's suspicions.

"Well forget *love*," Kit said on a sardonic grin. "Do what I plan to do and marry for business. It's not too late to sire some heirs." Kit added the last cheekily.

García did not reciprocate Kit's cheerful tone. "Ah," he said, "but your heart is free, and mine is not. It would not be fair to a woman to take as wife, when I love another."

The three of them remained lost to their own ponderings for the duration of the tour, the only exception when García would occasionally point out landmarks or vulnerabilities in the property borders. The sun was already setting, casting out brilliant fiery shades of pink across the western sky when they returned.

After rubbing down their horses, they joined the hands outside the bunkhouse. Kit and Price were both surprised to see what appeared to be a real meal cooking over the fire. Badger had delved into his new role quickly.

"It's still no grand fare, not until Perkins returns with the supplies," Badger announced gruffly.

Kit smiled. She could have hugged the man; she was that pleased. It would have embarrassed him greatly, however, so she instead said, "Grand fare or no, it smells delicious."

She turned to García and explained, "All we've had 'til now was a bin full of old potatoes and beef."

García's surprised expression took on a hint of guilt.

Kit continued, "Badger's grandson Samuel has been delegated to gardening duties and just today, Badger here took over the cooking routine. Already, I can see what an excellent decision it was, too." Kit beamed at Badger, who in turn, uncomfortable with such praise, grumbled and resumed preparing the meal.

A wide, flat cast iron griddle covered the fire and on it were flat little cakes of some sort. Badger was piling stew-size chunks of beef mixed with green peppers on them and serving them onto tin plates or napkins; as they had little in the way of dining ware there wasn't enough to go around, but they made do with what they had. The smell of the tender bits of beef and spicy peppers made Kit's mouth water. Badger handed her the little shell-wrapped meat and when she put it to her mouth, she wasn't disappointed.

"Mmm," she fairly groaned her pleasure, "what is this?"

García chuckled, "It's a tortilla. How shameful your mother never served any in her house. I shall take her to task for such a disservice she has done you children."

"Enjoy tonight," Badger spoke, "that was the last of the masa harina from the chuck box. Tomorrow we will be back to mealy potatoes."

Kit popped the last bite into her mouth and groaned again, savoring its juicy flavors. She opened her eyes to find Price's hazel eyes locked on her. She realized he must be trying to convey Badger's admission of lack of food as a reminder she needed to speak with García right away to discuss the ranch's financial details.

Without shame, Kit licked each of her fingers. Price's eyes never left her. *Good grief, the man is impossible,* she thought, *message received.*

Not wanting to dirty her newly cleaned clothes, she quickly rubbed her hands together to rid her fingers of any residue and turned to García, "If you are finished, there are some matters I'd yet like to discuss with you."

García, who had had his tortilla served on a napkin, used the unoiled parts to wipe his face. García was ever the gentleman. Kit did not question García's claim to Spanish nobility. Unlike her mother, who most none would believe to have been born a proper aristocratic lady from America's mother shores, kit chuckled to herself. She wondered how he had endured a friendship with her brassy, untraditional mother all these years.

Kit was glad Price hadn't followed them to the house. It was embarrassing enough to have to lead García through the squalid shelter, but at least he couldn't be certain just how poor of condition it had been when she arrived. Price DID know. Which meant he would know Kit hadn't seen to fixing a bit of it, not

143

even attempting to clean it as it desperately needed, despite having been there over a fortnight already.

"Don't go toward the kitchen," she cautioned García. Despite the oil lantern she carried, it was quite dark in the house. Still, she thought she saw García's lips form a grim line.

"Lo siento, Kit. So deeply sorry. I should have better seen to your care when we arrived."

Kit shrugged, then remembered he probably couldn't see the response, "It is of no matter now."

"Yes, you are your mother's daughter, nothing can knock you off your feet for long."

Kit wasn't so sure about that. She never felt she possessed a whole lot from her mother. And despite Grayson not being her blood father, she always felt she was more like him. But she accepted the compliment gladly. She would love to be thought of as fierce a being as her mother.

"I realize that my inheritance from my parents will cover costs up front for the ranch's needs, but it won't last its longevity. I have had no luck finding ledgers of any sort to help me learn where the ranch stands funds-wise. Also, I won't inherit until I marry, but my men will expect payment by the end of the month. There will be other expenses as well that might not be able to accept credit on my parents' good name. What do I do for funds in the meantime?"

In the frugal light, Kit saw García retrieve a leather-bound booklet from his vest. "I'm afraid you will be disappointed with what you find here. There is no money currently coming from the ranch, as you will learn when you go through the book." He handed it gently over to her.

"There's no money? None at all? But it's a cattle ranch, there must be profit to have somewhere."

"I raise sheep. Morgan, whether to spite me or simply contradict me—I'm unsure—sold everything to do with the sheep rearing and invested in cattle. Only, he never saw it to a profitable end. He sought loans from The Commerce and Agricultural Bank in Galveston, at first. When the bank discovered the loans had been used to cover Morgan's gambling habits instead, they cut him off and demanded their money back. He then came to me, but I had no incentive to help the weasel. If he lost the ranch, I as the original landowner would

have first opportunity to purchase the land back from the bank."
García gave a frustrated sigh.

"If only I had known his next plan to thwart me. When I
denied him, he went to Kingston, who was happy to lend the
money. At the time, I could not figure out why, but I knew it
could not be in Morgan's favor.

"I did not discover the details of the deal Morgan had made
with Kingston, until Morgan's death..." García eyed Kit
seekingly.

Kit assured him, "No worries, you may be blunt. I never knew
the man who truly sired me, so I have no feelings concerning his
death."

That wasn't entirely true, she admitted to herself, as she
certainly harbored quite a bit of animosity and resentment
toward the biological father she had never known.

García continued, "Morgan promised to marry you off to
Kingston's son. That way, Kingston would own the ranch upon
Morgan's passing."

"But, but, that's absurd! I was legally adopted by Grayson
Stone as a child. Morgan had no rights to me. Indeed, records
would not even show him as my biological father. According to
my mother, my biological father's brother, Jonathon Morgan,
claimed Livvy and I as his and allowed for my mother to forge
his name to our birth documents. And as I said, after marrying
our mother, Grayson appealed to the courts to adopt Livvy and
me as his own."

García gestured with his hands for her to calm, "It is of no
matter, because later, without Kingston's knowledge, Morgan
returned to the McKinney, Williams, and Company firm and
legally altered his will again. This time leaving everything to you,
with the stipulation that you marry."

"Why?" Kit asked, perplexed. "Why would he give everything
to me? Then demand I marry in order to keep it? And what
happens if I don't marry within the six months stipulated?"

"Because," García replied, "he wanted his blood, *anyone* with
his blood, to keep hold of a potential fortune. Not to mention, it
was a way he could thwart me, and Kingston as well. If Morgan
couldn't have the ranch, no one else would either. That was how
his mind worked.

"If you do not marry, I fear Kingston will gain the ranch. He will certainly have grounds to purchase it from the bank and I do not have the funds to fight him in a financial war." García's eyes slowly swept downward, saddened and defeated.

There was certainly a lot of pressure for Kit to come up to scratch. It didn't go unnoticed that her uncle didn't appear to have a lot of faith in her ability to procure a husband before the looming date, either.

Chapter 16

The following morning, Kit woke to Price's knocks on her door informing her García was already saddling up to leave. The sun hadn't even shaken hands with the moon yet, Kit grumbled to herself. Couldn't he at least wait for the breakfast fire and a decent cup of coffee?

"Here you go."

Kit squinted her slow-to-waken eyes in Price's direction. His frame filled the doorway, one arm bent above his head, resting against the open-door hinges, his other arm extending a tin mug with steam rolling off the top. *Bless the man.* He really was a saint. At least in this moment.

"Thank you." She rubbed circular motions over her eyes with her fingertips and tried to blink some of the dryness away, before accepting the warm mug from his hands. "Why do you think he's in such a tarnation hurry to leave for?"

Price chuckled, "Probably misses having a real bed to sleep in."

"Yeah, well, so do I," she replied testily.

The inky blue stain of dawn was only just fading from the sky, making way for the warming orange glow of the sun to fill its place by the time they saw García off.

~

"What's on the agenda for the day?" Price asked, watching Kit curiously. She seemed restless to him, uncertain perhaps; a feeling he cognized she was wholly uncomfortable with. The Kit he knew always had direction. Of course, she had always preferred responsibilities centered around the animals and she certainly had a lot more than just that on her plate these days.

She scuffed her boot in the dirt and sighed. He could tell her internal wheels were churning with thought. More than that, though, her brow was creased with worry. He wondered what she and García had discussed at the house last night.

He wanted to reach out and comfort her. No one was around, leaving them in semi-privacy behind the security of the barn. Still, it wouldn't be appropriate and after their little scene at the lake, he wasn't sure she would welcome his touch, innocent though his intentions were.

She pulled forth a book from the pack at her side and held it up in answer to his question.

"This. I plan to read through the ledgers and see where we can magically come up with some money for the ranch. If I can't come up with a profitable plan, I fear I'll be stuck marrying Kingston."

So that's what was on her mind. As much as he respected García and regarded him a friend, his neglectful actions toward Kit had him a little infuriated.

"Listen, about what García said yesterday. I know he would never intentionally hurt you, but I don't think it fair of him to encourage you on this path. And I can't imagine your mother would allow this, if she knew. She married for love, after all. What if you marry for business now, only to fall in love with someone you meet later?"

Kit's silver eyes hesitantly found his and a sad smile curved her lips, "I don't think 'love' has ever been or will be in the cards for me."

"Why not?"

"Because it isn't, okay?"

No, it wasn't okay. The sad smile she had shown told him she wanted more from a marriage than a business arrangement.

"Why, Kit?"

Frustrated, she jammed her thumbs into the pockets of her pants and kicked at the dirt—something he noticed she often did when uncomfortable or organizing her thoughts.

She spread her arms wide when she brought her gaze back to his and answered, "Because I'm different!"

He thought her face pink with anger, but quickly realized it was embarrassment.

"I'm not," she sputtered, searching for words. "Men don't..." she looked away, "find me attractive."

"How can you possibly believe that?"

"Please. Livvy is my twin, but we look nothing alike. At the barn at home, I know some ranch hands who were fired just for following her with their eyes. They never followed me."

"What about that Russell guy?" Anger flashed in his eyes at the reminder.

She rolled her eyes, "Do you think me a fool? I knew he was only feigning interest in me in hopes he could catch a Stone heiress before his chances diminished when we left for the academy once again. And he knew he could never have Livvy."

"Then why did you kiss him, for God's sake?"

"Because I was curious! And I didn't know if I would ever get another opportunity. I just wanted to know what it felt like to be kissed, at least once in my life."

She paced as she explained, "But then you had to ruin it."

At first Price thought she referred to the way he had ended her kiss with Russell.

"With Russell, I thought kissing highly overrated, but then you kissed me and, well, it was quite a lot better."

Her guileless revelation had his body taut all over with the need to remind her just how good it was.

"And each time you have kissed me, I've felt these strong stirrings throughout my body. I'm not sure how to describe it, but I quite like the feeling," she stated boldly.

Price nearly choked. Christ, didn't she know what she was doing to him? Talking like this? Telling him these things?

"What if, what if it doesn't feel like that with anyone else?" she asked.

God, he hoped not.

"What if no one else even wants to kiss me. Or, or touch me?"

That was fine by him. In fact, if anyone else tried, he'd kill them.

He wanted to demand she marry him. But he knew she didn't think him suitable for ranch life. Lord only knew why; had he not proven himself over these last weeks?

No. She wouldn't listen to reason, but maybe, just maybe, he could get her to fall in love with him.

She wanted lessons in the art of seduction? Perhaps he should give her what she wanted. Only, in the end, hopefully he seduced her enough to fall in love with *him* before she decided to implement his teachings on someone else.

It was a risky plan.

He studied her face; cheeks lightly dusted with freckles over a pert nose; the intensity in her silvery eyes. She had no clue her speech resembled more closely that of a courtesan than the innocent she was. She wasn't trying to illicit an aroused response from him. Kit was never coy. She was direct. Practical.

Except that nothing about her was *practical*. Nothing about this entire situation was *practical*.

He'd promised his best friend he would safeguard the forbidden treasure he'd secretly coveted the past two years. What had he been thinking?

She was aggravating in the way she worked fastidiously, easily able to ignore him in the process. And yet he admired that work ethic. Her drive to always see a job well done. The way her work always took on a nurturing touch, so contrasting to her curt, gruff manner. Her intentions often discreet, hidden by her soft command, such as when she would order the kid to fetch the water because she knew *he* needed it. Her care for others was always at the forefront of her duties, and often unnoticed.

But he noticed.

He knew what he felt for her was deeper than a simple infatuation. More than lust. He longed to hold her, to love her. To take care of her, the way she took care of everyone else. Someone who saw all the little things she did and let her know they were appreciated. Someone who would look after her needs while she was busy seeing to others.

She was the only one for him.

She didn't feel the same, though, that was the problem. But perhaps this was his opportunity to convince her she could come to love him, too.

"You are plenty attractive, Kit. Never doubt it. And any man would be lucky to have you for wife. *But,* if it would help to build your confidence, I could teach you in the ways of seduction."

A sweet smile crossed her face, before it was chased away by a concerned frown, "But the other day you acted as if the very idea would cause you to retch your breakfast."

"I was caught off guard," he replied lamely. "I was angry at myself for not fulfilling my promise to protect you."

"And seducing me won't encroach on this 'sacred promise' you made to my brother?" she asked saucily.

"Ah, but I won't be seducing you, not to the point of ruination at least. And besides, it is you who will be seducing me." He did feel a niggling sense of guilt for betraying his friends' trust. But in a way, he *was* protecting Kit. At the very least he was preventing the wildcat from looking elsewhere for such 'studies.'

A radiant smile grew across her face. How could anyone have compared her to her sister and found her wanting? Price's chest hitched and he knew he would spend the rest of his life keeping that smile fixed on her face.

If only she would let him.

Chapter 17

A problem arose before they could initiate their first agreed upon lesson. Actually, two problems. The first being Whitney Kingston, and the second, the Perkins duo.

"Rider approaching," Bernardo replied at Kit's shoulder. Bernardo, or Badger as she'd called him before learning his real name and becoming friends of a sort, was helping her design a greenhouse. Bernardo's grandson Samuel, as it turned out, had a natural knack for horticulture and was already becoming quite the gardening expert. It was because of his own experiment that they had had bell peppers to add to the meal the night García had visited.

Kit put another post in place. "Probably just Perkins returning with his sister. They are expected any day."

Kit peeked a glance at Bernardo. He made it clear he was none too happy with her decision to bring a woman of ill-repute to the ranch. He respected her decision, however, and agreed to assist with protecting the young woman in case some of the rowdier, less trustworthy men decided to force unwanted attentions on her.

His lips pursed in a grim line, he answered, "No. There is no wagon."

Kit stopped straightening the post against the leveling string and looked toward the path leading up to the ranch's arches. A black horse.

"Kingston," she guessed.

Bernardo gave her a curious look, "That is a good thing, señorita, no? The faster he proposes, the faster the ranch becomes yours in truth."

"Or his, rather." Kit wasn't too pleased to admit such an ugly consequence.

"Laws are not like in eastern states. Women have more rights here. Whomever you marry, make sure your rights to the ranch are protected."

She smiled kindly, "Thank you, Bernardo. I promise to do my best."

She hoped Logan would return before then. He studied law for fun. Her brother had the crazy dream to pursue politics and change laws for the Indian people of the United States. She hoped his plans met with success and he didn't get killed hunting down whomever murdered Albert Sidney before then. Perhaps he would find the murderer quickly and return here in time to ensure legalities were on her side before any nuptials took place. She gulped.

Kit folded her deerskin gloves and tucked them at the waist of her pants, as there was aught else she could do with them. Guessing that it was Kingston, she excused herself and asked Bernardo to find Samuel to ensure the boy took a break. The kid would work all day and never stop if someone didn't force him to. She smiled; he was really a great kid. He was going to be one hell of a man someday.

Kit heard some of her cowhands greet Kingston as she sneaked around the back of the horse barn out of view and darted toward the house. How embarrassing! She still didn't have a housemaid and no refreshments at the ready as he'd requested, and she looked the same sweaty mess as last time he'd met her.

There was nothing to be done about her clothes. It was impractical to change attire just to take another walk and see the man off. She still had a full day's worth of work to finish after all. She quickly ran her fingers through her long brown strands of hair and rebraided the thick mass to hang off her shoulder. At least all of the wind-tousled strands were back into place. The fly-aways at her temples refused to be subdued, though; it was a battle she'd lost her entire life. She took some of the honeysuckle water Samuel had gifted her. Price had laughed, knowing the kind gift came of necessity due to her lack of laundering skills, but she had been thankful all the same.

Kit still wasn't brave enough to use the tub on the backside of the house, but now that she knew her way to the cropping out on Hackberry Creek, she tried to sneak away there at least twice a week to bathe. The honeysuckle fragrance was a treasure. She splashed a bit of it at her neck now and buttoned the top button of her blouse.

Thankfully the sky was merciful today and scattered thick fluffy clouds about, blocking much of the sun. The breeze would cool the work-induced sweat from her skin and the fragrance water would mask any odor she may have worked up. Feeling more refreshed than when she'd met him on his former visit, she returned to the barns, where she assumed he would be waiting for her.

She'd been wrong.

She no sooner trounced down the steps from the house and nearly crashed into the man.

He grabbed her arms to balance her, "Ah, Miss Stone. I've found you."

"Oh! Indeed you did." She smiled brightly. Not too brightly, she hoped.

As he peered behind her at the run-down abode, she nervously wracked her brain for a way to distract him. The rotting home before him was hardly a compelling point in her favor.

"I do apologize, but we are in the process of replacing a housemaid so I'm afraid we shall have to take our refreshments up by the long building." She tried to steer him away from the house, but he held firm.

He smiled down to her, still holding his arm in hers, "That is of no matter, my dear. No need to concern yourself. In my hasty desire to see you again, I rudely forgot to send ahead a missive of my pending arrival. So, it is I who should apologize to you." He brought her hand up to his wet lips and brushed his wiry mustache across the back of her bruised and scraped knuckles.

She resisted pulling her hand away, knowing it would be impolite. But she couldn't help feeling completely uncomfortable with the gesture. For one, his mustache tickled and ruined the effect of his debonair attempts, and for two, she was embarrassed for him to see her unladylike hands up close.

Her hands were rough and dry from years of being exposed to harsh mountain winters and hard work. Currently, the very hand that received the kiss was sporting a fresh bruise and scratches from her recent rescuing of a calf.

She had been riding to the river crop-out to bathe one evening when she spied the calf bawling from the wrong side of the pasture. She stopped to help it over the dividing stumps and back onto the side with its mother. She'd had to pull aside one of the stumps and wrangle the hefty one-hundred-pound calf through the gap. Once on the other side, in its frenzied state to return to its mother, the calf bowled Kit over and its sharp little hooves stamped her hand.

"Would you like to show me the house?" he asked, bringing her back to her current discomfiture.

"No! Ah, that is, um," she stumbled along, "without a housemaid, I'm sure it wouldn't be proper to be unchaperoned in such closed spaces." She looped her arm through his and turned him back toward the working barns before he could continue his perusal of the squalid remains of the house.

Unfortunately, they turned and were met with Price's disapproving glare.

What was he doing? Him lurking like an angry shadow over her interlude with Kingston was hardly productive to her plans to procure him as a husband.

"Actually, Mr. Kingston, I'm afraid my ranch foreman has emergent news I must first attend to. If you would so kindly excuse us for a moment?"

When he looked as though he might refuse, Kit added, "If you head toward that long building, Bernardo will fetch you that refreshment we spoke of." She smiled in what she hoped was a felicitous manner.

He bowed politely, though he gave Price a look that said he was none too pleased to have been interrupted. Once he was far enough up the path to be out of earshot, Kit exploded.

~

"What are you doing here?"

Cayt Lawson

Her newly coiled braid swung about in her fury, but Price couldn't help but think she looked adorable.

"I came to remind you about our deal. No 'practicing' with anyone but me."

Kit eyed him suspiciously. He knew he was behaving like a boor and giving her reason to doubt his intentions behind the lessons. Lessons they hadn't had a moment to implement yet, much to his frustration.

"No need to fret so, about my reputation. I prefer practicing with you and keeping my reputation safe as well. Not to mention, my fumbling attempts at seduction are hardly what I want to offer my intended."

Before Price experienced an apoplectic fit, Kit added reassuringly, "Not that I've decided yet who that may be.

"I'd like to master the art of kissing before I go around kissing someone else," she added sincerely, causing Price to see red again.

He tamped down his rage at the thought of her kissing someone else.

"Is that all you wanted to tell me?" she asked. "I don't want to keep the gent waiting. He's quite an opinion of himself, I think."

Price grinned. She did not sound impressed with Kingston's hauteur. With the relief that knowledge brought, he nodded to her. As he was left with the lovely view of her backside as she walked away, the somber reminder came—she had to marry within six months, whether she was interested or not.

∿

"Sorry to have kept you waiting," Kit smiled up at Kingston as he approached. She sent a nod of thanks to Bernardo for supplying her guest with a cold cup of water. He tipped his hat and returned to the site where they were constructing the greenhouse.

"Shall we take another stroll?"

Kingston tapped his fingers along the dingy tin cup he held. The humble drinking ware yet another point not in her favor. His squinted eyes scanned over her head and she realized Price was his target. His expression was one of displeasure.

"When is your brother due to return, again?" he asked, masking little his contempt for Price.

"Do you have a problem with my foreman?" Kit addressed frankly.

He broke his concentrated gaze from Price and worked a small smile onto his face for Kit, "Not yet."

Before Kit could prod further, he procured with a flip of his fingers a crisp parchment and extended it to her.

"I'm afraid I cannot stay long. I was only coming today to deliver you this. It's an invitation. There is to be a jamboree held in the town of Onieda in honor of the new marshal. There will be dancing, good food, and good company." He smiled on his last words, displaying the full row of his top teeth, giving the impression he was insinuating himself to be the "good company" to which he referred.

"You may remember passing through it on your way here. It's just north of Canyon."

She nodded, taking the printed invitation from him, "I remember." It was the town where her brother Logan had met up with the Texas Rangers. Perhaps they would have word there of him.

"It's about a full day's ride from here," Kingston's words penetrated her thoughts of the possibility of receiving word on her brother, "I'll set up accommodations for you at the Yellow Rose Hotel."

"That won't be necessary but thank you."

Kingston's mustache quirked up on one side as his lips twisted in a knowing smirk, "Did García happen to explain to you the disastrous state of finances Morgan's ranch was left in?"

Kit did not like Kingston's smug features or the fact that he seemed entirely too knowledgeable about her finances. She supposed it made sense, though, being he was the son of Cornelius Kingston, the man who loaned Morgan money with intentions of easily procuring this ranch.

Still, Kit didn't like being lorded over, and this man seemed to think she—along with her ranch—was going to be easy pickings. She hoped other suitors made themselves known soon, for she wasn't sure she could go through with a marriage of convenience to *this man*, even for the sake of keeping her ranch.

It wouldn't hurt to remain diplomatic. No sense in burning bridges before she even knew the direction she needed to take.

She plastered an agreeable smile on her face, "Indeed, well, then I suppose I have no choice but to accept your kind generosity."

His brown eyes gleamed and crinkled at the corners as he offered another large smile. He then bent over her hand, wherein he planted another wet kiss.

His smile shifted from his face when she added, "Of course, you must make accommodations for my stand-in-guardian and ranch foreman as well. It wouldn't do for a lady to be seen gallivanting about town improperly chaperoned, after all." She smiled smoothly.

It also wouldn't hurt to needle the condescending pig of a man a little.

He gave a curt nod, "Of course. I will see it is so."

Next, he was calling for his horse as if he was already in command of her ranch hands. She gritted her teeth at such high-handedness, but kept a smile fixed to her face as she waved him goodbye.

Not one hour had passed after Kingston's departure, before Frank Perkins rolled in with the supply wagon.

And his sister.

Lily Perkins was not at all the dewy-eyed girl Kit had formed in her mind when she thought she was rescuing her from an unkind life. In fact, the chit looked wholly more woman than Kit herself did, despite Kit being nearly three years her senior.

The beautiful, voluptuous young woman smiled brightly as the men gathered to assist with the supply wagon. She greeted them all cheerfully while twirling her pink parasol. Each bob of her head sent the few artfully placed strands of copper curls bouncing...along with other assets about to spill forth from her bodice.

Kit rubbed her temples, what had she been thinking bringing the woman here? The men were never going to work a full day's work with this woman about. Already they were doing less hauling goods from the wagon and more gawking at the gorgeous creature in the pink confection, smiling and waving as if she were on display.

She felt Bernardo appear at her side, "You having second thoughts?"

Disgruntled at having been caught out, she squared her shoulders stubbornly and attempted to keep the bitterness from her voice, "No. I needed a house maid. Now I have one."

She thought she saw the silver whiskers above Bernardo's lip twitch in a gloating smirk as she walked from him toward the woman. She saw Price appear before Miss Perkins and offer his hand to assist her from the wagon.

"Why, thank you, kind sir." Miss Perkins tipped her head and partially curtsied before Price, causing Kit to wonder if the piled mass of hair on the woman's head would tumble forth from its straining pins.

Kit then watched as the girl put her hand on Price's bicep and coquettishly exclaim, "Oh my."

Kit rolled her eyes and made her way to the woman all the more quickly, wanting to put an end to this flash show.

"Hello. Miss Perkins, I presume?" Kit extended her hand to shake.

Instead, Miss Perkins daintily held her fingers out as if awaiting a gentleman's kiss. "Hello, dear boy, have you come to assist with my luggage?"

'Dear boy?' Kit's teeth gritted at the insult. Before she could emit the growl working its way up her throat, she heard Price chuckle.

"I'm afraid you are mistaken, Miss Perkins. This is your new boss, Miss Catherine Stone."

Price was still smiling charmingly at the young, frilly-gowned baggage before them. Kit eyed him suspiciously.

"It's Kit Stone, actually." Kit extended her hand once more in greeting to the young woman.

"Oh! Oh, do forgive me. I wasn't expecting Miss Stone to be attired in men's wear."

Kit smiled tightly, "That's quite all right. I wasn't expecting my new housemaid to be attired in a dress made for promenading about town."

The girl finally came to her senses and had the good grace to blush.

"Follow me," Kit said, picking up two of the girl's bags, leaving the third at the girl's feet. When Price attempted to pick up the bag, Kit shot him a threatening look.

This was a ranch. The girl came here to work. The sooner she understood her role here, the better.

To her credit, Miss Perkins picked up her bag and followed quickly behind Kit without another word.

When they reached the house, Kit explained to her, "We'll bunk together for now. I'm not entirely sure what state the other room is in or if there even is one."

The girl's brows crinkled, "Isn't this *your* house?"

"Recently inherited. And as you can see," Kit stopped before the porch steps and gestured toward the weathered boards siding the house, the rot erosion eating its way up the door frame and the broken steps, "It's quite a dump."

The girl's dark gray eyes widened in shock and she cast a look of disbelief Kit's way.

"Listen," Kit said, "did your brother happen to explain the job details to you? I mean, you are here willingly, right?"

The girl nodded.

"I'm not going to sugarcoat it. The job—it's terrible. The inside of the house is much worse than the outside. I haven't explored the house, because the stench from the kitchen is so strong, I feared losing the contents of my stomach."

Kit watched as a grim line wobbled across the girl's face.

"I hope your brother was clear about what your duties would entail, but if not, I'll understand if you decide to return to Canyon."

"No! That is, I'd prefer not to return to Canyon. I-I'm up for the job." The young woman's spine straightened, and she proceeded up the steps, skipping over the gap where one of the boards had rotted through. Kit's respect for her grew.

Kit helped get her set up in the room they would share, then deciding it would be in their best interests to start with the kitchen, they braved the stench and got to work.

Miss Perkins soon realized the folly of wearing such a frilly contraption and requested a moment to change. When she returned, she was wearing a gown far more suitable for the task at hand.

Kit smiled her approval, "I can take you seriously now."

"You don't like pretty dresses, I take it?"

"It's not that so much. It's simply that I can't work well in one and—"

"And you're one who is always working, aren't you?" Miss Perkins finished for her. Kit thought perhaps she was being insulted again, however, when she looked over, the young woman's eyes only shone with respect.

Miss Perkins then held out the plain brown skirt of softly worn material as if for inspection.

"It's the ugliest item of clothing I own, so I figure it will do."

"All the better, Miss Perkins," Kit replied, "because we may have to burn these clothes when we're done."

Neither of them laughed, for it was the truth.

"It's Lily, just Lily."

"Well, Lily," Kit spoke, taking the olive branch, "how about helping me sort which of these dishes are salvageable?"

Chapter 18

The two women had worked until the sun faded from the sky and cast shadows over the ranch. Price knew they must be utterly exhausted and near ready to retire for the night. He hoped bringing food would make his presence less unwelcome.

Price knocked at the door but didn't wait for an answer before entering. He hadn't seen Kit all day and he was too happy to finally have an excuse to check on her. Knowing as he did how she abhorred remaining indoors, he was anxious to learn how she faired.

Initially, he had thought Kit would settle the new maid in, explain what she was to do and then rejoin the men. He supposed he should have known her better than that; she wouldn't abandon the new girl to attend such grueling duties alone. Even if Kit didn't seem to get on with her.

That was another matter worrying him throughout the day. Kit's inauspicious introduction with the lively Miss Perkins did not predict a smooth transition for either of them. He had tried to warn Kit that hiring a woman of such ilk might bring on trouble. Kit had thought a frightened young girl would show up, happy to have been "saved." Kit had been too sheltered to understand the harsh realities women faced in the world.

In a way, the seventeen-year-old Miss Perkins—who had just spent who-knew-how-long working in a brothel or of her history prior to that—had already seen more of the world than Kit. The uglier side of the world, but it had wisened her all the same. One thing was for certain—she wasn't a lost hapless girl. She was a woman and she seemed downright pleased with a man's attentions.

Kit was the opposite of the ostentatious Miss Perkins, preferring instead to remain low key, in the background, unobserved through life. He was sure the two personalities would clash badly. Being cooped up together all day, Price figured it was high time he checked to ensure both women were well.

"Hello," he called as he entered. "You ladies survive the day?" he half joked.

Both Kit and Miss Perkins appeared through the archway adjoining the kitchen to the living area, dragging their tired feet. Price noticed at once the incredible difference they had made on the interior of the house.

"Wow," he exclaimed, looking around. "You ladies certainly didn't waste any time. It is spectacularly improved. Almost even livable."

Kit exhaled and brushed a few strands that had fallen loose from her braid away from her face, "Yes, no thanks to you."

Miss Perkins seemed to regain her vigor once more upon seeing Price in the room. She straightened and began touching her hair to ensure it had remained in its styled updo.

She smiled brightly, "Why, you naughty man, you've surprised us and caught us at an unflattering disadvantage. We're in quite the state of dishabille."

Kit rolled her eyes, "You will have to accustom yourself to being seen in work attire, Lily. This is a ranch, not a dance hall."

Price grinned, "I'm surprised you know what a dance hall is."

Kit blushed, "Well, Lily talked about the subject, incessantly, today."

Before Lily could manage a response, Price interjected, "I thought you may have worked up a hunger by now, so I brought you both supper."

"Oh, how kind," Lily simpered.

"What about the men?" Kit asked, visibly concerned.

"Everyone has eaten but you ladies," he assured her.

Kit sighed her relief. Price took in her disheveled appearance. More than her frayed braid, dirt-smudged cheeks, and the darkened stains at the knees of her pants was the fatigued look in her eyes that told how truly spent she was. The woman would work herself to death.

He wanted to sit her down and rub the tenseness of the day away, but that was out of the question. Even if Kit would allow it, which he was certain she would not, there were prying eyes observing them.

He darted a look in the maid's direction and her gray eyes danced suspiciously, confirming his conception. He needed to guard his feelings for Kit more closely. He wouldn't want his weakness to stir rumors leading to questioning her reputation.

"Well, I shall leave this with you." He handed the cut slab of wood being used as a makeshift tray with two bowls of beef stew balanced on top over to Kit. "If you ladies do not require my assistance for anything else, I'll be on my way."

"Price," Kit called, "wait. Could you see about fetching another cot for Lily from the bunkhouse? I forgot all about it."

She handed one of the bowls to Lily and then plopped herself down into the rawhide-upholstered chair. Lily yawned as she seated herself, only somewhat more decorously, into the wooden rocking chair adjacent and began eating her stew.

Kit's request for help was a testament to just how tired she was. He looked her over with growing concern and concluded she could use a warm soak in the tub. If only she would allow him to help her more. If he could convince the stubborn woman to marry him, he would ensure she was well-cared for whether she agreed or not.

Knowing she wouldn't appreciate his concern and would instead interpret it as believing she appeared weak, he nodded to her and left to see about transporting another cot up to the house.

∾

Both women retired after rearranging the room to accommodate the two cots and all of Lily's many things. Kit thought, with much incredulity, that the girl must have packed more with her than Kit even owned.

Despite being utterly exhausted, both women remained awake. *In part, due to Lily's inclination for chatter,* Kit thought with an ornery toss of her head as she adjusted her pillow.

"I think Mr. Price has some strong feelings for 'the boss lady.'" It was too dark to see Lily's face, but Kit could almost hear the sly grin in the girl's words.

Throughout the day, Kit's opinion about her new maid fluctuated from annoyance with the woman to believing they could be friends. At the moment she was returned to feeling irritated.

"He's simply a close friend. Practically family for as long as he's been attached to my brothers."

"Looks more like he's attached to *you*," Lily quipped, "after all, your brothers aren't here."

"He's here as a favor to them."

"Right, as he has nowhere else he could be."

"You don't know Price. He's a man of honor. If he made a promise, he would never betray it."

Lily grunted her disbelief, "Whatever you say, boss."

Definitely annoying, Kit decided. Her new maid was an absolute pest.

They both lay there, staring up into the darkness at the ceiling. Kit shrugged deeper under her quilt, thinking about what Lily had said.

Price wasn't here for *her*. Well, he was, but only because Logan had coerced him into promising to help her with the ranch until he returned. True, Price had proposed marriage to her, but that had been in jest. And, yes, he was helping her practice her seduction skills, but only to fulfil his promise to her brother to keep her safe. He just didn't want her searching elsewhere for "practice" and possibly ruining her reputation. That was all, she assured herself. What did Lily know, anyway?

Kit surprised herself when she continued conversation instead of closing her eyes and sleeping as she ought to have been doing. "So what was your life like in Canyon?"

Kit was curious, though she asked cautiously, knowing it was none of her business. The way Lily behaved, though, gave Kit the impression she had enjoyed working there as a *fallen* woman.

The silence stretched into the night and Kit wasn't sure if Lily had fallen asleep or was too offended by the question to reply. Then she heard her sigh.

"I'm not what you think I am."

Kit waited for her to explain.

"I never worked as a prostitute in Canyon," she then hastened to add, "or anywhere else."

Kit's brows shot up in surprise.

"I wanted to. Or, thought I wanted to. Now I'm glad Madam La Verne wouldn't permit it."

"Did you grow up in Canyon?" Kit asked, wondering where the girl's parents were.

"No, I moved here from Tennessee with my half-brother Frank about two years ago. My ma died when I was six. Our pa, he was a mean 'ol drunk."

Kit began to regret her prodding questions, but kept quiet as Lily continued, "Frank, he can be a mean one, too, but he doesn't succumb to the drink as often, so when he decided to move on to California, I asked him to take me with him. He wasn't too keen on the idea, but I told him he could drop me off in San Francisco and I'd find work there. I thought maybe I could be an actress or a dancing girl."

Kit could hear the girl's smile in her voice.

"Only, Frank never made it that far. He hired on here at Morgan's ranch and I got stuck in Canyon. There's no theatre or dance hall in Canyon," Lily voiced her irritation.

"There is a saloon and a brothel, however," Lily sighed. "I wasn't averse to the idea. Men already seemed to fancy me at the time. I figured it would be easy money. If I saved up, I could pay my own way to San Francisco. No one there would ever need know how I got there.

"But," Lily continued in a disgruntled voice, "Madame La Verne wouldn't hire me on as a prostitute. Said I was too young."

Kit couldn't help but agree and sent a small prayer of thanks to Madame La Verne.

"She let me hire on as a serving girl in the saloon instead and said if I still wanted to work as a dove when I turned eighteen, she'd let me. At first, I was angry with her decision. I couldn't earn enough as a serving girl to live on and save up for San

Francisco, see? But as I had little choice, I agreed to it. It didn't take me long to realize how ignorant I had been about that line of work."

Kit thought she heard Lily's voice harsh with tears and it made her heart ache.

"The ladies there were kind to me. Two of them had even been to San Francisco. They told me all about their lives there." Lily sniffled, "After a time, I no longer desired to live in San Francisco, but I didn't want to stay in Canyon either. I'll be eighteen before the year is out...and I was running out of options."

Kit understood. Lily's dreams of a grandeur life as an actress had been demolished by the harsh hammer of reality.

"Thank you." Lily's voice was uncharacteristically humble, "Thank you for bringing me here and taking a chance on me. I'm aware of the risk to your own reputation in doing so. I know when I arrived, I may have given the impression that I-I was every bit of the scarlet wanton my former occupation painted me to be. I just, I just didn't want to hold my head down in shame or garner pity. I guess I wasn't sure what role to play."

Kit smiled, understanding. Everyone put on an act from time to time. The girl had only been putting on a brave face as she ventured into another unknown in her life.

Kit exhaled as she gathered her next words, "I appreciate your honesty. And while you may fancy the stage and think yourself an actress, just know you don't have to play a factitious role here. I think you will find that I, myself, am fairly direct and prefer dealings in this manner."

Kit heard what sounded part scoff, part laugh from the other side of the room, "Ha! Yes, I learned as much already."

Kit smiled, "I must say, I am relieved to find that display you made upon arriving to be merely a charade. But I'm not sure I believe you entirely."

"Well, I may not be the harlot you imagined me to be, but I am still a woman," Lily replied cheekily. "Men admire me, and I admire them right back."

Kit suppressed a groan. Lily may end up causing trouble yet. "Well, so long as the 'admiring' doesn't get out of hand."

Chapter 19

Two more weeks passed with everyone seeming to have fallen into their own groove. Lily proved herself a worthy investment daily when it came to her work efforts. She applied herself whole-heartedly and definitely knew her way around household chores better than Kit.

Kit was able to return to ranch duties, which pleased her greatly. With Lily around, they were able to make use of the copper tub on the back porch to bathe in, since they could trust one another to keep lookout and protect each other's privacy.

In many ways it was nice having another female around to talk to. It reminded Kit of days with her sister. Kit tended to keep too busy to ponder her nostalgic feelings, but every once in a while they crept up on her. Mainly, her worry over her siblings and how dearly she missed them. She planned to post a letter to home on her visit to Onieda for the town celebration.

She dreaded the social engagement looming at the end of the week. She would be expected to dance and the only two people there she would know were Whitney Kingston and Price. She hadn't heard word back from García on whether or not he would accompany them.

On one hand she hoped he would attend, but on the other...well, she wasn't looking forward to the conversation revolving around her ranch prospects. No more suiters had come calling on her. She began to fear Kingston may be her only option to keep her ranch. And it was a rather unappealing option.

She hadn't been able to maneuver any more practicing sessions with Price. That was the downfall of having a maid around. Kit never had any privacy. Lily had her nose everywhere, but especially wherever Price seemed to be. Kit rolled her eyes skyward. Apparently, when Kit had expressed her disinterest in Price, Lily took that to mean the man was free game.

"When do you expect Mr. Price to come check in on us?" Lily popped her head in the doorway. Much to Kit's despair, there was no door and therefore no lock.

Together they had spruced up the tiny alcove off the living room which had obviously previously been used as a study. No books lined the walls, only a lonely desk and chair. The desk and chair were surprisingly of good quality mahogany, though. Kit harrumphed as she wondered how her sire had been able to afford the fine furniture.

Kit was planted at the desk now, going over every detail in the ledgers, desperately hoping the numbers would start to make sense. She wouldn't be suffering at all had the rainstorm not interrupted her morning and forced her inside.

Since she was stuck indoors, she could think of no excuse to prevent her from cracking the book open once more. Of course, making sense of the numbers would certainly have been made easier if Lily would cease her constant interruptions.

Kit set the tattered leather-bound book down on the desk and rubbed her palms across her tired eyes and down her face before answering Lily's question, "I don't expect Price at all."

"You know he will come, rain or not." Lily grinned.

Kit ignored her implied comments, "Speaking of rain, it sounds as though it has finally stopped."

Lily quieted to listen, a wholly astonishing feat.

Then they heard the door swing open and boots kick the threshold divider before entering.

Lily raised her brows and flashed a smug smile.

"I swear, the rain barely had time to give the ground a good soaking, the sun is already turning all to dust again. The drops of water on the walk up here were sizzling off my skin by time I made it to the porch." Price's voice rang through the small house.

Kit decided to ignore Lily still gloating in the doorway.

"In here," she called to Price, curtly. "What do you want?"

"I knew being shut in all morning would make you beastly." Price winked at Lily who giggled shamelessly at his jest. None of which did anything to improve Kit's mood.

An arch of her bold, dark brow was her only response.

"Miss Perkins, you're looking lovely, as usual."

Lily touched her copper coils hanging loose from her chignon. An appearance that looked artfully designed if one asked Kit. She certainly hadn't worked hard enough today to knock any curls loose. Kit's errant hair never appeared so charming after hours of work, she sniffed.

"Why, thank you, Mr. Price," Lily flirted.

"Would you mind doing a favor for me?" Price asked

"Anything," Lily answered, rather suggestively.

"Samuel needs help in the garden, would you mind giving him a hand? I told him I would fetch a basket from the house, but I also have news to depart to Miss Stone."

Lily's smile wavered across her lips.

Poor Samuel had a case of puppy love over her. To Samuel, a boy of fourteen, seventeen-year-old Lily didn't seem out of his reach. Lily, however, disagreed.

No matter how rudely Lily treated the boy, he was never discouraged. Samuel set up camp around Lily the way Lily had around Price. Lily didn't disguise her distaste for her admirer from Kit, but she did make an effort to conceal her ill manners from Price.

"Of course," Lily bobbed her head demurely and walked quickly from the house in search of the produce basket.

"Didn't want to get dirt under your fingernails, Price?" Kit asked drolly.

Stepping into the room, he seemed to fill the small space, "Wouldn't dream of it. I have work gloves after all, would be silly not to use them."

Kit shook her head and returned her attention to the ledgers before her, effectively ignoring Price.

"Actually," Price interrupted, "I just wanted a private moment with you."

A tingling sensation pooled in her belly. Her heart began to pound, and she thought Price had come to enact more lessons on kissing.

Apparently, she was becoming a wanton, herself.

She started to stand to better welcome his advances, until he spoke.

"I wanted to ensure all was well with the ranch finances. That is to say, I'm aware the ranch's finances are strained, but your apparent distress over the book you constantly carry about caused me to wonder if perhaps the numbers were askew in some way?"

Well. Well, that certainly hadn't been what Kit was expecting from this encounter. She tried to cease the butterflies in her stomach. *Price hadn't sent Lily off to get you alone so he could kiss you. He came to help you with the ranch.* As he had promised her brother he would. She shook her head, what a ninny.

She adjusted her seat in the chair closer to the desk and sighed her frustration.

"Is there a discrepancy, then?"

"No. I don't know." She unconsciously smoothed the hair from her face, "I suppose it won't hurt for you to know, but obviously I want this information to stay confidential."

"Of course. I'll put on my solicitor's cap." Price grinned, and her heart lurched.

What was the matter with her? A few kisses here and there and suddenly her body was a craven.

She focused her attention back to the book and pushed open the pages to three years prior and pointed, "I can't make sense of it."

"Any of it? Or is there a specific page where it stops adding up?"

"My struggle is not simply adding up the numbers, it's cracking the code. My sire *apparently* felt necessary to disguise whatever nefarious means he was spending any profits on."

"Might I take a look at it?"

She swallowed uneasily. If he looked at it and made sense of it as she suspected he would, she would reveal herself for the halfwit she was. But as mortifying as it was, she did need help.

Price was the only one present she could trust and who she felt was competent enough to assess the numbers.

But how she wished there was someone else.

Would his eyes still shine with respect for her once he knew?

"I can't do it."

"I don't understand, what exactly can't you do?"

"I can't make sense of these figures and it's not just because of the intentional puzzle woven throughout. I-I've never been good with numbers." She looked down, dejectedly. There, she'd admitted it. Her ugly weakness. She was an incompetent. A failure.

~

Price watched as she struggled with her embarrassment, though he didn't quite understand. Kit Stone was an intelligent woman. Could she really be trying to tell him she couldn't perform simple math? That was absurd.

"I can add and subtract, of course. It's when I'm bombarded with information and patterns, like this. It's silly, I know. Ridiculously stupid even."

She explained, "One time, when we were children, Livvy had gotten it into her head that she should learn how to sew from scratch her own garments. She asked me to help her configure how many yards of material she would need. Of course, she just casually rattled off numbers, performing the arithmetic in her head. I simply agreed with her assessment, as I had no idea where to even begin calculating all the different measurements. Finally, I just told her I was headed to the barn and left her to her project.

"It's not as if I wanted to help her design patterns to cut and sew. But it's always bothered me that I *couldn't*. And still to this day, numbers present a frustrating obstacle for me."

Kit met his eyes then and he could read in their gray depths the fear and shame in them. He swallowed, trying to think of a comforting response to put her at ease.

Nervously, she said, "It's difficult to explain... I get this itchy feeling. Not physically, but mentally. A discomfort so great all I can think about is escaping it. It's as if my brain shuts down and blocks the numbers out even when I try exceedingly hard to remain focused."

"So, it's not a problem concerning basic arithmetic."

"No. I told you, it's a problem with processing too much numerical information at once."

When he said nothing, she gave a deprecating laugh, "Perhaps my brain is simply serving to protect me from boredom."

"Kit, you're not the first who has ever struggled with this particular area of study."

"Mathematics is hardly the only area I have struggled to focus on. It is only the worst one."

"Well, plenty of people find it difficult to pursue academia as well."

"Indeed, those that are infirm in the head."

"Don't speak of yourself as such."

Chastised, she folded her arms defensively across her chest.

"I think it's a condition some are inflicted with, that makes it difficult for one to concentrate or focus on a task. In fact, your brother, Luke, struggles with this as well."

Kit looked to him in disbelief. "No. Luke isn't like me. He's smart. He graduated from university. With YOU," she said pointedly.

Price shook his head, "Trust me, graduating from university is not an indicator of one's intelligence. I know plenty of ignoramuses who managed to graduate from a fancy university. One must first start with a seed of intelligence in order for education to help it grow.

"So, you're saying Luke isn't smart?"

Price, frustrated, responded, "No. I'm not say—" He shook off the rest of his sentence, "What I am saying is, *you are* smart."

Kit smiled, obviously enjoying the frustration she'd caused him. "So how did Luke make it through his studies then?"

"To be honest, he didn't. Not well, anyway. His marks were always low. High enough to pass, obviously. But only that."

"Hmm," she considered thoughtfully, "I never knew that about him. I always saw my big brother as remarkably successful."

"He is," Price stated simply.

Kit looked to him confusedly.

"That is what I'm trying to tell you. Academic pursuits are not the only standard in which to measure intelligence or success. Plenty of people with little to no education are very intelligent. They are simply smart and knowledgeable in other ways."

His green gaze looked to the ceiling as if searching the rafters for the right words. Then he snapped his fingers, "Take us, for example."

"*Us*...?" Kit looked to him questioningly and a blush stole her cheeks.

Price smiled, knowing she couldn't see him doing so, as her discomfiture had caused her to direct her gaze to the toe of her boots. That her mind had snapped to the reference of "us" as them being romantically coupled gave him hope.

But that was neither here nor there, he mentally reminded himself. For there was no "us." Not yet anyway. Price cleared his thoughts and continued, gathering her attention once more, "Yes, compare you and I, for example. I could never do what you do with a horse."

"Well, with training you could. Anyone could."

"No. Don't downplay your talents. Your mother enjoys training horses, but she could never get as much out of a horse as you do."

Kit smiled; it was small, but earnest. "Thank you," she said. Then she cleared her throat and with it the tender moment, "But that still doesn't solve my problem, and help me to balance these ledgers."

"See, that's the example I was getting at with Luke. He could never sit in a classroom. But when given the chance to apply those teachings outside of the classroom, he excelled greatly. It's in part why he, Logan, and I were able to make a fortune in the gold fields a couple years back."

"But this *is* outside of a classroom. And I still can't seem to wrap my head around it." Kit paced in frustration.

"Yes, you can."

She read frustration in his crisp green gaze. And if she supposed a guess, a tad bit of anger in them as well. She realized he truly didn't like to hear her speak ill of herself and a kernel of warmth furled within her. That he cared so greatly about *her* was surprising. Astonishing, really. No one else outside of her family had ever thought Kit special in anyway. Not even her family, if she were being honest.

She cocked her head and looked at Price, really looked at him, for the first time. It was a strange feeling to think of Price romantically. But perhaps, not entirely strange...

Price was oblivious to her inner discovery. He surveyed the room impatiently, his fingers tapping a quick procession against the desk. Then his eyes met hers and he announced, "Let's go for a ride."

"A ride?"

"Yes, consider it a lesson in mathematics."

Chapter 20

The fresh air cleared Kit's mind as Price had predicted it would. From the saddle she was liberated from confining spaces forcing her to crunch numbers. Except, ironically, all they had done on the ride was discuss numbers. Specifically, the coded calculations within the book of ledgers—the book holding all her ranch's history, as well as its secrets.

Price turned the details into terms she could understand, as if taking worn, chipped pieces of a puzzle and smoothing the edges out for Kit to fit them easily into place. She now understood why professors had praised him and why her brothers didn't take any financial risks without him; his mind was extraordinary.

Kit couldn't help but be in awe of him. His hazel eyes took on that marbled sheen as he excitedly worked Kit through the numbers. She'd never seen him so, so, in his element. And all the while he worked calculations and made discoveries of where profits were being eaten up from, he sat his horse like any natural born rancher.

His English boots may be polished, and he wore a knotted cravat around his neck, despite the ungodly Texas heat, but he was rather an impressive figure all the same. There was nothing dishonorable about taking pride in one's appearance, after all. In fact, it bespoke well of his character that he took such diligent care of his possessions. His horse included, something Kit could always respect.

"So, there you have it. And all in one afternoon's ride." The sun caught his bronzed hair as he flashed an arrogant grin her way, making him look nearly celestial, and her heart skipped a beat.

Her new feelings toward Price were terribly inconvenient. He would surely retract any statements regarding her intelligence if she continued staring at him like a ninny.

She cleared her throat, "Yes, thanks to you." A blush stole through her body as she smiled. She looked away for fear it would be as apparent on her face as it felt heating all of her skin.

Focus, Kit! She didn't want him to decipher her blushes for what they were. She didn't know his feelings toward her, and it wouldn't do to reveal herself before finding out. He had proposed to her when they arrived at the ranch, but it had been in jest.

Hadn't it?

She would need to analyze these new feelings more thoroughly at a time when she had some privacy from both Price, and her all-too-perceptive maid.

For now, she needed to redirect her foolish fancies of romance to the problem at hand: saving her ranch.

"We discovered what we already knew. There is no money."

"Yes, but we also discovered there could be money. With better management this ranch actually stands to have a future."

"But," she continued, "even practicing better money management, profit will be slow to come. I need a way to make money quickly. In order to pay off debts and invest in practices that will aid in bringing in more profits in the future."

She thought for a second, then blurted, "García raises sheep. He's managed to turn a pretty coin in doing so. He suggested that Morgan began investing into the obscure cattle market simply to nettle him."

"I can't imagine a man desiring a life of gaming and drink to intentionally sabotage his own finances."

"True," she sighed warily.

"Besides, I think the market for cattle will soon be on the rise."

"Perhaps not soon enough. I need to think of a way to bring in cash quickly. A way that doesn't involve marrying Whitney Kingston."

Price offered a small smile but didn't look her direction.

They both turned their thoughts inward, contemplating different avenues that would potentially garner the desired outcome. Neither coming to any readily conclusions.

Suddenly, Kit was distracted by a red flash in the brush up ahead. She knew distinctly what it was.

A horse.

~

"Price," he heard Kit utter his name in a harsh whisper, "there's a stray mustang just ahead."

He saw her unstrap her lasso and loosen a coil in her hand at her side. Surely, she wasn't thinking of running it down? He gave her a weary look and whispered back, "That doesn't make any sense. We're too far south, and a mustang wouldn't leave its band."

"I know. But I'm certain that's what it was. Let's circle around that way." Kit pointed toward the bank trail leading to the creek, "If it spooks, it'll run back up the bank and toward the ranch."

This seemed a futile endeavor; rounding up a wild mustang was a lot of work, especially with only the two of them to do it, and besides, what did she want with it anyway? Then he saw her silver eyes spark to life and realized what Kit probably didn't— she was missing home, her familiar routines, and breaking out a horse would bring her a calming sense of control.

He nodded and followed her lead. As their horses picked their path down the rocky bank, they came across the carcass of another horse.

"A young stallion," Kit proclaimed. "Looks like wolves got him." Their horses snorted and pranced a jittery sidestep around the dead stallion. Carefully, they made their way down the slope, leaving what was left of the rotting stallion behind. As they cleared the bend, the wild mare spooked and crashed up the bank as Kit had predicted she would.

Price saw Kit's smile broaden as she nudged her gelding into the chase.

Oh, hell. Price prepared for his mare to follow suit and race up the bank in hurdled leaps. He could ride good as most any *man*, but not Miss Catherine Stone. He gave reign to his horse urging her up the steep, brush-laden hill, and held on for dear life.

Kit Stone was going to be the death of him.

He breathed a sigh of relief as his horse scrambled to the top after Kit's. Kit was already in a dead run and gaining on the mustang. Now that he was on flat ground, he squeezed and sent his horse racing after Kit.

By the time he reached her, she was already slowing, her lasso stretched taut connecting to where it was looped around the mustang's neck. The wild bay mare trotted closer, giving up the fight with surprising ease.

Kit's eyes gleamed with pleasure; her pride shone only in the barest hint of a smile.

Her excitement was catching.

She cast a teasing smile over her shoulder, "Nice of you to catch up, Price."

"You didn't appear to require any assistance. And we both know how little you welcome my interference between you and your feral projects," he quipped.

She laughed, "Ah, you're learning, and faster than my brothers, I might add." Then she winked at him.

Was he dreaming or had Kit Stone just engaged in the art of flirtation? *With him?* He couldn't prevent the serious set of his features as he studied her, searching for more, other ways she could be signaling a growing interest in him.

Her attention was already turned back to the horses.

No, he decided. He had only imagined her flirtatious manner. She was simply exuberated over her catch, and the thrill brought about a more playful manner in her.

"Let's get her home, shall we?" Kit asked, grinning from ear to ear, unable to restrain her excitement.

Price nodded and tried to summon a smile for her. Silently, his thoughts dark, he imagined never sharing these moments with her again. If it came to be that she married another, he would never be on the receiving end of her rare, brilliant smiles, and they wouldn't return home together after an afternoon ride. He smothered his black mood and flanked the other side of the wild mare as they trekked the long ride back *home*.

The ranch hands gathered around the corral, admiring Kit's prized horse flesh.

"Qué estaba hacienda un mustang solitario en esta parte del pàis?

As some of the men hurried to latch the gate, Kit slid from her saddle, led her gelding by the rein and joined the others to peer through the split rails. Price joined her.

"What's it that Osa said?" she asked.

José, in his low, strained voice as if it was always an inconvenience to reply to her, said, "He asked how a lone mustang came to be in these parts."

"Well, she wasn't alone for long. There was a stallion with her, but he was killed by wolves. We came across what was left of him as we trailed her. My guess is the young stallion got lucky and stole her from another band and simply lost his way or was too inexperienced to realize his peril. It's lucky we came across her when we did, she might've turned into a meal, herself."

In his typical clipped tone, José sneered, "And just what are we supposed to do with a feral caballo?"

Price certainly didn't like the determined glint in Kit's eyes.

Kit grinned, "You'll see."

Chapter 21

"No, Samuel, I don't care to see the new 'breed' of flower you've created in the garden. I've enough duties of my own to see to here."

"I would be happy to help you, Lily."

"If you don't have enough work to keep you busy, perhaps I should mention to Boss that you're *bored*."

"But I am not bored. I enjoy spending time with you."

Kit had entered the house quietly, in search of her lucky horse. Her adoptive and true father had whittled a tiny horse from the wood of an aspen tree. His father used to make furniture, so he had grown up around woodworking and enjoyed whittling on occasion. He made Kit and all her siblings tiny animals and characters of which to play with when they were younger. But the horse he had made specifically for her was special.

It was smoothed down to the point now, from her constant handling, that many probably wouldn't recognize its distinct features anymore, but Kit never went anywhere without it if she could help it. She especially wanted it today.

Today was the day she would mount the wild bay mare they had all taken to calling Solitaire. She'd been handling her all week and the mustang had progressed well learning ground manners. That didn't mean the little mare wouldn't put up a fight when it came time to ride, though, and when that moment came, Kit would definitely want her lucky token in her pocket.

When she stepped into the house to retrieve it, she heard Lily speaking to Samuel irritably.

Poor Samuel, he was a wonderful young man, but not grown enough yet to catch the eye of a young woman who had already lived too much of the world.

"Samuel, look, I know you have a crush on me. I think you're a great kid. But that's all. You shouldn't waste your time on someone like me."

"I am not a kid. I am two years younger than you!"

"Three," Lily corrected.

"Not as of tomorrow."

Kit wondered if she should intervene or simply head back to the corral without a word. Against her better judgment, she tread quietly toward the kitchen, where their voices were coming from. She walked along the wall until she could peer around the archway consisting of thick beams dividing the kitchen from the living area.

She saw Lily facing the countertop, her back to Kit and the rest of the kitchen. Samuel sat atop the countertop to Lily's left, searching Lily's downcast face intently.

She saw Samuel tentatively touch Lily's hand and Lily pull away. Samuel retracted his hand, hurt, but not wanting to cause Lily discomfort.

"Someday you will see me as a man. And I'll be your man."

"That's awfully presumptuous," Lily snipped.

Samuel smiled until his dimples showed, revealing the charming rogue he would one day be, "Maybe it's just confidence."

Lily shook her head in exasperation.

"The flowers are for you, so you must take them. Do not fear they signify a bonding promise or some such. They are just flowers."

Samuel's athletic frame hopped down from the counterpane.

Kit began a hasty retreat so as not to be caught eavesdropping. Apparently, the kids could handle themselves and an intervention from her wasn't necessary. As she made her way out the door, she could hear Samuel's parting sentence to Lily.

"And you will never be a waste of my time."

Kit smiled and rushed out the door. She decided to take the long way around behind the horse barn, knowing Samuel would be exiting the house soon. He wouldn't see her hidden behind the barn.

Kit hurried back to the corral. She wanted to have this mare bucked out before she left for the town celebration on the morrow. Price was at the rail waiting for her when she arrived.

"Why don't you wait until after we return? What if you break something, and can't dance with any of your *prospective grooms*?"

Kit rolled her eyes. She'd been thrown from lots of horses, had the wind knocked from her on several occasions, but never had she broken any bones. She reached in her pocket and rubbed the smooth wooden horse. And she didn't expect to this day.

"Price?" she asked as if she had something important to impart.

"Yes?"

"Latch the gate once I'm inside, would ya?"

"Bloody hell," he grumbled.

A blanket and saddle were waiting for her on the top rail where she had placed them. She walked to the center of the corral. Solitaire's ears twitched and her large glassy eyes watched Kit's every move from across the pen.

She waited patiently for the dark bay mare to remember she trusted Kit. The mare was smart and far gentler than any mustang Kit had ever before witnessed. She seemed to have already accepted her fate. Perhaps she was even thankful not to have been left to fend for herself without a protector.

Solitaire eventually made her way to Kit and placed her muzzle in Kit's hand. Kit let her snort into it, then slowly turned her palm to the middle of the white stripe running down the mare's face. Gently stroking, she moved her soft, quiet hands along Solitaire's neck to her shoulder with one hand, while her other took hold of the short rope attached to the halter.

Kit spoke softly and cooed to her. When Kit turned her body so that it was side by side to the mare and stepped forward, Solitaire, having already learned the cue, stepped along beside her, willingly. Kit smiled and led her to the rail but left her untied. Kit looped a longer lead through the halter, not as long as the one she used to lunge her with earlier, but long enough to give the mare some freedom if she resisted at all.

Unaware of the crowd gathering at the fence, Kit calmly rubbed the blanket along the mare's neck and up, settling into place at the withers and along her back. Solitaire had already been introduced to the blanket many times over the past week, but it was still a relatively new experience for the horse. Next Kit brought the saddle to her side. With the rope draped loosely over Kit's arm, the horse had full movement of her head and brought her muzzle round to smell the saddle. Kit let her.

Gently, but without hesitation, Kit placed the saddle atop her back. The mare quivered. Kit was familiar with this particular song and dance. All week, the cowhands had been surprised by the mare's gentleness, especially coming from undomesticated lines. But Kit knew differently. It was a deceptive calm. The mare's intelligent eyes watched Kit now, waiting, always waiting.

Kit rubbed her hand soothingly along Solitaire's dark coat, so dark she was nearly black. The red in her coat appeared to warm and glow when the sunlight hit it, like a breath to a hot coal. Her personality was similar, for Kit could feel the fire within the mare growing stronger, the spark fanned with each submission into her captive world. The mare only appeared to be easily accepting of her new role and environment to someone less perceptive than Kit.

If Kit had an aptitude for anything, it was reading horses. And what she read in Solitaire's keen watchful eyes, every snort and pawing of her hoof scraping the dirt, and quiver that rippled across her flesh, was anticipation.

The same excitement raced through Kit's body, so she recognized it well. On the outside, both woman and horse seemed a part of a mutual routine, but below the surface both were teeming with life awaiting the battle to come.

Leaving the rope halter in place, Kit slipped the bosal over the mare's nose and slid the hackamore into position, reins already attached. Looping the long rope around the saddle horn, Kit led Solitaire by the reins to the center of the corral.

The mare tensed, tight like a coil.

Kit grinned.

Challenge accepted.

Price's heart pounded as he tried to remain impassive from outside the corral. He believed in her abilities to handle any horse that came her way, but that knowledge did little to quell the fear building inside. He worried for her safety and would rather she not take such risks, but there was nothing he could do to prevent her from following through with her training.

He knew from experience not to come between her and a horse. Carrying her from the corral certainly hadn't worked in the past.

Price swallowed, not taking his eyes from the bold woman in the center of the corral. He couldn't help but think her petit form looked all the smaller near the nine-hundred-pound animal. Kit's braid fell from her shoulder to hang straight down her back as she gathered the reins.

He saw the horse stiffen and rock backwards, slowly, paused like a loaded gun with a finger at the trigger.

An audacious smile quirked the corners of Kit's lips.

God, the mad woman was looking forward to the fight.

Price wanted to cover his eyes, but he couldn't not watch. The other vaqueros gathered around the pen, wondering if Kit would continue being the one in control.

In one smooth motion, Kit grabbed the saddle horn and swung her weight up into the saddle. In that instant, the mare released every might of her power as she shot into the air, landing on four stiff legs, before launching again.

How Kit managed to seat herself in time was a wonder to Price. Then again, the woman had always been a marvel to him.

He watched as the bronco sprang forward and Kit with it. As the front end of the horse came down, Kit leaned back, transitioning as the back end of the horse lifted into the air. The mare snorted and pounded the earth with each descent of a violent thrust in attempt to dislodge the rider.

Kit remained in control, her grip from on the rope keeping the bronc's head raised. The mare wasn't to be easily defeated, however, and continued to buck with jarring force around the corral. All the men around the fence seemed to collectively inhale a sharp breath when the mare sunfished first left, then right. All expected to see their boss's backside broken in the dirt.

But Kit never lost her seat. It was as if she could predict the bronc's every move.

"Never seen anyone grip rawhide like that!" Samuel exclaimed, wide-eyed, with awe.

José sneered, "I've bucked out plenty of rank broncs."

"Never seen you ride out a mustang," Bernardo, who had been on the ranch longer than any of the other vaqueros, stated firmly.

Osa uttered something in Spanish Price was able to translate to, "Best I've ever seen," as he stared out at Kit pulling the mustang around.

The other vaqueros nodded and muttered in agreement, all of their eyes shining with respect and...

Christ. They all looked as love struck as that young pup, Samuel, did following around after Lily. Kit would have no problem finding a husband after this, he grumbled.

They could all see the bronc breaking down, conceding to the fight. Her bucks reduced to crowhops. Kit had both reins bunched in her hands and steered the horse to the rail, then turned her the other direction. She was in control. The mare went where Kit led.

Finally, the mare tired and when Kit applied pressure, drawing the reins back, the mare slowed from a trot quickly to a walk and came to a stop in the center of the corral. Kit kept the mare at a stand while she rubbed her shoulder. The mare panted from exertion, but never hung her head. She was still listening, awaiting the next command.

"She's going to make a great little cow horse one day," Kit announced as she climbed from the saddle.

The dark bay stepped sideways nervously and Kit waited patiently for her to calm once more. When the mare stood still, Kit at her shoulder urged her forward and the pair made their way to the rail.

Kit looked up then to smile at Price, only to realize she had an entire audience of ranch hands looking on. Her smile slipped from her face, replaced by a shy grim line, awkward and ill prepared for such attention.

Once the horse was free of its tack it trotted out to the center of the pen and rolled away its sweaty itch in the dirt. A weary sigh puffed over Kit's lips as she watched the horse coat itself in a thick layer of grime, knowing the mare was going to require quite the brush down later. Then with saddle and blanket rested at the side of her hip held by one arm and the headstall draped over her shoulder, she turned to exit the gate. She brought her head up for the first time since spying the crowd and searched for Price. She sighed in relief to see him already working the latch.

Once she stepped from the pen, the men began whistling and cheering. Samuel and Osa appeared at her side and relieved her from the tack she was carrying, taking it to the barn for her. She rather wished they hadn't, she had hoped to use putting the tack away as an excuse to avoid all the praise coming her direction.

She wasn't accustomed to ending a training session with a horse to a chorus of cheers. She wanted to run. If she had broken the mare out home at Stone Ranch, there would have been no one to witness the feat. And if a few people had been around, they would not have batted an eye, for it would have been just another day. No, Kit surely didn't know what to make of this spectacle.

She trembled, much like the mare had when she'd feared the unknown. Then she felt a familiar warm hand at the small of her back.

Price.

She leaned into it some, happy to seek comfort in his presence.

He brought his lips near her ear, she felt him smile as he whispered, "You look as though you'd rather go another round with the mustang."

His words reminded her of her strength and how foolish it was for her to dodge the parade of compliments coming her way as if they were rotten fruit. She steeled herself and spread a welcoming smile on her face, turning toward the crowd.

Bernardo clasped her hands, "Well done, señorita Stone."

And Frank, "That was some good ridin'."

"Una gran vaquera."

"Buen espactáculo!"

Kit nodded thanks and shook hands as the men dispersed. José, she noticed, remained at the rail, his lip curled in disgust. She met his gaze directly, "A problem, José?"

He gave a short, jeering laugh, "No problem."

She felt Price stiffen beside her. Kit held her arm before him to prevent him from confronting José and creating a scene over nothing. José's contemptuous eyes broke contact with hers and he sauntered away.

"I don't trust him," Price said.

"He doesn't like me, that's all. So long as he doesn't cause trouble and he gets his work done, I don't have a problem with him. Hate to send him packing with no other prospects in line."

"Well you're a might more generous than I am, then."

Kit smiled as she turned to face him and jested, "And yet, you're the one they call the Saint."

He reached out and playfully touched the end of her unravelling braid. Suddenly she was very aware of how alone they were, the darkening sky providing even more seclusion.

"We leave for the town celebration tomorrow." Price's voice was low and throaty.

"Yes," she answered on a short breath, her racing heart already having turned her breathing shallow.

He stepped closer, bridging the gap between them and heat flooded her body. She prepared herself, anticipating his kiss, but instead he spoke, "Perhaps you will save a dance for me."

That was it?

Oh, her foolish body. Why could she no longer seem to think straight around the man? Here she was panting after him, wanting his hands on her, to be wrapped in his arms and being kissed senseless, and he? He was just fulfilling his role of guardian over her.

Irritated with herself, but also a little hurt that she wasn't inciting the same desire within him as he sparked in her, she replied, "Well, I don't think being seen dancing with my ranch foreman will aid in my hunt for a husband."

Price took a step back reflexively. She felt the cold night air assault her skin in his absence.

Price smiled tightly, "I see."

Unable to think of a suitable response, she simply tipped her nose in the air impertinently.

"Well, then, you may want to get in one more lesson."

Before she could grasp his meaning, Price pulled her to him, cupped her head back, and covered her mouth with his. Her brazen body melted into him, betrayer that it was, and her mouth softened in invitation. His hands fervently roamed her body. One hand bunched in her thick hair at the back of her head, the other sliding down to cup under her breast.

Feverishly, she explored him right back, running her hands along his trim waist to the muscled expanse of his chest and the bulge of his biceps.

Then with as little warning as the kiss had been initiated, it came to an abrupt stop.

"That was...your lessons seem to be working." Price's voice was a rough whisper.

Kit stood, momentarily stupefied. Then with realization of how little the kiss had meant to him, embarrassment in the eager way she had responded flooded her.

Irritably, she pushed away from him. In attempt to redeem any dignity that remained, she stated, "Yes, well, I think there should be no need for further *instruction* from here out. Thank you for your generous efforts, however."

Price bowed, then walked off in quick, angry steps.

Kit didn't have long to consider what had transpired between them, for Samuel rushed up to her in the seconds afterward.

"I brought the brush and a pail of fresh water," Samuel spoke excitedly, "I knew you would want to brush Solitaire down before supper." He sat the pail down clumsily with a clang.

His smile disappeared from his face when he finally noticed her demeanor, "Are you okay?"

She snapped herself away from her thoughts of Price and brought her attention to Samuel, "Yes. Never better." She gave her best impression of a smile.

The concern didn't quite leave Samuel's eyes, but he accepted her refusal to voice her troubles. To divert the conversation to a more pleasant topic, Samuel began chattering excitedly once more about her winning ride. He remained outside of the fence at the rail as she worked to rub Solitaire down and give her a drink.

"It was spectacular. Better entertainment than this ranch has ever seen! At least since I've been around," Samuel amended. Followed by, "You could have been killed!"

Kit laughed then, "Hardly. You know breaking out the young horses was my sole job back home, right? I've been working with unbroke horses for so long now, it's like second-nature for me. I can seat them pretty well."

Samuel, apparently not ready to give up on the drama, said, "Well, I thought you were going to hit the dust for sure, when that caballo diablo started twisting in the air in all directions."

Kit laughed, "That's called sunfishing. I'll admit I've had few horses that gave as good as that one. She's not the worst I've ever broke in, though."

"I think I'd like to try it," Samuel said.

Suddenly, an idea sparked. Kit knew how she would bulk the finances for the ranch.

Chapter 22

Later, everyone gathered around the cook fire as Bernardo ladled chili into bowls and cups.

"Perhaps you could pick up some more dinnerware while you are in town?" Bernardo offered Kit a sly smile along with a chipped clay bowl full of chili.

She inhaled the spicy aroma. Bernardo was possibly a better chef than Rita; all of his meals burst with flavor.

"Sure thing. Shall I use your monthly earnings to provide these essentials?" she quipped.

Bernardo playfully reprimanded her sassiness with a tap to her shoulder with the ladle.

She grinned in response and made her way over to the stump tipped sideways to serve as a bench. She settled in next to Lily who had already been served and was spooning the fragrant food to her lips.

Then José quite ruined the silly mood by inserting a snide question, "Are we to begin receiving monthly earnings, then?"

Kit sobered, "Of course. I have money I can borrow from my family to pay backpay, but I'd prefer not borrowing if the ranch can provide for it on its own."

José's response was a derisive snort.

The others around the fire grew quiet.

She sensed Price, more than saw him, and knew his hackles were rising. Before he could intervene, Kit delivered a calm smile and glanced around at the group, "Actually, I've come up with a plan. And it should bring in revenue quickly."

"Do tell," José invited with a snide tilt of his head and a condescending grin.

"A contest." Kit looked around, expecting to read excitement among the faces, but instead they stared back on her blankly. She resisted the urge to wipe her sweating palms against her pants.

Lily caught on to Kit's attempt at politic diversion and came to her aid. Cheerfully, she clapped her hands, "A contest? How lovely!"

José snorted his bemusement and began to walk off in a show of great disrespect. Kit gritted her teeth. That vaquero was deliberately shredding the remnant scraps of her patience.

Before he was out of ear shot, Kit explained to the rest of the hands still gathered around the fire.

"Not just any contest. A contest between all of the neighboring ranches to determine the best skilled vaquero of us all!"

The gleam in the men's eyes over the fire told her she had their rapt attention.

"We shall have the contest here and charge people to enter. Some of the fees will go toward prize purses for the winners, of course."

Out of the corner of her eye, she spied José slowly making his way back to learn more.

"We'll have a variety of ranching categories to compete in: calf roping, bronc busting, and steer wrestling."

~

Price couldn't keep from smiling proudly on Kit. She had come up with a strategy to save her ranch that was as unconventional as she herself was. It was savvy and played to her strengths. To think mere days ago she had been insecure about her ability to rebuild the ranch from its financial ruins.

Her excitement was catching and soon all the men were eagerly chatting about who would be competing in which category.

"And will you be competing?" José's goading tone hushed the party once more.

"Indeed, I will." Kit grinned back, refusing to allow José's bad manners to ruin the festive atmosphere.

"Excellent." He smirked, then took his leave of the group. For which, Price was certain, all were eternally grateful for.

The tension visibly left Kit's shoulders. Well, visibly only to him, he was sure. He knew she was making great efforts to appear unaffected by José's disrespectful remarks.

In fact, Price intended to discuss with her the dismissal of the sour ranch hand. She couldn't allow one worker to treat her thusly and expect the others to continue to respect her. The man was planting seeds of trouble for her and it was best if she uprooted him, before the situation could grow any further out of hand.

The rest of the hands were all merry and carrying on, voices loud with cheer again. Laughter filled the group as some shared stories about similar contesting events they'd heard about in San Antonio.

Kit quieted them for a moment again, all listened intently.

"There is much reason to celebrate tonight, hope for our ranch being one of the reasons and another being that tomorrow is this young man's birthday," Kit announced.

Samuel blushed beside her, obviously uncomfortable, what with the centered attention or for the reminder that he was still viewed as somewhat of a child.

"I will not be here tomorrow night, so we must celebrate tonight!"

The men cheered. Osa rushed off to the bunkhouse and returned with a guitar and some tambourines. Soon, Lily was being twirled around as dance and song broke out. Kit took a few bashful turns as well.

Price remained back, however. He wasn't ready to feel her in his arms, knowing his opportunity to do so would only ever be as fleeting as when holding her close during a country reel.

After a while some of the men began passing around their personal flasks of whiskey and other strong spirits. Price kindly refused when offered. He was too focused on Kit. He had learned much from the Stone brothers and one thing of consequence was that it never served well to mix a drunken state of mind with an important task.

And Price hadn't forgotten his most important task of looking out for Kit's welfare. Whether she felt she required his aid or not.

On the other side of the fire near the shadows, he caught sight of what appeared to be an argument ensuing between Lily and Samuel. It didn't take great deduction skills to conclude what the spat was about. Samuel took an angry swig from one of the flasks being passed around and stared obstinately back at Lily. She then ripped the flask from his hand and threw it to the dirt at his feet.

While the boy scrambled to the ground to rescue the spilling contents, Lily stomped off toward the house.

Price wasn't the only one who had noticed. He observed Kit make her way to Samuel. She attempted to soothe the boy's ruffled feathers, but he appeared unwilling to be comforted. Price rather thought the boy's pride had been too badly maligned to recover from with soothing words.

The boy returned to the fire with forced cheer and entered the raucous once again. Kit then made it known she too was retiring for the night and followed after Lily.

Price turned down another offer to sip from the communal flask as a drunken Osa stumbled into him. To which Osa was offended requiring Price to assure the large man that he hadn't been attempting to steal his guitar.

Extracting himself from a slurring story, mostly in Spanish Price couldn't recognize, took longer than Price had anticipated, and it was a great effort to catch up to Kit to ensure she made it back to the house safely. She didn't have a lantern after all.

As he neared her, he saw her back stiffen. He peered beyond her to see what had caused her to freeze. Then he heard Lily's voice.

"Keep your hands off me, José." Lily's attempt to push him from her went unheeded.

"C'mon. Stop with the maid charade. We all know what you really are."

As José forcibly pulled Lily toward him, despite the girl's efforts to jerk free from his hold, Price heard Kit's brave voice ring out.

"Hey! Release her."

José paused and opened his hands, freeing Lily. As he started to lift his face, sporting an arrogant smile toward Kit, no doubt to spew something equally as offensive to her, Price decided to take action.

Or rather, he decided nothing and, as his father would accuse, submitted to his plebian character that lacked all self-control. He dashed forward and swung his fist into what was left of the smirking scoundrel's teeth.

And, oh, had it felt satisfying. This time he *decided* to swing again.

José stumbled back, completely caught off guard by the attack.

Price didn't care. He had wanted nothing more than to smash the arrogant prick's face for some time. Before he could get another good hit in, Kit's angry voice sounded behind him.

"Price, that's enough!"

Price backed a step but remained poised to fight, lest the rotten wank decided to try to return the punishment.

José regained his feet and spit a swatch of blood from his mouth.

Kit stood beside Price looking directly to José, "As of this moment, you're fired. You shall remove yourself from this property at first light."

From there, Kit walked smoothly past the filth and into the house after Lily, without looking back.

Price circled around to stand between José and the house, crossed his arms and stared him down coldly.

José simply spit another swatch of blood from his mouth, used his sleeve to rid the red rivulets from his chin and cocked a bloody smile Price's way. Price remained in control this time, not rising to the bait.

He watched José's form fade deeper into the shadows as he retreated to the barns. Tomorrow's long day of packing and travel would now be made more tiring, because one thing was certain, Price would be sleeping with one eye open this night.

Chapter 23

José didn't waste any time leaving the ranch. Price had been surprised when the man made good on Kit's threat and rode while the stars still filled the dawn sky. He rode out on a Stone branded horse, of course, but Kit didn't make a stir of it. She was merely happy to foresee a future where she didn't have to suffer that man's constant rude behavior.

Even though the threat of José causing trouble was over, Kit had insisted on bringing Lily along. She worried for the young woman's safety with both of them away.

García met up with them along the road and took Kit's place at the reins of the wagon. Kit detested driving the wagon. For some reason she had insisted upon it when Price offered to drive instead. Odd, that. He couldn't think too much on her strange behavior, however, his mind was too preoccupied that his former plans of seducing Kit into loving him seemed to be shot.

Even if he could somehow repair the damage from their spat at the corral last night, they now had plenty of chaperones to ensure no close company between the two of them.

Price wasn't sure how he could win her over anyway. Nothing he did seemed to stir her. She would go to the town dance tomorrow night and find someone to marry. It wouldn't be him, and he would be trapped in this hell of longing forever.

They didn't stop in Canyon. Kit hadn't thought it a good idea. She was trying to protect Lily, he knew. It wouldn't make a difference, however, as he was certain the girl's reputation would be just as sullied in Oneida, being it was only the next town over.

It was slow riding with a wagon and the sun was already slipping behind the boardwalk buildings on the main strip when they arrived at the town. Despite the evening hour, Onieda bustled with activity; giving its best imitation of a real city, rather than the frontier town it was.

~

A yawn escaped Kit as they pulled in front of the Yellow Rose Hotel at the far side of town. "Away from the riff-raff," the snooty luggage carrier who met them at the door informed them. She was glad now that García had convinced her to allow Price to stay behind at the coach and stable rental. She didn't particularly like leaving her horse in the care of someone else, but she could trust Price.

All the speaking of her contesting plans to García along the road to town wore her out. She was relieved García approved of her plan to host a ranchero contesting event in way of raising immediate funds for the ranch. Not only did he approve, he seemed quite excited about the prospect. He made a lot of good suggestions and she was glad for his support, but she wasn't accustomed to an entire day of talking.

She also wasn't accustomed to driving a wagon, which she had done until García had met up with them around noon. Her back still ached from it. She wouldn't have had to drive at all if she'd taken Price up on his offer to drive. She had wanted to leap upon the opportunity, but when he offered, Lily had smiled delightfully in a way that seemed awfully inviting.

She wasn't about to subject herself to the nauseum of hearing those two flirt and banter with one another all day. She was glad Price hadn't questioned her fumbling awkward reason for driving the wagon. Blessedly, Lily had kept her mouth shut for a change, only offering Kit a knowing arch of her brow.

Inside the hotel, García graciously declined Kingston's hospitality and footed the bill for all four of them himself, which Kit was immensely grateful for. The hotel overseer looked uncomfortable with the arrangement in Kingston's absence, but he didn't argue. Especially when García pointed out how it would appear inappropriate for an unwed young lady to accept such an invitation, under the circumstances.

The circumstances being that Kit was not betrothed to Mr. Kingston, though he seemed keen on telling the world they were. García agreed she should not accept his proposal if she felt they were so ill-suited for one another. The fact that the man hadn't even offered for her yet but had taken it upon himself to spread word of their engagement was rather an irksome situation she would have to deal with. And soon.

She hoped to escape to her room and evade such dealings for the evening, but her luck wasn't to be.

"Ah, Miss Stone, you've arrived!"

Kit hoped her groan hadn't been audible.

"Mr. Kingston," she greeted and summoned the strength to smile.

"And this must be the rest of your party?" he asked, taking Lily's hand and brushing a kiss along the back of her knuckles. "The unexpected company of an additional beauty is never unwelcome." He flashed his large white teeth, in what Kit was certain he believed to be a charming smile.

Lily seemed to think it charming as well, if her giggle was any indication.

"My uncle-er-that is, García, and Price have also accompanied me. Do not worry, however, García transferred the rooms over into his name. It would have been unpardonably rude to accept your generosity, under the circumstances." Kit borrowed her uncle's line and decided to initiate the process of unentangling herself from Kingston as quickly as possible.

A look of irritation crossed his features so quickly, Kit wasn't entirely sure she had seen it at all. Perhaps she'd imagined it. Between her exhaustion and dramatic spectacle with José the night before, it was entirely possible.

"Well, that wasn't necessary, but I quite understand." Kingston's smile was tight. "I do hope you settle in well. I look forward to seeing you tomorrow."

He brushed smoothly past her and Lily and out the lobby door before Kit could address the engagement rumors. She sighed; tomorrow would be soon enough for that she supposed.

The next morning, Lily's excited chatter filled the room, waking Kit from a much-desired slumber. She pulled the pillow and sheet—both of which were cleaner and more comfortable than what she had been forced to use back at the ranch—over her head in an attempt to block out the girl's yapping and snuggled into the soft, cotton-stuffed mattress.

Her comfort was short-lived, however.

"Hurry, and wake! I want to explore the town!" Lily tore the sheets back, stealing the warmth from her cocoon along with her hope to procrastinate. She whipped her pillow across the room, hitting her target squarely in the chest.

Her target simply emitted a laugh.

Ugh, Kit should have requested separate rooms.

"What's wrong? You hoping if you hide out in the room all day, you won't have to run into Mr. Kingston again?" Lily asked slyly.

Yes, that was exactly what she hoped to do. She was in no hurry to have that uncomfortable discussion with Kingston today. Not to mention, things were still unsettling with Price. She wasn't sure *what* was going on between them, but she decided it would be in her best interests if she avoided him as well.

It was a far-reaching wish, she knew. For Price would be around as he *always* was. Kit wished she knew why she felt this strange distance between them.

It didn't even make sense. They had never been particularly close in the first place.

She didn't like these confusing feelings, one bit. In fact, she decided she was quite agitated with the man. How could he throw out a marriage proposal in jest? Then turn around and kiss her dizzy and senseless? Then claim to feel nothing for her? And have the indecency to act disgruntled with *her*!

Apparently, men were creatures prone to dramatics. Her brothers had always been that way, and she realized now the affliction must curse the lot of them.

"Come now," Lily cajoled from the window, where she had the curtains drawn to overlook the town below. "You know you want to meet with that ranger fellow to find out news about your brother."

Curse the red-headed fiend; she knew just what would get Kit moving.

It was late morning by the time she and Lily made their way into town. Lily had tried to convince Kit to don a dress, but she'd rejected that absurdity. She couldn't be seen about town in her only dress and then wear that only dress to the dance later that evening. Lily had given her a pointed look that said Kit would regret that decision, but Kit sincerely doubted so.

To Lily's credit, however, she hadn't seemed embarrassed to be out and about with a lady who looked more like a vaquero. Kit knew most ladies—at least the ones she had met at the academy—would have been repulsed by the idea. Lily always surprised her and earned more and more of her respect. Kit would like to think them friends, but she couldn't negate the idea that perhaps Lily was only acting as a good employee and didn't want to offend her employer.

Although, if that were the case, one would think she would behave more obediently.

Kit left Lily behind in a hat shop, while she continued to the sheriff's office and post office with her letters. She had a letter for home she'd leave with the post and a letter to pass on through the rangers for her brother.

Much to her surprise, as she readied to step through the entranceway of the sheriff's office, Price stepped out. She nearly lost her footing as they collided, if not for his arms reactively reaching to steady her. She hadn't been expecting to see him again so soon, nor in such a close manner. The spice of his shaving soap tempted her to lean into him.

That thought was disrupted when he callously released her and stepped aside. Jarred awake from her foolish mind-wandering, she tried to recover her dignity. Obviously, Price was over giving "lessons." Perhaps he truly had never been affected at all. The thought stung. Especially since she had formed somewhat of a tendre for him in the process. No. He appeared rigid as ever.

"No word of Logan. If that's what you're here for."

"Oh." She nodded. Their stilted conversation was unusual, Kit wished she knew how to return to the former ease between them.

He seemed to be waiting for her to say more or to retreat.

She held up her folded, sealed parchment, "I'm just delivering this, in hopes Logan's friend may pass it on to him if opportunity arises."

Price seemed to search her face, for what she didn't know, but she almost thought he looked wistful. As if he missed being near to her as well. His demeanor changed abruptly as he asked, "Did you find Kingston, okay? Or should I say, your fiancé?"

Anger swelled in Kit's chest, blooming red in her cheeks, "As if I'd marry that pompous swell!"

Price looked surprised, "You didn't accept his proposal, then?"

"No, I did not accept. That is to say, I would not have, if he'd bothered to ask in the first place, which he didn't."

Price's smile just rankled her more. That he found sport in her tangled mess was irritating in the extreme. More irritating, however, was Kingston for spreading such falsehoods all across town. During a celebration that may provide her the only opportunity to find another prospective husband.

"That's where I'm off to after this and one other stop. I have to find the presumptuous scoundrel and reject the proposal he never delivered."

Price smiled and bowed his head slightly, "Good luck." Then he walked away.

Good luck, indeed. Ha!

He was supposed to be helping Kit initiate this ranching endeavor, but apparently, he would be no help at all to her in this.

Kit pushed those problems from her mind and entered the small compartment that made up the sheriff's quarters.

The sheriff sat behind the desk sipping off a mug of coffee and chatting with two other men. One of which was García, the other Kit recognized as Ranger McCulloch. The sheriff lowered his coffee and placed it back onto the desk when he noticed her in the doorway, and the other men directed their attention to her as well.

"Why, Miss Stone, hello." Ranger McCulloch tipped his hat toward her.

"Kit? Is everything well?" García appeared worried.

"Yes. I-I just wished to speak with Ranger McCulloch about Logan," she smiled sheepishly. "It appears I wasn't the only one who wished so."

García smiled comfortingly, "No word as of yet."

Kit nodded solemnly, not wishing to explain she'd already received such information from Price.

"I have a letter. I'd like to get it to Logan if possible. It's rather important."

García studied her.

She cast a smile García's way to assure him all was well before turning back to the ranger, "I was hoping you would know of a way to get it to him?"

"As a matter of fact, I'm sending two rangers north this afternoon, in hopes of locating him."

"You are?" She smiled brilliantly. Relief coursed through her. More rangers helping Logan would ensure his safety as well as speed up the process of him returning home. "Thank you, sir." She handed him her letter and excused herself.

Partway down the boardwalk, García called to her to wait up for him. Once he reached her, she smiled.

"Thank you," she said, "I know it was your doing why more rangers are being sent to help Logan."

"Actually, that was Price's doing."

"Oh? Oh... I shall be sure to thank him, then."

"I wanted to speak with you. You made it seem urgent Logan receive your letter. Is there a problem you haven't spoken with me about that I can help you with?"

Kit smiled, "Well, perhaps you can help. I was hoping for Logan's free legal expertise. You know he loves to study law in his free time in hopes of becoming a solicitor one day. I-well, I was hoping he could help me figure out a way to keep the ranch without marrying... No one seems all that interested in me," she admitted, embarrassment and shame evident in her voice. "Except for that awful Whitney Kingston fellow. And I simply can't abide shackling myself to a man like him for life."

García smiled, "I understand. Tonight the other ranchers will be in attendance at the fandango and will be able to meet you."

"I highly doubt that will improve my attractiveness."

García laughed, "Don't underestimate yourself, Kit Stone."

Chapter 24

Back at the hotel, Kit stirred restlessly waiting for Lily to return. *What was taking the girl so long?* She nervously ran her thumb over the soft frayed sleeve's hem of the only dress she had packed with her to Texas. The plaid was dingy and faded, but worse, she had outgrown the gown since last she'd worn it.

Had García *informed* her of the inheritance stipulations prior to leaving for Texas, she might have packed something more suitable!

If only Lily would return. She needed help fixing the dress and she was sure Lily would have an idea or two. The girl was positively obsessed with fashion. She waited impatiently for a time, until she suspected she was wearing a groove into the floor from her pacing. She tugged the silk brocade curtain over to peek at the town below; the fiesta appeared to already be underway.

Never mind waiting for Lily. The girl probably became distracted by a ribbon shop or some such, Kit released an exasperated breath. She would simply change back into her trousers and don her best shirt. She would rather look out of place in clothes she was comfortable in than appear to have had an attempt at looking pretty and fallen short.

Angrily, she shoved the shirt ends into her pants and belted the waist. She smoothed wrinkles from the shirt and assessed her form in the long glass mirror against the wall. She sighed; it would have to do. Just then the she heard the turning of the doorknob and Lily's giggling from behind the door.

Of course, now Lily appears.

To her surprise, however, Price entered the room with Lily. Their eyes caught as well as her breath. Then his eyes moved disapprovingly over her attire.

"Is that what you plan to wear to the town dance?"

Kit crossed her arms like armor, and defended, "Why not? This is my nice calico."

Price scoffed, "No, it's your *brother's* nice calico."

"I think the color looks rather fetching on me." She raised her chin a notch.

"Indeed," sarcasm dripped from Price's words. "You know all the other ladies will be attired in dresses, right?"

A growl escaped her lips, "Of course I know that."

Price and Lily exchanged a guilty look.

Lily giggled, "Oh, Mr. Price, don't be silly. Miss Stone was simply waiting for me to assist her into her dress."

"I *was* waiting, but the only dress—" Lily cut off Kit's explanation for why she couldn't or wouldn't wear her only dress.

"So sorry to have kept you waiting, Boss. But I'm here now and we can get started. You'll make a grander appearance if you show up late anyway."

Kit mumbled, "A grand entrance is exactly what I don't want."

Realization dawned on Kit. Lily was saving her from another humiliating situation. She sure hoped the girl had a few tricks at the ready, because once she saw the rag Kit had planned to wear, she was going to have her work cut out for her if she truly planned to make Kit presentable.

"Well, I'll leave you two ladies to get ready."

Before Price could make his exit, Kit called to him, "Could you tell García not to wait for us? He planned to escort us to supper before the dance, but now, we'll most certainly be late."

Price bowed, looking every bit of the Englishman he was, "Of course. And I'll arrange for supper to be sent up to you both." He winked, "Wouldn't want you too famished for the dancing this evening."

"Stop fidgeting, you look lovely," Lily scolded as they neared the town hall where the dance was being held.

It was cloudy and no stars lit the night sky, the only lighting came from oil lamps hung outside of the businesses along the board walk. A night breeze chilled her bare arms, despite the humidity. A loose wisp of hair Lily had artfully placed blew across her face causing an itch.

"Well, it's all this fluff you insisted on. I can barely walk, how am I going to dance?" Kit complained, irritably. "A better question, how will we all fit, dressed in as many petticoats as this?"

Lily laughed, "Relax. Besides, you're not nearly as 'fluffed' as you should be."

"The back of the collar is rubbing at my neck."

"You should be thankful I found such a conservative gown," Lily admonished while tugging her own low-cut bodice over the abundant swells of her breasts. "You don't quite have enough to hold up this style anyway."

Kit rolled her eyes.

"You'd simply be displaying your collar bone."

"Thank you for yet another allude to my small chest. My confidence is positively climbing."

Lily chuckled again, "Honestly, you look beautiful. That sky-blue color fairly makes your eyes pop. And the narrow V neckline with the frothy bit of material at the center is appealing, yet elegant. I've created a masterpiece of you, considering what I had to work with."

"Again," Kit drolled sarcastically, "thank you."

"Absolutely. Now, please do not ruin the image I've created with your gruff manner and awkward fidgeting. For goodness sake, stop brushing the flared sleeves up. They are supposed to be loose and flowy."

"Well, every time a breeze comes through, they wave and tickle my arms."

Lily shook her head, "You act as though you've never been draped in finery, yet you come from a wealthy family. I thought you attended balls and such at those fancy schools you attended?"

"I did," Kit spat, "but I never enjoyed them."

"Hold still a moment, a pin is loosening from your hair. Who knew it was so heavy?"

"That's another thing, every time I move my head I feel as though my hair will tumble down from this arrangement you concocted."

Lily ignored her complaint, "Did you never have your hair styled before either?"

"No, I've always tended to my own hair."

"Such a pity. All that gorgeous mass of hair always hidden in a braid or a spinster's knot."

"My hair is brown, not pretty, and the 'mass' is a nuisance."

"I doubt your future husband will feel that way," Lily smiled in her cat-like way.

Uncomfortable with the turn of topic, Kit pulled the handle of the door to open it, "Let's just get this over with."

The room was packed with people. Normally Kit would have preferred less of a crowd, but in this moment, she was glad for it; it allowed her to slip in unnoticed.

Lily's perky attitude deflated slightly as she observed the room, "I suppose I shouldn't be surprised to see people from Canyon here tonight. It's not often anyone in these parts gets to celebrate in such magnificent style. Oh, I see Mrs. Randall! She was always kind to me. I think I'll go say hi. Will you be kay?"

Kit nodded her head yes. She wouldn't allow her cowardice to spoil Lily's good time, "Of course. I need to search out Mr. Kingston anyway. I still haven't had the opportunity to reject his *kind offer*..."

Lily smiled, "Good luck."

Kit waved her off, "We'll meet up later."

As it turned out, she didn't have to look for Kingston. He found her.

"Ah, Miss Stone, what a pleasure."

We'll see, she thought.

"Hello, Mr. Kingston."

"Have you only just arrived?"

"Yes. I'm afraid my evening was somewhat delayed."

"Well, it was worth the wait." His eyes gleamed and a wolfish smile lit his face.

How was she to go about this, without offending the man?

207

"I had hoped to speak with you. I think there has been a misunderstanding."

"Oh?" His demeanor changed from smiling to defensive. Kit supposed there was no hope for it.

"The town seems to be under the impression that you and I are engaged to be married. When I have accepted no proposal and have not declared as much."

Kingston shrugged, "I hardly see that as a problem, Miss Stone. We would have announced our intentions soon enough. I thought it would ease your presence here if all knew you were under my protection."

Lord save her from all the male protection the world seemed to think she needed.

"Mr. Kingston, let me put this bluntly: I have not accepted a proposal—"

"Ah, I see, your feminine vanity has been offended. Shall I make a show of it then? Would that please you?"

"I beg of you do not." Kit ceased him from attempting a bended knee. "Please allow me to finish. I have not accepted a proposal from you and nor do I plan to."

Kingston's smile disappeared and he looked taken aback.

"Do I make myself clear?" Kit asked poignantly.

He dropped her hand as if bitten by a snake, "I'll not offer again, Miss Stone."

You didn't offer the first time, she bit her tongue to prevent herself from replying.

"I think you're making a big mistake," he stated, before straightening the cuffs of his sleeves and walking away.

She sighed, relieved the confrontation was over.

"Kingston didn't look too happy." Price's voice sounded suddenly at her side, startling her.

"Well, it was the man's own fault for spreading such tales."

"He didn't take the rejection well, huh?"

Kit snorted, "Oh, he's positively heartbroken over it, can't you tell?" She indicated with a nod in the direction of Kingston, already flashing his smooth smile at another lady who fluttered her fan and batted her lashes in return.

The corner of Price's lips quirked up, offering the barest hint of a smile, as was his way, "Care to dance?"

"Oh, Price, you know I have two left feet when it comes to dancing." Except the end of the word dancing came out loudly and drawn out in her surprise at being pulled onto the main floor.

Suddenly she was on the floor with a flurry of dancers. "Price!" she yelled in a harsh whisper. She hoped it sounded threatening, because she planned to do him bodily harm after all this was done.

The arrogant man didn't appear at all alarmed. Not that he would lower himself so indignantly as to emit feeling, but she could read the laughter in the glitter of his eyes as he swung her around.

It was a scotch reel, so the steps weren't intricate, but they were fast. Most of the ladies were laughing and moving fluidly through the steps. Kit couldn't laugh with enjoyment, however, as she was too concentrated on keeping her unusually slipper-clad-feet from skidding across the wood floor or tripping over the odd, uneven plank.

It was bad enough dancing with Price—someone she knew—but then it came time for her hand off and she had to join another group of dancers. She feared her attempt to return a friendly grin at the welcoming new faces came across as more of a grimace, and the endeavor nearly cost her her pride.

She fumbled with the recovery of the steps in time to be handed off once more into Price's safe hands.

The cheeky Englishman had the nerve to deliver a winning smile as he said, "You weren't lying when you claimed to be an abysmal dancer."

Kit grit her teeth and fervently hoped the music would cease and bring her mortifying shame to an end. Her prayers were answered as the musicians lifted bows from strings, leaving the paired dancers on the floor in wait of the next song.

Except her, she decided, she was getting out of there!

"You look beautiful tonight."

And just like that, her feet adhered to the floor instead of making quick their escape from the dancing area. Price's words molded over her like a soft, worn quilt.

"Th-thank you." She nervously touched the back of her hair where it tumbled down from the clips that held it pinned away from her face.

The first notes of the Waltz struck, and Price extended his hand to her. "You don't have to know this one very well. I'll guide you."

Her mind had apparently turned to mush from one silly compliment, for she took his hand and followed his lead.

He took her clasped hand into the air, elbows bent, and pulled her closer with his other hand. Her free arm extended to rest her hand on his shoulder, while his arm rested against the side of her breast, hand at her back. His left leg came forward, guiding her right leg back, then over a step, and forward once more, creating a box.

As he came forward again, and she back, he said, "You should bend your knees a little. It's just like riding a horse."

She quirked a brow at that statement.

"You would never sit stiff in the saddle, would you? No. You would let your body find the rhythm of the horse. It's the same thing."

Her brows scrunched together, thoughtfully.

"Don't think, Kit, just feel."

He stepped a little closer than was proper and she felt his muscled thigh against her person as he came forward, guiding her back and to the side and over again as if melded together; as if one body. She became lost in the feel of him against her, like in a trance as she floated to the music in his arms. She felt comfortable in her own skin for the first time on a dance floor and was able to enjoy it.

Chapter 25

Price was loathed to let her go after the reel. Her cheeks flush with the exertion of the dance, and probably a bit of hostile displeasure toward him, had his mind imagining all other activities that would enflame her cheeks so—namely those of the bedroom variety.

He loved all the different facets that made her who she was; the strong, bossy side of her, the compassionate, nurturing side, her awkward shyness in social gatherings, and the rarely-glimpsed soft, feminine side she displayed tonight. She was fearless, his Kit. He knew she was out of her element, yet she ventured forth, head held high for the sake of duty, like a regal queen.

God was she beautiful.

The pale blue of her dress only distinguished how silver her eyes were in comparison. Framed with the dark lashes sweeping her cheeks, the contrast was striking.

She wasn't aware of these features about herself, or how they affected any male looking on. And when the Waltz struck up, he quickly drew her in before she could decline. More than simply because he wasn't ready to give her up to the other gentlemen he was sure would be lining up to dance with her soon, but because he wanted her to know, wanted her to *feel*, how beautiful she was.

She shouldn't be hiding in the corners of ballrooms. She shouldn't have to accept marriage proposals out of desperation. She should know her worth and her power, and have as many choices as she desired.

And maybe—maybe—she would discover he was one of those choices and choose him.

He pulled her closer as they moved to the steps of the waltz and as she began to relax, she transformed in his arms. Her eyes closed, she smiled on a sigh as she surrendered herself to the rhythm of their bodies.

And it was nearly his undoing.

The song was coming to a close, he would have to release her.

"Thank you," she smiled up at him as they came to a standstill. "You were right, as soon as I imagined I was riding, the movements felt natural."

He inhaled a sharp breath and tried to suppress the erotic images conjuring in his mind from her innocent words. Tried not to allow them to stir his primitive desires.

Instead, he raised her silk-gloved hand to his lips and pressed a kiss.

"I wish I could dance the rest of the evening with only you," she confided.

He wanted her to look up at him, wanted to see her eyes. Was she saying she wanted something more? Did she have feelings for him?

García joined them then, however, and claimed her for the next reel. Price made his way over to the refreshments table and watched as Kit twirled around the dance floor, seemingly more comfortable and even enjoying herself. Every once in a while her eyes would seek him out and they would share a smile before she found her next circle of hands to join.

Price was feeling quite optimistic. Perhaps she had feelings for him after all.

"She has no idea what you're thinking." Lily appeared beside him, arms folded across her chest and smiling smugly.

"That obvious, am I?"

"To everyone, but her, I'm sure."

"Care to dance?"

Lily accepted his proffered hand and he led her out on the dance floor to join the merriment. He endeavored not to be rude to his dancing partners, but his eyes wouldn't cease searching for Kit.

Lily called him out on it, "You're not being very discreet, you know."

"My apologies. I shall strive to do better."

Once the dance finished, he and Lily departed once more to the refreshments table. He filled two cups with lemonade and offered one to her.

"How chivalrous of you."

Price laughed at the girl's wit. "It is the best apology I can manage at the moment in regard to my poor performance on the dance floor."

He let his eyes scan the room while he sipped, "Do you suppose she went out for some air? I don't see her anywhere."

"No," Lily replied, then smirked, "I think you're not looking hard enough through the throng of gentlemen gathered near the other table."

Like a kick to his guts, he spied the party of men Lily indicated, and sure enough Kit was at the center, being fawned over by them all. As he started forward, he felt Lily's hand at his chest.

"Whoa there, English. You can't go barging over like a jealous lover. Because you're not her lover. Are you?" she asked with a mulish tilt to her head, reminding him that others would believe just that if he went over and caused a scene. Thus, ruining Kit's reputation.

The rest of his evening was spent watching Kit take turn after turn on the dance floor with one cowboy after another.

García tried to approach him, but even he sensed his foul mood and didn't converse long.

He had thought Kit might be considering him, but obviously he had been wrong. As usual, he was just her learning tool. He watched sourly as smiles she had delivered to him earlier were now offered as little gifts to the men crowding before her.

To make matters worse, Kingston meandered his way over to him. Looking in Kit's direction, he smiled and said, "Women are fickle beasts, aren't they?"

No, not fickle, he thought. *Not Kit.* It was his fault for reading more into her words than she had intended. And he wasn't about to stand here and demean her with the fool Kingston.

"Sounds as though you're a bit sore after being rejected. Do have a care, Kingston, or people will fear you felt a great deal more for her than you did." Price adjusted his cravat and tugged his lapels into place before walking away.

~

"Oh, so you own the ranch southeast of mine," Kit asked Mr. O'Rien.

"Yes," the young man answered. He was near the same age as Kit, perhaps a year or so younger. Kit wondered why he would be looking to marry already. If he were inflicted with love for her, she might understand, but she knew that wasn't the case. She decided simply to find out.

"Listen," she started as they strolled along the edges of the dance floor. Kit had needed a reprieve from the dancing. The unfamiliar slippers pinched her feet something awful. "Why are you here?"

He smiled kindly, his youthful eyes intelligent, "I suppose 'for the town celebration' isn't the answer to what you're referring to."

She released an airy puff of laughter, "No. I realize my ranch comes with a lot of land, but it also comes with a lot of debt. Are you truly ready to sacrifice your future for land?"

"You're referring to my age, now, I recollect. And yet, here you are, ready to make that very same sacrifice."

"True, but I'm not like most women, I suppose."

"No, I see you are not." His words warmed with the compliment.

Kit blushed.

"Since you seem to be a straight shooter, I'll be honest with you as well. My pa died six years ago, and I had to step up and learn to fill his shoes. Then, my ma died little more than a year past. I have a sister...she's just a girl yet. I'm looking for—"

"For a woman to step into her mama's shoes," Kit finished for him.

He nodded affirmatively while looking down at his boots as he walked.

"I'm afraid, I'm not that woman."

Seeing his solemn look, she added, "I doubt I'll make a good wife let alone a good mother. I just don't think that situation would be fair for any of us. Including your sister."

"I appreciate your honesty," he finally said.

"Likewise," she smiled.

She happened to catch a glimpse of Price across the room. He was with Lily *again*. Seemed as though those two hadn't left each other's side all evening. Apparently, he preferred the attention of big-bosomed redheads. He hadn't come to rescue her from all the unwanted attentions of the many ranchers all evening, instead he had been too busy flirting with her maid.

Out of the corner of her eye, she noticed Leighton O'Rien smiling.

"What?" she demanded testily.

"I see you weren't entirely honest with me."

"What do you mean?"

"I understand why an arrangement between us isn't agreeable. But you've appeared disinterested in all the men here tonight. Save one." He grinned and nodded in Price's direction.

Her face heated and she was certain she must look crimson from the tips of her ears to her toes.

"No. That is—he is just a friend. And my ranch foreman." Uncomfortable with the conversation, Kit attempted to divert it, "Truthfully I'm hoping to avoid marriage entirely."

O'Rien's blue eyes lit with surprise, "But I thought you couldn't inherit unless..."

"Yes, that is indeed the current stipulation, however, I am hopeful my solicitor will discover a way around that detail. Especially if I can raise enough funds to pay the debt."

He smiled, "You look awfully certain. Have a plan in mind?"

"Why, I'm so glad you asked," she replied smartly. "I am putting on an event. A competition between ranchers to show off their prowess. Roping calves, wrestling down steers, bustin' broncs," she shrugged, "those sorts of things."

She continued, "There will be cash prizes for the top three winners in each category."

O'Rien looked surprised again, but decidedly enthused, "Do you have the means to put all of this on? Where will you get the horses?"

"I don't have all of the exact details worked out yet. But it's going to happen. And soon."

"I hope I'll be invited?"

"Of course," Kit smiled. She decided she liked Leighton O'Rien. If she did end up forced to marry, he was the best candidate of all the ranchers she'd met tonight.

If only she could get Price out of her head.

She twisted her head in search of the man constantly occupying her thoughts of late and found him once again on the dance floor. And once again with Lily. They appeared fixated on one another.

An unfamiliar emotion rolled over Kit.

She turned to Leighton who was holding out his hand, "Have your toes recovered enough for a dance?"

"I'm sorry, suddenly I'm not feeling all that well. I think it best if I retire early. Excuse me, please."

She didn't wait for his response. She knew it was unpardonably rude, but she had to get out of there. She had thought Price might have felt something for her, but it was now abundantly obvious he was attracted to women of Lily's caliber.

Kit could never compare when it came to physical attributes. Lily was everything men looked for in a woman, curvy in all the right places, a flirtatious demeanor and biddable nature. Kit had no curves whatsoever, didn't know the first thing about flirting—and didn't care to learn—and had too much of a stubborn streak to ever be considered biddable. All in all, she was an unattractive prospect as a wife or anything else...

She dashed out of the hall and trekked swiftly down the boardwalk, leading back to the Yellow Rose Hotel. In her hurried state, she didn't hear the boots hitting the boards behind her.

Chapter 26

Kit felt a hand curl around her arm. She swung around in alarm only to see Price glowering at her.

"Where are you going?" he demanded, as if he had any right to.

She ripped her arm from his grasp, "Where does it look like I'm going? I'm tired, I'm headed back to my room."

"Are you meeting someone there?" His green hazel eyes were piercing but it was his accusation that cut the most.

"How dare you imply such," she spat defensively.

"That's what your *lessons* were for, weren't they?" His jaw clenched.

She gritted her teeth and shook with the amount of control it took not to punch him. Instead, she said, "If I was meeting someone, I don't know why that should be any of your concern."

"You should know that William Caid's ranch is in just as much jeopardy as yours. And Josiah Fleurs is too old for you," he began listing the gentlemen ranchers who had sought her out tonight.

"Oh, for the love of—I'm not meeting anyone, I told you!"

"And Leighton O'Rien, you seemed pretty chummy with him. Did he mention he isn't so much in the market for a wife as he is a mother for his eleven-year-old sister?"

"As a matter of fact, he did. Whatever I choose to do, and whoever I chose to do it with, is of no concern of yours! Now, why don't you get back to your precious Miss Perkins. I'm sure she's growing lonely without your undivided attention upon her."

With that, she fled as quickly as the smooth-bottomed slippers would allow back to the safety of the hotel.

And he did not pursue her.

∼

Curled up under the blankets on her bed—even though it was far too warm for comfort—Kit feigned sleep when Lily arrived back from the dance. Her friend was discourteously loud, which Kit was certain to be intentional in order to wake her.

Kit ignored her.

Price may have confided in Lily about her suspicions of them having romantical feelings toward one another, and that wasn't a conversation Kit was ready to have. She first needed time to sort out *her* feelings. If Lily *wasn't* aware of her and Price's confrontation outside, her friend probably wanted to chat the night away about what a wonderful evening she'd had dancing with Price. And Kit wasn't about to listen to *that*.

Kit tried to sleep in earnest, but to no avail. Nothing felt right. Her blanket was too itchy, she was too angry with Price and Lily—as irrational as she knew the anger to be—and the rain was all wrong.

Normally, she found the steady pour of rain soothing, but tonight even it was out of rhythm. Somewhere nearby outside, the rain was beating down on what sounded like a sheet of tin, perhaps an old saw blade sitting out at the mill nearby behind the town. Like an orchestra out of tune, the uneven pitter-patter further grated Kit's nerves.

She tossed and turned for hours until she was sure Lily was sleeping, then rose from her bed to pace. She needed an outlet for her agitation, and she needed escape from the itchy coverlet.

Why had Price been so angry with *her*, anyway? *He* was the one who kept changing his attitude as often as a newt shed its skin. He would look at her in a way no man ever had before, make her feel things she never thought to feel...and then he would turn around and treat her as though she were a troublesome child he was watching over.

Were the feelings only on her end? That seemed to make the most sense. The confusion hadn't come about until her insides had started fluttering like a net full of butterflies whenever she looked at Price. She wished she could return to feeling nothing for him. She wasn't even sure what exactly she *was* feeling for him.

Was this attraction?

Or was it love?

All she knew was she was sick of feeling twisted up like a rag being rung out to dry. It wasn't pleasant. She was usually sure of herself. She came to this dance to discover her options of marriageable men, to make a good impression, and hopefully find an ideal partner to help her run the ranch.

But all of the men had paled in comparison to Price. With Price, she could speak about Livvy, her brothers, her parents...and it was comforting, because she knew he shared her love and fondness for them. He was her brothers' friend, but he was hers, too. She was sure he would rather have been helping Luke along with Logan, but instead he was here...helping her.

At her brother's request, she reminded herself.

Still, all her brother had asked was that Price keep her safe. Price needn't have lifted her spirits during the moments homesickness got the better of her. He needn't have assisted her with trying to find a husband. He needn't have taken her riding and allowed her to make sense of the ranch's financial tangle.

He didn't solve her problems, though he easily could have—he was that smart. He believed in her to do it on her own and he'd wanted her to believe as well.

He grumbled and worried for her safety at times, but when she broke out the mustang, he hadn't protested or tried to stop her. He never intervened or tried to take over the running of her ranch, though he could have in the beginning and the hands would have followed him over her. He disagreed with her decisions sometimes, but he never prevented her from carrying out her plans. Instead, after resigning to her decisions, he always lent his support.

When Lily came, he was the first to step up and disregard her reputation as a fallen woman. He was kind and patient with Samuel. He was intelligent and strived to ease the communication barrier between her and the vaqueros who didn't speak English.

He rarely showed his emotions on his face. One had to pay close attention to the subtle movements. The simple quirk of humor at the corner of his mouth after delivering a smooth quip. The way his watchful eyes widened in congratulating Kit on every small victory.

The way he always seemed to sense what she needed in her moments of weakness. His hand at her back to give her strength. Or slipping his hand discreetly in hers when she needed to know she wasn't alone. When she found herself in over her head, he was always at her side.

Kit couldn't imagine any of the men she'd met tonight ever being all those things. None of them would ever take the time to understand her the way Price did. Would they let her fight her own battles just to see her face when she won? Would they stand beside her running the ranch or would they stand in front of her?

She knew where Price would stand. He would be where she most needed him, before she even knew, most likely.

But would he want to stand with her? Until death did them part?

Aghh, Kit was getting nowhere with this repetitive monologue. She needed sleep. She lay down, this time peeling the itchy coverlet off the bed entirely and pulling only the soft quilt over her in its place. Then she closed her eyes and hoped for sleep to come and offer respite from her mind's constant workings.

Chapter 27

The rain persisted all hours of the night and into morning. Kit must have finally drifted off but was rudely awakened by an urgent knocking at the door.

"Kit. Kit! Wake up!" Price yelled from the other side.

Bleary-eyed, she crept to the door silently as not to wake Lily who had begun to stir. Still in her night gown, she only cracked the door, "What do you want, you ogre? It is ill-mannered to wake ladies from their beds before the sun has risen!" she shouted in an angry whisper.

"The town is about to flood; we've got precious little time to get out of here."

Her sleepy mind tried to process his alarm and make sense of his words, "The town is about to flood?"

"Yes. Apparently, that is common here." Price shook his head, clearly unimpressed with the idea that people built their town in such a location.

She blinked at him, still dazed with sleep.

"Get dressed. Wake Lily. And both of you hurry. García went to hook up the wagon. I'm going to meet him and grab our horses. Meet us outside."

Lily joined Kit at the cracked opening of the door, "I'm awake."

Kit finally snapped to. She nodded to Price, clicked the door shut, and she and Lily got to work.

Packing hadn't taken them long. When they reached the bottom of the stairs, no man occupied the lobby desk to assist them. They carried their bags out the door and gasped when they saw rivulets of water already filling the streets. Nearly every bit of the street was covered in water and it was rising, already halfway level to the boardwalk.

García drove the skittish horses to the door. Price hopped down from his horse to throw their trunks into the wagon, then helped Lily into the wagon.

"You riding?"

Kit answered with a nod. When she stepped down into the pooling water, it submerged the entire bottom half of her boots. She felt the force of the water pushing against her with each step. Her horse waited anxiously for her, nodding his head, and sending his reins flopping. She grabbed hold of them, swung up into the saddle and eased Blue forward.

They rode at as quickly of a pace as safety would allow and when they were free of the water, clipped along at an even faster pace, each soaked and in a hurry to get home. Everyone was too uncomfortable to make conversation, which was all the better for Kit who hoped to avoid it anyway.

García offered to accompany them the entire way, but Kit shook her head. It wasn't necessary and his clothes were still damp as well. She assured him they would be fine and made plans for her to visit his ranch soon.

Kit was happy to let Price drive the wagon. She heard he and Lily whispering occasionally, but she was too tired to care. She allowed Blue to clop along behind the wagon and tried not to think about Price and Lily's budding relationship.

Bernardo and some other vaqueros eagerly met them as soon as they crossed the arched entryway to the ranch, to assist them with the horses.

"You've made it in time for supper," Bernardo smiled in greeting as he took the reins of her horse.

She tried to force a smile in return.

"You don't look well, señorita Stone." His brown eyes studied her, filled with concern.

"Onieda flooded and we had to leave in a hurry. The rain followed us all the way to Canyon. We're all soaked clear through and exhausted to boot."

"I see that. You ladies should retire to the house. We'll take care of the horses and I'll see to it Samuel brings a tray with supper to you both."

Kit normally always saw to the care of her own horse, but after a night spent tossing and turning and a morning spent riding away from a town being washed away by a river of rain, she was happy to accept his kind offer.

"Thank you, Bernardo." She clasped his hand kindly.

She ignored the look of concern on Price's face as she joined Lily in walking to the house. The men would see to their luggage.

Price kept his distance the rest of the evening. All the better for Kit. Lily, on the other hand, made it clear she was unhappy with Kit. She hardly spoke through their evening meal and upon finishing, clanked her fork noisily atop her plate and rose in a huff. Lily disappeared into the kitchen and Kit to her office.

Too tired to work, but too early to retire for bed, Kit mostly sat at the desk and thought about the rodeo plans. It wasn't until she heard Lily ready for bed that she decided to do likewise.

When she entered the room, Lily was already in her own bed, under covers, facing the wall. Kit changed quickly and assumed the same position in her own bed, counting as she lay there awake until Lily piped up, as if on cue.

"I don't know why you pretended to be sleeping when I came back to the hotel last night. Or why you haven't spoken as little as three sentences to me since."

Kit smiled; she knew her feisty maid wouldn't stay silent for long.

On a sigh, Kit explained, "I had had a row with Price after I left the dance."

"Fled the dance, more like. What caused you to run away? Price and I were worried that young pup of a rancher had insulted you."

"No, no such thing. I-I was feeling conflicted over some things and wished to sort them out."

"That behavior seems very unlike you. And it still doesn't explain why you seemed angry with me."

Kit turned over to face Lily's side of the room.

"Do you have feelings for Price?" Kit blurted, surprising even herself.

"Every woman has *feelings* for Price," Lily answered in her usual saucy tongue.

Kit wrinkled her nose, not liking that answer. "Do you love him?" she clarified. Somewhat embarrassed by her own question and nervous for her friend's reply, she fiddled with the hem of her quilt as she waited.

Instead of answering her, Lily asked in return, "Do you?"

Kit reflected thoughtfully, "I-I don't know."

From the other side of the room she heard Lily's exasperated sigh. She then rolled over to face Kit's direction and said, "Personally, I'd have to believe you dimwitted not to."

Kit smiled.

Lily smiled back.

"I'm afraid to have feelings for him," Kit explained. "Love was never in my plans."

"Mine either. But if it happens to sneak up and bite me one day, all the better."

Kit thought on that for a moment and twiddled the corner of the blanket between her fingers. "What if he doesn't love me?" She paused. "What if he's in love with my beautiful, flame-haired friend?" she finished, emotions raw in her throat.

"I knew it!" Lily shouted, followed by a short laugh, "You were jealous!"

"No," Kit began to deny, then relented with a roll of her eyes, "Well, perhaps a little."

"I'm flattered, but you're wrong. Price has little interest in me."

Kit couldn't help but inhale a breath of relief.

"I could help you, you know."

"Help me?"

Lily folded her arms beneath her head and offered an arched grin, "On winning over your Englishman."

It was Kit's turn to surprise Lily, "If you mean by way of seducing him, I've already tried that."

The darkness of the room did not hide Lily's jaw-dropping surprise, "Why, Miss Catherine Stone, for shame!" Lily laughed, "There are more sides of you than I ever would have guessed."

"Yes, well, as I said, I wasn't successful."

"Perhaps you were going about it wrong."

"I don't see how that was possible, Price was the one instructing me."

The whites of Lily's eyes could be seen as they widened yet again.

Kit explained from the beginning. Afterwards, Lily said, "Well, it doesn't sound as if you ever actually tried to use your newfound knowledge on *him*."

"No," Kit admitted, "but during our lessons, I practiced on him. You'd think if it was going to work at all, it would have then."

Lily smiled, "I'm not so certain that it didn't. But no worries. I'll bet I can teach you more about seducing men than he ever thought to teach you."

"I don't know... I'm truly horrid at the practice."

"Now *that* I am certain of. But with my help, you'll have him panting after you like—"

"Samuel pants after you?" Kit teased.

Lily pulled a comically grotesque face before picking her slipper up from the floor and whipping it across the room to hit Kit's legs shielded beneath the quilt. Kit laughed.

"You'll see," Lily stated. "We'll start our plans on the morrow. Let's get some sleep now."

Kit agreed, feeling buoyantly hopeful. And sleep came easy to her that night.

∾

Hours later, Kit's peaceful slumber was disturbed by Lily's choked cries and the smell of thick, heavy smoke.

"Kit, wake up. Wake up!"

Her eyes stung when she opened them. Lily was shaking her desperately to wake her, yet she could barely make out her form in the dark smog filling their room. When she opened her mouth to question what was going on, smoke immediately filled her throat and caused her to gag.

"Let's go," Lily coughed.

Kit grabbed Lily's hand and together they crouched below the rising smoke to the door. They opened the bedroom door to see flames licking toward them as they spread across the living room floor. The front door was partially blocked.

In that instant, it didn't seem likely they could make it before the exit was entirely consumed. Kit glanced around frantically for something she could lift that was heavy enough to break through the paned window across from them. The chairs were already burning, and the fire grew closer.

"What are we going to do?" Lily cried

Before Kit could determine how best to proceed, the entry door slammed open. The fire roared stronger, but raced along, eating up the floor from the door to the office at the back of the room. A narrow path opened up near the front of the room to the door.

Price entered, shouting, with his arm shielding his face. Panic filled his voice, "Kit! Kit! Where are you? Lily!"

Kit grabbed Lily's hand and raced the narrowing strip to Price, nearly barreling through him out the door.

Once free of the house, Price grabbed both of them and rushed them farther out of harm's way. A line of men were forming with buckets being passed along full of water from the well. But their efforts couldn't fight the growing flames. The entire house was consumed in an instant, flames roaring to the sky.

Funny how the fear didn't take hold until it was nearly over. Kit could do nothing more than watch her would-be home blaze orange against the night sky as it burned.

Price wrapped her in his arms, wiping soot from her face, distracting her from the scene before her.

"Are you burned anywhere? Are you hurt?"

Kit could only shake her head. It was as if trapped in a nightmare. Then she remembered, "Lily. Is Lily safe?"

Price closed his eyes, relieved Kit seemed to be fine. He nodded, "Yes, she's already been taken to the bunkhouse. Bernardo and Samuel are seeing to her."

Kit nodded and exhaled through her lips, then rested her head against the safe plane of Price's chest. She couldn't recall how long she remained that way, curled against him, her head tucked beneath his chin.

It wasn't until Price turned his head to shout some orders to the men and began walking her to the bunkhouse that she broke free of the shock.

"No. We should stay and help," Kit insisted.

"There's nothing to be done."

"But what if it spreads?"

"An unlikely probability given the distance from the house to any of the other structures. The men are going to push some dirt forward to form a barrier, just in case, but it appears to already be dying down."

Kit turned her eyes to the glowing mass again to ascertain for herself. It did appear to be shrinking. Strange how something so fierce could be so fleeting. She shivered.

Price, in his low, soothing voice, said, "Come, let's get you to the bunkhouse. You need to drink some water and you shouldn't be out here in your night dress."

Chapter 28

Kit and Lily ended up sleeping the rest of the night in the tack room stall on some horse blankets with Price standing guard. An arrangement Kit believed developed out of desire to protect the ladies' reputations, but Kit learned otherwise as she awoke to voices.

"Yes, please deliver this message to him. As quickly as possible."

It was Price's voice; he was whispering instructions to one of the hands presumedly. No response was voiced, and Kit didn't see the person.

Still sprawled on a pile of blankets, Lily gave a small snore. Kit inched closer to the stall door to see who Price had spoken to, but no one else was there.

"You're awake." Price spoke with his back yet turned to her, startling her with his perceptiveness.

"Who were you talking to?" Kit stepped farther into the doorway, remaining cautious in case other men were around. She was quite scandalously dressed in one of Price's loose-fitting cambric blouses. Her gown had reeked of smoke, as had Lily's, so both of them had been lent some of the men's shirts to sleep in for the remainder of the night. Price's shirt was plenty big enough to drape over Kit and cover her in all the pertinent places, but Lily's form, being robust as it was, had required one from Osa.

"Ramirez," Price answered, "I sent him to fetch García."

Kit swallowed, her throat still raw from the smoke, "Yes, I suppose that is a good idea."

Kit sighed and leaned her head back against the door frame, "What are we going to do now?"

Price turned his head her direction as if to speak but stopped before his mouth formed words, as if they froze on his tongue and he couldn't remember what he'd been about to say. His hazel eyes darkened, forming a deep moss green as he studied her.

She rubbed the back of her neck, where it ached from sleeping on the lumpy saddle pads and blankets. Noticing Price's intense gaze locked on her, she self-consciously touched her wild, sprawling hair. She hadn't taken the time to braid it away from her face yet.

She became acutely aware of her scantily-clad state as his eyes traveled down her form, barely hidden beneath the thin fabric of his shirt. Her heart pounded. She wasn't sure if she moved closer to him, drawn to him by some unspeakable force, or if he had moved closer to her. She could see his nostrils flare and wondered if he too was experiencing difficulty to inhale normal breaths. His gaze dropped to her lips and her eyes closed, body poised in anticipation of a kiss.

And then— "Ugh, I smell like a smoked horse." Lily woke.

Guiltily, Kit hurried back into the room behind the wall, hidden from Price's view once more.

Her voice cracked, "Ah-h, Price, could we borrow a change of clothes?"

"I need a bath," Lily complained, sitting atop the piled blankets.

"Clothes are already on the way." Price's voice didn't seem quite normal. Was it just Kit, or had Price been as affected by her as she had him? She allowed a small smile of hope.

Complaints filled the barn as Lily exited the stall, "I can't wear these. I look utterly ridiculous."

"Why? They are just men's clothes. I wear some most every day," Kit assuaged, feeling a bit needled by her friend's appellation over the wardrobe that was quite common for Kit.

Lily growled, "Yes, I know, dear. And they aren't necessarily becoming on you either."

Kit simply rolled her eyes, not taking offense to her friend's contrariness.

"They're meant to be practical, not 'becoming.' Feel that freedom. The range of motion your legs have now." Kit strode purposefully from the barn in search of Price, leaving Lily behind to bemoan her fashionless fate.

Though, if she were being honest with her friend, she did share a bit of discomfort over her loaned clothes. Hers had come from Samuel and they were a smidge tight in some areas. She ought not squat low or sit a saddle in them, or it could prove rather embarrassing.

~

He'd run from the barn, like a coward making good his escape. Seeing Kit in nothing but her morning glory—her hair tumbling down wildly about her shoulders to the middle of her back and wearing nothing but his shirt—had devastated him. He'd ached with the desire to kiss her, to do plenty more than kiss her. And with people all around them, too. He needed to have more of a care with her already fragile reputation. If it hadn't been for Lily reminding him of their surroundings, he might have been her ruin.

Walking around to the front of the barn to await Kit worked effectively to cool his ardor. Seeing the smoking remains of her house reminded him of the nightmare that roared to life last night. Rage filled him, knowing Kit could have been amongst the burning rubble right now. She almost lost her life because he hadn't been diligent enough in his guardian duties.

He heard the thudding of boots approaching, "Last night still doesn't seem real, but here's the proof..." Kit came to stand beside him, her eyes scanning the pile of ashes. "I don't know how it happened. Neither Lily nor I recall leaving a lamp burning. And from what I can remember, the fire appeared to have originated in the kitchen. We don't even have any wall hangers in there. We just transport the one lamp back and forth from room to room. The lamp should have been in the room with us."

"It wasn't a lamp."

"You think the stove, then?" Her brows knit together thoughtfully.

"No." Price hated the news he was about to deliver. "I found hoof prints, tracks, riding to and from the house. I don't think an accident occurred. I think someone intentionally lit your house on fire, knowing you were in it."

"You mean—"

"Yes," he gritted his teeth, fighting the surge of anger coursing through him.

Kit stared out across the smoldering ashes, before tilting her chin a notch and asking, "Who do you suppose may have done it?"

"I don't know."

"Do you think José may have hidden and waited for the opportunity?"

"It's possible."

"Show me the tracks."

Price walked her around the far side. She observed the turned earth and crescent indentations made from horses' hooves.

"They seem to be coming and going toward the northeast." She narrowed her eyes, following the tracks fading across the property.

Price swallowed, "I know. I should have noticed a rider approaching from that direction, heard his horse, or knew when the fire was set at the very least."

She placed her hand on his arm. She may forgive him, but he wouldn't forgive himself.

"Who was posted as guard on the night shift?" she asked. "The tracks look as though they lead right to them."

"Frank Perkins." Price met her stunned gaze.

"But that's Lily's brother, so it couldn't be him. Lily was in the house with me. Where is he now?"

"We're not sure. He hasn't shown up. Even if he didn't see the fire from where he was stationed, he should have returned long ago for his switch."

Price would have thought José behind the fire, but Frank's disappearance was suspicious. Kit's expressive face showed her thoughts were with his.

"I sent Bernardo and Pedro hours ago to follow the tracks and ride to the northeast post to see what they can find and to report back. I wanted to wait for you, before I investigated myself."

"Thank you." Her voice was dry yet from the fire, "But you should have woken me."

"You needed to rest," he demanded, implying no argument.

An unexpected rider reined in his horse at the entrance. Samuel raced toward him and accepted an envelope from him.

"A mail carrier?" Kit voiced her surprise.

Samuel ran the letter to them, "It's for you, Mr. Price."

Price thanked Samuel and the boy rushed back to his own chores. Kit stared on perplexed. "Is it from my family?" she shamelessly inquired.

Price smiled, "No. It's from my brother."

"In England?" Kit fairly shouted her surprise.

"Yes, mail travels faster here than in the mountains, due to all of the forts along the way from here to the port in Galveston. I sent a letter from Onieda as soon as we arrived. I like to keep my brother apprised of my whereabouts."

Price tucked the unopened letter into his pocket, apparently that was all he seemed inclined to say on the matter. Kit, buzzing with curiosity, might have plagued him further on the topic of his brother, but at that moment two more riders emerged from the tree line, ponying a third horse.

It was Bernardo and Pedro and it appeared another rider rode seated behind Pedro—Frank, Price assumed, as it looked like his horse being led alongside Bernardo.

They rode at a quick pace and pulled the horses up in front of them. Frank's body wavered like a ragdoll from the back of Pedro's horse.

Bernardo spoke, "We found him nearly unconscious."

Kit gave a scrutinizing assessment and asked, "What happened, Frank?"

Frank continued to hold the back of his head. In a pained voice he said, "I don't know. Last thing I remember was hearing a horse nicker from the weeds. I was going to investigate, when I was hit from behind. Hard enough to knock me out. By time I came to, the sun could already be seen through the trees. I felt too sick to stand right away. That's when Bernardo and Pedro rode in."

Kit raised her chin in gesture to Bernardo and Pedro, "Help him to the bunkhouse and get him cleaned up. Price and I will take care of his horse." The men nodded and Frank groaned as they rode off.

Kit and Price led the sorrel mare back to the stable. Kit looked the horse over and felt for injuries, determining her to be fine.

Over the mare's back, she said to Price, "José is the likeliest suspect."

Price agreed, "We should still ride out and look everything over ourselves."

Kit nodded.

As they saddled their own mounts, a clap of thunder rent the sky.

"We'd better hurry," Kit exclaimed.

❧

The skies opened up and released a torrent of rain upon them before they ever made it to the scene where Frank had been attacked. By time they made it to the small outbuilding that served as a wind barrier intended for blizzards and the like for the night watchman, the tracks were all but washed away. The three-sided shed was big enough for a man and horse if need be.

Price shouted over the rain, "Well, what do you want to do?" He shifted his horse closer to hers and tried to offer her his hat to shield her from some of the rain. Normally Kit had her own, but the fire had swallowed it. The only thing of any importance she'd grabbed from the room as she and Lily fled for their lives was the small wooden horse she always kept nearby. It was in her saddle bags now, as the pants she was wearing were too snug to allow anything to fit in the pockets.

She refused Price's hat. She welcomed the warm rain and let it cleanse the last of the smoky odors from her hair and skin. She was about to tell Price they should head back, when a strange smell filled the air.

The hair on her arms stood on end, she looked up at Price to see if he was experiencing the strange sensations. His eyes grew big with alarm and his mouth opened as if to shout, but at that second, a bright flash of light and a booming roar the likes of dynamite filled all of her senses. Blue jumped sideways and it was all she could do to hang on and make sense of the world. It all happened in the blink of an eye. A bolt of lightning. It had struck less than two wagon lengths from them.

Regaining focus, she saw Price lying on the ground and his mare at a full run back the direction they'd come.

"Price!" Kit scrambled from her saddle as quickly as soaking wet trousers plastered to her skin would allow. Her horse, Blue, sidestepped a couple of times making the process more difficult, but she couldn't blame the horse for being skittish. She was still shaken up herself.

She reached Price and rolled him over, "Price!"

"I'm fine." His simple reply instantly unknotted the tightness in her chest.

"Hypatia bolted."

"You just fell off?" Kit asked, confused. She'd thought perhaps he'd been struck himself or that the current had run through the ground and jolted him.

He pulled himself forward, rubbing his back. With an irritated expression, he stated, "Yes, I just fell. Not everyone can bloody seat a panicked horse when they've been nearly struck by electricity shooting down from the wrathful sky above them."

Kit realized she'd unwittingly stung his pride, "I'm sorry, it wasn't my intention to imply you should have done a better job of controlling your horse. I only sought to determine whether you or Hypatia had been shocked. The way you were sprawled on the ground, I thought the worst."

"Had the wind knocked from me, is all." She helped pull him to his feet and another flash of light zigzagged across the sky followed by a clap of thunder.

"We'd better get into the shelter."

Kit walked Blue into the lean-to and found the inside wasn't what she'd expected. The entrance and first few feet were intended to house a horse. There was plenty of wall to shield the animal. Even a small hanging manger on the back wall for hay in winter months; empty now. Beyond that area was a raised platform, higher than her horse's back, with a built-in ladder up the front of one side. Clearly it was meant for the night watchman to rest.

Kit left Blue saddled. They wouldn't be staying long and re-saddling with wet tack could cause sores. He was content enough to rest and wait patiently. She rewarded him with a few pats to his neck, then walked to the ladder.

"You coming? Standing in the opening is a good way to be hit by lightning," she called to Price.

Price broke his concentrated view of the outside and gave her a dry disgruntled look, followed by some grumpy mumbling. He followed her up the ladder to the loft.

She paused at the top, surveying the small space. It was simply a flat wood floor, but it appeared clean. Guard riders were expected to bring their own supplies along for their shift, that way nothing could be left behind and stolen. There was a cutout for a window, with a wooden door that opened downward like a flap, to view out. It seemed to be doing an all right job keeping the rain out.

"Are you going to finish climbing up? Or are we going to stay suspended on the ladder the duration of the stay?"

Price was in a mood, she thought. Probably still smarting from his fall. She scrambled over the edge of the ladder onto the platform. There wasn't enough room to fully stand. She walked hunched over to the far side of the wall to give Price enough room to join her and sat down.

She wished she had grabbed her blanket roll now, to sit on. She hadn't deemed it necessary to unstrap from the back of her saddle knowing they likely wouldn't be utilizing the shed long enough to fully dry. Not to mention, the humidity was too stifling to wrap up in a blanket. Her bum was protesting that decision now, however, sitting on the hard floor.

She looked to Price, "You seem distracted."

~

Price was distracted. Climbing the ladder with Kit's perfectly rounded arse in his face, in pants that appeared to be painted on, had caused all manner of sense to flee his brain. Or perhaps he'd lost his senses from the fall. Either way, he couldn't very well share what his mind was focused on with her.

"Just wondering if Hypatia ran back to the barn or if she's just out grazing somewhere with all my supplies still in my saddle bags."

Kit laughed, "Well, at the rate she was running, I'm sure she was headed back to the barn."

"I blame the trainer," he teased, knowing either Kit or her mother had trained Hypatia at one time. He'd purchased the mare from Stone Ranch the first trip he'd made there after the entire family had ragged on him about the tender-footed thoroughbred he'd proudly purchased back east.

A dark brow arched over her glittering eyes, "Oh? And pray tell, what should the trainer have done differently?"

"Well, for starters, not make a ranch horse that will balk in a thunderstorm."

"Lightning nearly struck her!" Kit protested gamely.

Price stretched out his legs, leaned back against the opposite wall as Kit, and folded his hands behind his head. "If a proper trainer can't produce a horse that won't dump it's rider in an electric storm, then at the very least, have it trained so that it will return when the rider whistles."

Kit scoffed, "I think you've read too many dime novels."

They both grinned for the entire absurd conversation.

Kit tipped her head back and sighed. When her eyes settled on him again, she looked thoughtful. Both of them began to speak at once.

"Price, sometimes I feel—"

"Your eyes are remarkable."

Kit looked down shyly. He could just see a pink bloom rising in her cheeks. He wasn't sure why his tongue decided in that moment to blurt out what he was thinking, but he didn't regret it. There was something between them. He could feel it. And he didn't think it was one-sided.

He continued watching her. When she finally looked to him, she said, "I've always hated my eyes. They are in likeness of my blood-father, or so I am told, and a constant reminder that I'm not truly my father—that is, Grayson's—daughter. Livvy got our mother's eyes..."

He was surprised by her admission, as the unusual light gray coloring of her eyes—especially in contrast to the dark sooty shade of her lashes and brows—was near mesmerizing. He never would have thought her eyes to be a feature she didn't like about herself. In fact, he wouldn't have thought Kit gave much thought to her physical appearance at all. There was so much about herself she kept hidden from the world, even those she loved most. Her sharing her insecurities with him now was an intimacy he didn't take lightly.

He also understood, probably more than anyone else, where her vulnerability stemmed from. He didn't want her to feel ashamed or dislike herself...

"You and Livvy both seem to have an equal blend of physical traits from your parentage."

~

It was a correct judgment to conclude she and her sister had inherited a blend of characteristics from their parents. Kit couldn't help but feel she'd been given the weaker traits, however. Kit didn't share a lot in common with her mother, in personality or looks. Her mother was loudly affectionate—a description that may not make sense but was entirely accurate.

If one were to paint a picture of her family, Kit's mother would be the sun; Livvy the rainbow; her father, Grayson, the steady line of the horizon; her brother, Logan, the wind that silently rustled when willed or brought a soft breeze when one needed it most; her brother, Luke, would be the loveable, yet mischievous pup thieving drying clothes from a line; and Kit? She would be a tree or a bush beyond the horizon, so quiet and remote, she went unnoticed by the eyes of most.

Livvy took after their mother in personality and in appearance. Any resemblance to her mother Kit had stopped with her small stature and dark hair. While Livvy had taken on the golden appearance of their sire—or so they were told, they'd never actually met the man—the rest of her seemed a replica of their mother. Livvy even shared their mother's golden eyes and paired with her coloring, gave her an almost leonine look.

Kit wasn't jealous of her sister, exactly, though she did seem to inherit all the height, beauty and grace in their lines—it was only...well, perhaps she was a mite jealous. But there was an underlying fear, too. For if she wasn't like her mother, did that make Kit like her sire? A man she had never met, but despised all the same?

"Personality, however, is learned," Price continued. "You've not to fear in regard to similarities to your sire. There is so much more of Grayson in you. I think anyone who knows you both would see that right away. Your father—because for all intents and purposes Grayson is your father—is a great man. Your mother a strong, but kind woman. You were lucky to have such personages to look up to as role models."

Kit met Price's eyes, his words a balm to her soul, and she knew he understood her fear. Not just because of what he had said, but the irritation in the words as he spoke them. She sensed he was all too familiar with the fear, himself.

For the first time, Kit wondered about his past. Did he hate his father? He never returned home to England after graduation. Instead he remained with her family and even entered into a war with Mexico rather than return home to his own family.

Kit couldn't imagine abandoning her family. And she couldn't imagine Price doing so either. He was too loyal. But perhaps they had abandoned him...

"And do you take after your father?" she asked, hoping he would continue to tell her about himself.

He hesitated, his hazel eyes reflecting sadly as he replied, "It works both ways, I think. I learned what type of man I *didn't* want to be from my father."

There was so much pain behind his words. Kit wanted to hold him, comfort him, and take it all away, but she didn't know how to cross that emotional bridge. She had no right to touch him.

Price retrieved the envelope from his inner pocket. Kit's eyes lit with avid curiosity.

"I was happy to leave England after my mother's death. Life with my father had become unbearable. My only regret was leaving my younger brother behind."

Kit interrupted, "You feared your father would treat him poorly as well?"

"Miles is six years younger than I and Father never sought him out to deliver cruel punishments before, but yes, I worried that perhaps in my absence he would take my place for punishment."

Kit swallowed, realizing again how blissful a life she'd led. Her parents had never laid a hand on her or any of her siblings. She couldn't countenance such brutality.

Price continued, "I'm one year younger than Randall, our elder brother. The heir."

"Was he terrible to you as well?"

"No," his eyes stared off, "he simply treated me as if I didn't exist."

Kit's eyes softened with pity.

"I think perhaps he feared our father as well and it was for the best. Or perhaps in his own way, that was how he offered protection. Our father especially didn't like us found together. We learned that quickly in our youth."

Kit thought that odd, but family structures amongst the peerage were quite peculiar from her knowledge.

"Randall was too busy to play, our father said. After Miles was born and grown big enough to keep up with me, we grew quite inseparable. We pitied Randall and his responsibilities."

Price scanned the letter, reading.

"Is your brother well?" Kit asked once Price folded the letter and tucked it away once more.

Price smiled, "Yes, he is."

Hesitantly, Kit wetted her lips before saying, "You're nothing like your father. He sounds an awful man," she soothed, "and you are one of the finest I know."

Shy after her admission and uncomfortable under Price's tender gaze, an attention she was unaccustomed to, she broke the moment uttering, "The storm seems to have passed. We should probably head back. I'm sure Hypatia made it back by now and the ranch hands will be worried."

~

Price hadn't thought to be thankful his horse dumped and ditched him, but now that he was to ride back double with Kit, he thought it may have been a stroke of good fortune. Kit was just about to swing up into the saddle, when his luck was ruined by a familiar voice shouting at them from a distance.

García galloped his horse up next to them. "Where the hell have you two been?" he demanded. "Your men said you rode out hours ago into an electrical storm."

His dark brown eyes shot accusingly to Price. Kit didn't seem to notice.

"Well, it wasn't an electrical storm when we left. It hadn't even begun to rain, so we thought if we hurried, we could make it out to investigate before any tracks were washed away."

García pulled the reins on his horse that was still hot from the run. After one last suspicious look to Price, he replied, "Yes, Bernardo informed me about the situation. Did you find the tracks, then? Did you find any evidence confirming José responsible for nearly burning you alive in a house fire?" García reminded them all just how serious a situation they were in.

"No, we were too late," Kit stated.

García raised a questioning eyebrow.

Price thought it prudent he allay any more accusations, "Lightning nearly struck us. I was thrown from my horse and the damned mare took off. That's when we decided to wait out the storm in the guard shed. As you can see," Price said pointedly, "from our yet soaked attire, we weren't there long. And we were just about to head back now that the storm dissipated."

García nodded acceptingly, "Well, let's get back then. We can go over details once you've both had a change of clothes."

"Kit, why don't you ride with me," García suggested.

Price had looked forward to holding Kit during the ride back, but obviously that wasn't to be the case. Kit didn't respond to García's prompt right away. Instead she looked uncertain.

Price whispered at her shoulder, "What's wrong?"

Kit whispered back frankly, "I don't like other people riding my horse."

Price curtailed a laugh, "Just moments ago you expressed an exalted opinion of my character. Now, you don't trust me with your horse?"

"I do think highly of you as a man, but that doesn't include your equestrian skills," she grumbled, before thrusting the reins of her horse into his hands and stalking indignantly away to climb up behind García on his horse.

Price couldn't help but smile; the woman was far too adorable when her ire was up. She gave him a threatening look from her seat behind García that wiped the smile from his face. He had the impression his equestrian skills—or lack thereof, according to Kit—would be under considerable scrutiny the rest of the ride back to the barn. There was no one he knew who could handle a horse better than Kit Stone, so he was certain he wasn't about to pass muster. And this was surely a step back in winning her favor.

Damn.

Chapter 29

"Gather whatever you have left. You will be staying with me until new housing arrangements can be made."

Price inhaled, certain García's order was not going to go over well with the ferocious little wolverine of a woman before him. To his astonishment, however, she complied with an indifferent nod.

Lily, on the other hand, was ecstatic to be living elsewhere than a tack stall. When one of García's men arrived with the wagon to carry them off, Lily cried her delight.

"Please say we are headed into Canyon right away. I can't stand to be in these clothes a second longer."

"No need, Rancho Rivera has everything you need for the time being," García said.

Kit gave a look of uncertainty but didn't argue. Price knew she was in for a surprise when she reached García's ranch. It was even grander than Stone Ranch and unlike anything Kit had probably seen before.

While García was busy assisting Lily into the wagon and issuing orders to his driver, Kit gestured for Price to follow her.

"What is it?" Price asked once they were out of hearing range from the others.

"I know García thinks I am going to remain at his ranch until a new house can be built, but my place is here, with my men. I am going with him for now because I do need supplies, clothes, bedding, and the like. But I will be back as quickly as possible. I'm leaving you in charge until then. Please tell the men I'll be returning soon."

Price knew better than to argue with her. He knew he would do the same in her situation, so why should he persuade her otherwise? Besides, he didn't like being parted from her, especially when her life was possibly being threatened. He knew García would do all he could to keep her safe, but he feared the older man saw Kit as a foolish youth rather than an equal, and knew Kit would balk at the restrictions he was sure to put into place. Whereas Price would simply stay near her.

Of course, he hadn't been able to prevent the fire that had almost killed her. Perhaps García could better protect her.

Her eyes searched his expectantly, probably waiting for him to protest.

"Okay."

She sighed.

"If I learn anything new about the incident," he added, in regard to the fire investigation, "I'll bring word myself. I'll come about midweek, whether I have news or not. Will that be sufficient time for you to replenish supplies?"

Kit tipped her freckle-dusted nose toward him in an affirming nod. She looked, not distrustful, but pleasantly surprised by Price's plan.

"Thank you," she said earnestly.

A niggling of guilt settled and tensed in his shoulders. She wouldn't have thanked him had she known he'd only proposed coming for her by midweek because he feared she may run off on her own if he didn't, and he wanted to ensure she was afforded protection.

He realized he'd underestimated her, though, when she smiled and said, "I won't come back on my own. I'll wait for you. But you had better arrive on time."

"I will."

She placed her hand on his chest and stepped forward as if they were going to conduct another lesson. Price held his breath and resisted the urge to look around, knowing they were exposed to anyone happening by, not wanting her to retreat.

But she did.

Everything within urged him not to let her go.

But he did.

～

Kit couldn't believe her eyes. It was nearing nightfall, but torches lit the way from the extravagant archway to García's house, enabling them to see even in the dark just how beautiful and grand a home it was.

The adobe-style house rose above the ground like a palace erecting toward the sky. The smooth curving archways over walkways and windows only lent to its grandeur and loveliness. From the drive, a balcony covered in vines that would surely flower soon could be seen extending from a second-story window. Kit could see lighting farther off in the distance from what appeared to be a small town housed on the ranch itself.

García grinned proudly.

"García...your home...it's..."

"Not what you expected, I take it?"

Kit shook her head. She had to prompt Lily to step forward, who was frozen, mesmerized by the lavish structure.

"Welcome to the Rivera hacienda."

He ushered the women inside and servants attended them right away. García ordered baths prepared and ladies clothing fetched. Then he left them to settle in for the night, agreeing to meet first thing in the morning at breakfast to discuss plans.

Kit and Lily certainly didn't argue. Instead, they followed the kindly maidservant down a lit hall to where they would be staying.

Kit was almost sorry she wouldn't be staying longer.

～

Price reached the barn and hopped down from his mare. Everyone was supposed to meet back at the barn for lunch and go over any discoveries they made. Tomorrow was the day he was supposed to fetch Kit and they still didn't have any new information to go on.

The vaqueros who had ridden out in different directions on the search began arriving to the barn, all shaking their heads. All but Frank who came riding in at a full gallop.

"Price! I found something!" Frank shouted. He didn't dismount from his horse, "José's body. Far north, just off the road to Canyon."

Price jumped back into the saddle, "Take me to him." He whistled to Osa who was still saddled as well and gestured for him to join them. They set out urgently to inspect the body.

Price wasn't sure what he had been expecting, but a half rotted and eaten carcass wasn't it. José's body must have been there for some time. How long, Price couldn't be sure.

The man's clothes were torn in a few places, but mostly intact. Price could see where a bullet had entered his body right through the heart. Flies abounded and the smell was as appalling as the sight. The man's guts were exposed from vermin making a snack of him.

One time in the process of gutting a deer when Price was first learning to hunt, he had accidentally torn the intestine with his blade and the smell of warm fecal matter and digestive juices had made his eyes water and nearly caused him to vomit. The smell of the rotting corpse before them was even worse. He pulled the handkerchief used to keep dust from his nose and mouth over his face, but it barely helped abide the smell.

He quickly assessed the rest of the body and noticed José's boots were missing. His holster on his strap was empty as well signifying his gun had also been stolen. How odd... Had José worked alone and just met with bad luck running into a common thief on his way to Canyon? Not much traffic between Kit's ranch and Canyon, so it seemed unlikely. Which would mean José hadn't worked alone, and his partner had shot and killed him. But why?

Price pondered on the many questions throughout the night. The next day, he sent Pedro and Ramirez to fetch a ranger from Onieda, if the town could spare one. He thought Kit would want that much done at least. He assigned Bernardo and Frank in charge while he was gone—the ranch still needed to be run, after all—and ordered everyone to stick in numbers of two or greater.

Kit was rather enjoying her stay with García. His home was lovely, and the people of his hacienda were kind and welcoming. It was an entirely different environment at his ranch than her own. It gave her new vision for the future of her ranch.

"Do you like your new clothes?" he asked from where he sat across from her at the rounded table on the veranda. She loved breakfasting out there, it was as if she was amidst a fairytale garden.

"Very much, thank you. In fact, they fit better than my old clothes lost to the fire. Those had only been hand-me-downs from my brothers," she smiled. "These blouses and trousers tailored to fit me are unlike anything I've ever worn before. Ma almost never hired a seamstress, except for gowns when we were to be ushered off to that dreadful academy. She's not too keen on having visitors at the ranch, nor leaving the ranch." Kit and García shared a chuckle over her mother's strange ways.

"We shall need to begin building your new home right away. I was thinking to send some men to Onieda this week for lumber," García stated.

"What supplies do we need to build a house like this?" She gestured around her to the adobe-structured walls, "It's beautiful."

"Thank you. If you would prefer an adobe home, then that is what you shall have."

"I wonder if I can build my ranch into what you have someday," she said dreamily, remembering their walks through the small imitation town he had full of shops and gardens, right on his property. She was especially dazzled by the fountain in the center of the village. She never dreamed García lived this way all these years. And to think, he'd never had anyone to share it with, she reflected sadly.

The next time she saw Price she would tell him how she felt. Time was too precious. If he didn't feel the same, he would move on once Logan returned and she would see very little of him in the years to come.

"I'm not sure the contest will pay for all the extra supplies we'll need now. Indeed, I don't even have a place in which to

Seduced by the Saint

host it, my place being under construction." Kit drew herself back to her present reality.

"Have you received word from your parents, yet?"

Kit shook her head no. She knew her parents were probably busy trying to locate Luke and helping Livvy. Besides, even if they could spare the time to wire Kit some money, she wasn't certain they would. They did not realize how important it was to her.

"Why not host the contest here? It's the perfect setup and we could split the proceeds," García graciously offered.

Seeing Kit opening her mind to the idea, he continued, "I would keep only what was earned by services provided by my tenants, such as room and board and meals. You can keep the competitor's entry money plus admission profits."

García had already offered her the use of eight of his unbroke horses, so it would save a trip herding them back and forth. Plus, he did have the perfect setup. His gathering pen could easily be turned into an eventing arena. It already had pens attached for sorting during branding and castrating time.

"Deal," Kit said and shook his hand across the table. They continued discussing their new plans and Kit could see García was as excited about the event as she herself was.

They were laughing over a memory García shared of his brother joining just such an event near San Antonio in their youth, and how his pants had been ripped in front of the crowd from a steer horn, when Lily rushed to them from around the corner, clearly alarmed.

"Mr. Price is here."

García looked somewhat perturbed, curiosity mixed with alarm piqued in his coffee-brown eyes. Kit averted hers, not wanting him to read how *un*surprised she was.

Instead she rose quickly and followed Lily, García right behind them.

Kit tried to keep the smile from forming across her face. It had only been three days, but it was so good to see him. His gaze found hers and locked on her as if she was the only thing in his sight. Did the others notice?

She looked away and slowed her step so as not to appear so singled out. She even allowed García to greet Price first, though she was dying to talk to him. Price didn't allow her to remain shyly on the fringe of the conversation for long.

"You look well." His clear hazel eyes cut a direct path to her, causing her to blush.

Drat the man.

García led them back to the comfortable seating on the veranda and requested a fresh pot of coffee be brought out.

Price's long legs must have been folded below the table, for he seemed too tall for the delicate furniture. He was dressed in his typical English trousers and hunter green jacket, complete with neck cloth. Funny how she used to judge him pompous based on the care with which he took with his appearance. Now, she realized, he took care with all details in his life, especially where his friends were concerned. His hair, mussed from the wind on his ride over, gave his overall neat form a rather rakish look.

"She would," Lily elbowed her discreetly. She'd been staring after Price like a lovesick schoolgirl and missed the last bits of conversation. Thankfully, Lily was there to help her recover.

"Kit, you were just telling me how you would enjoy a walk along the pecan orchard, were you not?" Lily prompted

"Y-yes. Indeed, I was."

A man dressed in dusty riding attire appeared on the gravel walkway, "Señor Rivera? Señora Diaz is having another emergency and has requested to speak only and directly with you." The man sounded irritated.

García simply laughed, "That is quite all right, Rafael. I will speak with her."

Rafael gave a slight bow of his head and departed.

García laughed again and explained, "Señora Diaz is my oldest tenant. In fact, she was my nursemaid as a child and a friend to my mother. She has an emergent situation nearly every day that namely requires my company. She is a sweet woman and I am quite fond of her so I indulge her when I can."

He gently dabbed his face with a linen, though Kit was certain there was nothing to which to dab, but that was García's way. Much like Price. Both men were born to aristocratic worlds, a world Kit would never truly understand. But she now realized there were good men to be found there, just as there were bad men in the one which she was born.

"If you three will excuse me? I shall not be long."

Once García was gone, Price stared openly at Kit and she returned his gaze. Electricity seemed to charge between them.

"Right, well, as much as I wanted to accompany you. *On the walk. In the orchard,*" Lily hinted conspicuously, "I just remembered I was to gather recipe instructions from García's cook to return to Bernardo. I'll join up with you after that." Lily's eyes twinkled devilishly.

Price waited for Kit to rise from her chair, then took her arm in his and escorted her down the gravel path to the main dirt road that winded through the hacienda.

"New boots," Price commented.

Kit held out her leather-clad foot to admire, "Wellingtons, too. A cobbler here was able to fit them to my feet, just this morning. Feels strange without my knife tucked inside, though."

Price couldn't resist a smile.

"I lost it in the fire. It was my father's Green River blade. He carved the handle from maple wood himself," she said nostalgically.

Price reached into the pack belted at his side and handed Kit a heavy knife. "You may have this one. It's nothing so precious," he said offhandedly. "That is to say, it wasn't crafted by anyone I loved or admired, but it's a good knife. I had it custom made. Commissioned a scrimshaw while your brothers and I were mining in California."

Kit fitted the smooth bone handle in her hand and slid the blade from its leather sheath. She inspected the quality of the blade that ran the length of her hand; it was sharp and well balanced. The design on the handle featured a small cluster of stemmed flowers in their natural wild state.

"It's columbine," she said, awed by the artist's ability to capture the starlet petals and beauty in the flowers that grew in abundance in the valley near her childhood home on Stone Ranch. A wave of nostalgia warmed her heart as she thought of home. And she was reminded again how dear her home and family were to Price himself, which made her love him all the more.

She studied the design some more, admiring its subtle detail, such as the delicate gold bands, small as root hairs, that ran in the shape of Vs, one inside the other. They were positioned near the hilt, pointing toward the blade like an arrowhead. It wasn't extravagant or flashy. One might not notice the details, thinking it plain. But if one looked closer, they would see the fine etching in the craftsmanship and the elegant beauty in the design. And even then, most would miss the subtle meaning behind the artful image—home, family, the things that mattered most in the world to Kit herself.

Like its owner, Kit thought, *one had to look with deeper understanding to truly appreciate how special it was.*

She couldn't articulate her feelings into words and so simply said, "Thank you." She felt she should say more. She wanted to say more, but she didn't want to sound like a sentimental ninny either. "It's perfect," she added and smiled softly.

They meandered a ways out of the makeshift village and into the pecan orchard, not talking a whole lot, but occasionally touching shoulders. It was a splendidly sunny day and the shade from the pecan trees was welcoming. Kit found it particularly romantic. She reached up and plucked off a cluster of low hanging blooms, running the grainy strands through her hands silently as she gathered her courage to tell Price how she felt about him.

Before she could form her thoughts into words, however, Price said, "Kit, listen...we discovered something, and it's not good."

She processed his words, effectively shutting out any romantic feelings for the time being.

"We found José's body. It doesn't make any sense," he continued.

She pursed her lips in thought after his explanation, "No, it certainly doesn't..."

"Unless he met up with someone meaner than he was..." he trailed off in speculation.

"I think it's time we send for a ranger."

"I already did."

"We need to get back to the ranch—my ranch."

"I figured you would say that. I take it you didn't tell García you planned to depart today?"

"No," guiltily, she looked down at the now bared stem she rolled between her fingers.

"Do you think he suspects?"

"I don't know. I'd rather leave a note behind and deal with his wrath later."

"Not like you to take the coward's way."

She fixed a steely gaze on him, "I'm doing what I must. I know he simply wants to keep me safe, but it's my ranch and I'm the one who should be taking care of it. If I were a man, he would never try to keep me from taking action and protecting my home and the people in my care. He's like family and I respect him a great deal. It's not as if this is an easy decision to make."

"García is a fair man; do you think he won't understand if you talk to him?"

"Don't you think I've thought about that? Painstakingly so over the past few days? True, he might understand. But he might not. And that is a risk I'm not willing to take a chance on."

Price stayed her nervous hands from their busied state of stem rolling, "I know you care about him. I only asked to be certain you wouldn't regret your decision, not because I'm against you."

Kit sighed, "I regret that my decision will hurt him, but I do not regret the decision to stand with my men and protect my ranch."

Price nodded, affirming his agreement, "Shall we ready the horses, then?"

Chapter 30

Yesterday's plan went smoothly. Lily had done her part and been ready with their packs, waiting by the road. Price had packed all their new belongings on his mare while Lily had ridden behind Kit and they rode out without incident while García had been preoccupied.

When García hadn't shown up at her ranch late last night, Kit figured he was either too angry with her or had acquiesced to her decision. She discovered she'd been wrong on both accounts when he'd rode in this morning, along with Ranger Captain McCulloch.

She braced herself for a humiliating set down in front of her men. Instead, García had ridden directly to her, climbed from his horse, and using his horse as a barrier from the rest of the men gathering to greet the ranger, took her hands and asked for forgiveness.

"Kit, I am sorry I have behaved as an ancient patrician. I should never have tried to treat you as a delicate flower, when I know you are not. It is difficult to suppress a lifetime of cultural imprint, even as I have observed with my own eyes how strong and capable women truly are. I did it out of love."

"I know you did," Kit stated considerately.

"But that does not excuse it. My hope is you will forgive me. I did not come this morning to intrude or play protector, but only to offer my aid as I would to any of my neighbors, but especially to one I consider family."

Kit smiled, "Thank you."

"So, what is the plan?"

García followed Kit to greet Captain McCulloch.

Her men hung back, awaiting instruction, while Kit, Price, García and the ranger conferred.

Kit explained all they knew at this point and asked the ranger what he suggested.

"I agree, it is unlikely your former ranch hand was working alone. He could have had a partner and that partner could have killed and robbed him for spite, but there is something else you may not have considered. A comrade would have had little incentive to assist in a murder, unless you paid your ranch hand quite handsomely before he left?" A sardonic smile twisted the ranger's thickly-mustached lips, expressing his doubt over the last question.

"So, what are you saying?" Kit asked in her typical direct manner.

"I think you are underestimating how badly some men wanted this ranch and how your decision not to marry any of the men interested in it may have put you in danger.

"Kingston is a very powerful rancher in this territory, and he has invested heavily in this ranch already with the expectation it would be his one day."

"You think he hired José?"

"It's very possible. José could have turned to him looking for work and been more than willing to help wrack some revenge on you.

"One thing I know is word has had time to get back that you are still alive. It wouldn't surprise me if there are other 'Josés' about ready to remedy that."

"What do you suggest we do? Go around asking all the ranchers in the area if they have it out for me?" Kit drawled sarcastically.

"No, that is what I'm going to do," the ranger said. "You should divide your men up and very carefully search the borders of the property. More than likely, there is someone hanging about with ill intentions; either ready to finish the job," he looked to Kit, "or to run back to whoever is behind the attacks, to inform them of your movement. Now that rangers are involved, they will want to make their next move quickly to kill Miss Stone.

"We shall split up and patrol the property; if someone is waiting, it will probably scare them off. If we're lucky we'll be able to catch the informant and glean out some information for ourselves," the ranger smiled wickedly.

"It's still a possibility José was just sick and violent and had friends equally so and this was an isolated incident," Kit said hopefully.

"It's a possibility. But an unlikely one," Captain McCulloch replied.

∽

Price didn't like being separated from Kit. They divided into four groups. Three groups consisting of two-to-three people to search the property borders and one group consisting of all the remaining vaqueros to stay behind working the ranch. They couldn't spare any more workers; it was a large ranch and they were already sparse on help with the everyday runnings of it.

Price had wanted to go with Kit, but García had volunteered and he couldn't very well argue with the man who was the closest to an actual guardian Kit had at the moment, especially without causing an embarrassing scene. García, Kit, and Frank Perkins had formed one group. Frank was considered the most trusted cowhand after Bernardo, since his own sister's life had been endangered in the same fire that had nearly claimed Kit's. It was unlikely he had any involvement with the sinister acts taking place.

Not that Price or Kit had suspected any of the rest of the cowhands, but while Captain McCulloch didn't come out and say it, he strongly implied another of the vaqueros could have been in cahoots with José or working for one of the neighboring ranchers—Kingston being their prime suspect.

Price had paired with Captain McCulloch leaving the third group comprised of Pedro and García's man, Miguel. Bernardo had been left in charge of the vaqueros.

He and Captain McCulloch were to ride along the east perimeter, it was the largest area to cover, but also the easiest terrain to navigate. Unfortunately, that allowed his mind to continue worrying over Kit. She was well protected, he knew. She herself was quick and sure with a gun, plus she had García and Frank Perkins with her.

Still, he didn't like not being there to protect her himself.

∿

It occurred to Kit she never told Price how she felt about him. She wished she had found a moment before this morning. It was never the right time. Well, she had felt certain their walk amongst the pecan trees had been the right time, but then Price had spoken of their departure plans and her guilt over García had chased all romantic notions away.

Tonight, she resolved, tonight she would ask Price if he wanted to marry her.

No, that was preposterous. Women didn't propose to men...

What else was she to do? She didn't want to wait around for him to offer for her. That may never happen. For all she knew, his feelings didn't run deeper than the desire she felt in him when they kissed.

Then again, what if he did want her, but didn't think she would accept him?

She had spouted often enough her annoyance with him and doubted his abilities on more than one occasion in the past. She winced, her past attitude toward him certainly wouldn't encourage a proposal. To be fair, she hadn't known she would fall in love with him, then. She hadn't thought to fall in love with anyone.

Love was a strange emotion. She'd never felt so twisted up inside. All she knew was, somehow, she needed Price to stay with her. The prospect of him leaving her behind once her brother returned to reverse the inheritance requirements left her with an empty, aching feeling inside.

She was deliberating on exactly which words to use tonight that would make the prospect of marriage to her appealing to Price, when a gunshot sounded right next to her.

The startling explosion froze her temporarily with fear as her mind crashed back to the reality of her surroundings, struggling to piece together in an instant what was happening. After she was sure she hadn't been shot, she looked around. *Who had fired?*

"García!" she yelled as he crumpled and fell from his horse.

Drawing her gun, she rushed from her horse to where García now lay bleeding on the ground. She crouched over him, making a quick scan of the area. Frank was still in his saddle, gun drawn as well, searching the area.

"Per-Perkins..." García uttered weakly, clutching his side. Before Kit could make sense of his statement her gun was kicked from her hand.

She looked up in time to meet Frank's boot as it connected with her chin and sent her sprawling backwards to the ground. *Frank?* Frank had kicked her... Had Frank shot García? Had he shot José?

She recovered quickly, ignoring the questions burning on the tip of her tongue. She sprang to her feet, ready to rush her attacker, only to be grabbed and held firmly from behind.

"You're every bit the spitfire I imagined you'd be," the man behind her hissed in his struggle to keep hold of her. The voice sounded familiar to Kit, but she couldn't place it.

Her jaw ached where she'd been kicked. She saw García still lying on the ground, his hand pressed to his side in effort to stymie the blood flowing forth. Frank stood over him leering.

"He won't last long. I don't want another gunshot raising alarms. We need to get out of here fast. They hired a ranger, he's out with her gent patrolling the east side as we speak. One gunshot might not have them running, but we'd better get quick, just in case."

Anger welled within her, "Frank, you son of a bitch!"

"My, my, the Stone Ranch Princess has a filthy mouth, doesn't she?" the voice from behind chortled.

Striking back swiftly, the heel of her boot connected with the man's shin and in quick succession, he released her. She darted forth for Blue who was standing patiently nearby.

But she didn't make it.

The man who had loosened his grip from her tackled her to the ground. She hit hard, him landing atop her, expelling the breath from her lungs. He quickly bound her wrists together with a course rope that dug at her skin.

"Hurry up, get her on a horse and let's go," Frank ordered.

The man lifting her from the dirt grumbled back, "Would be easier if you'd help. She ain't as light as she looks."

The man pulled her to her feet and then slung her over his shoulders like a burlap sack filled with potatoes, then thrust her into the side of her horse, missing the target of over the saddle. Her face smashed against the hard leather and scraped up the side as he attempted to maneuver her over the hump of the saddle again.

Once she was positioned halfway over, she took the opportunity to twist and kick out, while grasping the leather on the other side of the saddle with her fingertips. Her mark hit true and as the man went flailing backwards, Kit pulled her other leg around to sit the saddle and kicked Blue into a run.

Her horse barely hit a single stride before Frank drove his horse into their path. Frank grabbed up Blue's reins as the horses collided. Blue tossed his head and danced angrily at the mixed signals. Kit didn't bother diving from her horse, with her hands bound she wouldn't be able to run quickly, and with them on horseback, they'd catch her quickly enough.

They hadn't shot her yet, but she didn't know if that was a good or a bad thing. They obviously wanted to take her somewhere. Perhaps if she stayed sitting up in the saddle, she could kick Blue into a run when less expected and tear the reins away from Frank.

That was a big *if*, since she didn't know how far or where they planned to ride to.

She wasn't sure if her plotting had been transparent on her face or if Frank was simply smarter than she'd given him credit for, but she was to be denied the opportunity to attempt another escape as Frank brought his horse side-by-side to hers and conked her on the head with the butt of his gun. Kit felt herself slink across the saddle as the world faded to darkness.

Cayt Lawson

Groggy, with a dull ache coming to life in her head like a beat of a drum growing louder and louder, Kit started to rouse from her forced stupor. Her body was stiff and sore, and she realized she was bent over the side of her saddle with arms still bound and her feet now as well.

At least they were still riding. She'd feared stopping and being unconscious with these men.

She tried to remain quiet and assess her surroundings, but it was clear they were no longer on her land. The sun was high in the sky, so she guessed it was only partway into the afternoon, indicating they hadn't ridden all that far yet.

She leaned into the steady pace of her gelding to absorb the bouncing movements caused from her position over the saddle, while trying to think of a way to escape. She wondered if García were still alive. Had Price realized by now what had happened? Would he and the ranger find her in time?

The horses came to an abrupt stop and she jolted forward with a slight roll; of course, all her horse's movements felt jarring from the angle she was at. She didn't hear the men dismount their horses, perhaps it was all the blood flow to her brain. Her head felt heavy as a shovel full of mud.

She didn't hear them approach her, but she felt hands untying the rope at her boots and then grab her hips to drag her from the saddle.

She fell right to the ground as her legs were nothing but tingling hollowed stalks, unable to support her. She felt more beat from their rough handling over these short hours than any whooping she'd taken from a bronc in her lifetime.

"Get up," the man working with Frank spat and shoved her toward a small building. She wondered where they were, certain they hadn't ridden for more than a few hours. The horses weren't lathered, so they hadn't been travelling at a grueling pace either. There were trees and brush surrounding the area and Kit couldn't see much of the land beyond the old shack.

Frank was seeing to the horses and he was taking the saddles off, implying they would be holed up in this shack a while. Kit didn't like the thought of that.

The hand at her back shoved her forward again and it was all Kit could do not to trip over the rain-rotted threshold of the little wooden building. Once inside, she whirled around to get a first look at the man helping Frank.

And she couldn't have been more surprised than if she were witnessing a dog birth a litter of kittens.

Russell.

Shock must have been clearly expressed on her face, for he laughed, "That's right. Didn't expect to see me again, didja?" His speech was as appalling as his pickled breath.

Retreating a few steps, Kit looked for a safer location within the shack to position herself against him.

Russell had worked at Stone Ranch, what on earth was he doing in Texas?

"What are you doing here?" she asked bluntly.

"I followed ya." His eyes gleamed. She didn't like what she read in them.

Her mind swirled to make sense. Frank entered then and she concentrated her fear into anger and narrowed in on him. He ignored her, hanging up his saddlebags on a wall hook for coats, instead.

"What the hell is going on?" she demanded.

"I'll tell you, you little bitch," a malevolent grin spread across Russell's face. "You went around, thinking you were too good for everyone. You had your daddy and brothers to protect you at home to run off men like me who you didn't deem worthy enough. But then you had to go and reject a right rich bloke."

"That's enough," Frank spoke.

Kit cast a glance from Russell to Frank through the suspicious squint of her eyes. "Kingston," she stated more than questioned.

Russell grinned widely and laughed, his eyes sending eerie chills down her spine.

"Christ," Frank spat.

"Not like she wa'n't gonna find out."

Kit decided it was in her best interest to keep Russell talking. "So, you followed me all the way from Stone Ranch. How did you know about Kingston's plan?"

For that matter how did Kingston have a plan? She *hadn't even known she would reject him until she did.*

"I didn't. Just came to get what I was *owed.*"

Kit had a feeling she knew exactly what Russell had in mind.

"But it wasn't easy to get to you, what with your watch dog always around."

Price.

Then you went to that fiesta in town and I followed you there. That's where I heard Kingston talking with some others. He wasn't none too happy with you." Russell laughed. "I offered him my services to help get you and even take the blame if lawmen come around. In return for a very specific payment."

Kit had heard enough from him.

"What about you, Frank? What's in it for you?"

"I'm not so sadistic as," he gestured toward Russell, "all that. Ain't nothin' personal. I just need money—money Morgan was supposed to pay and never did."

"But I planned to pay back wages including his debts. I had already said as much."

"Perhaps I wanted more than that."

"Was José involved at all? Who shot him?"

Frank answered, "Nope, but I knew he'd make an easy scapegoat, so I stopped him before he could get to Canyon."

"Stopped him with a bullet," Kit accused.

Frank simply shrugged and pulled a spindle-backed chair from the table to plunk down in. Russell remained leaning against the wall, checking the doorway every once in a while, but mainly just locking eyes on Kit.

"But your own sister—Lily—she was almost killed in the fire along with me!"

A lazy smile curled Frank's lips, "Ah, my sister. She knew about the fire. See, good brother that I am, I included her in my plans, much to my everlasting regret. She been wanting to go to San Francisco an awfully long time.

"She ended up forming an attachment to you, though, I guess. She won't make the mistake of saving your life again. She knows what's in store for her if she does."

Lily knew about the fire. She'd been in on it the whole time...

The betrayal cut deep. Kit tried to suppress the wrenching ache in her guts. To distract herself from grieving her loss of friendship, she asked more questions.

"Kingston wants me dead..." she said thoughtfully.

"No. He wants you for a bride."

That didn't make any sense, if what Russell had implied was true... She risked a glance at Russell. He knew exactly what she was thinking.

"Oh," Russell laughed, "he don't need no pure bride. Just one with a fortune attached her name. Ain't so special, now, are ya, princess?"

"But, what about heirs?"

"Heirs?"

"Surely, Kingston will want a pure bride," she swallowed the dry spit in her throat, nervously, "to ensure any heirs are his?"

Russell threw his head back and chortled, "Oh, you think it's the young Kingston gon' marry ya? No, see he *is* the heir. It's the old bastard gon marry ya."

Kit tried to think back, she'd briefly met Cornelius Kingston during her stay in Onieda for the festival. He'd been polite to her, but she'd met him only after rejecting his son, so she had kept her distance as much as possible, and he seemed to keep his as well.

Her mind swirled. How had this evolved into such a nightmare?

∽

A single gunshot echoed across the land. Already on edge, Price's insides filled with unease. Captain McCulloch stayed him with rationale. They were late for returning to the ranch for their noon meal meet-up. Perhaps Kit had fired to alert them of the time.

They moved along at a clipped pace, unwilling to ignore the shot could have signified danger. When they arrived back to the ranch, Pedro and Miguel were waiting for them, but Kit's party wasn't there.

Price slanted an uneasy glance to the captain.

Just then Bernardo came running from the barn holding a pair of fancy boots Price recognized as José's.

"Where did you find these?" Price demanded.

Bernardo looked to him, fear burning in his serious eyes, "Amongst Frank Perkins' belongings. He left his stuff all over the bunkhouse, in the way of everything. I was tossing his mess back to his side of the room when I discovered them."

Dread hit Price in the gut like a bullet. Kit wasn't safe.

Captain McCulloch asked, "How are these boots significant?"

Price explained as he retightened the cinch on his saddle, "They belonged to the ranch hand we had initially suspected. The one who was shot. Bernardo just found them among Frank Perkins' things. Frank was assigned to ride with Kit and García."

Captain McCulloch followed Price's lead and they rode out again. Price prayed he wasn't too late.

The plan had been for Kit's group to start in the northwest corner and make their way toward the northeast. Being that they had searched for a few hours, they had probably been close to the middle before the gunfire was heard. They decided to start there and separate in either direction. If they found something, they'd fire off two shots in quick succession, so the other would know to follow.

They never ended up implementing the plan, however, because as they neared the property border where they planned to split, they found García lying amidst the buffalo grass and sage.

Before his horse could come to a complete stop, Price was dismounting and running to García.

"Bloody hell. García!" He dropped to his knees and lifted García's head, "García, can you hear me?"

García's eyes fluttered open.

"Thank God," Price cried out.

Captain McCulloch appeared at his side, "Let me take a look at him."

Price paced the area and observed the ground finding churned dirt leading off steadily into the wooded landscape to the northeast. The tracks would be difficult to follow over the hilly and dense terrain.

"I don't think the bullet hit any major organs, but he's lost a lot of blood."

Price returned, his eyes looking to the captain, seeking the answer he probably wasn't free to give.

"We need to get him back quickly, and then there's a chance."

Seduced by the Saint

García's hand reached up and clasped the captain's strongly, willing himself to live, then faintly he uttered on raspy breath, "Frank and another man have her."

Price nodded, "They took Kit. Do you know where?"

In the barest of movements, García shook his head slowly side to side."

"Take him back, Captain, and send for more of your men. I'm going after them, but if it is as we discussed, then Frank and the other men are merely henchmen and I'm sure they will be meeting up with more or whoever hired them soon. We'll need as much help and as many lawmen as we can get and fast."

The captain nodded. Price helped transport García and lift him up to Captain McCulloch on his horse. Just then another rider appeared.

It was Lily.

Her dress bunched around her legs over the saddle and her hair sprang wildly from her tear-stained face. Her uncharacteristic appearance was alarming.

"Oh my God," she covered her mouth with her hand as she spied García's bloodied, weak form being hauled up into the saddle. "Oh no."

Price's hairs stood on end and he realized, *she knew*. His eyes narrowed in on her and she had the good grace to look frightened.

"I'm sorry. I'm so sorry," she cried.

"Your brother set the fire, didn't he? That's why you knew to get out."

She nodded.

"Why did you save Kit, then? Why did you save her then and not tell her? Why save her only to let her die now?"

"I didn't know—I didn't know her when I—when I agreed to help. And then when I did, I tried to save her," she blubbered.

"If you wanted to save her you should have told us your brother was behind the attack." Price's words were hard, he had no warmth to offer the disgusting woman before him.

"I wanted to, he said he would kill me, too. I didn't know what to do. You have to believe me."

Price climbed into the saddle, "If anything happens to her, I'll see you hang as an accomplice to murder."

"They aren't going to kill her," she hurried between sharp intakes of breath forced from crying. Her words stopped him.

"Do you know where your brother may have taken her?"

Lily nodded, "To an abandoned shed between the town of Canyon and Kingston's ranch. I think it used to be a homestead before Comanche's ran them out years ago. I've never been there, but I don't think it's far, Frank rode off plenty of times in an afternoon alone."

Captain McCulloch interrupted, "García needs immediate attention, I've got to get him back to the ranch. I'll take the woman back with me."

Lily swallowed fearfully, understanding she was being placed in the custody of the law. Hesitantly, she offered, "I could go with you, Price. I could help you save her."

Price recognized the fear in her strangled words and realized she was more afraid of running into her brother than she was of going back with the ranger. Price didn't want to take pity on her, but found himself relieving her of the duty, saying, "No, you will just slow me down."

Relief washed over her features and she closed her eyes, thanking Price for the kindness she didn't deserve. When her eyes opened, they looked to him, haunted, "Price? Hurry. Even if they don't plan to kill her, it doesn't mean they won't hurt her."

Chapter 31

"We don't have much time before the boss shows up to collect her. I want to git mine before that," Russell spat.

Averting her eyes so that filth of a man couldn't read the fear within, she slowly scanned the room for an alternate escape route, all the while commanding herself to take slow, calm breaths. She couldn't allow these animals the satisfaction of seeing they had succeeded in scaring her; that would be a costly mistake, one that could easily give them the upper hand. She needed to regain control.

She surveyed the room, but all there seemed to be was the table at the center with four chairs seated around it, the coat hooks along the wall near the entrance, and a small window toward the wall across from the door. Cupboards lined that wall from the window to the wall adjoining where Kit stood. Russell paced from the window to the door across from her.

Outside, the horses could be heard nickering softly. They were obviously penned up nearby. Just on the other side of the wall where Frank and Russell congregated, Kit guessed. If she could get out, she could get to the horses quickly. She didn't need a saddle or even a headstall for Blue; she knew if she squeezed her legs against his sides, he'd run, and he'd go in the direction of home.

But she did need her hands freed.

The weight of her knife could still be felt strapped against her leg, inside her boot, so she didn't think they knew about it. If they had felt it while tying her feet, they would have confiscated it, surely. She breathed a little easier for having it.

"Maybe you ought ta see what's bothering them horses," Russell's blatant suggestion was met with an obstinate glare from Frank.

Frank and Kit both knew why Russell wanted Frank to leave; a reason that made Kit feel as though a pile of worms wriggled wildly in her stomach. She tamped down her nausea and tried to think.

She didn't want Frank to leave the room. So far, he was the one preventing Russell from violating her. Not that he cared a whit about Kit, but he seemed to like things clean and organized. And quiet. This place certainly wouldn't be any of those things if Russell attacked her.

On the other hand, if Frank left, she'd only have one of them to contend with. She still had her knife in her boot. If she could get to it in time without Russell seeing, she could kill him or maybe wound him severely enough to allow her time to escape.

She'd never used a knife to kill anything before. She knew how to deliver a fatal blow in the technical sense, knew where to stick the blade, but she'd never done it before. She was equal parts repulsed by the prospect of killing someone and frightened she wouldn't be successful. She didn't even want to imagine what her fate would be if she failed.

She waited, wondering what Frank would decide to do. He seemed to think he was in charge and he didn't appear to take kindly to being ordered about by a young lunatic like Russell. They had a stare off for a few seconds, and to Kit's surprise, Frank stood.

"I've gotta take a piss."

A spark of excitement flared in Russell's eyes and a grin spread wide across his face, "Take your time." He spoke the words to Frank, but his eyes never left Kit's and she feared she could see into his shallow black soul.

"You've got ten minutes," Frank asserted his dominance in their little union once more. "Doubt you'll need more time than that." He scoffed.

Kit turned to face the wall behind her, leaving her back to Russell. She hoped he thought her simply frightened. Carefully, during their exchange, she raised her leg until she could grasp the bone handle of the knife Price had given her. She squeezed it as if thinking his name could somehow lend her strength, and slid it smoothly from its sheath. She hoped the table and chair helped conceal the movement. Both men seemed too engaged with one another at that point in their power stand-off, neither spoke a word to her; she hoped that meant she went unseen.

Her hands still tied in front of her, she rolled the handle in her hand so the sharp edge of the blade was facing out. She wasn't sure if she would have enough time to raise her hands, so she would have to strike him in an upward motion.

She heard Frank's spurred boots clunk across the floor and out the door. She tried to keep her breathing quiet so she could hear Russell's movements, but her heart thundering in her ears made it difficult.

"I've waited for this for a long time," he spoke, his voice carrying nearer.

She didn't say anything, couldn't trust her voice not to give her away.

He chuckled and she felt his hand brush her hair away from her neck. She clamped her jaw tight and her nose flared to feed more air to her lungs while she focused on remaining still. She repressed the urge to flinch away from his touch. Her arms being tied restricted her range, she needed him close. This was her only chance. Any number of possibilities could result if she failed. They would take her knife and she'd not have an opportunity like this again.

He was so close now his acrid breath furled amongst the tiny hairs at her nape.

"I expected more vigor from you," disdain dripped from his words. He trailed a finger down her arm. Then in a violent grip, his fingers curled around her, digging into her flesh. She knew what he planned next.

In one forceful motion he yanked her around to face him. As close as he was, he never saw her hands.

"I'd hate to disappoint," she hissed. She raised her hands, locked firmly around the knife, in one swift motion. Slicing upwards over his body at an angle as she did, ensuring a deep slash across his throat. She thrust the blade with all her might, prepared for any resistance against the blade.

His surprised cry never made it past his lips, instead it gurgled out in the blood flowing from his neck.

Her need to escape didn't allow for time to dwell on her actions. She shoved him aside and he fell to the floor. Quickly, she turned the blade inward to saw through the ropes at her wrist. Ignoring Russell's gasps for air as he drowned in his blood, she reached for his gun.

Her hands trembling and slippery with Russell's blood made it difficult to cock the hammer and she almost dropped the gun. Kit thought her pounding heart would explode in her chest when Frank entered the building at that exact moment. With teeth gritted, she drew the heavy weight of the loaded pistol, aiming for Frank's chest and pulled the trigger. Without hesitation she thumbed back the hammer and squeezed off a second shot, thankful Russell had kept his gun loaded.

Frank jerked with each shot, then fell forward, crashing to the floor where he lay unmoving for several seconds. Kit glanced swiftly to where Russell lay. He'd stopped struggling and was either dead or close to it. She picked her dropped knife up from the floor and wiped the blood clean from the blade across her pants, then slipped it back into the sheath inside her boot.

Frank still hadn't moved. She stepped cautiously closer, being as his body blocked the only exit, she needed to get past him. She didn't know how long she had before Kingston or more of his men might show up. Especially after firing two shots.

Blood seeped around the left side of Frank's body, pooling on the floor, and she could see the two massive holes where the ball had torn through him and exited his back. Certain he too was dead, she clicked the hammer back to be ready in case Kingston's men had arrived unnoticed when she'd fired. She then stepped carefully around his body and outside.

Colt drawn, Kit looked thoroughly in all directions. Seeing no trace of other riders, she dashed toward the pen holding the horses. She spotted her saddle, along with the others in front of the pen, resting on its horn in the dirt—much to her displeasure. Her headstall had been thrown in the dirt as well. But at least her saddlebags were still strapped to the back of the saddle. *Thank goodness for small favors,* she thought begrudgingly.

Seduced by the Saint

Quickly, she grabbed up her headstall. As she was about to enter the gate to retrieve Blue, she heard a rider approaching. Instinctively, her hand reached for the Colt Walker.

"Kit!"

Price.

She sagged with relief, released the hammer on her gun slowly and put it away.

~

Price had been close when the gun shots fired and he raced the rest of the way in the direction he'd heard them come from. He spied the shack and hadn't slowed, instead riding in with gun drawn. He jumped from the saddle of his horse but was surprised to see the dead body of a man lying in the doorway of the little shack. Looking around, he spied Kit at a pen that held just four horses, two of which he recognized—one was Kit's the other García's.

Kit appeared fine, ready to collect her horse from the pen and saddle up; a completely normal scene, which is what made everything more bizarre. Cautiously he inspected the building from the doorway. The body closest to him was that of Frank Perkins. He could only vaguely see another body lying on the floor, but it was sheltered by table and chair legs making it indiscernible to identify. Price noticed the pool of blood spreading from the body. One thing was certain, whoever he had been, he was dead now.

As he put pieces together in his mind, he realized Kit was in the middle of escaping. He picked up his pace, wanting to get to her. Fear must have been writ on his face for he could see her eyes already trying to communicate to him she was fine. He looked her all over, inspecting her for injuries. Though she wanted him to believe she was fine, he found to his horror that she was covered in blood.

"Kit! God, where are you hurt?" Despair tremulous in his voice, he reached her and cupped her face in his hands, tipping her face to his.

"I'm not hurt. I mean, I have some bumps and bruises, but the blood isn't mine."

There was no triumph in her voice. Only fear, exhaustion, and sadness.

"Please say you found García", she said, searching his face.

He nodded, "Yes. Captain McCulloch took him back to the ranch to fix him up. He thinks he will survive the shot." Price may have led her to believe they were more optimistic than they were, but she didn't need extra worry at the moment.

He pulled her to him, enveloping her in his arms with her head tucked beneath his chin, fitting her to him as closely as possible yet knowing it could never be close enough.

His chest rose and fell in rapid sequence, the fear from moments before of not knowing if she was dead or alive still coursing through his body like a poison.

"I thought I was too late. When I heard the shots, I thought—I thought..." Price trailed off, unable to finish the ends of those sentences.

She pulled far enough away from him to see his face. He knew he should let her go. Holding her wasn't proper. Neither of them had made any declarations toward one another, but he didn't want to let her go.

A smile wobbled across her lips, "I shan't lie, I feared I wouldn't make it out of that mess either."

Her humble bravery astonished him. She had sadly expressed before that she didn't share any qualities with her mother, but she did; she shared her fighting spirit. They were survivors.

Without quite knowing he was saying the words, he uttered, "You're remarkable."

She smiled shyly and looked to her feet. He tipped her chin back up to meet his eyes. She should know how amazing she was. He wanted her to feel all the things he already knew her to be.

"We need to go."

But, of course, she wouldn't allow him to. She had always avoided being the center of attention, deflecting compliments and loving gestures with a thankful line of a smile and redirecting focus to someone else or work.

One day, he'd not let her shrug off and deny how spectacular she was.

But right now, she was correct, they needed to leave.

"I presume the other body in the shack wasn't Kingston's," he said, allowing the conversation to revert to business.

She stepped from his arms and returned to catching Blue from the pen to saddle. "It was Russell Martin," she said, casting her eyes off into the distance stoically.

Price traced his brain to match a face to the name but couldn't seem to place it.

"Followed me all the way from Stone Ranch," she continued.

Russell Martin. Now he knew who he was. Fury surged through him, but he remained quiet, allowing her to explain.

"He planned to...to hurt me..." she trailed, and Price knew exactly how the man had planned to hurt her. "Somehow he discovered my rift with Kingston and ended up working for him. Kingston's on his way here and I don't know how many men he will bring with him. He has it in his hair-brained skull that I'll marry him." She slid the leather strap through the cinch and tied the knot, pulling the end through and securing it with a forceful tug before positioning the stirrup back into place.

"See this?" she asked, holding up a shiny new Colt Walker. "Russell had this. Doesn't it look like the one Luke had come up missing right before Russell was fired?"

"Easy to tell," Price walked over and held out his hand to inspect it, "Luke had his initials engraved on the bottom." Sure enough, LRS was written across the bottom of the handle. He passed it back to Kit to see for herself. With a disgusted curl of her lip, she placed the gun into her saddle bag.

"Suppose I'll have to give it back to Luke. There are only four shots left in it. Mine's loaded," she explained as she holstered her own Paterson at her hip. She then proclaimed, "But I'd like to get me one of them Walker pistols someday."

Wasting no more time, they swung up on their horses and rode out.

"How close do you think Kingston is?" Price asked over the galloping of their horses.

Kit replied, "I don't know. Frank and Russell didn't seem to know either. They unsaddled the horses as if we'd be there a while, but they were keeping lookout as well."

"My guess is Captain McCulloch is on his way and when he finds us, we should probably double back with him and catch Kingston while he's off his ranch, away from most of his men."

271

"Good plan. We'll see what the captain thinks of it."

When they rounded the next copse of trees, Kit pointed at the three riders approaching and smiled, "There he is now."

"No, that's not him. He rides a stout gray. And I don't see a gray among those riders." Price and Kit both slowed their horses to a stop.

"Could be coincidence, people riding through from Canyon..." She trailed off, not believing the possibility herself.

Price looked to her, "Not likely."

The approaching riders were gaining on them fast.

"We can't outrun them on this terrain, and I don't know the land well enough to try." Kit licked her lips, thinking on a plan, "Turn back. Head for those trees we just passed," Kit ordered and took off.

~

Once Kit made it to the trees she jumped down from Blue, pulled the Walker from her saddle bag quicker than a man could blink and dodged behind the first solid tree she found to shelter her.

She assumed Price followed suit and turned to see where he was.

That's when the first gunshot exploded, and the shrill cry of a horse pierced the air. She heard the snapping of thin branches and brush as a horse crashed to the ground. It was too close to be any other than Price's horse.

"Price!" Kit screamed frantically, breaking from the tree, and running toward the sound of the crash.

Another shot cracked the air and splinters of timber peppered her face. The shot exploded a hole in a tree near her head as she ran through. Somehow, she managed to keep her feet running.

"Price!" she hollered again.

Answer me.

She needed to hear his voice, needed to know he wasn't dead.

"And where do you think you're headed, little missy?" A pair of thick, bearish arms grabbed her, halting her run so abruptly, the air nearly dispelled from her lungs. The arms didn't belong to the voice that had spoken, though.

Kit kicked wildly and reached around to bash the man holding her in the face with the handle of her gun. She hit him repeatedly, until he released her, and she was able to spring away.

"Don't make me shoot my bride, now."

The slow, smooth speech raised the hairs on Kit's arms. She froze still in her tracks knowing the man had more than one gun trained on her. Her eyes searched frantically through the blur of green until she finally spied Price's horse in the distance, lying still on the ground.

She didn't see Price.

Breath ragged from sprinting forced her to ask between pants, "What's your plan, Kingston? You think I will marry you willingly?"

He laughed from behind her. She couldn't see him, but she imagined his large girth shaking with the cachinnation. She needed to keep him talking. Captain McCulloch couldn't be far behind and should've heard the shots fired. That is, if he hadn't already been killed, Kit swallowed.

"None of this would have been necessary if Morgan would have done as he should. You can blame your daddy for all this bother." Cornelius Kingston's words caused her to grimace.

She started turning slowly to face him, not liking the man at her back. As she turned, she thought she saw Price out of the corner of her eye. She didn't focus on him, in hopes Kingston wouldn't notice him as well.

One of Kingston's men started walking quickly toward her. It was obvious by the man's bloodied and battered face, he was the one she'd pummeled with the weight of her gun. She should have shot him with the gun, she realized with disgust. And would have, had she not been so focused on making sure Price was alive.

If she fired now, Kingston would shoot her. Maybe not kill her, but she was certain he wouldn't agree "his bride" needed to *walk* down the aisle.

"Stop," Kingston ordered his man, halting him with his hand in the air. "No need to collect her." Kingston's dark eyes traveled questioningly to his third man, who Kit just realized had moved around to investigate Price's horse.

She watched Kingston's eyes narrow before he spat, "Find him."

Kit wanted to sigh with relief, knowing Price had escaped.

Before the third man could proceed, a shot fired from somewhere deeper in the woods behind him. Kit didn't watch as blood spread across his chest and he fell to the ground on his knees. She took that moment instead, while Kingston's arrogant face crinkled with confusion, to fire her own gun. But she wasn't the only one.

Gunfire peppered the air, exploding all around her. She hit Kingston and in the fraction of a second it took her to thumb back the hammer to shoot again, another gun fired next to her, killing the brute beside Kingston before his shot could find *her*. Still, she kept her gun trained on both men crumpled on the ground in front of her. Price hobbled his way to her side, his gun also aimed at them.

"Price!" she cried, shaking both from the elation of visual proof he was alive and the fear still drumming through her from all the events of the day. She wanted to throw herself in his arms, but refrained, knowing Captain McCulloch and perhaps more men with him were nearby.

She knew he sensed her need to be close to him. He took a discreet step sideways, meeting his shoulder to hers. She closed her eyes and swallowed, wanting more than anything for the nightmare to be over and to be able to have a private conversation with Price.

"Nice work on your end, Miss Stone." The ranger stepped into the padded down clearing where they stood.

She turned to greet him, "Nice timing on yours, Captain McCulloch." She extended her hand to shake his. Price secretly gave her other hand a gentle squeeze, before stepping around to greet the captain as well.

Chapter 32

It was nearing dark by the time they made it back to the ranch and the three of them were exhausted after having to round up all the horses and bodies.

Price rode Frank's horse.

Kit had seen his inner struggle when he'd untacked Hypatia for the final time. The animal had broken her neck and died instantly from the fall after being shot, resulting in little suffering, but that was little compensation for losing a good horse and companion.

Price's inattention to the captain's words on the ride back told Kit he was still silently grieving. She or her brothers might have allowed their moods to turn dark and foul in time of grief, but not Price; he would suffer alone, quietly. In the past she would have thought him unfeeling and shallow; a product of his English rearing in which he was trained to suppress anything as undignified as emotion. Now she knew better. He was one of the least selfish beings she had ever met, and he comported himself with steady control as to not burden those around him.

But more than that, Kit knew he didn't have anyone he thought would want to share in his burdens.

Kit, often misunderstood herself for being gruff and direct, understood his silence all too well. And when this was over, she hoped neither of them would feel alone in the world again.

They were met with the happy, relieved faces of her ranch hands—especially Bernardo who patted her on the back affectionately and beamed from ear to ear, expressing how dearly happy he was she was returned home alive. The other men assisted with the extra horses and the bodies while Bernardo saw to whipping up some food. Price pulled his saddle from the ranch horse and allowed one of the men to see to it, while he offered to take Blue for Kit. She'd longed to get out of the blood-dried clothes and was thankful for his help.

She couldn't bathe, though she desperately wanted to soak her entire body to wash the blood and death from her. With the house gone, all she could make use of was the well. And there was no privacy there.

First, she stopped by where García was said to be resting. She was relieved to see him sitting up. He appeared to be in good health for someone who had just been shot. He was relieved to see her, too, and informed her now that she was safe, he was happy to go home to his own bed, on the morrow, to finish recovering.

Kit couldn't blame him. If she didn't have this ranch to run, she'd want to stay on as a guest at García's ranch. She was feeling a strong urge for some modern comforts. Like a real bed. *And indoor bathing*, she groaned, forcing her tired feet to the well to wash up. Unexpectedly, she was met by Lily when she arrived.

The girl's gray eyes were red-rimmed from crying. Kit was too tired to muster up any anger at the moment.

"You'll never know how sorry I am," Lily hiccupped. "I thought I could do it. When Frank came to fetch me from Canyon, before I knew you, I thought I could do it."

Kit interrupted her, "You thought you could kill an innocent person for money?"

"No, the kidnapping was planned first. You were supposed to marry a rich rancher. Didn't sound all that bad to me. But then Frank thought it would be easier to kill you. I didn't want to help him. I didn't know what to do. You don't know my brother. He said he'd kill me, and I believed him. But I couldn't let you die. I had hoped Frank believed you had woken up on your own and escaped, but he didn't. Then Kingston increased how much he would pay to have you delivered alive. No one was supposed to die."

"What was your role in today's attack?" Kit asked darkly. "Did you get your theatrical practice in?"

"I didn't have a role. Frank wouldn't tell me any of the next plans for fear I would ruin them again."

"You should have told me everything after the fire."

"I was too afraid Frank would kill me... I wanted to tell you." Kit read the sincerity in Lily's eyes. "When García and the ranger showed up to help, I thought you would be safe. I never thought Frank would be bold enough to take you with all the men out hunting the border today. When you didn't return for lunch and I learned Price and the ranger had went in search of you, I went after them. I had a feeling I knew where Frank would take you."

Kit sighed, despite Lily's fear for her own life, she had attempted to save Kit twice.

"I didn't want to help Frank. You have to believe me," Lily begged.

"I do," Kit said, "I do believe you. And I forgive you."

Lily sniffled, "I don't deserve your forgiveness."

Kit watched the girl's lips tremble. Uncomfortable with the emotional display, and fearing Lily would begin crying again, Kit drew her in thinking to give her a hug but stopped when she remembered her blood-covered clothes. She looked down, gesturing toward the mess, and squeezed Lily's hands instead.

Lily wiped the tears from her eyes. "Let me help you. We'll heat water and fill a horse trough and give you a proper bath. I'll stand guard." Then realizing she perhaps wasn't trusted to stand guard, she said, "Or Price can. I'm sure he would remain a true gentleman and be happy to help."

"Thank you for the offer, but I'm afraid I'm too tired to wait for warm water. But if you could I'd appreciate help out of these clothes and for you to stand guard while I wash up."

Kit dumped bucket after bucket of cold water over her head until she was sure the blood had washed from her hair. The clothes would have to be burned, but at least she was no longer sticky.

Lily helped her carry a bucket of water back to their former makeshift bedroom stall and then helped her from the wet clothes. Once Kit was dried and in clean clothes once more, she excused herself from their stall to find the captain. His men were only just arriving to the ranch when she reached him.

They had ridden hard all the way from Onieda only to have missed the action. Kit ordered some of her men to put up their horses and offered them sleeping quarters in the bunkhouse. It was decided that tomorrow the rangers would take the bodies back to the town with them and investigate further to determine if Whitney Kingston had been involved as well. With all taken care of, Kit still had one important thing to do, so she set off in search of Price.

She found him in Blue's stall.

"You're still here?" she asked, surprised.

"I needed to change my clothes. I've just returned to finish brushing down Blue." His wrist did even flicks along Blue's back.

Kit picked up a brush and began stroking the other side. "I'm sorry about your horse," she said.

Price nodded and smiled his thanks.

Moments passed in silence. Kit stepped around to join Price on the other side. She resumed grooming the dirt-crusted sweat from Blue's coat but stepped closer to Price as she did until they stood shoulder to shoulder. It was a most ineffective way to groom a horse, but she went through the motions while she worked up the courage to speak her mind.

Electricity buzzed within at his nearness. She wondered if he felt it, too. Her thoughts scrambled, she searched for something intelligible to say.

"Thanks for coming to my rescue today," Kit voiced her sincerity.

Price expelled a puff of air for a laugh, "Not that you needed rescuing. You already had everything under control by the time I arrived."

Kit smiled, "Well, you helped. You didn't have to come after me." Her tongue felt thick in her mouth as she braved crossing the line of friendship, "I'm glad you did."

"Of course. I made a promise to protect you."

She felt Price still beside her as if he struggled with words himself. She pushed on. She needed to know.

"Is that the only reason you're here?" Her lungs felt constricted in her chest awaiting his reply. She too stilled, and for a heartbeat kept her eyes cowardly fixated on the horse, afraid to look at Price and find rejection in his eyes. Or worse, pity. She licked her dry lips and swallowed, trying to force her lungs to function at her command.

His continued silence forced her to meet his gaze.

His hazel eyes searched hers before answering, "No."

His hand slid over until it covered hers and each of his fingers found a mate to her own, intertwining them.

"No, that's not the only reason."

Lips parted, breathless with hope, Kit asked, "Do you love me?"

His eyes remained locked on hers, "I do."

"Would you be willing—that is—" She wet her lips with the tip of her tongue as she attempted not to botch this, "Do you want to marry me?"

Price tipped her chin up to see her face as he answered, "I do."

A bashful grin grew handsomely across his face.

"So far this has been a rather one-sided relationship. You didn't allow for my heroic rescue of you," he ticked a brow in mock reproach and continued to list, "and you didn't allow me to propose as a gentleman ought." His smile widened and she found herself grinning like a fool in return. "Tell me, is there anything I will be allowed to do proper?"

"Seduce me..." she advised with a saucy smile. "But as you should be familiar by now, patience isn't my strong suit, so I suggest you don't delay."

Chapter 33

Transporting the bodies to Onieda the following day had met with no trouble. Kit and Price had decided to ride along with the rangers, since they needed supplies from town, anyway.

While there, Kit posted another letter to her family informing them of her upcoming nuptials and expressed her sorrow they wouldn't be in attendance for the ceremony. She still had not received word from them, but that wasn't surprising. Mail delivery through the stagecoach wasn't all that reliable, it was possible they hadn't even received her first letter.

It saddened Kit that her family wouldn't be present, but it couldn't be helped. A speedy wedding was necessary in order to legalize the ranch in Kit's name and begin to pay off all of its debts.

Not enough evidence could be gathered to prove Whitney Kingston had been an accomplice to his father's plans of abduction and attempted murder. She didn't think the young Kingston would try to carry out more attempts on her life with the law now closely involved, but she thought paying off Morgan's debts to the Kingston ranch would aid in that decision. Even so, she wasn't about to let her guard down anytime soon.

And neither was Price.

She never would have imagined there could be so much joy found in sharing the burdens and even the smallest details of one's life with someone. And yet, with Price, all of those small details were brighter and shinier somehow. Something as mundane as him meeting her with coffee in the morning, because he knew she would be a bear without it, was special. No one had ever thought of her needs in such ways before. No one had ever cared to spend time with her simply because one enjoyed her company. And she'd never enjoyed another's company to this extent either.

People on the street turned peculiar looks her way. She knew she looked a ninny, but she couldn't find the gumption to care. Let them gawk at the permanently fixed smile on her face and her airy gate, she thought. She fairly skipped her way to the lumberyard where she was to meet Price. They were putting in an order to have delivered to the ranch to begin rebuilding. Price agreed to her romantic ambitions of building an adobe-style home; perhaps not one quite as grand as García's, but lovely all the same.

They would first need a quickly-built dwelling to reside in while the construction took place of the other. They couldn't very well continue sleeping in the barn with the horses. So that plan was in motion.

She found Price already mounted on a borrowed ranch horse, holding Blue's reins in hand as he awaited her, a troubled expression across his face.

"What's wrong?" Kit asked, swinging up into the saddle.

"I received a letter from my father."

They steered their horses to the south road leading back home, keeping a brisk walking pace. Kit remained silent, waiting for Price to explain.

"My older brother passed away in a carriage accident." Price swallowed. Kit remembered Price telling her he wasn't close with his eldest brother. Even so, it must be difficult for him to digest.

Suddenly she realized what that particular news signified. Price's brother was heir to the earldom and Price was next in line. With his brother's death, Price was now the heir...

Her mind raced. Surely, he would now be obligated to return to England to see to matters. It was as if lightning had struck, leaving a zigzagged line across her heart, bringing rolling clouds of gloom to cancel the sunny life she had been planning. If he left, there could be no marriage between them. She couldn't give up the ranch she'd just worked so hard to obtain. And he couldn't stay. The inner storm battered the walls of her chest painfully.

"I'm sorry," she managed to croak out and hoped the sound of her heart breaking couldn't be heard.

Each struggling with their inner turmoil, neither paid much attention to the road. Luckily for them, the horses knew the direction of home and continued on the path with little guidance.

Licking his dry lips, Price continued, "It's not what you think." Riding side by side, he easily reached out and covered her hand resting on her thigh as she rode. Then he looked to her, "Kit, I'm not leaving."

Kit sucked in a long, much needed breath, "You're not? But how can that be?"

"I'm not the heir," he said plainly. His jaw muscles worked painfully. "My father, that is the earl," Price coughed, working through his emotions, "has proof of my bastardy. A letter my mother wrote on her death bed, which he included, details all." He looked ahead silently, processing his thoughts.

"It makes sense," he said after a moment, "he writes that he always suspected as much. That in itself explains a great deal..."

The pain of rejection was cutting him anew, she could see the hurt in his eyes.

"It's a comfort, actually," he lied. "Before, I thought it was something inherent in me that disgusted him. Try as I might I could never earn his affection or his respect. No matter how well my marks were in school or how successful... Now I know. It was my mixed blood. Nothing really at all to do with *who* I was, but rather *what* I was.

"It's strange, though," he continued. "The man was never fond of me, there should be no love lost, and yet, it feels as though I've lost both a brother and a father. Two brothers actually."

Kit looked to him questioningly.

"My father, that is, the earl, declares that he is having me proclaimed deceased and if I ever return home, my presence could harm the position of my younger brother, Miles."

Kit recalled Price speaking fondly of Miles. She knew now where the greatest source of his pain stemmed from.

"I'm to have no more contact with either of them. As far as Miles knows, I am dead. It's for the best."

"I would hate for someone to make that decision for me," Kit pointed out. "Don't you think he would rather continue a relationship with his brother than have a spotless reputation amongst the peerage?"

Price huffed at her ignorance of the way the world of aristocrats worked. "He would indeed. That is why it is better this way. He would go to battle to fight our father for me and in the process only harm his own future. If he believes me dead, his grief will be short."

Unlike Price's grief, she thought, *that will extend his lifetime over a callous separation.*

The pain in his eyes belied his words, "Now he may live a full, happy life, unencumbered by a bastard brother who would only cause conflict between him and his father, and his position in the world."

She squeezed his hand comfortingly as he had hers. She hadn't a way with words. What helped her through times of hardship was riding fast into the wind with no imminent destination. Perhaps she could give Price that—the freedom from one's own tormented mind.

"Let's not head straight home," she said, veering Blue off the road where it met the edge of her property.

~

The glint of determination in Kit's eyes should have been alarming. One never knew what she planned when that look came over her. Price didn't think *she* knew half the time.

He was grateful, though, for her effort to distract him from the dark, aching void spreading throughout his heart at the thought of never corresponding with or seeing his younger brother again. Of being severed off from his life.

"I think we should hunt you up a new horse. What do you think?"

Price smiled at her less than subtle maneuvering. "I think you're quite mad. We've a house to build and a ranch to run. When do you expect you'll find time to train a wild horse? You haven't finished that other little mare we wrangled up last time we went on a jaunt."

"O' ye of little faith," she bantered. "Perhaps you simply prefer Stone Ranch bred horses. I suppose I cannot disapprove of such an opinion."

"Your humble character is truly shining through."

Kit snorted a laugh.

Their wedding was yet a month away, entirely too long of a wait if one asked him. It made sense, however, to give García time to heal. The ceremony was to be held at his ranch after all.

As they traveled, they searched for signs of disruptions made to the land or fencing. So far all looked well. A huge relief. Price hoped the days between now and the wedding would remain calm. He wasn't sure his patience could withstand further delay.

When Kit turned south again, Price knew exactly where she was headed. She was so easy to read if one took the time. He smiled silently and allowed her to lead. The horses splashed through Hackberry Creek and he followed Kit up the trail path to the shady ledge that overlooked the crossing.

This was where he and Kit had met for her seduction lessons.

He raised a suspicious brow her direction to which she attempted to ignore, except for a barest hint of a smile that gave her away.

She had given him fair warning about lacking patience. The woman was fit to drive him mad. Kit slid down from her horse and pulled her saddle, signaling she planned to remain at this spot for a while.

Price felt his skin heat and it had nothing to do with the burning Texas sun.

"I was thinking, we could both use a good washing after the last few days," she said, her innocent voice nearly believable.

"Indeed." He uncinched his horse and sat his saddle and pad on an outstretched tree limb. Then he said, "You should know, I'm not about to let you steal this from me."

"Steal what?"

"The seduction. You said that role was for me."

"I also told you not to take too long."

"Minx."

"Why don't you come over here, Englishman, and help me with these," she instructed coyly, beginning to unbutton her white gingham blouse.

"Oh, I'll help you all right."

~

In two swift steps he reached her. Kit had hoped her extended lessons from Lily, conducted secretly during their stay at García's after the fire, were working. But when Price reached her, instead of slowing to enjoy the act of undressing her as Lily claimed he would, he scooped her up inelegantly in his arms. By the time she realized his intentions, it was too late to escape.

"Price! You dunderhead, don't do it!"

"Your clothes look as though they could use a sound washing as well."

"They're new. Priiiice!"

He threw her over the bankside into the deep, cool running water below.

Again.

As she splashed into its depths, she concluded she must have erred in her training. How mortifying.

She thought to remain underwater indefinitely so as not to face him, but then a large splash next to her indicated he'd joined her.

When she surfaced, he was already pursuing her like a wolf its prey. The strong muscles in his neck and shoulders glistened above the water where absence of a shirt exposed them. Getting a foothold in the gravelly river bottom, she held herself still, awaiting her capture, wanting to be caught. She realized the tables had turned. And she shivered with anticipation.

When Price reached her, she allowed him to guide her. He drew her closer, his hands running along her back to her bottom, lifting her. She instinctively wrapped her legs about his waist, cradling the aching, wanting core of her against him.

She let her eager hands slide over his shoulders and down the slick, corded muscles of his back, then around to feel the expanse of his chest, allowing for them to glide down the strong bulge of his biceps as he held her. She wanted to touch him everywhere.

It was a heady feeling.

His smoky gaze dropped to her lips followed by his own. Softly, he tugged at her bottom lip until she opened for him and his tongue slowly mingled with hers. A deep moaning worked low in her throat. Her entire body felt hot and the tingling sensation at her core throbbed. She squeezed her legs to press more firmly against him, her body desperately seeking what she didn't yet know.

His kissing became more rapid and he broke from her mouth, leaving them both ragged in breath as he frantically found the place just above the delicate bones that collared her neck with his lips. He used his rough, stubbled jaw to nuzzle, scrape, and suckle until her fevered body felt tormented with pleasure.

She tipped her head back, arching her neck, exposing her breasts, bobbing in the water, begging without words for him to take his feasting mouth there.

In case he needed further encouragement, she squeezed her legs around him again. She smiled at the power she seemed to wield, as he elicited a feral growl and moved his mouth lower.

His arms still holding her, hands cupping her bottom, he gave a firm squeeze in return as his lips roved over the thin, wet, clinging fabric of her shirt over her nipples, reclaiming his power. A sharp cry of pleasure escaped her.

Deftly, his fingers worked to release the buttons.

"Blast, this would have been easier before the water," he rasped between pants.

Kit arched her brow as reminder that he'd been the one to hastily toss her into the water.

"Yes, yes, I know," he said on an exasperated breath before claiming her mouth once more.

This was not the soft slow kiss of before, but a consuming, devouring need as strong as her own.By time they broke to regain breath, she felt the warm breeze kissing her wet skin and realized Price had carried her to the grassy bank. He laid her down, covering her with his own body and finished stripping her wet shirt away to resume the thrilling, torturous caress of his tongue to her breasts.

Sinking into the ground with zero protest, she succumbed to the blissful, artful lips placing design over her body, reveling in the new sensations she found at dragging her hand up the naked masculine thigh sidled over her.

One of his hands twisted in her hair, cupping the back of her head as he licked and suckled at her bounty, while his other roamed lower to the waist of her pants. She twisted her body in slow effort to help him peel them down around her hips, and lower, until she was free of them.

Completely naked before him now, a feeling of shyness came over her. He adjusted himself until she could feel the thick ridge of him nestled between her legs at their jointure. It throbbed against her as if it had a will and mind of its own.

"You're so beautiful," Price whispered above her, while gently moving a strand of her hair away from her face. "I love you."

"I love you," she returned.

"Our wedding isn't for another month..."

"I don't want to wait," she assured.

He nodded and sighed his relief.

Then his smile sobered, "The next part may not feel particularly pleasant, but I'm told it's a short-lived inconvenience and then everything is going to feel..." he struggled for the words.

"As it did moments ago?"

"Better. God, so much better," he smiled and brought his lips back to hers.

Her trust in him unwavering, she allowed her hands to resume their perusal of his body as he brought her to a fevery peak once again.

He slid the bulging length of his cock against her most sensitive pulsating center, back and forth, until the smooth, slippery feeling was as though satin meeting silk. And then his thick, swollen rod found her opening and he slowly pushed forward, entering her.

Her body accommodated him as he filled her. She winced at a small discomfort of pressure, but then it passed as he said it would. His slow, steady movements as he slid back and forth within her sent heat spiraling through her once again. She wrapped her legs about him as she had before and pulled him deeper as he thrust.

She moaned and tipped her head back, melting away beneath him, leaving only the tingling, growing pleasure spreading

287

throughout her body. Slowly at first and then faster and faster, like a fire racing to consume her. She bucked and rocked against him harder, seeking the unknown. Wanting to end the sweet torment, while at the same time wishing it never to end. She desperately...needed...

And then, all at once she found herself exploding within, crying out as she reached the pinnacle of ecstasy, the likes of which she'd never known or could ever have imagined.

Price stiffened above her on a final thrust in the throes of passion before lowering his body closer to rest against hers. He nuzzled her cheek with a gentle caress of his lips, their panting breaths mingling together as they returned to an even state. She stroked the strong muscles of his arms as he withdrew from her body to rest beside her.

They lay there for a time, allowing the sun above to bake the water from their naked skin. The scent of honeysuckle traveled on the breeze and Kit wondered if they'd always have this heaven on earth.

Price gathered his dry clothes from the perch above bringing them to the bank below where she remained stretched in the grass, her face to the sun, and eyes closed as she fought her dreamy state.

"I was going to share my clothes with you while yours dried, but if you keep sighing and posing so invitingly, we may have to pass the time in a different manner."

Kit smiled lazily and rolled onto her side, drawing her eyes open to see him. Her newfound confidence made her bolder. It was hard to be shy around the man who'd just spent the better part of the afternoon worshipping every inch of her body.

"I find that an exceedingly agreeable proposal."

He grinned and her heart did a little flip.

"Unfortunately, your body may disagree with your passionate ambitions."

She conceded she was a little tender. "Traitorous vessel," she snarked, eliciting a laugh from Price.

He tossed her his large shirt, which she slipped into while he donned his trousers. Then they collected her wet clothing and traversed up the hill to perch, where their horses remained grazing a small distance into the brush on the other side of the trail. They laid her clothes onto a large boulder clear of shade from the trees, so they could dry. Then Price wrapped his arms around her as he stood at her back and planted a soft kiss into her hair. They stood silently peering out across the water and the land from their cliff-like cove.

The breeze blew some of her rebel strands of hair as well as her sigh of contentment away from her face.

~

Price buried his face at her neck for another kiss. He couldn't seem to be close enough to her.

"You've no idea how often I dreamed of you this way."

"You never said."

He sputtered a laugh, "I never believed you would ever see me as good enough."

Kit looked down solemnly, "All the time, I was the veritable snob I accused you of being. How on earth could you have ever loved me?"

"Because you're remarkable, and talented, and clever, and feisty. How could I not love you?"

She smiled, "I'm so glad you do and stuck with me until I came to my senses. Thank you. I can't believe I was set on living in this world without *this*. I would have missed so much and never known. Or worse, learned what I had missed, too late."

He hugged her tighter if possible. Then, she patted his arm, and he knew she was about to break the sentimental moment. Kit never was one to gush about her feelings. She was a tough woman. He was glad he was the only one to know her this intimately.

He smiled as she said, "No worries, dear, you'll always be enough. Even if you can't cut it as a cowhand," she teased, "I'm sure I can find a use for you around here doing something."

She turned in his arms to face him then, giving him full view of the saucy smile she wore on her lips as she circled her arms around his neck. Reaching up on her tip toes, she kissed him soundly.

It pained him to have to break the kiss. But it was necessary if he was to prevent them from getting lost in another rapturous moment.

"I think your clothes are dried by now. We should be getting back, before they send out riders to look for us."

Reluctantly, she nodded her head in agreement.

After dressing, and re-saddling the horses, he noticed her expression turn troubled.

"What is it?" he inquired.

"I was just thinking about the riding competition I'd planned. A shame for it to be postponed. We need the money after all."

"Kit, need I remind you, you were recently nearly killed and your house burned to the ground? I don't think anyone is expecting you to continue with those plans. Besides, are you forgetting you're marrying a man with a small fortune?" He quirked his lip up in one corner.

She swung up into the saddle, "You know I can't accept that."

"No, I do not know that. Why ever not? Women bring dowries into marriage with them all the time to be used at a husband's disposal. How would this be any different?"

Her face remained grim and focused. *Dashed annoying, stubborn woman.*

"I want to prove to myself I can do it. On my own."

Price expelled a frustrated breath and studied her face.

"I'm thinking we could have it around the time of the wedding."

Protests formed at the tip of his tongue, but he held them back and waited for her to finish.

"Everyone will already be gathered at Rancho Rivera, anyway. It wouldn't make sense to gather again at a later date and take up valuable ranching time and resources again."

He studied her as she rambled on justifications for keeping to her original plan. He realized it was important to her in more ways than one.

"You think it will be fun and had your heart set on whooping all those vaqueros at the bronc busting."

"No," she began weakly, but cracked once she saw him grinning. "Well, perhaps I was hoping to trounce some of them."

He ran his hand through his hair in thought. Apparently, his delayed response caused her to prickle defensively.

"This is still my ranch. You can't stop me from proceeding with the events."

290

He interrupted her tirade quickly, "I would never make such a futile effort as to prevent you from something you already had your dogged mind set to. Nor would I dream of denying you just about anything. But might I make a small request?"

Her silver eyes looked to him skeptically.

He continued, "Please, might we have the damned competition in the days *following* our nuptials? I'd prefer my wife standing at my side without her face potentially battered from a bucking horse during our vows. And I'd like at least one honeymoon night following the wedding ceremony."

Kit laughed then, "Fair enough. We have a deal."

"Excellent." Had he just gained bargaining ground with his future wife?

He was still congratulating himself when Kit tossed over her shoulder, "If you can beat me back, I'll give you another preview of the honeymoon night."

A cloud of dust she kicked up settled around him while he scrambled to get his horse into a gallop to catch up.

Chapter 34

A second honeymoon preview was not to be borne. When Price and Kit arrived back to the ranch, a surprise awaited them they could never have predicted.

"Catherine Mary Stone," the furious voice of Ann Stone could be heard as they pulled up to the barn, "where on earth have you been?"

Kit's mouth gaped open like a fat trout on a line and he was sure he didn't look any less stunned himself.

Then the woman materialized from the barn, Grayson Stone not one step behind her, arms crossed over his barrel-shaped chest and daggers for eyes. Directed straight at Price.

"Mother..." Kit spoke as if she were seeing a hallucination before her. A bright smile soon transformed her face, "Pa!" She leapt from Blue and it was apparent it was taking all of her collective control not to charge him with a hug. Instead she walked briskly and stood before him. He reached out for her and drew her in. Their paternal embrace would have been a far more tender moment, had Grayson's stormy gray eyes not continued piercing a hole through Price's skull.

Price looked to Ann. He didn't seem to fare any better under her judgment.

"I can't believe you're here!" Kit shouted gleefully.

"García wrote us before you ever made it to your ranch and informed us Logan had handed off his brotherly duties of you and taken off in chase of a mysterious shooter. We had no choice. It's highly inappropriate for you to stay under guardianship of a bachelor who is of no relation to you." Ann spoke curtly and sent a look sharp enough to cut glass in Price's direction.

"So you never received any of my letters?"

"No."

"Oh my goodness, so much has happened. You will hardly believe it!" Kit began, pacing back and forth as her mind boggled where to begin. Meanwhile Price, obliviously to Kit, stood under grueling scrutiny of her parents.

Price cleared his throat. "A-hem. How about telling them the good news first?" he suggested hintingly.

"We're building a house like Uncle García's! Have you seen García's ranch?"

"*Not* that news."

Kit's brows drew together questioningly until the situation at hand dawned on her. She'd never before thought she'd find herself in such a predicament.

"Oh! Oh, yes." She smiled and walked to Price's side. He tried to move over a step to provide space between them as he was certain her father might kill him if he didn't, but Kit slipped her arm through his and clung to him tightly.

She smiled brightly and announced, "Price and I are engaged to be married."

It was Mr. and Mrs. Stone's turn to display shock-stricken faces.

"Come, let me tell you everything over a cup of—oh dear! I forgot, we've no accommodations for you. The house was burned down."

"Yes, we quite heard," Ann gritted, clearly unhappy with the events surrounding her daughter.

"Your sister is helping your maid to pack a wagon. We are all to stay with García for a spell. We shall discuss all of the details there."

"Livvy is here?" Kit's heartache was heavy in her words.

Her parents' faces lightened for the first time since greeting them.

"Yes."

Kit didn't wait, she had to see her sister. Had to see for herself if her sister was healing. She spied her at the wagon with Lily. They appeared to be talking. Kit's heart deflated some. She could tell, even from the distance she was, that Livvy had not returned to her former self.

Her sister would normally have been a bouncing ray of energy, chattering like a magpie, and smiling from ear to ear to be "adventuring" and meeting new people.

And while her sister was smiling, it didn't reach her eyes. She wore politeness like a cloak. A cloak that dampened her vibrant spirit and hid it away. That inquisitive, never-to-be-ignored spirit that had annoyed Kit through all their childhood. The one Kit missed dearly.

Suddenly, Kit felt unsure how best to proceed with her changed sister. Should she call her Lavinia? Her sister would have insisted before, but Kit had never adhered to such in the past. Should she now? Then again, perhaps what her sister now needed most was normalcy. Kit tossed the quandary around in her head some more, irritated that something as simple as saying hello to her sister had been reduced to this. Fury for the man who'd caused her sister and their family such distress filled her anew.

Kit shook it away and focused again on deciding which words to proceed with when greeting her sister. Kit thought on which she would prefer if she were in Livvy's shoes, sensitivity or normalcy? Of course, she and Livvy were not very alike in most things.

It occurred to Kit, now understanding how the act of physical intimacy worked, how truly violent and scary it must be for someone forced into the act. She and Livvy's first experiences had been drastically different from one another. Livvy had loved the professor, though, or at least believed she had. And yet the man had betrayed her. How that in itself must have hurt, Kit pondered.

Inhaling a shaky breath, Kit gathered the courage to speak to her sister, deciding on the use of her sister's beleaguered nickname.

"Livvy," she called out in greeting.

Her sister froze at the side of the wagon and turned slowly. She did not remonstrate Kit for the name as she would have in the past, instead she wore only a wan smile. Kit walked the remaining steps to her and took her hands.

"I'm so glad you're here."

Livvy glanced down and nodded silently.

"I see you've met Lily," Kit smiled. "She's been a wonderful help to me. As well as a giant pain in the arse. Which means you two are sure to get on famously."

Livvy cracked a real smile then, "Indeed. She has been regaling me of the little adventures you've had since you arrived."

Kit took her sister's arm then and steered her away from the wagon, "There's so much I want to tell you."

"Yes, it sounds as though this inheritance has been a dangerous undertaking."

Kit studied her sister, trying to read if there had been a seed of jealousy in her words. Kit had seen the ranch as an impossible hindrance to her life in the beginning and hadn't given much thought to the fact that Livvy *hadn't* inherited a ranch.

"Oh, don't look at me so. If this is what you want, then I'm happy for you. It's certainly not something I would wish for," Livvy supplied, "especially now." She looked away solemnly again.

"I've truly missed you."

"Whew," Livvy expressed an animated whistle reminding Kit of her former self, "what those words must have cost you." Her eyes glinted with her teasing.

Kit bumped her shoulder into her in turn and they laughed.

"Do you know the details surrounding my peculiar ranch inheritance? I assume García filled Mother in when you stopped by his way."

"Before then, I should say," Livvy answered. "Once Mother discovered you were here unchaperoned and dancing attendance upon men in order to select a husband, well, we were packing the same afternoon she received García's letter."

Kit smirked, "Ironically, she was the one who forced me to leave in the first place."

"Perhaps she had some regrets about that," Livvy offered, "I tried to tell her she shouldn't worry about you taking up a husband, that you would never marry, but she wouldn't listen."

Kit felt her face pinken.

Livvy looked aghast, "Kit Stone, have you gone and married a southern rancher?"

Kit, "No. I'm engaged."

Livvy's eyes widened with shock, "Well. Well, I suppose Mother had right to worry. Then again, knowing you, you probably made a practical arrangement. I admit, there was a time I would disapprove, but now... Well, I think a practical union rather smart if one is contemplating marriage. And I trust you would make a splendid business choice."

"While I am happy to receive such unexpected praise, you should know, the man I am engaged to marry is Price."

Livvy gaped in shock once more, "Price? The man you adamantly tried to make me believe you couldn't stand to breathe the same air as?"

"The one and the same."

"My, my, my. And to think I argued Price's abilities as a proper guardian for you. I told Mother he was always an utmost gentleman."

Distress crossing her features, Livvy looked to Kit and asked wearily, "He never... Please say he never...took advantage of you?"

Kit squeezed her sister's hand comfortingly, "No. He did not. Price is, as you said, an utmost gentleman." Then Kit eyed her sister teasingly and added, "A veritable saint."

Instead of making Livvy laugh, however, Livvy shuddered and said, "Sometimes men are good at making the world perceive them exactly how they desire to be seen."

"Very true," Kit agreed quietly, adding, "But I think you know Price better than that. He's exactly as the world sees him. And more." A happy sigh escaped Kit's lips.

"I can see you are exceedingly happy with the arrangement. And that makes me happy as well." Her sister bumped into her arm lovingly and Kit squeezed hers in return.

"So where is your *Saint*?" Livvy asked.

"Oh, heavens! I left him with Mother and Father!"

"The poor man," Livvy laughed. "We should rescue him."

"Is that an offer to help?"

"Of course, why ever would I be disinclined to help my sister save her beau?"

"For the same reasons I would be disinclined to aid you: to see you squirm under our parents' wrath."

They both laughed, remembering each of their devilish moments from childhood.

"Perhaps just a little," Livvy smiled.

Chapter 35

Rancho Rivera
July 15, 1852

The month flew by very slowly in Price's estimation. He and Kit were never permitted any time alone with one another. In fact, Price had remained behind at the Morgan Ranch while Kit stayed on with her family at García's, except for the last week prior to the wedding. But even staying under the same roof had permitted no privacy for them.

Unsurprisingly, there had been another uproar when Kit's parents discovered her plan to continue with the competitive eventing during the weekend of their wedding.

Kit's father thought it an abhorrent idea, while Kit's mother was in support of it; which meant, of course, that the eventing was still to take place.

Grayson wished Price luck, stating he was marrying into a family with a history of producing the most stubborn women on two continents. Price had laughed, albeit nervously, since he was fairly certain that assessment to be true.

The eventing was to take place on the morrow. Kit had promised him one wedding night before she would attempt to do herself in on a mad horse. Those weren't her words obviously, since she seemed to believe herself invincible.

The ceremony itself had went off without a hitch, thankfully. He was a married man now and *finally* he would have Kit to himself once more.

Price sipped from a glass and watched dancers twirl about the courtyard of the Rivera hacienda. Dusk was upon them, so García had oil lighting and candles prepared to keep the courtyard lit. It was quite beautiful. Too bad his wife wasn't admiring the view with him.

His new bride had disappeared with her sister to "freshen" themselves. Price had a feeling Kit was cowardly escaping the party. She hated large gatherings of people as equally as she hated being the center of attention, so it was no surprise to him she was avoiding her own party.

He would appease the crowd a while longer and then disappear as well *with* his bride, he smiled. His father-in-law came to join him, standing at the outskirts of the makeshift dance floor. His attempt to be friendly was negated by the almost feral gleam in his eye. At least, Price thought amusedly, it wasn't directed at him this time.

He followed his father-in-law's line of vision leading to García dancing with Ann. Price noticed right away what he already suspected. García's attempts to hide his love for Ann would no doubt fool most people, but it didn't Price, and by the looks of Grayson's jaw clenching and unclenching, it wasn't lost on him either.

Hesitantly, Price quietly declared, "You know."

Grayson sighed, "Yes."

Price couldn't help but feel a swell of disbelief over Grayson's calm admission, "How can you stand it?"

"Because...he's a good friend. I trust him. I know he would never act upon his feelings. He's been there for us both, our entire family, all these years. I had hoped he would find someone—someone else—but he could walk the earth ten times over and never find another as special as that woman right there."

Grayson's eyes were locked intently on his wife and Price felt the full force of his words.

"And," Grayson continued, "I happen to agree. So how can I expect him to move on when I know I never could?"

Caytt Lawson

Grayson was a stronger man than he, then. Price didn't think he could watch another man look on at Kit in such a doting manner.

"Besides, I pity him. Think about how hard it would be to love someone eternally, who loved another? It must be torturous for the man."

Price didn't have to wonder too hard. That had almost been the case for him, or so he had believed at one time.

The dance ended. García bowed to Ann and parted ways through the crowd and Ann floated back to her husband's waiting arms, smiling.

"Have you tired from dancing yet?" Grayson asked his wife.

"As if you could be so lucky," she teased.

"Never let it be said your husband failed to turn you up on the dance floor," Grayson quipped back. "Of course, if I cannot tire you here, perhaps we should remove our energies to a more private section of the house."

Ann giggled, returning her husband's flirtations. Price was sure the tips of his ears were singed pink. Where *was* his blasted wife?

As if he'd spoken the question aloud, Ann pointed beyond him, "It appears your wife is trying to make good her escape from her own party. You may want to go catch her."

Price didn't have to be told twice. He shoved off in pursuit of his vexatious, yet extremely gorgeous, wife.

~

"Kit."

Oh lord, she'd been caught out, she jumped, startled, until she recognized the voice belonging to her husband. She sighed, "Thank heavens."

"Thank heavens is right. You left me stuck alone with your parents once again. And they are truly a scandalous couple."

Kit laughed knowing he must be referring to her parents' infernal lack of discretion when it came to displaying their affection for one another.

Then he surprised her, "I do hope we can be just as scandalous."

She smiled up at him.

"Were you planning your escape without me?"

"I'd rather hoped you would make quick notice and seek me out."

Price chastised her cowardice with a look.

"I'm sorry. I couldn't take one more moment in that dress or running into another guest I'd be forced to make small talk with. Who knew García would invite all of two towns in addition to all of the neighboring ranchers to our wedding?" Kit placed her hand to her forehead in distress.

They strolled hand in hand to the other side of the house, the entrance there was blocked by people as well.

"It's a lovely night," Kit suggested, "and I don't think I received a thorough examination of the orchard on our last visit."

Price gave a gentlemanly hook of his elbow in which Kit gladly accepted and they sneaked off together in search of the pecan trees.

As they strolled beneath the twinkling stars, they discussed the future plans for their ranch.

"What are we going to name our new growing spread?" Price asked. "A ranch should really have its name carved across the arch over the drive entrance, don't you think?"

"English noblemen," Kit harrumphed, as if she knew more than the three she actually did. "Always concerned with the inconsequential things. I assure you I have greater priorities than naming our newly acquired dump."

When they reached the shelter of the trees, he pulled her into his arms and her body melted like butter against him. The man had turned her into a right wanton. She turned her face up to meet his, expectantly.

But instead of kissing her, Price's lips quirked in that way she'd come to know he planned to deliver a cunning, witty retort.

"I was thinking we should call it 'Saint's Ranch' after its newest co-owner? It has a good ring to it, doesn't it?"

Kit smiled to him coyly, beckoning him to kiss her. Her eyes glittered with arousal. He lowered his mouth and just before his lips met hers, she minxed, "Ah, but you're no saint..."

And at his wife's encouragement, Price set to prove just how *un-saintly* he could be.

Cayt Lawson

<u>**Readers!**</u>

Thank you for taking the time to read my book. I hope you enjoyed Kit and Price's story. Please feel welcome to leave a review as your support and feedback are invaluable to me as a writer!

Read on for a preview of <u>Kissed By A Devil</u>; the story of Livvy Stone and Gabriel Hart. Book 2 in the *Stone Ranch Series*!

Kissed By A

Devil

(An Excerpt)

Columbus, Missouri
October 4, 1851
Female Academy of Columbia

"Howdy, Miss Stone."

Ugh, there he was again. Was he following her from shop to shop?

Lavinia Stone didn't bother hiding her annoyance, "Gabriel Hart, what on earth are you doing in the library?" she asked slyly, knowing how it irked him when she insinuated his academic interests inferior. "I wouldn't imagine you'd have much use for books, as you already know everything." Her voice rose with biting sweetness.

"Well, I mostly just come to speak with the lovely Miss Porter." Gabriel tipped his hat toward the desk where the librarian, Mr. Porter's, daughter sat prettily.

Miss Porter returned Gabriel's wave with a saucy, knowing smile.

Of course, Gabriel would be sniffing around Miss Porter's skirts, she thought; he and every other male without the sense to see past twinkling sapphire eyes and a perfect, pearly white smile.

Livvy self-consciously ran her tongue over her upper teeth behind her lip, noting where both lateral incisors jutted slightly more forward than her two front teeth. She despised how her overly pointy cuspids gave her the resemblance of one of those blood-sucking night-dwellers she'd once read about in a gothic novel. How she wished her smile as lovely as Miss Porter's.

Though why Livvy was allowing a tingle of jealousy to fetter at her mind over Gabriel Hart, she didn't know.

She visibly shook her insecurities from her mind. Professor Blake thought her smile charming. Why should she care if Gabriel Hart preferred that of Miss Porter? She should encourage his interest in the woman. Perhaps then he would see fit to follow *her* around the town and disrupt *her* day!

~

Gabriel thought he saw a twinge of jealousy flicker over Liv's features. Exactly the reaction he'd hoped to inspire by flirting with the coquettish Miss Porter. Miss Porter was now eyeing him expectantly, however. Not one of his most well executed plans, he admitted. The woman was known to most all but her father for her lascivious nature, and her inability to hook her claws into Gabriel served only to make him more enticing to her.

He may have succeeded in stirring some jealousy in Liv's cold heart, but he had probably reaffirmed her belief that he was shallow and unrefined as well.

The spoiled brat should look into a looking glass.

Liv—or Lavinia, as she was recently wont to instruct him to call her—had cast her judgment of him long ago; labeled him a course rancher from Texas the first day they'd met. He should forget about her. She thought herself too good for the likes of him and she was right.

But try as he might, he could not. The memory of their kiss still burned sweet on his lips...

Thank You

Thank you for reading. If you enjoyed the preview of *Kissed By A Devil*, be sure to sign up for my Newsletter where I will offer free giveaways and exclusive excerpts from my upcoming books! To sign up for my Newsletter, simply head over to www.caytlawson.com and click on the Newsletter tab.

Again, I'd like to encourage you to leave an honest review and I sincerely thank you for choosing to read my book!

Acknowledgments

I would like to thank all of my friends, family, and readers for their encouragement. My mother and grandmother for an adventurous childhood and for providing strong female role models to look up to. A huge thank you to my dad, father-in-law, and stepmother-in-law for all their continued love and support throughout the years. This definitely would not have been possible without them! And finally, thank you to my husband and children, for their unwavering faith in me to achieve this goal.

About the Author

Cayt Lawson is an avid reader of Historical Romance, favoring stories set in Regency England and the American Frontier. She was raised on a quarter horse ranch in the state of Michigan and traveled the rodeo circuit with her parents as a young girl. The modern cowboy lifestyle she grew up in greatly inspired her love of the American West, and the romanticized time in history sparked her desire to explore other remarkable periods of the past.

Cayt currently spends most of her time trying to keep up with her three energetic, young children and—much to the detriment of her husband's sanity—adding animals to her growing hobby farm. When Cayt isn't reading or caring for her beloved children and critters, her time is spent researching and thinking up new stories.

To read more about Cayt Lawson visit her website at www.caytlawson.com.

www.ingramcontent.com/pod-product-compliance
Lightning Source LLC
Chambersburg PA
CBHW031549240626
47153CB00002B/443